DUTY ACCOMPLISHED

DUTY ACCOMPLISHED

The Drieborg Chronicles

Book Two

Michael J Deeb

Dear Joan,

The adventure continues.

Mike

iUniverse, Inc.

New York Bloomington

Duty Accomplished

iUniverse books may be ordered through booksellers or by contacting:

iUniverse

2021 Pine Lake Road, Suite 100

Lincoln, NE 68512

www.iuniverse.com

1-800-Authors (1-800-288-4677)

ISBN: 978-1-4401-0127-4 (pbk)

Printed in the United States of America

Duty Accomplished is for all my family and friends

*I have fought the good fight, I have finished the race,
I have kept the faith.*

Timothy 4:7

My undergraduate degree was in history with an emphasis on American studies. My Masters degree was also in history with a similar emphasis. My doctorate however was in management studies. Following the Masters degree, I was in education for nineteen years most of which saw me teaching American history. Nineteen years in education most of which included the teaching of American and world history and historical research techniques to students at all levels.

My personal life saw me as a pre-teen spending time regularly at the Grand Rapids, MI public library reading non fiction works of history. This passion continues to this day. Teaching at the college, university and high school level only increased my passion for such reading and research.

Since 2005, my wife and I have lived in Sun City Center, FL. I write daily. In the fall of 2007, I finished the historical novel Duty and Honor. this sequel Duty Accomplished, is the result of several hours a day of work. There is a third novel planned in the Drieborg Chronicles.

Prologue

Begun in April of 1861, the American Civil War was a conflict that most believed would be settled after one or two battles. But by December of 1864, the conflict had caused the death of over five hundred thousand military personnel, with no end in sight.

By the end of 1864 most people in the North and South longed for the war to end. Despite this, Abraham Lincoln, the war candidate of the Union Party defeated the peace candidate of the Democratic Party in the November elections; so the war continued.

The Federal Navy had blockaded the major ports of the states in Rebellion, so that cotton and tobacco rotted in Southern warehouses and the Confederacy was cut off from Europe's consumer goods and war material. Southern railroads were either destroyed controlled by the North's forces, or too antiquated to be efficient. Thus, food and supplies needed in the Confederate war effort seldom reached those in need. By the end of 1864, the replacement soldiers available to the Confederate armies were primarily old men and boys. And it wasn't until the spring of 1865 that the Confederate Congress authorized the recruitment of black men for their army. This came too late to even be implemented.

The North, on the other hand, had no such problems. Their pool of soldiers seemed bottomless and over 150,000 Negro men volunteered for service by the end of the conflict. The railroad system in the North was the best in the world. War supplies and food were plentiful and available at the point of need.

In the winter of 1865, a serious effort to begin formal talks for peace failed. Even a meeting of representatives from the two sides failed to materialize because President Lincoln would not accept the demand of the Confederate president that the independence of the Confederate States be recognized as a precondition to such talks.

So it remained for the opposing armies to continue the fight until one or the other was destroyed. It appeared to most observers of the day that the forces of the United States government would be the victor in that death struggle. General Grant's much larger Union army had trapped Lee's Army of Northern Virginia at Petersburg, a rail center just south of the Confederate capital of Richmond. Then, in the fall, General Sherman's army captured Atlanta, Georgia, a very important rail center. From there his forces turned east, fought their way to the sea and captured Savannah, Georgia in December. By January Sherman was ready to move his Union army into the Carolinas against a much smaller Confederate force.

Lowell, Michigan

The weather in Michigan during December was unpredictable; wet snow one day, rain the next. Today it was very cold and windy. The glass of the windows protected the family from the pelting of icy snow.

Major Michael Drieborg had been home on leave at his parents' farm near Lowell since early November. The blustery weather did not bother him in the least. He had spent the previous two winters practically living out of doors as a member of the Michigan Cavalry Brigade. He wasn't always a major, however.

As recently as three years ago, his rank of major in the United States Army would only have been held by a man who was a graduate of West Point, probably fifty years old, or more, with least twenty years of continuous military service.

But war between the Confederate States of America and the government of the United States changed all that. When the war began there were fewer than thirty-five thousand men in the entire army of the United States. When the thirteen southern states left the old Union and formed the Confederate States of America most of the career soldiers and most of the senior officers resigned their commissions in the Union army and joined the armies of their home states.

But rapid promotions were given in the Union army to those with past military service, and appointments were given to thousands of others with no military service.

At nineteen years of age, Mike joined the Michigan Cavalry Brigade in mid-1862 as a private and was rapidly promoted, the result of various circumstances. His last promotion to the rank of major came when he was awarded the Congressional Medal of Honor.

Like his father, he was six-foot-two, blond haired and blue eyed. He was rather tall for a cavalryman of that era. He was still a bit underweight since his escape from Andersonville Prison four months ago. But his mother's cooking had helped solve that problem.

Mike had to report for duty in Washington, D.C. the first week of January, 1865.

✶   ✶   ✶   ✶

He and Julia were in the barn alone. He was feeding the animals. She was lending a hand and talking with him. Two weeks ago they had told his parents of their intention to marry. Since then, the family left them alone at such times.

Mike stopped for a moment, leaned against his pitchfork and watched her pour some grain for the family's two cows. *What a marvelous woman. She's beautiful; smart too.*

Julia Hecht had been staying at the Drieborgs' farm since last October. She had lived with her parents on their Maryland farm and had accompanied Mike's family back to Michigan from the award ceremony in Washington when he had been given the Congressional Medal of Honor by the president himself. She was the sister of his late wife Eleanor who had died the previous summer.

She's gotten a bit taller since I saw her in Washington, Mike mused. *I don't remember her filling out a dress like she does now either; pretty; very pretty. I like her long brown hair pulled back and tied with a ribbon too.*

"Let's go over this again, Michael. Just when do you think we'll get married?"

"You know I can't answer that, Julia. In the first place, I don't know how long this war is going to last. In the second place, neither you nor I know if your parents will allow us to marry right now. Remember, until you are eighteen they must give their approval."

Julia stopped what she was doing and faced Mike with hands on her hips. "The war should have nothing to do with it, Michael Drieborg. I recall that it did not stop you and my sister Eleanor from getting married."

A year ago this past October, Mike had married Julia's older sister, Eleanor. The newlyweds had visited here last year at this same time. After he returned to duty in January 1864, he was part of an attack on the Confederate capitol of Richmond. Mike was captured in that engagement and sent to Andersonville Prison in Georgia. It was during his imprisonment there that his wife Eleanor gave birth to their first child. Shortly after, though, she died.

Mike paused and considered what Julia had just said.

What a feisty lady! He smiled, looking at her facing him with such determination. *She is not going to let anything get by her. I might just as well get used to that.*

"You know, Julia. You're right. It didn't stop your sister and me then. And, it shouldn't stop you and me now." It was Mike's turn now to look intently at her. He dropped his rake and put his hands on his hips, mimicking her stance. "But you tell me how we are going to get your mother's approval."

"You just leave that to me, Mister Washington hero," She responded quickly with some passion. "So when my parents approve our marriage, the announcement will be made in my church. Isn't that what you just said?"

My Lord! A few weeks ago, right here in this barn, she tricked me into asking her to marry me. Now, she has done it to me again.

Mike stepped toward her with his arms outstretched to hug her.

She held up her hand toward him. "No, Michael; none of that. Answer my question first."

"All right, you get your parents approval and we'll marry as soon as possible afterward. Now come here young lady; this hero needs a hug from you."

Trip East

It was a bitterly cold afternoon when Mike and Julia's train arrived in Detroit, behind schedule. Heavy snow had delayed their journey some from the western Michigan town of Grand Rapids, so they were worried that they might miss their connecting train bound for Cleveland, Ohio. They heard the conductor shout, "All aboard!" as they struggled with their luggage against a strong wind to catch that train. They just made it.

Once on board they were relieved to be out of the icy wind. But they quickly discovered that their new passenger car was hardly warmer than the outside temperature. In 1864, trains used by the average traveler were not very well insulated against the outside cold and were poorly heated, if at all. This railroad car at least had a potbellied stove at the far end of the aisle. Someone was feeding wood into it. So it didn't give off much heat yet.

Our travelers could still see their breath turn to vapor.

"Here Julia, move closer," Mike urged her. He put his arm around her and pulled a blanket over their laps. As the train pulled away from the station, they could see that the cloud cover had blown off and the sun had brightened the countryside.

"We can't see much outside, Michael," Julia observed. "The frost on the glass of our window is too thick."

"Give that stove a chance," Mike urged her. "We'll feel the warmth soon. It will heat up this car before you know it and that frost will melt. We should see a lot of countryside before we arrive in Cleveland."

"Actually, I don't mind the chill, Michael," Julia smiled. "It feels nice and cozy being held by you under this blanket."

"It is nice, isn't it? Mike agreed.

"But the stove is at the far end of the car, Michael. It would be much warmer if we moved closer."

"It probably would, but you'd soon be surprised how hot it will be down there. Besides, Julia, it is safer with our backs against the wall at this end of the car. The only way anyone can enter this car is through the door at the other end."

"Are you still worried about Carl Bacon, the fellow who attacked you in Detroit last month? I thought he is in jail for that."

"I'm told that he is in federal prison. But with his father's money, he has a long reach. So it's better to be safe than sorry."

"Is that why you've had your pistol on the seat beside you the entire trip today?"

"Yes it is. I'm not going to let anyone hurt you."

They were both quiet for a while. In the silence Mike leaned his head back against the seat and closed his eyes. He began to remember this same train ride a year ago.

Julia's older sister Eleanor sat at my side on that trip. She was my wife then.

I had met their family in December of 1862. Fifteen miles or so outside of Washington, my cavalry troop was on patrol duty in the Maryland countryside. It was as cold and windy a day as any I had known in Michigan. It was snowing too. Another trooper and I, a man called Swede, were riding together on this patrol. As we came over a rise we noticed smoke coming out of a farmhouse chimney in a valley ahead of us. Darkness was not far off, so we could also see light in the windows.

As we rode into the yard, I remember seeing a short, stout man standing just outside the open doors of the barn. It was sort of comical because he looked like illustrations I had seen of Santa Claus on the holiday catalogue at the general store. His red wool cap had flaps tied under his white beard. His winter parka and pants were red as well. With red cheeks and nose to top it off, I expected him to bellow "ho- ho- ho," or see reindeer in the barn's corral.

"Velcome boys," he said. "Put your horses in da barn and come to da house for a varm drink."

That's when we met the entire Hecht family. The Swede and I returned to the farm during our time off to help with farm work. It was great; the Hechts were great. We even spent that Christmas with them.

The following July of 1863, I was wounded at the battle of Gettysburg. According to the doctors in the field hospital, I had not suffered a mortal wound. But when all the seriously wounded filled the Washington hospitals, soldiers like me were put in the hallways of government buildings to fend for themselves.

Delirious with fever from infection and dehydration, I was discovered there by Congressman Kellogg. I had worked for him as an aide before being sent to Gettysburg. He obtained permission for the Hechts to take me to their farm. Mrs. Hecht was known in her farm community as a healer. She helped me regain my health. It was during my recovery there that I fell in love with her daughter Eleanor.

We married at her church in Maryland. I was still on convalescent leave from the Army, so two weeks after the ceremony we left her home to visit my family in Michigan. We spent two months at my parent's farm in Lowell. Then, last December she and I returned to her parent's farm in Maryland. Once I reported for duty in January, I never saw her again. She died In July after giving birth to our daughter. I was in Andersonville Prison, so I couldn't even attend her funeral.

Could it only have been a year ago that she and I traveled together?

＊　　　＊　　　＊　　　＊

"Michael, are you asleep?" Julia whispered.

"Hmmm?" he responded. "I don't know sweetheart. I guess I was sort of dozing a bit. Are you all right?"

"I'm fine Michael. But I want to ask you something."

"What is it, Julia?"

She sat up, turned on the seat some and looked directly at Mike. "When is this terrible war going to end?"

"You don't beat around the bush, do you?" Mike chuckled in response. "But to be equally blunt, I don't know."

"Michael," she prodded. "If I am going to be your wife, I need a better answer than that. Remember, I was in the room when you and your father talked about the war. You told him how you thought it was going. Can't you tell me, too?"

"Yes I can, Julia," Michael admitted. "I did tell my father what I knew about the war situation. And since you want to know, I should tell you too. Just keep in mind that I've been away from Washington for almost two months. Most anything could have changed during that time."

"Wait a minute. You know what might help? I have a map of the United States and the Confederacy I used when my father and I talked about this. I still have it in my bag, I think. Let me look." Mike rummaged around in his duffel bag. "Here it is, Julia. It even has all the major cities marked, too. Are you ready to start?"

**Civil War
United States**

"Yes I am. But first tell me, what does that line along the left side of the map represent?"

"That's the Mississippi River, Julia. Union forces control the entire Mississippi River from New Orleans on the Gulf of Mexico all the way to our border with Canada in Minnesota. This map shows the river ending at Chicago, Illinois. That city is right here on the shore of Lake Michigan. Actually, the river runs a few miles west of it." Mike pointed out.

"Farther south, though," Mike drew her attention to the state of Georgia on his map. "General Sherman captured the city of Atlanta this past fall. And I just read in the Grand Rapids Eagle that his army captured the port city of Savannah recently." Mike pointed to another two dots on his map.

"It seems that Sherman has almost 70,000 men in his army, and will soon move along north toward Charleston, South Carolina." Mike moved his finger to a dot north along the Atlantic Ocean. "There, he is opposed by a Confederate army less than half that size."

"Isn't Charleston the city where this war actually started?" Julia asked.

"Yes it is. South Carolina militia used cannon located on the shoreline of that port city to bombard the Union's Fort Sumter, which controlled the Charleston harbor. That attack started the war."

"North of that, in Virginia," Mike directed Julia's attention further north on his map. "General Grant has surrounded the Confederate capitol city of Richmond and its sister city to the south, Petersburg. His army of 150,000 men is opposed by General Lee's Reb army of about 50,000 soldiers."

"Do you see those places, Julia?"

"Yes, I can see where you are pointing; and I heard what you said. But I don't understand how two very small Confederate armies can stop our two very large armies. And, unless I'm mistaken, I heard you tell your father that our bigger armies have more supplies and better weapons, too."

"You're not mistaken. I did tell my father that."

"So why isn't the war over?"

"Well actually, for all practical purposes, it is over."

"Come on, Michael," Julia snapped. "Don't toy with me here. You said the war is still being fought. Soldiers are still dying. How can it be over, too?"

"The war continues right now because armies don't fight much during the winter. And in the early spring months of March of April, it's too muddy to do much either. But while there is very little chance anymore for the Union to lose this war, we probably have to wait until late April to win it. Does that clear up the confusion some, sweetheart?"

"Sort of, Michael. But let me think about what you said for a while. We can talk about it again, can't we?"

"Sure we can," Mike assured her. Then he held out his arms to her. "Get back over here, young lady. I still need some warming up."

"One more question first,"

"What's that?"

"If this war is virtually over, just what will you do after you report for duty?"

"Congressman Kellogg told me that I would be working with his Joint Committee on the Conduct of the War. He expects that our men who have been held in Confederate prisons will need a lot of help recovering their health and getting back to their homes. As I understand it, my job will be to make sure that happens."

"It doesn't sound like you'll be in any battles then," Julia surmised.

"Not according to the Congressman anyway." Mike assured her.

"All right, mister," Julia warned. "Just you make sure you aren't. Now, where are those arms you want to hold me with?"

*   *   *   *

I don't know what the future has in store for us. Mike thought. *The only thing I know for sure is that Julia and I will be sleeping in separate rooms tonight.*

CLEVELAND

Two scruffy looking men entered the lobby of the Weddell House through the Bank Street entrance. It was obvious to the man behind the front desk that they were out of place. This was the best and most expensive hotel in Cleveland.

They looked around some and watched people come and go. They saw where patrons were picking up keys and messages. They walked briskly to that desk.

One man turned the register around to read the names, and the other man opened his overcoat to show the well-dressed clerk a pistol stuck in his belt. "What room is Major Drieborg in?"

"Hotel policy prevents me from giving out that kind of information to just anybody, sir. Have you tried the American House or the Franklin House? He might be staying there. They might give out that kind of information about their guests; we at the Weddell do not. "

"I don't care a hoot for your fancy talk or your rules. Listen to me careful you dandified pile of crap. I know he's stayin' here. But you tell me what room Drieborg and his whore are staying in, or you will never get home tonight, or any night. Do you understand what I just said?"

Visibly shaken, the clerk could not speak or look directly at either man. "Answer me, or I'll kill you right now. Do you understand?"

"Yes sir. I understand." With that, he wrote a room number on a sheet of paper and slid it across the counter.

"I find you told anybody about us, you're a dead man. Do you understand that?"

"Yes sir, I do."

"Just to make sure, close your eyes and put your left hand flat on the counter. Do it now!"

As soon as the clerk complied, the second man brought the butt of a pistol down on the clerk's fingers. The two men were out the door into the snowy night before the clerk could even scream.

✴　　　✴　　　✴　　　✴

It was already dark outside; Mike and Julia were in their rooms preparing for their first real meal of the day.

"I don't know why you spent all that money, Michael. Not only did you pay for two bedrooms, but we have a living room in between besides. What did the desk clerk call it, a suite?"

"That's what he said. I sort of like the idea. After we return from the restaurant downstairs, we can spend some time together in this room before we each turn in for the night. It was a bit expensive, Julia. But you're worth it, aren't you?"

"I may be young farm girl, Michael, but I can tell when I'm being sweet-talked."

"Yes I am, sweetheart. Don't you like it, even a little bit?

Julia walked over to Mike and stepped into his warm embrace. "Actually Michael, yes I do like it. I hope you never stop."

Mike leaned down and kissed her upturned lips. They stood in the center of the room, hugging and kissing.

Her lips are so soft. I could do this for a while. Just calm down here fella, or you'll never get to supper or use that second bedroom either.

Mike held her away from him some.

"You probably don't realize just how much I love you, Julia. But I intend to do what I can to convince you."

"You can start right now, Michael, by kissing me again."

It was a few minutes before Mike could manage to push Julia away again.

"It's time for us to clean up for supper, Julia." He picked up her bag and led the way into her bedroom. He left, quickly.

In his room, Mike had striped to his shorts and washed. As he was finishing his shave, he heard Julia calling him.

"Just a minute, Julia," he shouted. Before he went into the sitting room, he wiped the excess shaving soap off his face, pulled on his trousers and put on a shirt. Just after he walked into the sitting room, the door to Julia's bedroom opened and she walked into the room.

Oh my God!

As with Mike, she too had partially undressed to wash. But unlike him she had not completely re-buttoned her underwear top before she stepped into the sitting room. So the garment gapped open barely hanging on her shoulders.

Arms wide at her sides, she held up a dress in each hand. "Which dress should I wear this evening, Michael?" she asked, smiling coquettishly at his obvious astonishment.

She is flat-out gorgeous! What a temptress. She wants me to see her like this. She doesn't want me to pick a dress for her to wear. I'll bet that she doesn't even want us to leave this room tonight.

My face feels like its on fire. Can she tell? The sight of her this way has my heart rate up too. Calm down, boy. Take a deep breath. The next move is up to you.

Straight faced, Michael told her, "I think the dress in your right hand would be fine Julia. But get on with it, please. Our reservation downstairs is in twenty minutes."

Mike turned his back to her and retreated quickly to his bedroom. Once inside he leaned against the shut door and waited for his heart to slow its pounding and the rest of his body to calm.

"Michael Drieborg!" he heard Julia shout from the doorway of her room. Then her door slammed shut.

Mike donned his dress uniform, sword and all, for this occasion. Then he took a seat in the sitting room and waited for Julia. When her door opened he stood up as she stepped into the room with a smile on her freshly scrubbed face.

Oh my! Fully clothed in that rather plain dress, she is still beautiful.

She raised her arms at her sides and spun in a circle before him.

"Does the major approve?"

"The major would be proud to escort the beautiful lady to supper. Would you allow me?"

$$*\qquad*\qquad*\qquad*$$

During dinner, Mike struggled to avoid talking about Julia's brazen display in their rooms. But Julia wouldn't let the matter be forgotten.

"Michael," she began smiling. "Do you realize that this is the first time I have been with a man, without a chaperone?"

"Julia," Mike responded. "I am very much aware of that. And, I am very aware of your beauty. But that stunt you pulled earlier this evening did not make it any easier on my resolve not to take advantage of you. I can't get that image of you out of my mind, thank you very much.

"Like what you , did you?" Julia teased.

"Yes I did; very much, thank you. I also like the perfume you are wearing. When did you get that?"

"It's nice that you noticed. Your sister Ann gave it to me for Christmas."

"All teasing aside, Michael," Julia continued. "I understand the duty you feel toward my parents to deliver me home safe and untouched. That is honorable of you; and I love you for it. But think a moment. You had your pistol on the train seat beside you today because you don't know if we are going to be attacked and killed by this Bacon enemy of yours. You're looking over your shoulder tonight too. On top of that, when you return to Washington, you might be sent to a cavalry unit to fight and possibly be killed. And you wonder why I want the man I love and will soon marry to make love to me, now?"

"I understand what you are saying, Julia. Believe me when I tell you that I haven't ignored your beauty or the strong desire I have for you, but it is also hard to ignore the obligation I feel toward your parents. They trust that I will not take advantage of you on this journey. How do I get around that, sweetheart?"

Julia had no quick answer.

After dessert, with Julia on his arm, Mike walked them into the lobby. The sight of an officer in full military dress was not all that unusual, especially in Cleveland's Weddell House. After all, the country was still at war. But Mike and Julia made a most handsome couple. But they did attract the stares of other hotel guests. Having been quite a celebrity in the nation's capital, Mike was used to such attention, especially when Congressman Kellogg's beautiful daughter Patricia had accompanied him. But Julia was surprised.

"Michael! Why are people staring at us?"

"They are looking because you are such a beautiful woman, Julia. The men envy me and the women are jealous of you."

"Am I expected to respond?"

"Yes. You can smile and tip your head in their direction, or you can coldly look away. I suggest you smile."

"Oh! My goodness, Michael!" Julia decided to smile.

"That's life in the big city, young lady, especially when you are seen with a war hero like me."

"Well I never. You forgot to add, a war hero with a big head."

They continued their walk down a hotel hallway lined with shops. These were not your small town general stores. On the contrary, these stores were stocked with expensive items only found in the very best homes, cut glass lamps, hand made crystal furnishings, jewelry, suits, dresses, dress hats and shoes were on display. There were no farm furnishings or work clothing here.

"Look at all these fancy things, Michael. I remember the homes in Washington where we were invited for tea. I saw lot of this kind of thing in them. I bet this stuff cost a lot."

"There's an old saying, Julia. If you have to ask the price, you can't afford it."

"Well then, Michael, we can't afford any of it. But it's still fun to look."

"Oh, Michael," Julia nudged him. "In this shop you can have your picture taken. Let's do it. Please, Michael? I would so like to have a picture of you."

"The picture you see in this display case is called a daguerreotype. It's the rage in Washington right now. I'm not at all surprised a fancy hotel like the Weddell has a shop like this. It would be great to have a picture of you with me too. Let's see if we can get it done tonight."

The shopkeeper suggested several poses they might consider. They chose one seated side by side on small couch, and another posing alone.

"We have to catch a train at eight o'clock tomorrow morning. Can we have them by then?"

"Not a problem. I'll finish them up tonight and have the prints at the desk in the morning. When you pay for your stay here, my charge will be included."

"Did you ever have one taken before, Michael?"

"Yes; last fall at a fashionable social function, one of the evening's highlights was to have a daguerreotype taken. It was great fun."

"What happened to your picture?"

"I must have left it at the office in Washington." *Actually, Patricia Kellogg has it. She probably has thrown it away by now. Truth be known, there were other daguerreotypes of me; that time I was in bed with a prostitute down on Hooker Street. I had been drugged and the photo was staged. Carl Bacon was behind that episode when I was a Congressman's aide in Washington. I think I'll keep that story to myself for now.*

"It's getting late, Julia," Mike reminded her. "We should be getting back to our rooms."

Julia looked up at Mike with a bright smile and squeezed his arm to her breast. "That sounds good to me, Michael."

Just the way she's looking at me, I know I could be in real trouble back in that sitting room.

✳   ✳   ✳   ✳

He was.

Mike had hardly dropped his belt sword and pistol on the sitting room table when Julia turned and was in his arms.

She reached up and pulled his head down for a kiss.

He's mine tonight, Julia thought. *I just know it.*

They continued to kiss as they stood in the center of the room.

Where did she learn to kiss like this? I don't care. I love it.

Before long, they had moved to the room's couch. Still in his arms, Julia whispered in Mike's ear, nipping his earlobe with her teeth.

"Will you always want to hold me and kiss me, Michael?"

"Of course, sweetheart," Mike assured her as he pulled her back into his arms.

"I am so afraid that when you return to duty I'll lose you to this terrible war; or to some beautiful Washington woman."

"We have already talked about my new assignment. It does not involve fighting, remember? As for another woman; I had an opportunity to have a life in Washington with the Congressman's daughter. I turned that down. But that's over. I love you Julia. I want to have a life with you, the baby Eleanor, Robert, and our children."

Julia slipped back onto Mike's lap and brought her lips to his again.

She put her hands on either side of Mike's face. "I want you to give me children, Michael. Make love to me now!" Julia urged kissing him again.

Mike pushed her back, "When we're married sweetheart. When we're married."

*   *   *   *

Mike jerked upright when a loud knock sounded on the sitting room hallway door.

"Major Drieborg," a man announced. "I have a message for you, sir."

"Could that be the picture-taking guy, Michael?"

"I don't know, Julia. Just to be on the safe side, though," Mike told her. "Get behind this table." He turned over the table in the center of the room. "I'll get my pistol before I open the door."

This can't be Carl Bacon again. He's in a military prison for trying to kill me last month in Detroit. But still, his father's money can buy most anything.

Gun in his hand by his side, Mike unlocked the door and slowly opened it. There was no messenger there. But Mike recognized a military grenade sitting on the floor by the door, and, the fuse was lit.

He slammed the door shut, threw himself across the room behind the round table and took Julia to the floor under him. Seconds later the bomb blew the door and part of the wall into the sitting room. It sent sharp wood splinters and pieces of metal flying through the air. Then, silence.

"Are you all right Julia?"

"I don't think I'm hurt. But I can't hear you very well. I feel like throwing up."

"Don't move. Stay behind the table," Mike ordered sternly.

Then he moved quickly to the blown-out doorway of their sitting room. Pistol in hand, he looked down the hall. He saw a man too poorly dressed to be a guest in this hotel walking toward him. The man had what looked like another bomb in his hand. Mike raised his pistol, and waited.

The man came closer and moved the bomb's fuse toward the lit cigar in his mouth.

He's going to light the fuse, Mike realized.

"Not again, you bastard!"

Mike fired and knocked the assassin to the floor with a bullet to the chest. The unlit bomb rolled harmlessly to the wall.

As Mike knelt by the bomb thrower he had just killed, he saw another man suddenly appear at the top of the stairway at the end of the hall. This man raised a handgun and shot at Mike; he missed. Without hesitating, Mike shot at him in response. Mike didn't miss. The impact of the bullet knocked the man backward, causing him to tumble down the stairs out of sight. Mike ran to the stairway and saw the man at the floor below struggling to stand.

As Mike walked down the stair he asked, "Why are you trying to kill me?"

The wounded man gripped the lower stairway railing and stood. "Nothin' personal Drieborg; just a job, ya understand."

Mike raised his pistol, "Who hired you?" He walked right up to the wounded man and put his pistol under the man's nose.

"Go ta 'hell, Drieborg."

"You first asshole." Mike shot the assassin in the face. The impact knocked the man against the wall. Then he tumbled down the staircase to the floor below.

Mike looked impassively at the wall where much of the man's brain and blood remained, turned and calmly walked up the stairs to check on Julia.

Its Bacon; no doubt in my mind. If he were here I'd kill that son-of-a-bitch and end all of this.

AFTERMATH

He no sooner had walked into the rubble of his sitting room that Julia rushed into his arms. She was sobbing and he could feel her body shake.

"Hold me, Michael, hold me close," she whispered.

"Drop the pistol, soldier. Put your hands on your head and turn around slowly," Mike heard. He released Julia and did as he was told.

Several men in uniform stood in the hallway, their pistols pointed at Mike and Julia.

"Easy now soldier," Mike was told. "Place yer hands a'top of yer head if ya please an stand really still. We're not used ta this kind'a thing in Cleveland's best hotel. Chief of Police Haynes will be here shortly. While we're waiting you can sit on the couch miss."

After Chief Haynes arrived, he and the police officers on the scene, sorted things out. Mike and Julia were moved to another suite. The police then took a written statement from Mike. And, the hotel clerk identified the dead man outside of Mike's room as the one who had forced information about Drieborg from him earlier that day. Chief Haynes concluded that Mike had acted in self-defense.

"We're going to post guards in the hallway for the rest of the night Major," Haynes told Mike. "We won't put up with this kind of thing in our city."

✳   ✳   ✳   ✳

In the sitting room of their new suite, Mike sat on the couch and held Julia close.

*She is pretty badly shaken ,h*e thought. *I'm pretty upset, too. Not because I just killed two men, but because I didn't have to kill the second one. I could have turned him over to the police. But I was in a rage and killed him out of hate.*

"You don't need to worry any more tonight, Julia. The Chief Haynes put two of his men outside our door. They'll stay with us until we leave on the train tomorrow."

"I don't care, Michael. I can't be alone again, not for even a minute."

Mike could feel her shake again. "Don't worry, sweetheart. I'm right here. I'll not leave you. We need to try and get some sleep."

Julia was trembling so badly that she could not even undo the buttons of her dress; Mike had to do it. When he finished, he took off her dress, unlaced her shoes and removed her stockings and underwear as well. He carried her to her bed. He even had to help her put on her nightgown. She curled up as he slid her under the covers and blew out the light.

He had barely stood up when Julia gripped his hand. "Please don't leave me." She pleaded.

"I won't, sweetheart," he assured her. "Let me wash up and I'll just be a minute" He went to the other bedroom. He threw his clothing on the unused bed, washed, put on his nightclothes and returned to Julia's room. But he didn't forget his pistol.

Mike placed the reloaded pistol on the bed stand. Then he joined Julia under the covers. In his arms, she fell asleep quickly. But not Mike; he was still reliving the explosion and the killings.

How will I ever explain to Papa why I killed that second guy?

It seemed like hours to him before he finally shut his eyes.

✳   ✳   ✳   ✳

The knock on the bedroom door startled Mike awake. He quickly reached for his pistol.

"Major, this is Sgt. Ryan, sir. "Tis six o'clock sir; time for you and the young lady to be havin' breakfast if ya' plan to make yer train to Philadelphia."

Fully awake now, Mike answered. "Thank you, Sergeant. After what happened last night, I'm still a little nervous about opening a door. Could you have the kitchen send up our breakfast with a pot of hot coffee? It will be better if we ate in our sitting room this morning."

"Yes sir. I'm sure they can do that; safer for all concerned that'a way, too."

Mike slipped out of bed and went into the other bedroom. He stripped, washed and shaved. Still in his underwear, he heard Julia shout in freight.

"Michael. Where are you?"

"I'm right here, sweetheart. I'm coming." Like last evening, before he got to her room, she appeared in the doorway. This time a flannel nightgown covered her from head to toe. She ran into his arms.

"I woke up and you were gone."

"You were sleeping. I didn't want to awaken you. I was just in the next room cleaning up, Julia. Besides, I had to use the chamber pot."

"Am I being silly, Michael?"

"Not entirely. But we do have to get ready. One of the policemen is bringing up our breakfast. Then we have to go to the train station; so you to need to get a move on."

"What happened after that explosion last night, Michael?"

"I killed the man who put the bomb by our door. There was another man with him. I killed him, too."

"Have you killed men before, Michael?"

Be careful here, Drieborg. Remember, you're supposed to be a nice guy. She might not understand.

"Yes I have, Julia. I'm a soldier, you know."

"Didn't it bother you?"

"In the battle at Gettysburg, I was part of a group of men fighting another group of men. It's so impersonal and happens so fast, that it doesn't seem as though you killed anyone. In prison we killed men, other prisoners who were attacking us; self-defense didn't cause any of us remorse. We had to defend ourselves if we were to survive. Can you understand that, Julia?"

"But last night; do you feel remorse for killing those two men?"

"Not in the least. They were hired to attack and kill us. The only way for me to have stopped them was to kill them. I feel no remorse at all. In fact, Julia, I would do it again in a heartbeat."

"That doesn't seem like the gentle Michael I know."

"Bother you?"

"I know it shouldn't. But I never experienced anything like it. I know you carried your pistol on the seat in the train yesterday; but I never thought we'd be attacked. I'm just a naïve farm girl, Michael. Thank you for protecting me."

"Speaking of protecting me; did you take off my clothes last night?"

"Yes I did, Julia. You don't remember any of that?"

"What else did you do that I don't remember?"

"I brushed your hair some after getting you into your nightgown."

"And then you slept with me, the whole night?"

"Yes, I did; for protection."

Julia turned to go into her bedroom. Before she closed the door behind her, she looked back at Mike.

"I'm sorry I missed that part."

Me too, Mike thought.

$$\ast \qquad \ast \qquad \ast \qquad \ast$$

Later, they were finishing breakfast in the sitting room, when someone knocked on the door. Julia looked at Mike in alarm.

"Not to worry this time, sweetheart," he assured her. "Remember, we've had two policemen outside our door all night. They're still there."

As his rose to move toward the door, he noticed Julia hug herself and take a deep breath.

"Yes? Who's there?"

"This is Chief of Police Haynes of the Cleveland Police Department, Major. Can I have a word with you?"

Mike offered the police captain a seat and a cup of coffee.

"Thank you sir, and miss." Haynes sat and addressed them both. "The bomb thrower you killed last night was a local troublemaker. He and his accomplice were members of the same Cleveland gang. Both of them just got released from the Federal prison in Detroit. According to our sources, that's where the fellow who tried to kill you earlier this year when you were passing through Detroit is kept. We figure he paid these two. We're glad to be rid of them, I assure you. But the rest of their bunch might not take the killing so kindly. They might just come after you."

Mike moved to Julia's side.

"Don't worry, miss," Chief Haynes continued. "We do not intend to let them harm you."

"It just so happens that the Waddell House has several Ohio Congressmen staying here as guests. They were in a meeting room last night when all the commotion occurred. Congressman Clark from this very city was most interested when he heard who was attacked. It seems that he knows your Congressman; you too for that matter, Major.

He wired his colleague and received assurances that an escort will meet you two in Baltimore. For our part, two of Cleveland's best policemen will be with you on the train until you reach that city."

The hotel manager Bill Young joined them.

"Please accept our apologies, Major Drieborg, miss. The clerk who gave those attackers your room number has been dismissed. We have waived all room charges, even for these daguerreotypes you had taken last evening. We hope you will stay with us the next time you are in Cleveland and that the rest of your journey will be a safe one."

"Thank you, Mr. Young," Mike responded. "I'm sorry about all of this damage. And, thank you, Chief. It takes a load off my mind that I'll be able to get Julia to her parents safely."

"Major," the Chief continued. "Aside from our concern for every visitor to Cleveland, it is important that these toughs know that we will not put up with this kind of conduct in our city. As we speak, my men are rounding up as many of this bunch we can find. Miss, you can rest assured that we will do our best to get you home safe and sound."

BALTIMORE

It was barely light when Mike and Julia left Cleveland. With their police escort, they were the only passengers in their railroad car. As they reached each stop along the way, blinds were pulled and all were on alert with weapons drawn. In Philadelphia, the couple was hurriedly transferred to a southbound train for the last railroad leg of their journey. Lunch was served in their rail car. That evening, they were met at the Baltimore railroad station by a military escort and taken to a nearby hotel.

"This suite of rooms is a far cry from Cleveland's Waddell House, Michael."

"I would have preferred a nicer place for our last night together, Julia. But Captain Wheeler, the officer in charge of our escort decided his detail could best protect us here. The captain has the room to the right of this sitting room, and two of his men will stand guard in the hallway while the other two rest in the room to the left of our bedroom."

"With all this secrecy, how will my parents know where to find us?"

"He said that your parents have been notified. They are supposed to meet us downstairs by noon tomorrow."

"How are we going to spend any time together with guards all around? You were so standoffish on the train ride here, I couldn't believe it. Was it something I said?"

"Not at all, Julia," Mike assured her. "I would have liked nothing better than to give you all my attention. But for all I knew, we could have been attacked again; and I was nervous about that. That was then and this is now though. But" Mike held out his arms to her. "Come over here young lady, these arms want to hold you."

"I can do better than that, mister." She brought her lips to his. That took care of conversation for a while.

Still on his lap, Julia pulled back some from the kiss.

Julia sat silently for a moment looking down at the hands in her lap.

"What is it, Julia?"

"Last night. Is that what battle is like; explosions, with things flying all over? "

"Yes, only much worse. Everyone is screaming and yelling as you and your enemies attack one another. There's sort of an out-of-control madness about it. And, I know it sounds crazy, but you seem to shut off all the sounds of battle somehow and you don't think about anything; you just kill. When I was wounded, I was stabbed from behind; didn't even see my attacker."

"That's what happened to us last night, isn't it, Michael? We didn't see our attackers then either."

"Sort of, Julia; we didn't see the attack coming or the assassins who tried to kill us."

"That could happen again tonight, couldn't it Michael; even with guards outside our room?"

"Yes, it could."

"Are you going to have guards after you get back to Washington?"

"No, Julia. I don't think so."

"It sounds to me like that banker back in Lowell, Michigan will not stop these attacks until you're dead. With all his money he'll eventually find someone to kill you. He may not even be satisfied with that. He might be hateful enough to destroy your whole family. Is it silly for me to think this way, Michael?"

"It's not silly at all, Julia. Seems to me you're simply trying to see our situation as clearly as you can; right?"

She nodded in agreement. Mike pulled her closer. "I can't tell you how sorry I am to have gotten you involved in this mess, sweetheart. It might be best for us to keep apart until this Bacon problem can be solved."

Julia jerked out his embrace, and looked him sternly in the eyes.

My goodness, I never saw her so angry. I was just trying to protect her.

"If you're trying to get out of your marriage proposal to me, forget it! It will take more than a few bombs or this war to scare me off, buster! I intend to be by your side until both are settled. But one thing I'm not going to wait for is for us to make love. You got that?"

"Yes ma'am! Do you have any other orders for this lowly major who is hopelessly in love with you?"

Snuggling back into Mike's warm embrace, Julia purred. "Now that you mention it, Major Drieborg, yes I do. Let's talk some about the rest of our evening together. I gather we're going to eat supper right here in this sitting room; and later you and I are going to sleep in the same bed together. Is that right, Michael? "

"Yes, but don't get any funny ideas, Julia. Sleep is what we're going to do tonight; nothing else."

"Is that right?" Julia taunted, with that mischievous smile Mike had come to know. "We'll see about that." She looked up at Mike, put her hand behind his head and brought his lips to hers.

Tomorrow my parents will take me home. Tonight will be our last night together, maybe forever.

Julia's experience with boys had been limited to her schoolmates. She hadn't been attracted to those boys at all. In fact, she thought them a major pain to be avoided. Other girls at school, especially those who lived in the nearby town, thought otherwise. And they seemed to know ever so much more about boys; or at least they talked as if they did. One of the whispered secrets they shared was about kissing a boy on the lips; something Julia had never done before Michael, that is. They said that it was enjoyable especially if you parted your lips some.

That sounded ugly to me when I first heard it. But my sister Eleanor told me that it was true, if you were kissing someone you loved that is.

Tonight, I'm going to try that with the man I love, she decided.

So she opened her lips a little, then some more against Mike's lips. He stiffened in surprise, but she held his head tightly and kept her open lips against his.

That's right, Michael, just relax and enjoy.

Mike put his hands on her shoulders and gently pushed her away.

What has come over me? I should stop this. I always did with Julia's sister Eleanor before we were married, and with Patricia Kellogg despite her invitations.

"Please, Michael. Don't stop."

"We have to, Julia. I'm not made of stone believe me. Besides, I promised your parents. If we go on, I'll not be able to face them."

Before Julia could respond, there was a knock on the door.

My Lord! Not again. Where is my pistol?

"Major Drieborg? This is Captain Wheeler. If you don't mind, sir, the hotel people want to know about eating arrangements this evening and in the morning?"

Julia slid off Mikes lap and rushed into her bedroom.

"Just a moment, Captain." Mike answered. He straightened his jacket and ran his fingers through his hair.

"Come in, Captain. Miss Hecht is cleaning up in her bedroom. Please sit down."

$*$ $*$ $*$ $*$

Later Mike and Julia were served supper in their sitting room. Neither of them had spoken of the passion they shared earlier. Now, they were making small talk.

"I'm surprised. This stew is really good, isn't it, Michael?"

"Not bad. I prefer the biscuits your mother and mine make. This will do, though."

Julia certainly had me on the verge of giving in earlier this evening. Might have happened if we had not been interrupted. The touch off her lips was so nice.

I can tell just by looking at Michael that he wants to make love to me. That damn honor of his. I want him too, that's for sure. My hand is shaking so much right now that I can't even set my teacup down without it rattling against the saucer. Did he hear it? I know my face is flushed. Can he see?

"Do you want anything more, Julia?"

"Yes I do, Michael," She pushed her chair back, rose and stepped around the table.

For the second time this evening, Julia was going to tempt her Michael.

Forgive me, Lord! Mike thought. *She's right. There may not be a tomorrow for us, only a now. She's unbuttoning her dress.*

Mike stood, too.

"No, sweetheart," he protested. He put his hands on her shoulders and pulled her to him.

Julia struggled free, angry.

"Didn't you understand any of what I said to you earlier? We were almost killed last night. We could be attacked again tonight. Maybe killed this time."

"I heard every word you said and I do understand. And right now, I want you so much that I hurt. But we both know it's still not right."

Crying now, Julia stepped into Mike's arms.

✳   ✳   ✳   ✳

It was nearly midnight. The bedroom door was securely locked. Mike's pistol was within reach on the bed stand. The drapes were pulled back from the slightly open window. Moonlight and cool air flowed into the chilly room.

But under blankets, Mike and Julia were far from cold. Still too frightened to sleep alone, Mike slept with her He held her close until she fell asleep. It was not a good arrangement for someone who was having a hard time resisting her, even when she was fully clothed. But the memory of Cleveland was still fresh for her, and so was her fear of being alone.

"Michael?"

"Yes, sweetheart?"

"You're so quiet. I thought you were asleep."

"Fat chance, sleeping with you so close to me."

"We could do something about that, you know."

✳   ✳   ✳   ✳

"Clang! Clang! Clang!" The loud sound stunned Mike. He threw back the covers, jumped out of bed and gathered his clothing scattered on the floor.

"Julia!" he shouted sternly. "Get dressed right now." He put on his pants, jacket and pulled on his boots; picked up his pistol.

"I can see smoke coming under the door of our room. Take the water pitcher, Julia, and soak a blanket. Keep it with you until we see what is going on."

He heard a pounding on their bedroom door.

"Major Drieborg. This is Captain Wheeler. Get dressed, sir. There is smoke coming up the stairwell and into this hallway. Someone's sounding a fire alarm on the floor below. We best go down the back stairs to the ground floor."

Damn! It's Bacon again; Detroit last year; Cleveland last night; Baltimore tonight. When will all this end?

"Don't leave me, Michael." Julia pleaded. She hadn't bothered to lace up her shoes, but she had almost finished buttoning her dress.

"Bring that wet blanket, Julia. My pistol is in my right hand, so you stay by my left side."

He slowly opened the hallway door. The four guards and Captain Wheeler were waiting.

"The back stairs are this way, Major."

"Wait!" Mike ordered. "Captain, you and two of your detail move down the stairs first. I'll remain on this floor with Miss Hecht and the other two soldiers. We'll join you after you tell us the floor below has been secured. Is that clear?"

"Yes sir."

Smoke continued to build up on their floor.

"I'm frightened, Michael."

"Put the wet blanket over your head sweetheart," Mike directed. "Stay close; we'll be all right." He pulled her closer with his left arm.

He placed the two soldiers behind them a few feet facing the stairway at the far end of the hallway. They held their rifles loaded and ready. They waited.

I wouldn't be a bit surprised if there weren't two or three attackers on each floor. This time, one of them will survive to tell me who paid them. I'll get it out of him, whatever it takes.

Shots rang out on the floor below. Then, shots hit the wall by Mike's head.

"Get down and return fire," Mike ordered. "Julia, get into that corner."

Mike fired his pistol at a target down the smoky hallway. The two soldiers began firing in that direction, too. Their target lurched backward. Then there was silence.

From the floor below "Major, are you all right, sir?"

"So far we are, Captain. Have you secured your area?"

"Yes sir. We have taken one of them prisoner. He's wounded. What do you want me to do with him?"

"Hold on to him. I'll be right down."

Mike ordered the two soldiers on his floor to hold their positions. Then, he took Julia down the stairs to the floor below.

"Julia," Mike told her. "Stay with Captain Wheeler. I'm going back up to make sure that the hallway up there is clear. Then I'll bring our bags down." Julia was trembling and clutching his arm.

"Be strong now. I have to do this." He pulled her hand away and ran back up the stairs.

"All right, men, one at a time, down the hallway," he directed. "All this smoke probably came from a smoke bomb, not a fire. But move carefully."

First one man moved a few feet, then the other, then Mike. Halfway down the hall, they found a man, dead. Otherwise, the area was deserted. Mike searched the man's pockets and found written directions for the attack; nothing else.

By this time, the local police were on both floors. They interviewed Mike and Captain Wheeler. Julia was taken to another suite under guard.

"I'll only be a minute, Julia." Mike promised.

A Baltimore policeman spoke to Mike. "We know that dead man upstairs. He's a local tough for hire. The wounded one you captured is new to us. He's probably from out of town."

"I'd like to question him if you don't mind," Mike proposed. "If I could take him into one of these rooms for a few minutes, I think I could reason with him."

"Go ahead Major," the police officer offered. "Leave some of him for us though. We have some questions we'd like to ask, too."

Mike pushed the man into an empty room and closed the door behind them. The fellow's hands were handcuffed behind him and he limped from a minor gunshot wound to his leg. He turned and saw that Mike held a very large knife.

Mike put the point of the blade under the assassin's chin and pushed upward just enough to force the man to his tiptoes. Blood trickled down his neck.

"Do you know who I am?" Mike pulled the knife back some.

"I heard that other army guy call you Major Drieborg. But I guess that's who you are."

"Was I your target?" Mike brought the knife back under the man's chin. He lowered it some so the man could answer.

"Yep. We were to kill you, and anyone with you."

"Why?

"Don't know. It was just a job I was paid ta' do."

The knife was back. "Who paid you?"

"The head of my gang in Cleveland told me ta' do it and promised me fifty dollars in gold if I killed you. If you're askin' where the gold came from, I don't know."

"You don't know very much, do you?"

"I know my life wouldn't be worth a plug nickel if I ratted on my mates."

"Tell me this, mister tough guy. Would you get many of these jobs if you had only one leg?"

"But I got both legs."

"I've seen men lose a leg after minor wounds less serious than yours. Of course I could be wrong."

Mike held the man's shirt in his left hand and with his right plunged the knife into the man's wounded leg.

"Do I cut the rest of your wounded leg's muscles, or has your memory improved?"

"Stop; stop!" the man shouted. "I was told that some guy in the Detroit federal prison wanted revenge. Said you railroaded him. He's the son of a rich guy, a banker or something."

"You'll tell the police that?"

"Yes."

"You'll sign a statement for me, too?"

"Yes. But don't cut me any more."

"One more thing." Mike told him. "Are there any more attacks planned?"

"We thought we would kill you tonight. So I don't think so; at least not yet."

"What in hell does that mean; not yet?" Mike twisted the knife causing the man to moan.

"We promised ta' kill you, Drieborg. Bad for our reputation if we let you live."

Dayton, Maryland

"Captain Wheeler," Mike ordered. "I don't know how good you are on a horse, but you and your detail are leaving with me right now. We're going to take Miss Hecht to her parents' farm. Get your gear. The Baltimore police are arranging a wagon and horses for us. Your men can ride in the wagon. You and I will be on horseback."

I'm not going to give that hoodlum bunch another chance tonight. The police will escort us out of town. My guess is that the local toughs aren't much good outside of the city.

Within an hour they were well on their way out of Baltimore. Julia was bundled up in the wagon. Two soldiers were in the back with her and the other two handled the team of horses from the front bench. Everyone had a rifle. Mike had given Julia a pistol, just in case.

Without incident, they pulled into the Hechts' farmyard two hours before dawn.

Julia rushed through the doorway of the house into her mother's arms.

"My heavens, Michael," her mother gasped. "What is happening?"

"Julia can tell you, Mrs. Hecht." Mike assured her. "Ruben, can you and Kenny help us out in the barn?"

"Ya Michael. Just give me a minute to get dressed."

While the men were out in the barn, Mrs. Hecht and Julia rekindled the fire, brewed coffee and fixed warm food for everyone. Mike explained everything while they ate.

"I'm real sorry about all of this, folks. I don't think we've been followed. Before I turn in, I'm going to ride back up the road some just to make sure. Bill, a soldier in this detail can ride a horse, he says. He'll go with me. The rest of the men will get some sleep in the barn. We'll scout around some in the morning, too."

"Der are some blankets in da loft, Michael," Ruben told him. "Kenny, bring dem down for da men. Den ve go to bed again."

✶   ✶   ✶   ✶

"Papa. Did you see how Julia hugged Michael before he left the house just now?"

"No Mamma. Vat do you mean?" Ruben was pulling on his nightclothes for the second time that night; so was Emma, his wife.

"I think there is something between them, Papa."

"It is late Momma. Come, sleep now. You can talk mit Julia in da morning, ya?"

✶   ✶   ✶   ✶

Emma was up baking bread at the usual hour. Ruben was sitting at the table smoking his pipe and drinking his first coffee of the day.

"Julia," Emma greeted. "It is so early, dear. After all that you have been through, why don't you stay in bed for awhile?"

Julia moved to Ruben and gave him a hug. "That's all right Momma. I want to help get things ready for the men this morning. What can I do?"

"All right, since you are up and dressed anyway, set the table. Then when the bread is almost ready you can scramble some eggs and fry some bacon. I want them to have a good meal before they leave for Washington this morning."

While Julia was getting the table set, she told her parents of her stay in Michigan. They were full of questions about baby Eleanor, too. But before long, Emma couldn't resist asking.

"I couldn't help noticing how you and Michael hugged one another. Is there something between you two?"

"Michael and I wanted to talk to you about this together; but yes there is Momma. He asked me to marry him and I accepted."

The room became quiet. The only sound in the room was that of the burning wood crackling in the fireplace. Ruben put his mug down and just looked at his wife. She stared out the kitchen window, her back toward Julia.

Before anyone spoke again, the outside door opened and Mike could be heard stomping the snow off his boots in the entryway. When he entered the room, everyone looked his way.

Oops! They way everyone is looking at me, I'll bet Julia told them of our plans to marry.

"Good morning everyone; can I have some of that hot coffee, Ruben?" Mike asked rubbing his cold hands together.

"I'll get it for you, Michael," Julia offered.

Mike stood by the fireplace, warming up, when she handed him a mug of black coffee.

She stayed by his side and faced her mother.

"Michael. My mother asked me if there was something special between you and me. I told her that we intended to marry. Do you want to add anything?"

"Only that I want you and Ruben to know that during my stay at home, I came to realize that I loved Julia very much. And, I believe she will be a great mother for little Eleanor and Robert. But I ask that you allow her to marry me."

Julia moved closer and held Mike's hand.

What is Momma worried about? Is she still mad at Michael?

"We have the soldiers in the barn to take care of this morning. We will talk of this after they leave. Is that all right with you Papa?"

"Ya Momma," Ruben agreed. "Ve talk later."

Julia objected. "Momma, you know very well that Michael will leave with them. If you and Papa need to talk with us about this before you give permission, it has to be now."

"If Michael has to leave, he will leave. After all, he has his duty to perform. When he has the time, maybe he will come back for that talk. We will see. Come now, finish setting the table. You still have eggs and bacon to fix for the men."

Emma Hecht was the boss in this house. Julia did as she was told.

But Ruben could speak for himself too. He broke the silence. "Sit down here mit me, Michael. Tell me about your father's harvest. Vhat are da crop prices like in Michigan?"

The two men talked as though nothing unusual was going on. Julia looked at them in dismay.

Men! How can they do that? Michael's going to leave after breakfast for only God knows how long; maybe forever. And, he's gabbing away with Papa like nothing important should be decided before he leaves. Has he forgotten that he promised to marry me? Men!

Shortly, the soldiers joined them for breakfast.

Afterward, everyone gathered in the yard to see them off.

Mike had yet to join them. He stood in the house's entryway holding Julia in his arms. He could feel her tremble, even through his heavy greatcoat. She arranged a wool scarf around his neck and caressed his neck with her warm hands.

"Momma makes me so mad, Michael, I could scream."

"Well don't. If you keep your calm and don't make a big fuss, things will work out Julia. Please watch that temper of yours. Harsh words are hard to forgive and even harder to forget. We don't need that. We'll be married, sweetheart. Promise me you will be patient with your parents; please."

"I know you're right, Michael. I'll try. But it won't be easy. You just take care of yourself soldier. Promise?"

"Yes, I promise. I'll be back to visit as soon as I can get some time."

Oblivious of those waiting for him outside the doorway, he kissed her one more time. Mike reluctantly pushed Julia away, put on his slouch hat, pulled on his riding gloves and left the house. Tears welled in her eyes as she watched him ride away.

God bless you, Michael. Bring him back to me, Lord.

WASHINGTON CITY

Mike and his escort arrived in Washington City without incident. The escort stayed with Mike until he went into Congressman Kellogg's office building.

Kellogg came out of his private office as soon as he was informed Mike had arrived.

"My lord, man, you have had quite a time getting back here in one piece."

"It was all quite a surprise to me as well, sir."

"I want you to tell me all about it, of course. But right now you and I need to meet with some people about the prisoner-of-war issue. You can bring me up to date on the other matter over lunch."

For the next several hours they met with a number of people and discussed the plight of Federal soldiers recently released from Confederate prisons. Medical personnel laid out the problems these men faced. Men responsible for clothing, equipment, transportation and pay gave their suggestions as well. Each specialist also presented the Congressman a written analysis with recommendations. As soon as they were alone, Kellogg told Mike what was expected of him.

"I want you to review these after lunch today, Mike," he directed. "You know my office manager, George Krupp. He'll get you an office to use. If you need anything, ask him. He's arranged lodging for you, too. First thing in the morning tomorrow, you and I will go over these documents with your notes and recommendations. Any questions, Mike?"

"No sir. You seem to have everything covered."

"Good. Now, let's get out of here for some lunch. How about the Willard Hotel; that place is always fun? The food's not bad, either."

*   *   *   *

The two men stood in the doorway waiting to be seated. "Not much has changed since were here last October, Congressman," Michael observed.

The hotel's large dining room was crowded and full of cigar smoke. Waiters delivering trays full of food were everywhere. Those with empty trays virtually ran between the tables on the way back to the kitchen.

"Not much at all, Mike. The Willard is still the largest hotel in Washington. It's the only one with indoor plumbing and toilets for its guests, too. This restaurant probably serves the most meals per day in this town. It is quite a place."

"You might remember the last time we had lunch here together. I told you then that there is much more going on here than just eating and drinking. Even today, bribes are surely being offered and taken in this very room; right now, probably. Men are meeting with Federal officials to gain a commission or a government contract. More government related decisions are made here than in any other place in Washington outside of the president's office. There are probably Confederate spies in this room right now, too, trying to pick up information useful to their cause. Look around us. Can you spot any spies; or see any bribes being paid?"

"I'm afraid not, sir."

"Here's our waiter, Mike. I'm going to have the chicken potpie. For all I know, it could be made with horsemeat or alley cat; tastes good, though."

"After my stay at Andersonville Prison, I can stomach most anything. I'll have the pot pie, too."

After sweet potato pie and coffee, Mike joined the Congressman in smoking a cigar.

"I don't recall you smoking, Mike."

"Sorry to ruin my image, sir. But I must admit I've picked up some bad habits; an occasional cigar is one of them."

"I won't even ask about the others," Congressman Kellogg chuckled.

'Thank you, sir."

"After you were attacked in Cleveland I got a telegraph message from my colleague, Congressman Clark, about it. That's when I arranged for the military escort to meet you in Baltimore last night."

"It seems the Washington reporter from the Grand Rapids Eagle was in Cleveland, too. He wrote a story about the attack on you and Miss Hecht for his paper. My aide there telegraphed me a copy. According to the story, the Cleveland police were quite impressed with how you handled yourself. After the attack in Baltimore last night, that would make three attempts to kill you. Tell me about them, would you?"

"Yes, sir." For the next half an hour or But Mike told of the three attempts on his life; the first in Detroit, last November; the second in Cleveland two nights ago; and the third in Baltimore last night.

"It sounds to me that Harvey Bacon has paid for all three attempts," Kellogg concluded.

"It would seem But if you can believe the confession I got from one of the assassins last night," Mike confirmed. He handed the Congressman the written statement the wounded man made and signed.

"This confession could be very useful. I have some thoughts about how this vendetta might be stopped. First, I'll have my aide back in Michigan have a talk with the Federal marshal in Grand Rapids. Second, my friends at Old Kent Bank might be interested in opening another office; maybe Lowell is ready for a new bank. And third, the Federal authorities might be willing to tighten security at their Detroit prison where it applies to one of their inmates, Carl Bacon."

"As usual, sir," Mike observed, "You have come to my rescue again."

"We can't have a holder of the Congressional Medal of Honor a walking target for any tough Harvey Bacon's money can buy; now can we? Besides, Mike, as I've told you before, we don't need any more dead heroes. We need men of honor like you alive and able to help us heal the country once this terrible war has ended."

"Thank you, Congressman. You know that I will do anything I can to help."

"I know that, Mike," Kellogg assured him. "Right now, we need to get back to the office. You don't realize it yet, but you and I have a busy schedule in the next few weeks. It starts this afternoon with the work I assigned you. Get a good night's sleep tonight too because starting tomorrow we will be busy selling our plan to help the released prisoners of war.

"We start with a meeting with President Lincoln in his office, then with members of Congress and the Senate. We'll meet with the press, too; and we will use evening social events to interest people in our project. The people of this town who count will remember the dashing Major Drieborg, I think. We need them on our side, too."

As the two men left the building, Kellogg asked Mike one more question.

"Patricia told me that you two could not work things out. How are you coming with the problems of parenting your daughter and your stepson?"

They walked a ways in silence.

It's out now. I don't know how this will affect his attitude towards me; but I must tell him.

"Well, sir." Mike told him. "Julia Hecht consented to marry me. You might remember her when you had my family and the Hechts at your home last fall. She is my late wife's sister."

"She is very pretty too, as I recall. I expect she will be a fine mother for your stepson and your little daughter; and a fine wife for you, too. Actually Mike, I was not all that sorry to hear of the decision you and Patricia made. You made an attractive couple, but I had come to believe your marriage would not have been a happy union for either of you."

"She and I came to the same conclusion, sir."

*   *   *   *

Later that evening Mike was settling into his rented room. It was sparsely furnished and came with breakfast and supper. But it was fine for his purpose. Even so he was surprised at how much it cost; even a small bedroom in a boarding house was expensive in wartime Washington. He had a closet for his uniforms, a dresser for his other clothing, a bed and a small writing desk, all for nearly half of his monthly pay as a major.

I'm really tired. But I need to let my folks know that I am well; Julia too. So Mike sat at his desk.

Meeting with President Lincoln

"Please be seated, gentlemen. The President is expecting you and the major."

They did as they were told and took chairs by the door. The room was crowded with men hoping to see President Lincoln. They all wanted something from him. He didn't want to see any of them, actually; so only a very select few would make it beyond his secretary today.

"The President is ready for you, sir; and the major too of course."

If looks could kill, Mike thought. *The Congressman told me that most of the people in this waiting room today will never get to see President Lincoln; we just waltzed in as though we owned the place.*

The president stood with his back to one of his office windows. He was reading a document in the bright sunlight that came in over his shoulder. He looked up when the door was shut behind the two visitors.

"Congressman Kellogg, Major Drieborg, welcome." He greeted the men while walking over to them with his right hand extended. They both shook his hand.

"Welcome back to Washington, Major, from your recent leave. It looks as though your mother's cooking has agreed with you."

"Yes sir, it did. And thank you for the welcome."

He directed the two men to chairs by the fireplace and sat facing them.

"I have been reading your documents, Kellogg; I must say your analysis clearly identifies the problems faced by our poor soldiers recently freed from Confederate prisons; and your recommendations make sense. What can I do to help?"

"We need you to publicly endorse our project, sir; have Major Drieborg assigned to the Committee on the Conduct of the War; and direct the Secretary of War to give him written authority to commandeer resources needed to accomplish these recommendations."

"I can take care of those requests, Congressman. And, since I was re-elected handily last fall, my endorsement of this project might carry some weight with the public. It's a slow news time right now with the armies in winter quarters, the holidays over and the Congress out of session. The press just might give this project a lot of attention.

"Meet with my secretary, Kellogg to set up my announcement to the press. Invite whomever happens to be in town from the Congress and the Senate. You and the major must be there too, of course. Be sure to wear that medal I awarded you last fall, Major. Reporters have short memories, so I'll remind them that you received the Congressional Medal of Honor; and that you were once a prisoner at Andersonville. They need a non-political person to focus on, you see; it should make it easier for them to support our project.

"I suspect that there are thousands of families anxious about their loved ones being held in Confederate prisons, Kellogg. It won't hurt their support of the war effort either if we tell them of our concern and of our plans to help the freed men regain their health and return home."

The president stood signaling that the meeting had come to an end.

"We appreciate your support, Mr. President," Kellogg asserted.

On the way to the door, Lincoln put his arm around Mike's shoulder.

"How is your father, Major? Jacob isn't it?"

"He's fine, sir. He'll be happy to know you remembered him."

"He and I and your father-in-law, Ruben, had a nice conversation when they were at the White House for your medal ceremony. I enjoyed their company immensely."

"Please give them both my regards."

"Yes sir, I will."

Meeting with Congress

The next day, Mike sat at a special meeting with the Joint Committee on the Conduct of the War. He and Congressman Kellogg had privately met with the Committee Chairman and several of its key members to go over the details of the plan.

The Chairman began the meeting. "Good morning, Major Drieborg. I'm pleased that you could join us. The purpose of your presence today is to explain this project to the members of the committee. Please proceed."

"Thank you, sir."

Over the next hour, Mike went over the entire project with the committee. He identified the severe malnutrition, dysentery, rickets and depression most of the freed soldiers suffer; and the solutions proposed by federal medical experts. Based upon sheer numbers he gave them estimates of clothing, equipment, transportation and payroll needs.

"My heavens, Major. I had no idea of the enormity of this problem. Do we have enough medical personnel on site to care for these men? And if not, where will we get them?"

"To answer your first question, sir; we do not have properly trained personnel available at this time. Let me explain what I mean by properly trained. We have many doctors in the field who are trained to treat battlefield wounds. We have very few equipped by training or experience to deal with the maladies these men will be suffering.

"The answer to your second question, sir; we don't know, actually. We intend to ask doctors and nurses from the civilian work force to help out on a volunteer and short term basis."

"We feel sure that we can supply clothing and food through existing channels current stores. Transportation can be supplied through a combination of military and civilian methods"

"Any other comments or questions for the major?" asked the chairman.

"I have a few of both, Mr. Chairman."

"Mr. Webster, the Congressman from Tennessee, has the floor."

Last fall, this fellow and I had almost come to blows during my last appearance before this committee. This guy is still so fat he can't even sit up to the table. This is ten o'clock in the morning and I can smell the alcohol on him from across the table. I don't like him any more now than I did when he went after me last fall. What did Congressman Kellogg call him, a Copperhead; a southern sympathizer; he said that to his face in front of this entire committee.

"It is good to see you looking so well, Major." he began. "Just to be sure; aren't you the man who led the attack on fellow prisoners at Andersonville Prison and bragged about killing several of them with his own hands? "

"Yes sir. That was me."

"I just read that you are still killing people; two in Cleveland a week recently; and another one the following night in Baltimore. Is that true as well?"

"Yes sir. It is. And aren't you the Congressman who voted to end prisoner exchanges and let our imprisoned troops rot in Confederate jails because the Rebs wouldn't exchange our Negro soldiers they had taken prisoner?"

Mike could see the man's face redden. "I see you are still disrespectful of authority, Major. But tell me, with your penchant for killing wouldn't you better serve the interests of our war against the Confederacy if you were assigned to a combat unit? "

"I think so too, sir. But, President Lincoln thinks otherwise. He told me that he believes I will accomplish more working with our newly released prisoners of war than I could as a combat cavalryman."

"I'm in the habit of following orders, sir," Mike continued. "I think it's called doing ones duty, Congressman."

The man's face reddened again. His jowls shook, he fumbled with the papers in his hand and he fumbled for words.

"Don't get smart with me, young man," he sputtered. "You wouldn't like what I can do."

My heavens! This guy is easy to goad. He's still a real asshole, too.

The committee chairman cut in. "Thank you for taking the time to be with us today, Major. Rest assured you have the full support of this committee."

"I'm not finished with this fellow," bellowed the fat Congressman Webster from Tennessee.

"Yes you are, Congressman," the chairman told him. "This meeting stands adjourned."

An Evening in Washington

Kellogg's office was shutting down for the day. The office manager and Mike were having their umpteenth cup of coffee of the day. He reminded Mike of this evening's engagement.

"The Congressman will pick you up at your rooming house at eight this evening. Dress blues are required; don't forget to wear your medals. And remember, it's a dinner, so don't snack too much beforehand; and for heaven's sake, don't drink too much at the party either."

"I've got it on my schedule, George. But thanks for all the reminders anyway. That makes three dinner parties he and I will have attended this week. I hope these things do some good for our project."

"Judging by the invitations coming to our office, you are doing something right Mike; you're a hot item, as they say, since you visited with the president and he endorsed your project. People want to be able to brag about your being on their guest list."

"I must admit, the food's good and the people are interesting. I'm just getting tired of the grind of it all. I wish Julia were attending with me. It would be fun showing her off."

"The Congressman's daughter Patricia is in town. Why don't you ask her to go with you? She's a beauty and would be welcome in everyone's home."

She's a beauty all right. I'm not sure she would welcome me as an escort, now that her father has told her that I intend to marry Julia Hecht. Besides, how could I explain that to Julia?

"She is beautiful, George; and she could be a great help in gaining support for our project; but it would not be a good idea for us to be together."

"Do you still have feelings for her, Mike?"

"No George, I don't think so. In the past, she could just walk into the room, and I would get aroused. That part is over, I'm sure. But it wouldn't be appropriate. Not any more. Besides, Julia would probably skin me alive."

"Want to stop for a drink on the way to your room, Mike?"

"Not tonight, George. I'm going to write Julia and get ready for tonight's dinner party. But thanks. Some night when I don't have to go out again would be better."

"See you in the morning."

*   *   *   *

Dearest Julia,

As I put pen to paper, I am in my rooming house getting ready to attend another dinner party with Congressman Kellogg. This afternoon I told his office manager that I would love to have you as my companion instead. Escorting you would be so much more enjoyable.

The Congressman and I have gone to several of these evening social events since I visited with President Lincoln last week. I am told that by attending this type of social event and meeting Washington's powerful people, more support will be gained for our project.

You can be sure, sweetheart, that there are no bullets flying around the homes where these dinners are held. In fact, I am safer here than you and I were during our return trip.

I'm sorry I was not able to visit last weekend. My assignment here has turned out to require long days and late nights, too. I'm in the office very early by Washington standards. I meet all day with people who must supply the various things our freed prisoners of war will need.

Our greatest and most scarce need is for medical personnel. Tomorrow I'm going to meet with people at the Sanitary Commission. This organization provides nurses for our military hospitals. We will need a lot of them. We'll need a lot of doctors, too. I wish we had a dozen as skilled as your mother to help these men regain their health.

Some good news is that I have arranged to be free for a couple of days the week after next; so I plan to ride out to the farm. I need to hold you in my arms again, sweetheart, I can hardly wait.

You and I should be able to talk everything over with your folks then, too. Be patient sweetheart.

I love you

Michael

DINNER PARTY

Mike was standing in a circle of men and women. One of the ladies spoke directly to him.

"So you are the fellow who was attacked by a dozen assassins in Cleveland recently. I was told that you killed several of them single-handedly."

"Not quite, ma'am. I am the fellow who was attacked by two local toughs in Cleveland," Mike politely corrected her. "In self defense, I did kill both of them."

The man at the woman's side, a United States Senator, spoke up.

"The comments my wife made are a reflection of the talk around the afternoon tea tables, Major. If even half of the exploits they attribute to you are true, I would petition the War Department to send you against General Lee immediately. You'd have this war over in a week."

"But weren't you and your military escort attacked again in Baltimore, just a few miles from here?" another lady asked. "And you killed several of your attackers there too, didn't you?"

"Well, mum." Mike responded with a slight bow. "You are correct; there was an attack on us there as well. One attacker was killed, another was wounded and captured."

Congressman Kellogg stepped into the group.

"Excuse me ladies, gentlemen, I need to borrow the major for a moment. Please excuse us." He gently pulled Mike toward another group of people across the ornate living room.

"Oh, darn," one of the ladies lamented to another. "I wanted to invite him to tea next week. I would like to introduce him to my daughter. I understand he is a widower."

"Get in line, my dear," her husband chuckled. "There are a good number of young girls who would like to walk that young fellow to the altar, including Kellogg's daughter Patricia. I'm told he already turned her down."

Across the room, "General Halleck," Kellogg began. "You might remember Major Drieborg. He assisted your successful effort to liberate Andersonville Prison last fall."

"Of course I remember him, Congressman. Sorry to hear of all that fuss on your trip back here from your leave, Major. I'm told you handled your attackers rather well. Having worked with you on that Andersonville project, I'm not surprised."

"Thank you, sir. I was beginning to wonder if I wouldn't be safer with General Sherman's army in Georgia."

"Let's hope that's all behind you, Major. The President has directed me to cooperate with the Committee on the Conduct of the War and this proposal of yours. But whatever my office can do to help, we will. Have Kellogg's office set up an appointment for you with my staff."

"Thank you, sir. I'll do that tomorrow."

At the dinner table later that evening Mike was seated between two of Washington's most influential matrons. After the soup and before the salad, Mike was interrogated.

"Major," one began. "My husband, the Congressman, has told me horrifying tales of what those heathen Confederates are doing to our soldiers in their prison camps. Don't you agree?"

"Agree with what, ma'am?"

"Why, that our soldiers in their hands are suffering terribly, of course."

"Oh, yes ma'am. You're right, they are suffering terribly."

The lady on his other side joined the conversation. "He should know, Mildred. You were a prisoner at that awful Andersonville place; weren't you, Major?"

"Yes ma'am, I was. I managed by the grace of God to survive. But thousands of others I saw there did not. As more and more of our soldiers are freed from southern prisons, we should help them regain their health and return to their homes safely. Don't you agree, ladies?"

Both agreed between bites of bread and sips of wine.

"And our husbands too, don't they, Mildred?"

"Of course," the other pledged. "By the by, Major; I'm so sorry to hear of your wife's passing. You men don't appreciate how dangerous birthing a child can be. How is your little daughter doing?"

"Fine, thank you, ma'am. I left her in Michigan where she is being cared for at my parents' home." Before the meal was much further along, the two women would pry some more.

The lady on his right whispered to him. "She's one to talk. She never had any children of her own. She is her husband's second wife. She has raised her husband's children from his first marriage, though."

During dessert and coffee, the Congressman's wife on his left asked, "I thought you and Patricia Kellogg were going to marry. At least, that's what everyone assumed."

Mike almost choked on a piece of chocolate cake.

How in heaven's name can I ever respond to that? It's like being asked if I have stopped frequenting the brothels on Hooker Avenue. I'd convict myself of past bad behavior if I said yes; and be guilty of scandalous behavior if I said no.

"Really, Mildred," the lady on his right chided. "That is so personal."

"It seems to me that he has a right to know what people are saying about him. Don't you agree, Major?'

She has me trapped. I have to say something.

"Of course, ma'am," he began. "I appreciate your giving me that opportunity, too. Believe me." He stopped right there and took a sip of his coffee and thought about what he might say.

"Well?" the lady on his right prompted.

"Until this terrible war is over, I don't think it would be fair of me to ask any lady to raise another's woman's children alone. Don't you agree, ladies?"

"My heavens." The busybody was visibly aghast. "You have more than one child?"

"Ladies and gentlemen," their host interrupted. "May I have your attention? Join me in a toast." All the men at the table rose; everyone took their wine glasses in hand; "to President Lincoln and victory over the Confederacy!"

"Hear! Hear!" all responded. "Now ladies, if you will excuse us, the men will retire to the study for brandy and cigars."

Saved; thank you, sir. I can only imagine what else those ladies would have asked.

✳   ✳   ✳   ✳

Later in Congressman Kellogg's carriage, he and Mike talked about the events of the evening.

"I think the evening went very well, don't you, Mike?

"I think but sir. At the dinner table I was sandwiched between two determined scions of Washington society. They were determined to know why Patricia and I are not getting married. I was struggling with their questions when our host interrupted with a final toast and the adjournment for brandy and cigars. Thank the Lord for that."

Kellogg chuckled at Mike's description of the scene. "I noticed you over there. It didn't seem to me that you were doing much talking."

"Thankfully, they did most of that."

"As irritating as that can be, we are gathering a good deal of support for our project. Just remember that. We have another one of these dinners tomorrow night."

"Whatever you say; I'll see you in the morning, sir."

WASHINGTON

Another week of whirlwind activity passed. It was late in the afternoon. Mike was finishing up his report on the last meeting of the day.

"I wish you would wait until daylight Mike" George Krupp urged. "You'll be fresh with a good night's sleep and this snowstorm will have blown itself out."

"You're probably right, George. But I don't care if it is almost dark; I'm leaving for the Hecht farm right now. All I have to do is walk down to the livery stable and saddle my horse. In two hours or so I'll be at the farm; have a warm supper and Julia in my arms.

That's worth the risk. Besides, I can make that ride in my sleep. Darkness and a little snow will not be a problem."

"All right Mike. Just be careful. Enjoy your two days away. Remember though, you have a ten o'clock meeting here the morning of the third day."

THE HECHT FARM

I know George's arguments for waiting until tomorrow morning make sense. But, Julia's mother, Emma has not grilled him. It's been three weeks since I returned to Washington. I'll bet Emma has counted each of them and has told her daughter that I could have visited if I were really serious about being a husband to her and a father to little Robert. But snowstorm or not, I've got to go tonight.

It was dark, and very wet snow had been falling for the better part of the last hour. He had stopped now and then to wipe off his horse and shake the snow off his slouch hat and greatcoat.

But he noticed the snow was rapidly piling up on the road. It became so deep that his horse began to struggle some getting through it, even at a fast walk.

Come on, boy. No more stopping. Michael thought out loud as he patted the horse's neck. *Temperature is dropping and the wind is picking up. It's getting hard to see more than a few yards. And, once this snow starts drifting we might miss the road markers. No more easy pace for us boy; we've got to move faster.* He kicked the horse's flanks with his boot heels to spur it into a trot.

As they moved through the countryside at a fast trot, Mike could hear his horse snorting with the effort. Its coat was so hot, steam rose into the night when snow hit it.

"Good boy, good boy," Mike leaned forward and murmured in his horse's ear. "Only a couple of more miles now." He patted its neck in confirmation. "We can slow down some now." The horse began to walk when it felt Mike's legs press against its sides.

It was still slow going, but in another twenty minutes Mike stopped his horse at the top of a rise and looked down on the Hecht farm below. "Here we are, boy." Mike rubbed the horse's neck in assurance. "Let's get you comfortable in that barn."

Mike removed the saddle and all the other leather gear before putting his horse into a stall. There he gave it feed and water. As he gave it a good rubdown, he could hear Sgt. Riley shouting at the riders in his troop as though it were yesterday.

I don wana tell yas again; yer horse comes first or ya will be in the infantry afore ya know it.

Mike couldn't help but laugh. He paused in his work and thought of Riley and the others.

They're all off in the Shenandoah Valley somewhere with Sheridan's cavalry. Look after them, Lord. And while you're at I, Lord, look after Julia and me with her Momma.

When I walk into her home in a few minutes, do I dare hold her in my arms right in front of her parents? Anyway, I hope my arrival is a pleasant surprise for all of them.

Mike entered the outside door of the house, hung up his greatcoat and hat, stomped the snow off his boots and knocked on the inside door.

When that door opened, it was Julia's younger brother Kenny who saw Mike first.

"Hey Mike," he shouted in surprise. "Look who the cat dragged in everyone; it's Mike."

"Michael!" Julia shouted and ran across the room into his arms. He returned her hug.

Does she feel good! Why should I have worried about hugging her in front of the family; she doesn't?

After a moment Mike reluctantly stepped back. "Hi everyone!" he began. "I hope you don't mind my just showing up. I wrote Julia that I arranged for two days off to ride out here, but there was no time to notify you in advance of the actual day I could come."

Ruben rose from the table and approached Mike with his hand held out in greeting.

"Not to vorry, Michael. You are velcome here anytime. Come, sit down. Julia, get him some warm drink. Have you eaten yet?"

Everyone peppered him with questions. He did his best to answer between chewing and swallowing the food they warmed up for him. Over pie and coffee he finished telling them all about his duties in Washington and what he knew about his future.

"I had hoped to arrive earlier this evening and visit with little Robert before his bedtime. But that weather is scary out there tonight. With all the snow and wind, I almost missed the last road marker a mile or so back; pretty heavy drifting."

"You can sleep in da loft mit Kenny tonight, Michael." Ruben told him. "It is time for bed now, everyone."

*   *   *   *

Ruben and Emma were in their bedroom.

"You ver so quiet after Michael arrived, Mamma," Ruben commented.

"I listen now, Papa. Michael has many fine qualities, I know. But I remember how he forgot us so quickly last fall after President Lincoln awarded him that medal. I still have not gotten over that. I worry that he will forget us again. He still must prove to me that he can be trusted, Papa. I think he has not earned my trust back; not yet, anyway."

"Momma, remember dat he rode all da vay out here in dis storm. He could have waited for it to blow over. I tink he vill be fine for our Julia and for Robert, too."

"We will see Papa," Emma sighed. "I hope you are right. We will see."

*   *   *   *

Mike and Julia stood by the fireplace, kissing.

"I missed you so much, Michael."

"I missed you too, sweetheart."

I want Michael to hug me and caress me right now; right here. I don't care if Kenny is up in the loft right above us. I don't care if he sees and hears everything.

Julia ran her hands up his back and pulled him to her. "I wish you could make love to me Michael," she whispered.

This is not like me. Here I am standing in the Hecht living room kissing their daughter like this. I've seen so much dying; the dreams and plans of so many men destroyed. What if I never return? That's why I want to do more with Julia, right now. But I can't.

"I've missed holding you and kissing you, Julia." Mike whispered in her ear, as he kissed her lips again.

Oh! My, that feels so good. Kiss me more, Michael.

Julia brought one of her hands up behind Mike's neck and held his lips to hers

This is not the place for this. Michael thought.

So he just held her against him for a few more minutes as he calmed down.

She allowed him to lead her to her bedroom door. Before he left her and climbed into the loft above he gave her one last hug.

"I love you, Julia. Goodnight, sweetheart."

DETROIT

The Federal prison was located by the Detroit river. High walls with several guard towers surrounded a three-story building on all four sides. The building's few windows had bars on them. All in all, the place did not look very inviting. It was wartime, so military courts had sentenced most of the prisoners who were there.

Basement cells were called 'the hole' by inmates and guards alike. They were rooms just five feet by five feet with six-foot ceilings, and no window. Prisoners were placed there as punishment for having broken a prison rule; there were sometimes other reasons for such solitary confinement.

This afternoon, a prisoner had been brought from one of these cells to a main floor room for interrogation. This small space was somewhat bigger than the cells below, but not much; at least a man of average height could stand up. A table and two chairs were bolted to the floor. The only light came in through a single window placed high on one wall.

After two weeks in a basement cell, the man was physically weak, hunched over and disoriented. The light hurt his eyes and he could barely hold up his head. When the door of the room slammed shut, he jerked erect.

"How have you liked your new cell the last two weeks? You've had no one to talk to; no light; a pot to piss in; swill for food? Even a little shrimp like you could barely stand up straight in that little dark box."

"Why? Why have you done this to me?" the prisoner managed to rasp.

"But you've wondered why you can't walk around our prison any more like yer shit don't stink; get mail from yer big shot daddy; have money in yer pocket; cigars to pass around; some alcohol to share?

"You dumb shit. You get some lowlife toughs to attack a major in the United States Army, and you wonder why you're in solitary confinement?"

The interrogator stood as though to leave.

"Wait! Wait; please. Don't send me back to that hole."

"That depends on what you tell me."

"Anything; I'll tell you anything."

"We'll see. First off, what is your name?"

"Carl Bacon."

"Well, Carl Bacon, why are you in prison?"

"I was sentenced by a military court over a training camp incident. I was set up."

"That's a pile of crap! Everyone in this place says he was set up. What did you do in Detroit last November? Remember that, Carl?"

"I shot at the guy who put me in here, just to scare him."

"What's that guy's name, Carl?"

"Guy named Drieborg. He's been a pain in my ass since we were kids together in primary school; picked on me all the time."

"Funny thing, that's the name of the guy who was attacked in Cleveland three weeks ago. How did you arrange for that attack, Carl?"

"Don't know anything about that."

The interrogator was out of the room before Bacon could protest.

"Take that piece of shit back to solitary."

"No! No!" Carl shouted. But two burly guards dragged him down the stairs to his dark cell anyway. They pushed him inside and slammed the metal door behind.

I don't belong here. They have no right to do this to me. I wasn't in this pit but a day when I threw up whatever they fed me the day before. In the dark I knocked over my chamber pot. I've been sitting in my own shit ever since. I begged them to clean it up. My clothes, mattress and blanket stink with it.

Calm yourself, Carl. Remember who put you here. Think of how sweet it will be to get revenge. Think of kidnapping one of his sisters maybe; lock her up somewhere just like I am now; strip her and have some fun with her. Think of what things you could do to her, all tied up. Will it be Susan or Ann? Then let her go and make the whole family live with the shame of what I did to her.

That's it. Think about that. But first, you must survive this.

*   *   *   *

A week later, he was back in the interrogation room.

"Welcome back Carl. I hope your memory has improved since our last visit. Who knows; if you cooperate, I may even let them clean out your cell. Where were we when we ended our last conversation? O yes, I remember. Tell me how you arranged that Cleveland attack on your old friend Drieborg."

"They'll kill me if I tell you."

"Who will kill you, Carl?"

"Those guys in Cleveland have contacts here; guards, prisoners; I don't know who exactly. But they told me I'd be a dead man if I talked."

"Carl, listen to me carefully. How did we know about your connection to them and their attack on Drieborg in Cleveland? Think about it, Carl. You didn't tell us. They did, you stupid shit. One of the attackers was captured in Baltimore. With a little bit of persuasion he told the Federal marshal all about you. Drieborg killed another member of his gang in

Cleveland. We know that guy. He was just released from here. Are you beginning to get the picture, Carl?"

"So now, the Army wants to hang your sorry ass. This is wartime, Carl. They can do it if they want to. But maybe we can keep you here; protect you from the gallows. The only way you can save yourself is to cooperate here, right now!"

My God! I'm damned if I cooperate and damned if I don't. But survive one day at a time, Carl. The longer I live the better my chance for revenge.

"If I tell you everything I know will, I be out of solitary?"

"Depends on what you tell me, Carl. We'll see."

He told his interrogator everything.

"I read a story in the Grand Rapids Eagle about Drieborg being this big hero home on leave. It just got me real pissed me off. But I was talking some trash about him being the guy who railroaded me into prison and how I wanted to kill him."

Carl went on. "Some guy overheard and told me he was going to be released soon and could arrange to kill him for me; on the outside. A hit would only cost $500. But I got the money and gave it to him. When I found out when Drieborg was going to return to Washington, I passed the train schedule on to the same guy."

"What's the guy's name?"

"He called himself Harry. He said he had connections in Cleveland and that no one would be able to connect me with the killing. Just before he was released, he told me the price had gone up; it would cost another $500. I had to get the money sent to a post office box in Cleveland. I was in too deep by then, so I had the money sent."

"That's enough for now Carl," the interrogator told him. "We're going to check out what you have told me. If you're blowing smoke up my ass, it's back in the hole for you. For the time being, I'm going to let you wash up, get some food and clean clothes. Your new cell will even have a window. You had better hope we get these guys, Carl, or you might be soon swinging from the end of a rope."

Yes! Yes! I'm going to be clean and have some decent food. And, I'm going to survive this after all; I can feel it. I'll get you yet, Drieborg.

HECHT FARM

"Hey, you two sleepy heads," Julia shouted up toward the loft. "Rise and shine. There's work to do on this farm. That includes you Major Drieborg, Washington City big shot. You haven't got school today, Kenny, with all that snow last night; so there's work for you too."

All right; all right I'm awake. My goodness! It's still dark outside. That long ride out here last night must have really worn me out. I haven't slept that soundly for a long time.

"Get used to it, Mike," Kenny told him. "She's been like that since you brought her home. Are you sure you want to wake up to that every morning?"

Kenny was fifteen now. Average of height, he had put on some muscle since last fall too.

He's a smart kid. Maybe he's right about his sister. There are a lot of kids his age fighting in the army, on both sides, Mike thought. *I hope this war ends before he takes a notion to join the fight. Or, before he's drafted.*

"Coming Julia," Mike shouted. "Give me a minute to get my work clothes out of my bag, and I'll be right down."

By the time he and Kenny had dressed and visited the commode by the outside door, breakfast was ready.

"Could I have some coffee, please?" he asked.

"Goot morning, Michael," Ruben said. "Vould you like to help mit da milking after you take care of your horse?"

"I had better, Ruben, or that daughter of yours will probably take one of those big cooking spoons to me."

"Very funny, Michael," Julia said smiling. "Maybe you've forgotten how to milk a cow since you worked in your father's barn a few weeks ago?"

"You can ask the cow after I've tried to get milk out of her, Julia. But you can watch. If you don't like my technique, you can take over."

"All right you two," Emma interrupted. "I warmed some biscuits from last night. Eat while they are warm. Julia and I will have your breakfast after the chores. There will be plenty of time for talk after that. Say the prayer, Papa."

In the barn, Kenny was feeding the farm animals; Mike and Ruben were milking the Hechts' two cows. For a while, all they could hear was the hiss of the milk as it was squirted into the pails. Eventually, both men got into a rhythm and relaxed enough to talk. His chores finished, Kenny had gone back into the house.

"What do you think of Julia and me getting married, Ruben?"

"We should talk about dis with Momma, Michael. She vill speak for herself, but I tink she vorries about you in Washington City, und da war too. Since you brought her home, Julia has told us how much she loves you. I believe her. But I need to hear from you about your love for her Momma does, too."

"I understand Ruben. Is it all right that we talk of these things with Kenny present? I must leave tomorrow night you know, weather permitting."

"Mit all dis snow Kenny will have no school. So it can't be helped. Da whole family, ve talk later today some I tink. But now, tell me about da attacks against you in Cleveland and Baltimore. Julia didn't even vant to talk about it."

Mike told him about their trip from Lowell and the attacks. He left out the part about making love with Julia.

"How do you feel about killing dose men, Michael?"

"I was given little choice, Ruben. If I hadn't killed them, they would have killed me and probably Julia too. I must admit though;

I fired to kill and did so without any hesitation. And I have felt no remorse since."

"I have not been faced with dat kind of situation, Michael," Ruben admitted. "But I cannot judge anyone who was. I hope dat I never have to make such a choice.

"So tell me," he quickly continued. "How is da war going?"

Lowell, Michigan — January 1865

It was Saturday; the Drieborg family had just finished their noon meal. The dishes were cleared. The children returned to the table and sat silently looking at their father, Jake. Their mother, Rose, took her usual seat too.

"All right, everyone," he announced. "Now we hear da letter from Michael I just brought home from town." All three children could read very well. So could their mother Rose. Jake read the Bible aloud to them many evenings; but he would rather listen to his children read.

Today he asked his eldest daughter Susan to read the letter. Jake sat quietly puffing on his pipe.

✳   ✳   ✳   ✳

Hi Everyone,

I hope this letter finds you all well. I saw Julia home earlier this morning, safe and sound. I reported for duty today too, and find I will be very busy working here in Washington; no real battles to worry about here, Momma.

In Cleveland, two hoodlums attacked us at our hotel. Julia was not hurt and I am fine as well. It turned out that I had to kill them both. They gave me no choice Papa. One of them told me that they had been hired to kill me and anyone who might be with me.

I am sorry to tell you that there was another attempt to kill us the following night in Baltimore. One of the attackers was captured. He as much as told me it was Carl Bacon's father Harvey who had paid them.

Congressman Kellogg thinks he can do something to stop this from happening again. We'll see. In the meantime, all of you had better be careful. God bless.

Your son

Michael

✳   ✳   ✳   ✳

When she was done, no one spoke. Rose broke the silence. "Papa, what are we going to do about these Bacon people?"

"I talked to da Justice of the Peace and our marshal this morning when I was in town. Dey believe da Federal marshal in Grand Rapids will soon take some action against Harvey Bacon. Until dat happens though, none of you will leave da farm without my permission. We all must be very careful. Der will be no more walking to school for now, either. Momma will have da lessons at home. We even don't go into town for awhile."

"In the meantime, can the Lowell marshal protect us from these evil people, Papa?" Ann asked.

"I don't think so. We do not control what da marshal or Bacon does. But we can protect ourselves. We are in control of dat. So today I bought another shotgun and two pistols at Yared's general store. I will show each of you how to handle da weapons. You start to learn dis afternoon."

MARYLAND - EMMA HECHT'S RULES

Little Robert was not so little anymore; he was almost three feet tall. Not bad for a boy three years old. Before anyone could stop him, he rushed out of the house toward the barn, coat open with no hat or gloves.

He ran into the building. "Mike," he shouted. "Where are you?"

"Over here. I'm milking one of the cows, Robert."

The next thing Mike knew, the little fellow had jumped into his arms, giving him a big hug.

"I thought you were never coming back."

"I told you that I would," Mike reminded him. "And here I am."

"To stay forever?"

"No. I can stay today and tomorrow. Then I'll be back from time to time until the war is over. After that, you and I will spend a lot of time together."

"That's great, Mike. Grandma says breakfast is ready. Come on. She gets mad if the food gets cold."

Some things are the same in all home, Mike thought.

Back in the house, everyone gathered around the table.

"Papa," Emma instructed. "Say the prayer."

A good farm breakfast was always served after morning chores, usually between six and seven o'clock. This morning, the Hecht meal consisted of biscuits, gravy, bacon, eggs, milk and coffee. Since he returned to Washington City, Mike ate breakfast on the run; a quick cup of black coffee and a slice of day-old bread in the boarding house. This farm meal was a feast.

When the dishes were finally cleared and everyone was sitting around the table enjoying a cup of coffee, Ruben lit his first pipe of the day.

"Momma," he began. "I tink it is time ve should talk of Julia's vish to marry Michael." It was not a question. Then he settled back in his chair and was silent.

"Wouldn't that be great Momma?" Kenny exclaimed.

"But Michael," Emma began looking him directly in the eye. We are in no rush today; tell us about this idea you and Julia have; talk."

"Michael and I love each other, Momma. And, we want to get married."

"That's true," Mike added. "We came to realize this when I was home on leave last month. It was not something we expected; but it happened anyway. I would like your permission to marry Julia."

"What of your duties in Washington, Michael? What of the war? What will happen after the fighting is over? What of baby Eleanor and little Robert?"

"I'm not little anymore grandma," the youngster interrupted.

"Sorry, Robert, I forgot." his grandma assured him. "We call you Robert now."

Over the course of the next hour, Mike explained what his job in Washington would demand of him. He also told them what he understood about the current war situation and what was expected to happen in the spring. His view of the post-war was speculation, based mostly on rumor.

"I've told my parents that I want to return to farming after the war. I have already paid for eighty acres of land right on the river next to my parents' place. We have talked of sharing equipment and helping one another. I am saving money for a house and barns too. Julia and I have talked of this, and she wants to live on a farm, be my wife and be a mother to Eleanor, Robert and our children, too."

Julia interrupted. "Because I am not of age, Michael knows that you must give me permission to marry. We are asking that permission of you now."

Emma had a few more questions.

"Julia told me you had written to her about attending dinners and other social gatherings in Washington as part of your duties. Tell me about that, please."

Michael went into great detail about how evening social events play a part of Washington power structure. "Just last week, General Halleck, who is in charge of all the armies, told me to contact his office for an appointment to discuss how he can help me do the job the president wants done. He was at the same dinner party. I would not have had that opportunity to meet him otherwise. Important people attend these things. They ask me questions. I attempt to interest them in the project of helping newly released prisoners of war. They in turn use their influence to help me accomplish my job."

"Congressman Kellogg's office manager, George Krupp, schedules these events for the Congressman and me. He told me that there are more invitations than he can satisfy.

I wear my dress blues, sword and all; and at his insistence, my medals too. Kellogg keeps reminding me how important it is for us to attend these events. But as part of my job, I go with him. It makes for a real long day. I am at the office by eight in the morning; have meetings all day long; clean up and change to my formal uniform in the evening; and attend a dinner party until late at night. The next morning that routine starts all over again."

"I would rather be working on the farm, believe me. But I am a soldier who must serve in whatever capacity I am assigned."

"Would Julia live with you in Washington?"

"She and I have not talked about that, Emma," Mike responded. "I would want her with me, of course. But it wouldn't be practical. In the first place, decent housing is very scarce in that town. Right now

I spend a third of what I am paid for a ten by ten room in a rooming house, breakfast and supper included. Better housing is much more expensive. Aside from what I pay for lunches and the cleaning of my uniforms, I am trying to save the rest of my pay to build our home after the war."

"I would love to have Julia accompany me to the evening events I must attend. But at those events the focus has to be on the project I'm working on, not on the beautiful wife of Major Drieborg."

"And then there is the travel," Mike continued. "When I return from my visit here, I am scheduled to join General Sherman's army in Savannah, Georgia. Evidently there are thousands of recently freed Union soldiers there. They are in dire need of medical attention, clothing and transportation home. My team's first assignment is to help them. I don't know how long I will be there. But Sherman's army is planning to move north into South Carolina very soon. So preparations must be made to care for more released prisoners. It may be a month or more before I can return."

"For Julia to be left alone in Washington would not be safe, either. She would be much better off staying here."

"Michael!" Julia exclaimed, petulantly.

"I'm sorry, sweetheart. It's just not practical for us or safe for you to join me in Washington."

Ruben finally spoke. "Tank you for your honesty about dis matter, Michael. I tink you are telling us vhat is best for Julia. Ve must, too."

"It is almost the end of January, Momma," Julia said rather hotly. "You should have no objection for us to marry at Easter time, in April. Besides, I will be of age to decide for myself in June."

"We will talk about this again, Julia," her Momma decided. "Michael does not have to leave until tomorrow afternoon. Papa and I will talk with both of you some more about this before he leaves. What do you think, Papa?"

"Dat is fine mit me Momma."

All this time Robert was sitting on Mike's lap. Mike was amazed that the boy had remained quiet throughout the conversation.

"Mike," the boy urged. "Play soldiers with me by the fire." Sure enough, Kenny had carved wooden figures for him. Some had been painted blue and others gray; he even had several mounted cavalrymen and some wooden cannons. They both were soon on the floor setting up for a battle.

"I'll be our side and you be the bad guys, Mike." He directed.

"How can I be the bad guys, Robert; I'm an officer in the Union cavalry?"

"You can be the good guys next time. All right?"

And so it went for a while. Mike never did get a chance to be the 'good' guys.

"Time for your nap, Robert," Julia announced.

"Just a little while longer - please?" Robert pleaded.

"Nope. Not a chance. But maybe Michael will read to you a little in the bedroom."

Sleep came quicker than the end of the story.

"He really needs these short naps," Julia told Mike when he returned to the room. "Robert does everything at full speed. It's as though he's afraid he'll miss something."

"I think my parents would like to talk in private. Kenny has some schoolwork to finish. So why don't you and I go to the barn for awhile?"

They no sooner had closed the barn doors and thrown the latch, they were in each others' arms. After a long kiss, Julia pulled Mike toward an empty stall. She threw a horse blanket down over the loose hay there, lay down, and beckoned Mike to join her.

Julia didn't have to entice Mike for him to become passionate; at least not much.

I love the way Michael kisses me now. No more stiffness; his lips are soft. It's like a shock. I can feel it to my toes.

"Don't stop Michael."

*   *   *   *

"Well, Papa," Emma began. "Tell me what you think of Michael's proposal? Can we trust him?"

"I tink so Mamma."

"How can you be so sure?"

"I remember last fall vhen he visited us. He vas not sure vat he should do about Robert. So ve sent him avay. He knew den dat he could marry Congressman Kellogg's beautiful daughter, vork in Washington und live in grand style. But she told him dat she vould not be a mother to Robert. Michael could have her und all da rest, but he had to turn his back on Robert. Vat did Michael do, Mamma? He turned her down; and told us he vanted to keep his promise and be a fader to Robert.

"Den, back in Michigan, Michael somehow discovers dat he loves our Julia. How did dat happen, mMmma? I have no idea. It is not important dat I know how dat happened. But I believe him when he tells me dat he loves our daughter. Dat is enough for me. What about you, Momma?"

"What you say makes sense, Papa. But I am still nervous about all of this. I believe Julia loves Michael very much. I'm just not so sure about him yet. Maybe by Easter time when they want to marry, I will be."

"Fine, Mamma; but what do we tell dem now?"

"We hug them and say they can marry this Easter."

SAVANNAH, GEORGIA

General Sherman's army had captured Savannah in December 1864. In a telegram to Washington, he said it was a Christmas present to President Lincoln. Now, in the winter of 1865, Sherman's 70,000 men were poised for the invasion of the Carolinas.

"An army loses it toughness sitting around too long," he bellowed. "And this army has sat on its ass too long as it is."

"General," his aide Colonel Robert Taft began. "You might remember sir that General Halleck told you he wants us to help with the released prisoner project the president has endorsed. He sent you a copy of the plan. You gave it to me. Well, a Major Drieborg was assigned to get it done; he's here to see you about it."

"Damn it all!" Sherman erupted. "What's the matter with those people in Washington? Don't they know we're fighting a war out here? First, they wanted us to capture Atlanta and Savannah overnight and now they want us to capture Charleston yesterday.

"Their supplies haven't been able to keep up with us; so we've lived off the land as we fought. At the same time they have expected us to feed, clothe and hug every darkie who happened by; and now they want us to waste time coddling every former prisoner we freed.

"I've told you, the longer we stay in one spot, the more those asses in Washington will find stuff like this to hold us back. We've got to get back on the attack."

"Yes sir," Colonel Taft agreed. "But the president personally endorsed this project."

"All right; all right. Before you show the major in, tell me about this almighty important project."

Before long, Major Drieborg was standing at attention in front of General Sherman's desk. Mike had been led through a larger room Sherman used for meetings with his staff.

This room had been a bedroom, so was much smaller and sparsely furnished.

"At ease, Major," Sherman directed. "Relax; I'm not going to eat you for breakfast. Have a seat. Colonel Taft here tells me you need a few men assigned to you, some supplies and travel authorization for the prisoners we liberated from the Confederate prison here. Is that about it?"

"Yes sir."

"Taft, I'm assigning you to work with the major here on this. You draw up the paperwork authorizing whatever you need, and I'll sign it. But it's going to be up to you, Colonel, to find the personnel and supplies. I got a war to run, not a nursery. Both of you understand that?"

"Yes sir."

"Any questions, Taft?"

"Respectfully, sir," Colonel Taft began. "I'm not on your staff to nursemaid a clean-up operation like the one Drieborg here is running. I'm here to fight Rebs. So I request you assign someone else to this job."

General Sherman virtually jumped to his feet. The violence of his movement sent his chair crashing to the floor behind him. "You hear me clear, Taft, and you hear me good," Sherman shouted, his face suddenly as red as his hair.

"You're here to do as you're told. You're on my staff because you have a big shot family back in Ohio and a bunch of pull in Washington. Still, it wouldn't trouble me a bit to break you to the rank of private.

How would that blue-blood family of yours like it if I assigned you to digging latrines for some infantry unit?

"If I get any more whining from you on this assignment, sonny, that's just what you can expect. I am holding you responsible for the success of this project. And, if I get any flack from Washington about it, I will bury you. Do I make myself clear, Captain Taft?"

"Yes sir. But I'm a colonel, sir."

"Not any more, Taft; you are now a captain. See how quickly I reduced your rank? Thank your lucky stars that I'm in a good mood. You can talk to me when this assignment is successfully completed and I'll consider restoring your rank. Now, get your whiny ass out my sight and bring me that paperwork I need to sign for this project."

LOWELL

Harvey Bacon was taking his usual Monday morning walk along Main Street. He wanted to be seen by all the business people.

If each of them doesn't owe my bank money now, they know they might need to borrow some in the future. That's how I've come to own this town. Seeing me reminds them of that.

He stood at the end of the street and watched as lumber was being unloaded from a wagon.

No one borrowed money to build anything on this street. What's going on here?

"What are you men doing?"

"Seems pretty obvious, doesn't it?" one worker snapped. "We're going to put up a building here."

"What for?" Bacon asked.

"We're told it's going to be a bank."

"This town has a bank. We don't need another one."

"Maybe so mister, seems there's going to be another one pretty soon anyway."

My Lord! Who would do this to me?

The Lowell Justice of the Peace was working at his desk when the door burst open.

"What the hell is going on at the end of the street, Deeb? Those workmen tell me they are putting up a building for a bank. What do you know about it?"

"Now that you told me," Deeb replied. "It would appear that those workmen are going to put up a building to house a bank. As you've told me many times, Harvey, you run this town; so you should know. Why ask me?"

"You're useless, Deeb. I don't know why I bothered to ask you." Bacon turned and stormed out of the building.

These two men would talk again later that day.

＊　　＊　　＊　　＊

Deeb entered Bacon's bank building accompanied by a burly man dressed in a black business suit. The badge of a Federal marshal was pinned to the lapel of his overcoat and a pistol belt was strapped around his waist. The two men approached a teller working behind the counter.

"Mr. Richards, "Deeb asked the teller. "Would you please tell Mr. Bacon I would like to see him in private?"

I can hardly wait to see Bacon's reaction when he finds out the purpose of this visit, Deeb thought.

A few moments later, the teller returned.

"You can go into his office now, gentlemen."

As the two men entered Bacon's office, he barely looked up from the papers in front of him.

"What do you want, Deeb?" Bacon snapped. "And who's this fellow with you?"

Neither man was invited to be seated in the chairs in front of Bacon's desk. But they stood behind them.

"Mr. Bacon," Deeb began. "Allow me to introduce the Federal marshal for this area, Mr. Kalanquin."

"Why are you here, Kalanquin?"

Still standing, the marshal began. "Information has come to our attention that you hired men to kill Major Michael Drieborg, an officer in the Army of the United States. The first attack was attempted in Cleveland, the second in Baltimore."

"That is absolute nonsense. I don't care if you are a Federal marshal, Kalanquin. You can't just walk in here and accuse an honest citizen of attempted murder."

"Oh, but I can. I just did. In fact, I am here to place you under arrest, Mr. Bacon; today; right now actually. You're going to spend tonight in a Grand Rapids jail cell. The Federal district judge will deal with you tomorrow. With the testimony we have, I would bet that you'll be joining your son as a prisoner in the Federal prison at Detroit.

"Get your coat, sir. You're leaving peaceably, or in chains."

By now, Bacon was on his feet behind his desk glaring at the marshal.

"He can't just barge in here and do this can he, Deeb?"

"As you so often have told me, Harvey," Deeb responded. "I'm just a small town lawyer; so what do I know?

"What I do know, however, is that this is wartime; and the Federal government's people can do most anything they deem necessary. I think protecting soldiers ranks pretty high on their priority list; especially soldiers like Drieborg, who was awarded the Congressional Medal of Honor.

"Harvey, I'd say you're headed for a stay in jail."

Deeb is a fool. My lawyers will get me out of this. That damn Drieborg family; I'll get them yet.

SAVANNAH

"Follow me this way, Drieborg. This mansion has closets as big as bedrooms. We can use one of those rooms down this hallway."

The newly demoted Captain Taft closed the door and turned in fury on Mike.

"Hear me real good, Drieborg; no hick farm boy from Michigan like you is going to jerk me around. I'm going to get my rank back; and you're going to help me. Not even Sherman is going to mess with a Taft."

Mike sat down behind the only table in the room. He sat back and said nothing for a moment or two; just looked calmly at Taft.

Are all sons of the rich such assholes? I grew up with one in Lowell, Carl Bacon. I probably didn't handle that very well. But he's the one in prison, not me. I've seen a few in Washington, too. Now this kid from Ohio, they all feel so entitled; as though their shit doesn't stink. I haven't met a one of them who is worth a damn; weaklings one and all.

But, in this case, you need me more than I need you. For now, let me see what you're made of.

"I think you had better cool down and sit down, Captain," he began. Mike paused until Taft was seated. "You got yourself into this mess with the general, not me. What I heard him say is that the only way out for you is for me to tell him that this project has been successfully completed.

"I may just be that farm hick from Michigan," Mike continued, leaning forward toward Taft. "But my rank was earned at Gettysburg, the Richmond Raid, Libby and Andersonville Prisons. You may have powerful family connections in Washington, Captain; but last fall the president himself pinned the Congressional Medal of Honor on this coat, and put these oak leaves on my shirt. He met with me again in private three weeks ago and approved this project. That's pretty powerful stuff, too. And I don't intend to let him down.

"You and I can both get what we want Taft, if we work together. If we don't, both of us could lose. So how about it? Do we help one another or fight?"

"You would help me?" Taft asked somewhat puzzled.

"Damn right, Taft. And, it won't cost your family a cent of their money. If you help me successfully carry out this project, I'll put your name front and center on my report to General Halleck and the Joint Congressional Committee on the Conduct of the War. You could be golden at the highest circles in Washington. Just imagine; you will have earned something on your own; without your family's money and influence. If you do not; well, you heard General Sherman. What's your answer, Taft?"

"All right farm-boy, let's get to work on that paperwork for the general to sign. What do you need?"

"Hold on, big shot. Is this a 'we' project or not?"

A bit startled, Taft paused and looked at Mike for a moment. "I get it," he smiled. "What do we need to have the general authorize?"

$$*\qquad*\qquad*\qquad*$$

Later in General Sherman's office.

The general looked over the requests he was asked to authorize. "My Lord," Sherman exclaimed. "You don't want much, do you, Major?"

Mike sat and did not respond.

My experience in Washington has taught me to let the written words speak for themselves. By speaking, I just provide more that can be questioned. Sherman has been told to help me by his superior, General Halleck. I've been careful to ask for nothing that will slow his army down, put their success at risk or is beyond his authority to authorize.

"You want a cavalry troop assigned to you; but not just any unit; you want this particular one. Sounds to me like you're afraid I'd assign some bunch of misfit foragers to help you.

"And all these supplies. Are you going to leave me any medical supplies? I suppose I should be thankful you'll allow me to retain some of my doctors.

"About all this food you want. I'll authorize you to have it; but I don't know where you'll find it. My entire army has fought and foraged its way through Georgia to get here. We took everything edible we could find and burned or killed the rest."

"Yes sir, I can believe that," commented Drieborg. "On my trip here from Atlanta, the men of the troop I rode with told me that the destruction I saw was actually forty miles wide, clear across Georgia to Savannah. All the way to this city, I don't think I saw one building or home standing; only the chimneys."

"Destruction is what this war is all about, young fella. It's time these secesh understand that and never forget it."

"But back to the supply issue," Sherman continued. "Even though some supplies have begun to reach us from the north, we are still far short of what we need. I wish I could eat as well as the men you're planning to feed with all of this food you're requesting. My army is going to have to live off the land once we move into South Carolina. Just like in Georgia, you're going to see a lot more chimneys standing in heaps of ashes in that den of Rebels."

"Moving your men north might be a problem beyond my control. We've destroyed all the railroads we could on our way here; and we don't yet control the direct routes through the Carolinas and Virginia. We have repaired a lot of rail line to the west. So supplies are just starting to come east from Atlanta.

"I'll authorize the movement by rail of the healthier former prisoners to Atlanta. But told that raiders are constantly tearing up roadbed and burning rolling stock. So your men might just have to walk at some point. That will be your problem.

"I'll authorize the ships you want to transport the sick men north; but the navy might not care what I authorize. The president's endorsement of your project will carry more weight with them than mine.

"My staff has already been told to help you and this crybaby Taft. So I'll sign this form directing them to help you, anyway. I'll also introduce you to my staff at this afternoon's meeting.

"I think that about does it. Now, I have a form for you to sign major; friend of President Lincoln; Congressional Medal of Honor winner. Read it before you sign it."

Mike read the document.

What a wily fox. This states that he has cooperated fully with the orders he received. And further, that he has authorized everything I have requested of him. I can't blame him. I'm just cleaning up the war's mess. He's still got a lot of war to fight. He has to protect his hindquarters in the meantime.

"Yes sir," Mike responded. "You have been most cooperative. And, while I'm at it, thank you for assigning Captain Taft to this project. Thus far, he has been most helpful. So I'll be glad to sign this statement."

"All right," Sherman thundered. "Get the hell out'a here, both of ya. "I've got a war to run."

✳   ✳   ✳   ✳

In his quarters later, Mike read a letter from home he had just received.

Dear Michael,

Papa just came back from town with some interesting news. It seems that there will be a new bank in Lowell. Remember when you wrote us that Congressman Kellogg told that you he had some ideas about how to bring the Bacons under control?

Papa thinks this is the Congressman's doing. Flyers have been passed out to all the farmers and businessmen. The new bank is called the Old Kent Bank and Trust. It is located in Grand Rapids, actually. In the flyer, they told everyone that they will charge less than Bacon's bank on any mortgage. Papa explained how it will work. You go to the Old Kent bank and apply for a loan. If your application is approved, they buy your old mortgage from Bacon's bank.

He says that if everyone goes to this new bank, the Bacon bank will be destroyed. That should end their influence in Lowell. We can only hope.

By the way, Michael; George Neal from your old unit is staying in Willi's barn bedroom. He came back here on sick leave and had nowhere to go. But when he came to pay a visit Papa and Momma asked him to stay. I am sure Momma's food will help him regain his strength. Papa says he can do some chores too.

Papa also bought guns in town today. He insists that we all learn how to use them. It seems that you are not the only one who is in danger. I never thought we would be fighting for our lives here in Michigan, too. But, as you already know, the Bacons are bad people. Papa is determined that we be able to defend ourselves.

We all hope that you are well. Other than the Bacon problem, we are fine. God bless you.

Your sister,

Susan

✳   ✳   ✳   ✳

Those damn Bacons! Now my entire family is in danger. All of this is my fault, too.

The Bacon kid, Carl and I were in grammar school together. He was a bully and even though I was younger, I was pretty big for my age; so I roughed him up some. No, I did more than that. I beat on him pretty good. When he tried his stuff on my sister Susan, I beat on him a lot.

A couple of years later I stopped him from beating on a little kid and in the process, I dunked him in the horse trough; on a Saturday morning in town in front of everybody. The parents of the kid he was hitting were afraid to press charges because old man Bacon owned the bank. He had a lot of power in town. But I was the one arrested for assault. The Justice of the Peace gave me a choice of jail or signing up with a Union cavalry regiment being formed in a nearby town. I chose to join up.

Carl was an officer in that regiment and he used his authority by ordering his men to attack me. This time, though he was the one arrested. He was court marshaled and sentenced to a federal prison. Then the attacks on my family began. Bacon's bank foreclosed on my parents' farm.

I made a deal with Congressman Kellogg to join his Washington staff as he wanted, if he would lend my parents the money to pay off their mortgage. After Carl was released from the Federal prison, he tried to kill me in Detroit as I was traveling home on leave. It was back to Federal prison for him. I think he is still there..

This past December, Julia and I were attacked on our trip back to Washington. It became clear that the Bacons were not through trying to get revenge. Papa is right; they must prepare to defend themselves.

Lord, please look after my family.

LOWELL

Jake Drieborg was standing beside his eldest daughter, Susan. She was a very pretty blond haired eighteen-year-old girl who stood about five foot seven.

She is da spitting image of her mother when we came to dis country. She can do most anything around da farm dat a man can do. She will make a fine wife for a farmer, if any young ones are left after dis war.

"How many more times must I fire this shotgun today, Papa? My shoulder hurts and I'm freezing out here."

"When you can load and unload without dropping a shell and hit da target two times in a row. Den you can stop for da day. You and your sister must be able to handle this shotgun and hit what you aim at.

"Do you think that because you are a girl, you shouldn't know how to defend yourself?"

"No. I understand why I must do this, Papa. But I'm cold, my shoulder is sore from the shotgun and I am almost deaf from the noise."

"Well den, you better hit what you are aiming at; if you want to go inside to our warm house, dat is."

Susan became pretty accurate firing the shotgun, but she fumbled a lot loading the gun. They had to work at it another twenty minutes before her father let her go into the house.

"Are you going to make Ann do this too, Papa?" she remarked sharply.

I'll bet my sister will find some way to get out of this. She usually can.

"You just take care of yourself, young lady. I'll see to your sister. Tell Jacob to come out here, and to bring his rifle with him."

I know that Jacob is good with his squirrel gun. I don't know if he can handle a rifle as well, though; especially when he has to fire, reload and fire again. We'll see.

"Dat's enough with your rifle, Jacob. Now I want you to fire dis pistol at da target."

Dis is not going so well. With the cold, he is having trouble loading quickly.

"We will spend some time tomorrow with da pistol, Jacob."

"It is much easier to carry a pistol dan your rifle. But I want you to have dis pistol with you when we go into town, Jacob. Here, put dis belt and holster on. I will carry one, too. I bought a small two shot pistol for Momma to have in her purse."

"Wow, Papa. No one better try anything with us Drieborgs."

"All of us have to be prepared and willing to defend ourselves, son. I hope word gets back to Bacon, and he stops dis fight he has started."

"We do dis again tomorrow, son. Now go into da house and send out your sister Ann."

When Ann joined him, she was very direct.

"What do you want me to do here, Papa?" she said tersely.

Like her sister, Ann was very pretty. Unlike her sister, she was slender and a bit taller. More importantly, she seemed to attack whatever she set her mind to with a determination that was very noticeable.

I can't remember a time when she failed to accomplish whatever she set out to do. I don't see her living on a farm, though. She will probably marry a town boy; a businessman of some sort. He will be successful, too; she'll see to that, I'll bet.

"You must be able to hit dat target two times in a row and reload da shotgun without dropping a shell on da ground."

"Then I can go back inside?"

"Yes."

"Please show me the loading part and how to hold the gun to shoot it."

It only took Ann about twenty minutes to master the required skills.

"Nobody better fool with any of us, by God!" she said as she handed the shotgun to her father and strode through the snow back to the house.

What fire I saw in her face; hatred almost. Dat Bacon boy is fortunate he is not her target today. Unless I miss my guess, she will not hesitate to kill any attacker.

And so it went every afternoon for the rest of that week. Jake wanted everyone to be prepared for the worst when they went into town Saturday.

✳   ✳   ✳   ✳

On Wednesday of that week, a neighbor dropped off a letter at the Drieborg house. It was from Michael.

After their evening meal, Jacob asked Ann to read the letter.

Dear Family,

I am fine and I hope all of you are too. Things have been moving rapidly for me here in Savannah. Since I wrote you last, I met with President Lincoln again and was assigned to set up help for our soldiers freed from Confederate prisons.

Yesterday I arrived in Savannah, where General Sherman's army recently freed thousands of prisoners. When I met with him today, he wasn't too happy to have his attention diverted from fighting Rebs by helping me on this project; but he will, anyway. The president seems to get what he wants. What a temper the general has; I'll sure try to stay out of his way, believe me.

He assigned a member of his staff to help me here. A guy named Taft. He's the son of some big shot in Ohio who has a lot of influence in Washington. Are all sons of rich men so spoiled? This kid never earned a thing in his life as far as I can see. I hope he is not just a Carl Bacon, named Taft. But I'm stuck with him, so we will see.

Before I left, I was able to visit the Hecht family at their farm. I rode out there after work one night and found myself in a snowstorm that was so fierce I thought I was in Michigan not Maryland. I almost missed the turn to their house. They are all fine and asked me to remember them to you. Ruben and Mrs. Hecht agreed to let Julia and me marry this Easter. We are very happy about that.

Julia promised to write you all about it. She sure misses you all, especially little Eleanor.

I do too, even changing her smelly diaper. Give her a hug for me.

It might not be safe for any of you to travel to Maryland for the ceremony, though; at least not until this Bacon business is cleared up.
I will write again soon.

Love,

Michael

SAVANNAH

"Gentlemen," began General Sherman to his staff assembled. "As soon as I can clear up a few items, we move north. One of those loose ends involves this Major Drieborg here. I have assigned Captain Taft, lately of this staff, to help him. I want you gentlemen to direct your people to cooperate fully with their project. The president wants it and General Grant has ordered it. Now, I am ordering you. Major Drieborg, please explain your project and what kind of help you need."

"Thank you, General," Mike began. "When you captured Savannah, there were approximately six thousand Federal troops held captive here. Having been a prisoner at Andersonville myself, I know that all of these men would have been undernourished and most, possibly thousands of them, in need of medical attention. These former prisoners of war look to you for this assistance. But you are a fighting force, not well suited to help them.

"The purpose of the project I have been ordered to direct is to deliver that help; and simultaneously, relieve you of the responsibility. But I need your assistance.

"First: We need you to direct your chief medical officer to meet with us as soon as possible. We don't plan to keep any of your medical personnel but a few days. But we need them to examine all former prisoners and identify what each needs medically.

"Secondly: We need you to direct your quartermaster personnel to meet with us too so that we can begin to identify what supplies are available for these former prisoners. Ships are expected this week, bringing food, clothing, medical supplies and some personnel; so we are not going to raid much of your supplies or your food. But we do need your personnel to help identify needs and to organize distribution. We also need you to assign us cooks to direct the preparation and distribution of food, until ours arrive.

"Third: We need help in identifying the former prisoners who have joined units in your command. With your permission, we will set up a registration post at division level. We need you to direct your command personnel to send all former prisoners to those stations. From there, we will direct them to the physical examination center we will establish at a medical facility in Savannah. We intend to also arrange for the payment of their back pay.

"And last: We don't want to disrupt your preparations to carry the war north, and we don't want to have to ask you to back us up every time one of your command personnel refuses to assist us. That would be disruptive for us both. But we need you to sign this authorization directing personnel under your command to cooperate with Captain Taft and me. Are their any questions, gentlemen?"

All the officers around the conference table and those sitting in chairs against the wall looked toward General Sherman.

"You heard the man," he virtually shouted. "Any one of you don't cooperate, I'll find someone to replace you. Ask Captain Taft, who you might remember was a colonel yesterday, what happens when I give an order and an officer drags his feet. We got a war to fight. We can better do that if we don't have to play nursemaid to thousands of former prisoners.

"Besides, I've been ordered by Grant to see to this. If I have to address this matter with any of you again, you'll regret it.

"But sign the damn authorization," he thundered. "All of ya."

LOWELL

For the first time in several weeks, Jake Drieborg went into Lowell on a Saturday morning. A pistol was strapped to his waist. His wife, Rose, sat beside him in the wagon. Susan sat in the back with a loaded shotgun cradled in her arms.

"I don't feel right about this pistol in my purse, Papa," Rose told him. "I can't even shoot it straight yet."

"Susan," Jake asked. "Momma does not want to carry da small pistol. You practiced with it. Will you put it in your purse, just in case?"

"All right Papa." Rose handed the small two shot pistol to her daughter.

"I'll drop off this grain to be ground at da Hatch and Craw elevator," Jake reminded them. "Den, we will all go to Jim Yared's General Store. I will stand by da door with the shotgun while you shop. After dat we will go to see Mr. Deeb, da Justice of da Peace. He will know any news about da Bacons; den we will go to da library for books before we pick up da flour at da elevator on our way out of town."

"Do we have to parade around town with all these guns, Papa?" Susan complained. "It feels as if we're guilty of something. Besides, it takes all the fun out of a visit to town."

"It does seem odd, Susan," her father agreed. "But we have to look after ourselves until da Bacons stop dis revenge against da Drieborgs. Fun will have to wait."

Mr. Deeb was at his desk when the Drieborgs came into his office. He stood and came around to greet them.

"Jacob, Mrs. Drieborg, Susan, welcome." He shook Jake's hand. " I haven't seen you in town for a while. I hope you all have been well."

"We have stayed away until everyone, even Momma here, has practiced with a shotgun and a pistol. We intend to defend ourselves against dis crazy Bacon. You heard of da attacks on Michael in Cleveland and Baltimore. He had to kill three men on his return trip to Washington."

"I read the account of the Cleveland attack in the Grand Rapids Eagle, Jake," he admitted. "I think everyone in town knows what happened there. Since you have not been in town for a while, you may not know, but Harvey Bacon has been arrested for paying for those attacks against Michael. Harvey has been in Federal custody in Grand Rapids for a week now. It seems to me that he will be sent to the Federal prison in Detroit, where his son Carl is serving his jail term.

"And," Deeb continued, "the Old Kent Bank out of Grand Rapids has opened an office here in Lowell. I think Congressman Kellogg had something to do with that. Old Kent Bank is offering lower interest rates on all loans. So people here are lining up to get money to pay off their notes at Bacon's bank. It looks to me that Bacon is finished in this town."

"Dat's a good thing, Mr. Deeb," Jake admitted. "But he still has his money. And I don't know if he has given up his hate for us Drieborgs. Even if he is in jail, he paid men his son found in dere to try and kill Michael. Thank God our son survived dose attacks. Now we must keep vigilant and be prepared to defend ourselves."

"I can't say that I blame you, Jake. I'm sorry that I can't offer much help. But Marshal Chapman, who has his office right here in Lowell, and the Federal marshal Mr. Kalanquin in Grand Rapids will respond if needed."

"Dey are both too far away," Jake reminded him. "By da time we could get any help, da attack would be over. No, we must look after ourselves. I hope da word gets out dat we Drieborgs are prepared to defend ourselves."

"By the way, Jake," Deeb continued. "The next time you are in town, Mr. Snell will be the Justice of the Peace. I have accepted a position as manager of the new bank in town.

Be sure to stop in and say hello when you're next in Lowell."

"Congratulations on your new job, Mr. Deeb. I am sure that people will be treated fairly with you there," added Rose Drieborg.

"Thank you, Mrs. Drieborg," Deeb responded. "I wonder if I could ask a favor."

Rose looked a bit puzzled at the request.

"What favor would you need from us, Mr. Deeb?"

"You might not know it, but I am not married," he began somewhat embarrassed. "I wonder if you would mind if I called upon your daughter Ann."

"Such a request is new to us, Mr. Deeb," Rose responded. "But if you want to become better acquainted with our family, you might attend mass at St. Robert's church with us tomorrow morning at 9 AM. We have seen you in church before, so we know that you are of the Catholic faith. We always stay for the social following the service. If you stay for that you can eat with us, and visit with our Ann then."

"Thank you both," Deeb responded happily. "I will accept your invitation, Mrs. Drieborg, and plan to meet you there tomorrow morning. Can I bring anything for the social?"

"No, that is not necessary," Rose responded. "You will be our guest this time. But thank you for offering."

"By the way, Susan," Mr. Deeb continued. "Allow me to congratulate you on your engagement to George Neal. I just heard about it. When is the wedding?"

"We haven't set the date, actually. But I expect it to be this spring. George is trying to arrange financing to purchase the bakery in Grand Rapids where he apprenticed before the war. The owner was killed last month in the fighting at Petersburg, Virginia and his wife wants to return to Lansing where she grew up. So she is looking for a buyer. George is there today, talking with her."

"If you like, have George come to visit me at the new bank office. I'll tell him what information we will need to consider financing his purchase. Maybe we can work something out."

"Oh thank you," Susan exclaimed. "We will both come to see you. Will next Saturday morning be too soon? "

"I should be settled in my new office by then. Next Saturday morning would be fine.

How about eight that morning? Will that work for you two?"

"We'll be in town then, won't we Papa?"

"Ya; we probably will, Susan."

"So Mr. Deeb, George and I will make it work. You can plan on us being there at eight."

*   *   *   *

As the Drieborgs left town, they had much to talk about.

"My, my Papa," Rose Drieborg began. "Our girls are growing up. First, Michael's friend George Neal asks us if he can talk marriage to our Susan. Now Mr. Deeb wants to court our Ann."

"Susan," her mother directed. "I will talk with Ann about this matter. You don't say anything right now. Besides, you will have your hands full telling George about the arrangements you have made for next Saturday with Mr. Deeb at the bank."

"Church tomorrow will be interesting, eh Momma!" Jake chuckled.

"I can hardly wait, Papa." Susan volunteered from the back of the wagon.

"Susan. Remember, not a word when we get home."

"Yes Momma. I know."

SAVANNAH

"What in heaven's name is this crap all about?" Stan Killeen spouted. "We're a cavalry troop, not nursemaids."

"May be, lad," Sergeant Riley agreed. "But 'tis an order now. And you're a squad leader; so get yer men ready. We ride for Savannah in one hour."

Stan had to be virtually ordered to become squad leader. Probably the best horseman and outdoorsman in the squad, he had resisted previous opportunities for command because he said he would not give an order that might cost a man his life.

Raised on a farm, Stan had become pretty proficient with animals. He spent some time as a lumberman in northern Michigan, working out of doors in all kinds of weather, before a cash bounty induced him to enlist back in 1862. Unusual for most troopers, he was clean-shaven. But at five-foot-seven and one hundred forty pounds, he was the typical size of most cavalrymen.

Back with his squad, Killeen continued to complain.

"It's bad enough that Neal is home on medical leave and I have to look after you bozos. Now Riley tells me our platoon has been ordered into Savannah to help nursemaid soldiers who have just been released from the Confederate prison there. How in hell can we help them? They need clerks and doctors, not combat cavalrymen."

"I suspect we'll find our soon enough, Stan," Bill Anderson calmly told him.

Bill never told anyone how old his was. But the other troopers in the squad figured him to be about forty. That would make him the oldest, by far. He and his wife had owned a general store in Wyoming, Michigan. She died from tetanus poisoning in the spring of 1862; he sold the store and joined the cavalry regiment being formed in nearby Grand Rapids the following September.

"It's gotta' be safer and better duty than dodging bullets from local militia or chasing Reb cavalry in the cold winter rain and mud of Georgia," Anderson continued. "Besides, we never got into Savannah after we captured it. I heard it's a pretty nice city."

"It could be raining cats and dogs and cold as a rat's ass, Anderson," Killeen growled. "And you would talk about the sun coming out any minute. Sometimes your positive attitude makes me feel like puking."

"Did Sgt. Riley tell you why our troop was chosen out of da entire Division, Stan?" Swede asked.

Gustov Svenson had volunteered, as had everyone else in the squad back in September of 1862. The bounty money paid to volunteers had lured him. He used it to repay the copper mining company the money he owed them for his passage from Sweden. They had brought him to Michigan to manage the mules and horses used in the mines.

"He didn't give me or the other squad leaders a clue, Swede. He just said we leave in an hour. But all of us had better get our gear together and our horses saddled. You know how cranky he can get."

LOWELL

Jake Drieborg had left his son Jake and his daughter Ann at the farm, while his wife, Rose, and their daughter Susan joined him in town.

"Remember, you two," he had cautioned. "It is a Saturday. Anyone Bacon might hire would guess dat we will be in town dis morning."

Jake's instructions were clear. "Be on da alert. Jacob, stay in da barn loft with your rifle and pistol. If you see any riders come into our yard, fire once over deir head with da pistol. No talking, Jacob, just shoot a warning immediately. If dey don't leave after you shoot, or if dey draw weapons, kill dem if you can.

"Ann," he continued. "I leave you here instead of your older sister because I believe you will not hesitate to shoot anyone who attacks our home. Besides, you handle da gun best of anyone. Have da shotgun loaded and by you in da house. Keep extra shells in your apron pocket. When you hear Jacob fire his pistol, go to da yard window in da kitchen with da shotgun. If you can see da riders in da yard, open da window and fire at dem just like we practiced with da target.

"Do you have any questions, children?"

"No, Papa," Ann responded.

"We'll be fine, Papa," Jacob assured him.

✳   ✳   ✳   ✳

It had been over an hour since her parents and her sister had left for town. Ann had just put baby Eleanor down for her morning nap. She was seated in a rocker knitting a scarf for Michael. She had always loved the back and forth motion of the chair. It seemed to soothe her. Today, however, it wasn't working. Maybe it was the shotgun by her side.

Could I really shoot someone? she wondered.

Her brother Jacob was positioned in the loft of the barn. There were double doors covering the loft opening onto the yard. Hay was lifted by means of a pulley from the ground and stored in that second floor area. He had tied these doors back, so he had a clear view of the entire yard. Even though he was comfortably seated on a bale of hay, the chilly February wind allowed him little chance of falling asleep. He was too nervous, anyway.

I hope I don't have to, but I promised Papa that I would shoot to kill. My brother Michael killed when he had to. He killed a bunch of men at Andersonville Prison, two men in Cleveland and another one in Baltimore. Please God; help me protect my home.

Another hour passed. In the house, Ann was standing at the sink looking out the window sipping some hot tea. She could see her brother in the barn's loft. Below, their dog Blackie was lying on the ground in the open barn doorway.

I can see Jacob rubbing his hands together. I'll bet he is cold. Should I take him something warm to drink? I had better not. Papa said for each of us to stay where he put us.

Just as she was turning from the window, she saw two men on horseback ride into the yard. As she lifted the shotgun by her side, she heard the dog barking at the intruders and a shot ring out from the barn.

"Get off our place" she heard Jacob shout.

Oh, my God! Both men have a pistol in their hand and are aiming at the loft, Ann realized. *They're shooting at my brother.*

By the kitchen window now, she heard another shot; then another. She saw that shooting spooked the horses of the two attackers. One jumped high on his hind legs; the other turned a complete circle. As soon as they regained control of their horses, the men fired toward the barn again. She saw a rifle fall to the ground from the barn loft, and heard a loud groan.

"I got him," one of the men shouted. "Come on, let's finish him."

Ann opened the window over the sink and aimed the shotgun at one of the intruders; aim, cock the first hammer and fire, just like Papa drilled.

The recoil of her first shot pushed her back into the room some and the barrel of the shotgun almost hit the top of the window frame.

What is that scream? The horse? I didn't mean to shoot a horse. How could I miss that badly; the man was only a few yards away? At least he's on the ground. The other man is still in his saddle. He's turning to see where the shot came from. He's raising his pistol and aiming at me. Oh Lord, help me!

She quickly raised the gun again.

Stay calm; pull the hammer back; aim and pull the trigger. Got him!

This time her target took the entire impact of the shot in the chest, knocked him clear out of the saddle. His pistol shot went high, hitting the window frame above her head.

I can't see the horses anymore; they must have run off. But both men are on the ground. The first one I shot is crawling toward the barn where Jacob is. Ann raised the shotgun again, aimed, cocked the hammer and pulled the trigger.

She heard a click; no shell explosion.

Damn, I already fired two shots. Calm down, Ann; take a deep breath. Now reload. Remember Papa's drill; raise the barrel; then push the lever to open the gun; let the two spent shells fall out; lower the barrel; insert one, then a second shell; close the gun until you hear it click securely shut. The man is still crawling toward the barn; can't let him get to my brother.

Loaded once again, she aimed, cocked the weapon, and fired. At the impact of the buckshot, the man's body virtually leaped off the ground, only to settle and remain still.

Good; he stopped crawling. Is that another shot I hear? Is Jacob firing; or is there another attacker? I can't hear too well; my ears are ringing. Must be my imagination?

Ann ran into her bedroom to a window facing the road. She looked through the curtains and saw a riderless horse standing in the road. Its left flank was covered with blood, and it was snorting loudly as it raised and lowered its great head.

Damn! I did hit it. Lord, forgive me. Why is it so quiet? Is Jacob all right? I want to go to help him. But Papa said to stay in the house.

It was only then that she heard the baby's loud cry.

Oh! I'm sorry Eleanor. All that shooting frightened you. Come to Ann. We'll rock some. That's right Ann's here now. No need to be afraid.

SAVANNAH

Mike and Taft made their way to the outskirts of Savannah. They were looking for the recently liberated prisoner of war facility, Camp Davidson. It was supposed to be adjacent to the city's hospital.

"That's a good location for a prison camp," Taft commented. "Where I come from in Ohio, people went to a hospital to die, not recover."

"We didn't even have one in Lowell," Mike added. "The local doctor cared for people in their homes."

As they approached the two facilities, they noticed that the two large doors in the prison stockade were open. Once inside the enclosure, they dismounted.

"I'm surprised to see so many men still here. There must be two or three thousand of them."

Throughout the enclosed area, men tended fires or huddled inside tents and leantos, called shebangs.

To their left, a man was stirring some sort of liquid in a large cauldron over an open fire.

"Soldier," Mike asked. "Who is in charge here?"

"Nobody I know of, Major," was the reply. "But you might check in the hospital. That's where we get our food."

Inside the hospital, the two Union officers continued their search for someone in authority. As they walked to the right of the entrance, they found themselves in a large open room that held upwards of fifty beds. A female dressed in a strange outfit was sitting by a bed, feeding a patient.

"Ma'am," Drieborg asked. "Can you direct me the person in charge of the prison?"

The nurse looked up. "You can call me Sister Mary, Major. I am a nun of the Catholic church and the order of Sisters of Charity. The nuns of my order are trained to treat the sick in hospitals. There are a few civilian patients here, but most of those here are soldiers. Some of them are Confederates, but most are Union men who were prisoners here. To answer your question more directly, Major, Dr. Woolworth is in charge of the hospital. He's around here someplace."

"Thank you, Sister."

"That starched white thing she wears on her head, looks strange. What's a nun anyway?" Taft asked of nobody in particular.

"As she said, Taft; she is a woman who is a member of the Catholic church. From what I have been told, women who become nuns take vows of poverty and obedience. They also take a vow never to marry, and instead devote themselves to God in prayer and service: like teaching or nursing. Most of these groups of women were started in Europe long ago. Rather than wear the latest fashion, these women decided to retain the style of clothing worn long ago in the country where their group began. Thus, you see the rather strange outfit Sister Mary is wearing."

"Interesting, Drieborg," Taft responded. "But it still seems weird. Besides, it doesn't seem natural for women to work with sick and wounded men, cleaning their wounds and bodies. Male orderlies should do that."

Mike laughed heartily. "Wait till you meet Clara Barton, Taft. She's going to be here soon to help with the nursing. She has recruited women like herself to work with the wounded in all sorts of conditions. She and many other women have worked on battlefields and assisted doctors at the operating table as well. She believes that women are much better suited by temperament to help men recover from wounds and sickness. I would guess that many thousands of our soldiers would have died if not for her and the other nurses she brought into our hospitals."

"How do you know so much about this?"

"When I was wounded at Gettysburg, I was treated at a field and at a regimental hospital. I did not have a wound that was life threatening, but by the time I reached Washington with thousands of other wounded, I was virtually unconscious with infection and fever. The medical practices and unsanitary conditions damned near killed me, not a Reb saber. Barton and others just like her have done a lot to improve the sanitation at hospitals; and she has recruited hundreds of female nurses, much like Sister Mary, to take care of our wounded and sick boys.

"I had the privilege of meeting and working with her when we liberated Andersonville Prison last fall. She is quite a lady, as you are soon to discover. She'll be here in a few days to help us. But don't listen to me, Taft. Get in her way and she'll run you over, big shot family or not."

"Keep those bleeding hearts away from my wounded," Taft insisted. "Give me a good male orderly any day."

"You had better hope and pray that you never find yourself on a field operating table, Taft. If the surgeon doesn't chop off your arm, leg or hand with a well used filthy saw, he might just stick his dirty finger into your wound to probe for metal, cloth or bits of bone. Should you survive that experience, the only help you will receive is from another wounded soldier assigned to give you all the whiskey and opium you want but deny you water."

Mike paused, exasperated with his companion, and resumed his search for the director of the hospital.

"I see a fellow down that hallway. He might know where Doctor Woolworth can be found."

"You have found him, Major. How can I help you?"

After the introductions, the doctor led the two Union officers to an office.

"So you want to know who is in charge of the prison. That's easy, gentlemen; no one I know about. Since General Sherman liberated Camp Davidson, we have provided what food we can and medical services; but the men are pretty much on their own as far as I can see. What is your interest?"

Mike explained the prisoner of war project to Dr. Woolworth.

"Captain Taft has been assigned by General Sherman to help. I would hope that you and your staff would help as well. Food, medicines, clothing and trained medical personnel will arrive soon by ship. May we join you in this facility to carry out our charge?"

"If you mean may you use space in this hospital for diagnosis, treatment and distribution: of course you may Major. This facility and my staff have always served the sick of this community. For some time now, we have also treated the wounded and sick of both armies. We intend to continue to do so. Any help you bring will be most welcome."

"We're not here to ask favors, Doctor," Taft interrupted heatedly. "We took this city from you Rebs. You'll help us whether you like it or not."

"You can save your anger for the battlefield, Captain," the doctor responded angrily.

"It has no place in our hospital. If there is nothing else, gentlemen, I have patients I must see." With that he rose from behind his desk to signal the end of the conversation. He extended his hand to Major Drieborg.

"Thank you Doctor," Mike said as he shook the physician's hand. "Can I meet with you at nine tomorrow morning?"

"Until tomorrow, Major." The doctor looked directly at Captain Taft and refused to shake his extended hand.

As soon as the two were outside the hospital, Mike turned on his companion with fire in his eyes.

"What the shit is wrong with you, Taft? Woolworth and his staff can be of great help in the success of our project."

"Come off it, Drieborg. He's just another high and mighty Confederate slaver who needs to be knocked down a peg or two."

"I don't think But Taft," Mike insisted. "I'll bet that we'll find that his hospital is filled with Union soldiers. Let's ask them if the good doctor and the nuns here need to be punished. From what I've seen so far, this place is a paradise compared to the other prisons and hospitals I have been in."

Mike warmed to chewing Taft out.

"How about I tell Sherman that your arrogant big mouth will likely sabotage this project? Remember, he promised you a job digging latrines for a front-line infantry unit. You want to test him on that?"

"I'm going to meet with Woolworth in the morning," Mike continued. "I will do that alone, without you and your damn fool attitude getting in the way."

"What am I supposed to do?"

"I don't much care what you do. At thirteen hundred we have a meeting with each of Sherman's field commanders, be there. Plan to keep your mouth shut then, too."

"You can't talk to me that way." Taft sputtered.

"Sure I can, Taft. I'm a major who is in charge of this assignment; and you're only a captain, remember? Keep in mind that one word from me and Sherman will assign you to a front-line unit.

"I may have to put up with you on this project, but I don't have to hang out with you. So get out of my sight. Your arrogant attitude disgusts me. Just be at Sherman's headquarters tomorrow at thirteen hundred hours. Consider that an order, Captain Taft."

Mike left Taft standing in the hospital hallway, mumbling angrily.

"We'll see about how well your project turns out, Drieborg; we'll just see."

✳   ✳   ✳   ✳

Mike walked back to the hospital and into a room that contained twenty or so patient beds. He stood in the doorway and looked around for a male nurse. He had to look into several such rooms before he finally spotted a man moving from bed to bed, evidently passing out food to patients.

He approached the man from behind.

"You wouldn't happen to know if a broken-down cavalryman named John Ransom who is pretending to be a nurse is around here, would you?"

The man straightened up and stood with his back to Mike.

"Can't be," he told the patient lying on the cot in front of him. "Tell me, soldier, is there a rather ugly Union cavalry officer standing behind me?"

"Can't rightly tell if he's ugly John; my preference is women actually," the man in bed responded. "But there is a rather tall blond-haired guy who happens to be a major in the cavalry standing there."

John put his tray down and turned.

"My God, Mike, it is you," John almost shouted. He put his hands on Mike's shoulders and stood quietly just looking at him. John wiped a tear from his own cheek. "I often wondered if you and Battist made it back to our lines. You're looking great, Mike."

Mike cleared his throat, swallowed hard and finally responded. "Lord, it's good to see you, John. I must say you look a lot better now than you did when I left you here last fall. You couldn't even stand back then, you were so sick."

"Feel better Mike, a lot better. I can even walk real well, too. They treated me fine here. The rest, good food and clean water did the trick. Got to give'em credit, these people saved a lot of our guys like me who were brought here from Andersonville. But wait a minute. Tell me what in hell you're doing here? Are you with Sherman's boys?"

"I've been sent by the president himself to see that the prisoners freed by Sherman's army are helped to become healthy enough to return home safely and with dignity. It's a huge job, John. I just had a brief conversation with Dr. Woolworth. The impression he gave me was that he and his staff will be glad to help. If my assignment can help his hospital serve this community too, that's fine with me."

"He's a straight shooter Mike, the nuns too. If he says he will help, he will. Is there anything I can do?"

"Now that you mention it, John, there is. I have a medical crew arriving soon. They are going to send the soldiers here who need special assistance to Washington area hospitals. You and the staff here can identify those men and save a lot of time. You probably have records identifying others who need food and clothing. We will have a lot of both. Could you help me with that, too?"

"Sure thing, Mike. Sam's still here too, you know. He'll help, I'm sure. Boy, will he be surprised to see you."

Mike and John left the hospital and headed for the prison compound.

"He should be over at that shack, Mike. Sam took it over after the camp was liberated. He's sort of in charge of food distribution."

"Hey Sam," John shouted. "Where the hell are you?"

"Hold your shirt on. I'm coming." Sam came out of his shack.

"Well I'll be a monkey's uncle. Do my eyes deceive me; or is that tall drink of water in front of me that big- shot officer, name of Mike Drieborg?"

The two men hugged in greeting.

"I'm glad to see you survived your escape last fall Mike. We never did know. But what in hell are you doing here?"

Mike and John Ransom explained the project to Sam.

"When you escaped from here last fall, Mike," Sam reminded him. "I was suffering from serious dehydration. John here had a bad case of scurvy and couldn't even walk. Thousands more here were malnourished. But with the help of these nuns at this hospital and a lot of good local people, we survived. With your project even more men can get healthy before they return home.

"So damn right I'll help. We can set up clothing and supply distribution right here in the prison compound. We have a good-sized shed to store stuff, too."

"Are the men here difficult to manage, Sam?"

"Naw; the guys here are pretty well behaved. Some men will always try to take advantage of others, though. So we had to do something about that. Do you remember Big Pete Mc Cullough from Andersonville Prison? He's in charge of our court here, too. He also runs our Regulators to enforce our rules. They keep a tight lid on things. I'm sure that his guys will help you. When do you expect your people to arrive?"

"They should be here later this week, Sam."

"But Mike," Sam continued. "Savannah's been stripped clean of anything edible; and the army claims they have no extra food, clothing or supplies for us. Where are you gonna get all this stuff?"

"It's coming by boat, Sam; should be in Savannah this week sometime."

"I'll believe that when I see it Mike," Sam said heatedly. "We have been given a lot of promises by those stuffed-shirt officers on Sherman's staff. Unfortunately for us, they have been real short on results. If it weren't for the doc and the nuns here, a lot of our soldiers here would have starved to death by now."

"You can see, Mike," John chuckled. "Sam's still a hard man in the trust department."

"Let's go meet with Mc Cullough, Mike," John suggested. "He's at the other end of the compound."

I remember Big Pet, Mike thought. *He was a big, tough looking no-nonsense guy. When he volunteered to be the judge for our prisoner court back at Andersonville Prison, I could see he was the right guy for the job. He could smooth talk anyone, but knock you flat with his big fists if he thought it necessary. His court sentenced six of the outlaw prisoners we called the Raiders to hang.*

I remember the Catholic priest Father Whelan, too. He begged for the lives of the six men. Big Pete heard him out and the pleas of several of the

other condemned men; banged his gavel and shouted, "Hang all of 'em."
And he did.

I also remember that one of the six Raiders hung turned out to be
my stepson Robert's natural father. My wife Eleanor had been told he was
killed. Was that a shock for me to hear him beg for mercy? I suppose that I
could have asked the court for his life. Instead I watched the trap door open
under his feet and I stood silently as he struggled for air at the bottom of the
rope, and died. I hope his son Robert never finds out.

The judge also handed out lesser punishments to at least another
hundred of the outlaw prisoners. My crew of Regulators followed up as a
police force to keep the peace in camp; his court backed us up every time. It
doesn't sound as though he has changed much.

"Dreiborg, you say," Mc Cullough shouted. "Where is that
scoundrel?"

The big fellow burst out of the shed that served as his courtroom.
He grabbed Mike in a bear hug, lifted him off his feet and twirled him
around.

"By damn, Drieborg," he declared after he set Mike back on the
ground. "You've put on some pounds since you escaped this place. But
what in hell are you doing back here, man?"

"The president sent me to bring you home, Mc Cullough."

"Don't pull a man's leg now, Major. I might just sentence you to
the stocks here if'n you're joking."

"No joke, Judge," Mike assured him. "Let's go inside your
courtroom and I'll tell you all about it."

When Mike was done outlining the project Mc Cullough quickly
responded. "Of course my men and I will help you, Drieborg. Every
one of us wants to get home. But after working with the likes of
Sherman's people, I've become like Sam here; I'll believe it when I see
it, don't you know."

"Hey, guys," Mike protested. "You all know me; I don't make
promises I can't keep. Are you going to help me out on this or not?"

"Speaking for myself," John Ransom said. "I'm totally in favor of
what you're proposing, Mike. But I will not tell all the guys in the

hospital that they are going home. At Andersonville Prison, we all suffered a lot with rumors of prisoner exchanges. You remember how the guards teased us with stories of exchanges at other prisons, but not at Andersonville? When Savannah was captured last December, we thought we would get all sorts of supplies and be sent north. But we're still here and still fending for ourselves. Thank God for the nuns. So I'm not going to be a part of getting everyone's hopes up about going home. You should understand our caution better than anyone, Mike."

"All right," Mike conceded. "Fair enough; I'll work through you three, Doctor Woolwroth and the nuns. My people and all the supplies should be here by week's end. You three tell the people here whatever you wish. There will be no talk of going home heard from me or my people. Will that do for now?"

The three men agreed and joined Mike in outlining procedures to implement the project at Camp Danville.

"By the way," Mike warned them. "I've got a guy assigned to me by General Sherman.

"He's from some big-shot family back in Ohio. Anyway, he's a bit arrogant and touchy about rank. I'll ride herd on him. But if you have any trouble with him, let me know. I don't want to give him any excuses to foul up this project or have cause to come after any of you. For Lord's sake, don't hit him, however much he might tempt you."

"Can't guarantee that, Mike," Sam told him. "You're the only officer I found in this here army who I can trust. You best keep this dandy Taft on a short leash. If you think my fuse is short, wait until you meet a lot of the other men around here. If that dandy gets too full of hisself he might not make it out of the gate here one evening."

The four men were still seated in McCullough's courtroom.

"Sam can really carry on, can't he, Mike," John chuckled. "Unless you have to rush off, tell us about your escape and what's happened to you since you snuck out of here last fall."

"Yah," Sam interrupted. "I'd like to hear how you finagled a promotion since we seen you last. Don't tell me they gave you that just for escaping from prison?"

"Sort of, Sam," Mike smiled. "But let me go back to the beginning. You remember, Sam; you didn't feel up to escaping with me so Battist went along. That Indian was really something. We traveled at night and hid during the day. More than once we went around farmhouses to avoid barking bogs. He said he smelled smoke from their chimney. I never smelled a thing; probably would have walked right back into prison without him.

"A Federal patrol picked us up. When we arrived in the first Union encampment, the colonel in charge invited me to eat with his officers, on the condition that I wash and change clothing. He told me that I stunk to high heaven. After Andersonville Prison, I just didn't realize.

"Anyway, I was sent to Kilpatrick's camp next. He sent me on to Washington where my old boss, Congressman Kellogg had arranged for me to meet with the president; ya, that's right, Lincoln himself. He asked me to help liberate Andersonville Prison. I agreed to do whatever I could, of course. All the while, the Congressman and the president were referring to me as Major Drieborg. I kept reminding them that I was a captain. They just smiled and told me that they would explain everything to me later.

"Well, eventually I found out that the president wanted to get a lot of publicity for this Andersonville Prison liberation project. Part of that effort centered on me. He decided to hold a big ceremony for the Northern press and Washington celebrities to award me a new medal Congress had created. It's called the Congressional Medal of Honor. So long story short, I became a major.

"To top it all off the Congressman surprised me by bringing my family from Michigan for the ceremony; Eleanor's family from Maryland, too."

"Oh ya, Mike," John cut in. "How are she and your child?"

"I didn't know it until I arrived in Washington," Mike told them. "But shortly after giving birth to our daughter, she died. Her parents named the baby after her, Eleanor."

"Wow. That must have been a shock." Sam observed softly.

"Yes it was, Sam. But I promised the president I would help on that liberation project, so my parents took the little tyke back to

Michigan. She's still there and doing well. After they returned home, I was involved in the planning and the execution of the liberation at Andersonville. There were still a few thousand prisoners there, mostly the sick. As it turned out, my job was to arrest Captain Wirz, seize his records and bring him back to Washington to stand trial."

"Well, good for you," McCullough exclaimed. "By my reckoning, that old bastard deserves to be hung. What happened to him?"

"After a trial Wirz was found guilty and hung last November."

"At least those damn politicians in Washington got that right, by damn," Sam announced.

"After that, I went back to Michigan on leave. When I returned to Washington, they assigned me to put this project together. And here I am."

"And it tis good to see you, Drieborg," Pete McCullough assured him. "We'll meet again when your people arrive. You can count on that."

"That's great, guys. In the meantime, I have a meeting with Dr. Woolworth tomorrow morning. I'll see you then."

HECHT FARM

Ruben had just returned from his weekly Saturday visit to Dayton, the local town. Impatient for mail from Mike, Julia had ridden along with her nephew Robert in tow. When she took her mother's list into the general store, she found a letter waiting for her.

"You go look at the candy, Robert," she directed. "I'll be right with you."

She went to a corner of the store and tore the letter open. *It's been weeks; I thought Michael would never write.*

Dear Julia,

I cannot tell you how much I miss you. What I would give to hold you in my arms right now. Tonight I am sleeping on the floor at General Sherman's headquarters in Savannah. The best hotel in town, the Pulaski House, refused to let him stay without paying, so he took over a very large home in the city, the Charles Green mansion. It has more rooms than a person could ever use. Sherman's people have not been very easy on the once stately home, so it's sort of a wreck right no; but at least I am out of the cold and rain.

My visit to the former prison here went well. Most of the former prisoners who were here before are still. That's because they have no place to go. Besides, the Catholic nuns who run the hospital located nearby, have been taking good care of the sick and have been providing food for all the prisoners. In fact, the nuns eat the same food they give the prisoners and patients. Two men who helped me survive Andersonville are here, too. It was great to see that they survived thus far.

The ships carrying supplies for my project should arrive this week. Then the real work starts.

I have no idea when I will be able to return north. I love you, darling. Be patient; we will be together sooner than you think. Take care of yourself.

Love,

Michael

She held the letter tightly to her chest. Mike's expression of love brought tears to her eyes.

She heard her name called and she felt a tug on her skirt.

"Julia," little Robert called out to her. He was pointing to the candy counter. "You promised, Julia," he reminded her. He was almost three now, just tall enough to see all the candy jars on the counter. "You said if I was good, I could pick out some candy."

In front of the candy counter Julia asked, "Did you pick out what you want, Robert?"

From the main counter of the store, she heard her name called again.

"Julia," the store clerk called. "We're clean out of the white cloth you asked for. Do you want to substitute another color, or place an order for what's on this list? It might take a few weeks, with the war and all."

"Thank you just the same, Mr. MacConnell," Julia told him. "But I need the kind and color on our list. It's for a wedding dress. I'm getting married you know."

""No, I didn't know. Congratulations. I can understand now why you need that particular cloth. Have you decided upon a date for the ceremony, Julia?"

"Why yes, we have. It will be the Saturday after Easter, Mr. MacConnell."

"If I can telegraph the order in, we might have it in two weeks. That should give you enough time to make your dress, don't you think?"

"Yes sir. I think so. We would really appreciate it."

"Julia," Robert called again. "You promised."

"Mr. MacConnell," she called. "Could you come over to the candy counter? We have some very important business to conduct here."

*   *   *   *

They were back on their farm before the noon meal. Ruben and his son Kenny carried the supplies from town into the house.

"So what is new in town, Papa?" Emma asked.

"Noting much, Momma," he answered. "The Petzold boy vas hurt at a place called Petersburg. He is in a Washington hospital."

"I hope they care for our boys there better than they did when Michael was wounded."

"Ya, Momma," Ruben recalled. "If it hadn't been for you, he might have died from da infection and da fever. I remember dat dey refused him water."

"And da Bernreuters' son, Hans," Ruben continued. "Da family had been told he is a prisoner, like Michael vas."

"We pray for them both tonight, Papa." Emma decided.

"I almost forgot, Momma," Ruben told her. "Julia got a letter from Michael. She seemed happy about it, so I tink he is all right. She vill tell you."

The dinner conversation continued to revolve around the news Julia and Ruben had heard from other families while shopping at the general store. The weather had turned colder and a light snow began to fall. The family would stay indoors until the late afternoon milking. So the dishes and food leftovers were cleared, little Robert was down for his afternoon nap and the Hechts were sitting around the table talking over a cup of coffee. Ruben, of course, was enjoying his after-dinner pipe.

"But" Emma began. "You got a letter from Michael. Tell us what he had to say, Julia."

"Well Momma, he says he is fine. He is in Savannah working with the prisoners of war there freed by Sherman's army last December. He doesn't know when he will be back in Washington. But at least he's not in the fighting; and he's safe."

"That's good to hear." Emma declared. "By the way, Julia," she continued. "If that material doesn't get here in time, we could alter your sister's wedding dress."

A little too heatedly, Julia refused to consider it. "That was Eleanor's dress Momma. She used it twice. That's quite enough. I'll wear this plain brown everyday dress before I'll wear hers."

✳   ✳   ✳   ✳

Before the two women could continue talking about this, a heavy knocking on the door startled the Hechts. Kenny was the first up to answer the knock.

He had barely had his hand on the latch when the door was shoved against him and a rough-looking man holding a rifle filled the doorway. Two other armed men followed him into the room.

The third man removed his slouch hat. "Excuse us, folks," he began. "I'm Captain Scott; my men and I are part of General Fitz-Hugh Lees' cavalry. We're on a raid into this part of Maryland and in need of supplies. The general insists that we pay for anything we take, so I will sign vouchers for everything. My other men outside are already in your barn taking grain for our horses, hams from your smokehouse and chickens and ducks from their pens.

"Ma'am," the captain spoke to Emma who was still standing by the kitchen window. "I see the empty coffee cups on the table, sugar too. None of us has seen real coffee or sugar for a long time. Unless you want one of these roughnecks to search through your pantry, I would appreciate it if you would pack up your coffee, sugar and flour for us to take, too.

"As long as you don't interfere, no harm will come to any of you. These two men here will stay in the house to see that you don't do anything reckless. Excuse me, I must check on my other men outside."

The raiders had little to fear. The Hechts were too stunned to do anything but sit silently and pray that no harm would come to them, as the captain had promised.

Shortly though, the man who had forced his way into their house began to move around the room. He moved behind Julia. He smiled while he caressed her long brown hair in his dirty hand.

Oh God, his hands are dirty and he stinks, Julia thought as she pulled away from him.

"Been a long time since I been close to a pretty girl like you, missy. Ain't she pretty, Ben?"

"Sure is, pard," the other soldier agreed. "Jus remember ta save some a that fer me."

Please Lord, let that captain come back into the house, soon.

And he did. All it took was a look from the captain and the soldier removed his hand from Julia's hair and backed away. As he did, he spotted a daguerreotype hanging on the wall. It was the picture Mike and Julia had taken in Cleveland the previous December.

Meanwhile, Captain Scott removed his slouch hat and approached Ruben at the table.

"This is a rough list of what we have taken, sir," he began. "As you can see, I have signed it at the bottom. After we win our independence, you can redeem this voucher. I hope we have not caused you too much inconvenience sir. But many distasteful things happen during wars. And thank you, ma'am, for packing up the stuff from your pantry. The men will really appreciate it."

"Captain, I think you should see this," one of the soldiers suggested. He handed the photograph he had taken from the wall, to the officer.

"It looks to me like you and your husband or beau, young lady," he said to Julia. "I can see that he's a good-looking fellow. I can also see he wears the insignia of the Federal cavalry. A Michigan man too, by the looks of it. Because of what those boys have done to my troopers with their repeating rifles and the way they have looted and burned our farms in the Shenandoah Valley , we call them the 'Michigan Devils'. We still will not harm you or burn your home as they have done to our farmers, but we will burn your barn and storage sheds.

"Corporal," he directed. "See to it; but I won't be a party to burning animals alive. But drive their livestock and plow horse into the yard. Put their wagon in the yard, too. Kill all their pigs, goats and sheep and any chickens and ducks we did not take. That should set enough of an example for the other Yankee sympathizers in this area. Sorry, folks." He threw the voucher on the table, picked up the sack of supplies Emma had prepared, and left the house.

The man who had touched Julia followed him. He smiled at her and gave her a wave as he moved toward the door.

"Maybe I'll see ya later, missy," he teased.

Ruben sat slumped in his rocker, too shocked and afraid for his family to protest. Emma sat ramrod straight, furious with the destruction being brought upon them.

"My God, Momma," Ruben finally said. "How will we survive da winter? Dey took all our smoked meat, killed our chickens, sheep and goats and burned our seed for da spring planting. It is like starting all over again."

"Come Papa," Emma directed firmly. "Julia, you stay and look after Robert. We and Kenny go outside and see what we can salvage." Roused from his shock, Ruben stood, got on his winter gear and followed his wife out of the house.

Fueled by hay and stored corn, the barn and storage sheds burned hotly in the overcast sky of the afternoon. The roof of the buildings had already fallen and little was left of the walls. The Hechts could feel waves of intense heat from the doorway of their house. But they kept their distance. But they rounded up their plow horse and cows and went to the pens to see if any other animals had been left alive.

None of the animals had been spared. "Papa," Emma said. "I think we can preserve some of the meat from the dead chickens if we do it today. Maybe we can preserve some lamb and goat meat, too. You and Kenny skin what you can before dark. Julia and I will get the water boiling to get ready for the canning."

"Ya, Momma," Ruben agreed. "Come Kenny, Momma is right. Let us see what we can do."

The Hecht family worked into the night; Ruben and his son Kenny outside skinning, and Emma and Julia inside canning. Long after dark, the family sat around the table and ate a late supper.

"What do we do now, Mamma?" Julia asked.

"I am too tired to think right now. We talk about it tomorrow, Julia; all right Papa?"

"Ya Momma, we are all too tired. Let us talk tomorrow."

SAVANNAH.

The ninety-some men in I Troop of Michigan's 6th Cavalry Regiment had been up since dawn. After taking care of their mounts, they ate and headed into Savannah. They had ridden on the town's muddy roads for the last three hours. A light rain had been falling, and the temperature was still at the freezing mark; not so comfortable for the men or their horses.

The commander of I Troop, Captain Lovell, rode at the head of the column of troopers. Alongside of him was First Sergeant Riley.

"This city is bigger than I thought," he observed. "We have been riding the streets within the city for some time." Lovell had been given command of I Troop after Mike Drieborg had been captured in March of '64.

"Most any city would seem large to a farm lad like you, sir. I'm a Detroit boy myself," Sgt. Riley responded. "This town's not much bigger, it seems ta' me. I'm just happy that no one is shooting at us from the houses as we pass by. Begging yer pardon sir; I think I'll remind the boys ta keep their carbines out an' their eyes peeled for trouble."

"Proceed, Sergeant," Lovell told him.

What a blessing that Riley is, Lovell thought. *His instincts have kept us alert and alive many 'a time since I've been in command of I Troop. I've learned a lot from him over the past ten months. Keep him safe from harm, Lord.*

I wonder if this Major Drieborg is really the great leader everyone talks about. Riley has told me a few things about him. The guy joined the regiment as a private, and was assigned to I Troop back in the fall of '62. Right off the bat the five other men of his squad selected him squad leader. He was just a teenage kid. Riley was his platoon sergeant then. After that, promotions came one after another until he was given command of the troop in January of 1864.

Riley says of him, that the men would have followed him into hell itself if he had led them. He hasn't been with them since the Richmond raid back in March of '64. He was wounded and taken prisoner then. Afterward, Riley brought the troop back safely to Union lines. Shortly thereafter, I was given command.

Now he is in command again. We'll see how it goes.

Riley had been with the troop since it was first organized in Grand Rapids, back in the fall of 1862. He trained most of the men back then; and now ran the troop with both an iron fist and a tender feeling for each of his men. A fire red head of hair topped his five- seven frame. He had a lean body shaped over two years in the saddle.

The men of I Troop who survived that initial training camp had learned to trust Riley. Early on he had driven their training, insisting that they thoroughly clean their cooking gear and weapons properly, change their socks daily, care for their horses as though their lives depended upon it, and look after one another. Seldom were men from his troop found at sick call, either.

"If I see any ayah at sick call, lads," he would remind them. "It better be from something the Rebs done to ya; or yer in trouble with me."

When Lovell next looked back at the column, he saw that each trooper had taken his Spencer carbine out of its scabbard. Each man held the weapon in his right hand and rested the weapon's wooden stock on his thigh as he rode. Riley had also moved each of the two columns of men about ten yards apart, so that they rode along the outside of the road on each side. Lovell could see his men looking at each house along their route for signs of trouble, too.

A rider galloping toward him from the front interrupted Lovell's thoughts. The trooper was a member of the Point Squad riding one hundred yards in front and leading the main body.

"Sir," the rider said as his brought his horse to a halt at Lovell's side. "The Point has reached the intersection where we are to turn off, sir. What are your instructions?"

"Direct the Point to hold the intersection until your relief moves past you. Do you have any questions?"

"No sir."

"Then proceed, Private."

To another trooper, Lovell ordered, "Ride back into the column and have Sergeant Riley report to me."

Shortly, Riley reined in his mount alongside his troop commander.

"Yes sir."

"Sergeant," Lovell directed. "Select a relief for the Point and escort them to the intersection ahead. It is my understanding that we are to turn away from the sea and go on the road to the southwest to reach the prison compound."

"Yes sir."

Shortly, Riley led six troopers past Lovell at a fast gallop, headed forward to the road intersection.

Maryland:

The following morning Ruben was lying in bed, awake. It was still dark and he could see stars in the clear sky. As exhausted as he had felt last night, Ruben didn't think he had slept much. He knew he had prayed, though.

Thank you, Lord, for protecting my family from harm and sparing our house. But I don't understand why you let dis happen to us. Now my family needs me to be strong, Lord. Help me find da strength to go on and da wisdom to see da way.

We will need money from da bank, I know. Like before, dey will give us a loan if dey think it is safe for us to Rebuild here. Our neighbors will help us with a barn-raising. Maybe our friends will give us some chickens, pigs and goats to start new flocks and herds; and seed for da spring planting, too. How will we replace all da food da soldiers took? Der will be no new money coming in until next fall's harvest to buy anything. Momma and I will talk about dis later.

I must be strong for da family. Help me, Lord.

After milking their two cows, Ruben joined his family for breakfast. It was strange that there was no aroma of freshly baked bread in the house; the raiders had taken all their flour. There were no eggs, bacon or coffee, either. But aside from fresh milk, Emma served leftover chicken from last night and day-old bread. The silence of the family only made the gloom worse. Little Robert was his usual self, though, full of observations and questions.

"Grandma," he began. "What happened to the barn? Was it an accident? Why did it burn? What happened to the chickens and the sheep and the pigs and the goats?"

Finally, Ruben gave him a believable answer. "Some Confederate soldiers burned da barn and killed those animals, Robert."

That just started the questions anew. "Why did they do that, Grandpa? Are they the men who killed my real father? I thought Mike was protecting us from them."

Da little fellow isn't da only one with questions. We must all talk about dis. Dis time even Momma is waiting for me to begin.

"Well, everybody," Ruben began. "You can see from da breakfast on our table dis morning dat ve don't have much food. Mit most of our animals killed, food vill continue to be a problem, I tink. Ve have no shelter for our cows or our horse. And we are in da middle of winter, a long way from harvest time."

"Are you saying that we have to leave the farm, Papa?" Kenny asked.

"That's dumb talk, Kenny," Julia snapped. "Of course we won't. Will we, Papa?"

"Dat is what ve must decide, Julia."

"Last night we canned a lot of chicken and pork, Papa," Emma reminded everyone. "But we won't have enough to last until we raise more chickens, pigs and goats. That means we will have to buy food. The Confederates took our coffee, sugar and flour, too. So we will have to replace that, also. Feed for our stock we will have to buy as well."

"Now dat da barn ashes have cooled," Ruben interrupted. "Kenny and I vill go out and see if ve can salvage any of our tools and equipment. I hope ve find enough of da horse harness undamaged so ve can use him to pull da wagon.

"Den ve meet again to talk. Does dat sound all right to you Momma?"

"Yes it does," Emma agreed. "We can talk on the way to church, Papa. It is Sunday. The Hechts still have much to thank God for."

"I wonder about that, Momma," Julia said sharply. "Where was God yesterday?"

"You just watch your attitude and your tongue when you talk about our God, young lady. Dress up Robert and take him outside. It is good for him to be out of the house and see everything."

"He will just pester me with questions, Momma." Julia moaned.

"He probably will," Emma agreed. "But if you are going to be his Momma after you marry Michael, you might just as well start doing what a Momma does, right now."

She knew her mother was right. "Come on, Robert. Let's join Kenny and Grandpa outside."

"How can you be my mother, Julia?" he asked. "My mother is in heaven. Am I supposed to call you Julia, or Momma?"

"We'll talk about that later. Right now we're going to get our winter jackets and shoes on, and go outside. So young man, button your jacket and button your lip until we get outside."

"All right." The little tyke agreed.

Ruben and his son were rummaging through the debris. Their work gloves protected their hands and a kerchief over their mouths and noses gave them some relief from the remaining smoke.

Kenny was at the front edge of the barn when he uncovered one of their tools.

"Hey, Papa," he shouted. "I found that metal pit-fork we just bought. The handle is blackened some, but it appears all right." He began to use it to move pieces of burned wood around.

Just then, Kenny saw two horsemen ride into the yard.

My God. It's those two soldiers who were in our house yesterday. I'm not going to let them push us around again, he thought.

One man dismounted and walked over to Julia, who was standing by her brother Kenny.

"Well, well," he said as he approached. "I told you that we might meet again, missy. This time, my captain will not interrupt us, will he Ben?"

"No pard, he sure enough won't."

As the solder reached for Julia, she slapped his face.

"You stink as much today as you did yesterday."

The man just brushed her arm aside and grabbed her around the waist from behind. Julia kicked and yelled for him to let her go.

"She's got spirit, pard. You save some for me now, hear?"

Before the other man could answer, Kenny shoved the sharp blades of his pitchfork into the man's back.

"Not today, you won't." Kenny grunted as he gave the blades one more push up and through the man's torso.

Julia was still in front of her assailant, so his companion was slow to see what Kenny had done. But as soon as Kenny pulled the blades out of the man's back, he fell to the ground. Then his mounted partner jumped to the ground, drew his big Bowie knife and walked toward the sixteen-year-old boy.

"We'll see about that, sprout."

In the house, Emma heard her daughter's screams. She looked out her kitchen window and saw the soldier approach Kenny with the knife.

This cannot happen. Yesterday was enough. I will not allow these animals to destroy my family. Papa is standing too far away and is unarmed. He can't help. But I can. I must. The shotgun Papa keeps on the pegs over the door. It is always loaded.

She took the shotgun from its place on the wall above the doorway and walked into the entryway. She held the weapon at her waist as she entered the barnyard. Three or four yards away, the Confederate soldier who was about to attack Kenny had his back to her.

Without hesitation, she fired one barrel of the shotgun at the man's back. With all his winter clothing on, the man was more stunned than seriously hurt. He spun around in surprise, and took a step toward his assailant.

She stepped forward, too. With only a few feet separating them, she stopped, calmly cocked the hammer of the second barrel and fired point blank into his chest. This time he was lifted off his feet and thrown to the ground on his back. Kenny moved toward him with his pitchfork, ready to finish him off. It wasn't necessary; the man was dead.

It had all happened in just a few moments. The members of the Hecht family stood in the yard and looked at the two dead soldiers. Ruben spoke first.

"Momma," he asked, hurrying to her side. "Are you all right?"

"Yes Papa. My knees are shaky, but I am fine."

"Julia?" he asked. "Are how are you?"

"I wasn't harmed, Papa. I'm just mad; furious mad."

"Momma, take Julia and Robert in to da house and stay with dem. Kenny you help me mit da soldier's horses. Be calm mit dem. We don't want to spook dem so dey run back to da soldier camp. Dey come after us for sure, den."

"I killed a man, Papa," Kenny blurted out. "I killed a man."

"You did a brave ting with da pitchfork, Kenny. Dat man vould have hurt Julia for sure; maybe killed her and den us, too, I tink. You had no choice, son. I was too far away to help."

"Will God forgive me, Papa?"

"Yes son," Ruben assured him. "You were protecting your family. You did noting bad God needs to forgive."

"I hope so Papa."

Then they turned their attention to the dead soldiers.

"Now we tie dese dead bodies on da horses. First, we search deir pockets for coins. Ve take da pistols dey carried too; nothing else, though." The two rolled the bodies in rain ponchos and tied them over the saddles on their horses.

"In the rubble, I found enough harness to hitch up our horse to da wagon. We do dat now."

"Why are we doing that, Papa?" Kenny asked.

"Because, Kenny," he explained. "When des two men do not return to deir camp, da other soldiers will come looking for dem. We do not vant to be here vhen dey do, I tink. So ve must leave our farm for good. You go now and hitch up our horse to da wagon. I see Momma and Julia in da house and have dem pack up. Go now, son. Ve must leave very soon."

Within an hour the wagon was packed and ready to leave. Even the two milk cows and the horses carrying the dead men were tied and ready to walk behind the wagon.

As they all climbed into the wagon, Kenny asked. "Papa, what are we going to do with the dead soldiers and their horses?"

"When da other soldiers come searching for dem, Kenny, ve don't vant eider da horses or da bodies found near our farm. So ve set dem loose down da road a few miles."

"What will we do with the cows?" Julia asked.

"Ve drop dem off at da Bierlein farm on the vay to town. Dey vill be glad to have dem."

'I see, Papa," Kenney said, surprised with his father's quick grasp of the situation and complete planning. "But must we leave our home for good?"

"It can not be helped, son. Now ve go to town. Until da war ends ve can never return to dis place."

Ruben's son was still stunned by it all. "Where will we go, Papa? What will we do?"

"We will be fine, son." Emma Hecht assured him. "You will see. We are survivors. Never forget what Papa says. Believe me, Kenny; we will survive this."

SAVANNAH

It was nearly noon when I Troop's Point Squad reached the prison. One of the six men rode back to the main column to report.

"Sir, we think the Point Squad has reached the prison. It is several hundred yards up this road. What are your orders, sir?"

"Sergeant Riley will accompany you, trooper. He will talk with Major Drieborg. The rest of the troop will remain here until he reports back to me."

The two men rode ahead.

When they neared the prison site, Riley noticed a tall man wearing an officer's uniform and a slouch hat standing in the open gate of the prison. He thought he recognized him.

He dismounted and walked toward the taller soldier.

"Well, I'll be," he shouted. "I thought I'd seen the last of ya, lad."

In their excitement the two men embraced without embarrassment, slapping one another on the back.

"I had hoped you were still with the troop," Mike said still holding Riley at arm's length.

"Only the Rebs could get me away from my men, Mike. And they sure tried hard enough if truth be told. Yer'a major now, I see. A'fore you know it, you'll be running this whole show, I'm thinking."

"I didn't get this rank for anything I can remember doing. But it seemed that the president had other ideas. I'll tell you all about it later."

"What in hell is I Troop doing here anyway, Major?" Riley asked. "We got our orders yesterday to report here to you. Not another word of explanation."

"I just thought you and the boys would appreciate a break from fighting. Besides, I need people I can depend on for this job. Since I knew you were in the area, why not ask for you? You object to my choice of I Troop?"

"Not a'tall, lad," Riley assured him. "But I'm anxious to know the rest of the story, though; so are the rest'a the men."

"You'll know soon enough." Mike assured him. "How far behind you is the rest of the troop?"

"They're less than a mile back." Riley told him. "The captain is waiting for my report before he brings them in. Where do you want us to set up Major? Not in that prison compound, I hope."

Mike chuckled. "Wouldn't Killeen and the other men of my old squad love that; setting up in a prison compound. No, I'm not putting you there. That's a hospital building over there, Sergeant. Behind it is a well drained pretty good-sized field. It has plenty of room for your picket line and tents. It also has a pretty nice stream running along the back. Remind your men not to use it as a latrine. It supplies the men in the prison with their drinking water.

"Once your men are settled, please bring the captain back here. I have an office just inside the hospital building. I'll go over everything with you then."

"Yes sir," Riley answered. He snapped to attention and saluted his former recruit; turned, mounted his horse and rode down the road away from the prison.

When Sgt. Riley returned with the rest of I Troop, Mike couldn't resist; he stood at the side of the road and watched as the men of the troop he once commanded rode by.

Most of these men reported for training with me in Grand Rapids back in the fall of 1862. Then, I was just an eighteen-year-old kid in a squad with five of these guys. We went through training together, fought at Gettysburg and in Virginia, too. They have been through a lot of fighting since the Rebs captured me in March of 1864. Thank you Lord, for looking after them.

*   *   *   *

Sgt. Riley and his troop commander Capt. Lovell reported to Mike as ordered.

"Come in and be seated gentlemen," Mike greeted. "Help yourself to some hot coffee. I was even able to commandeer some sugar from General Sherman's kitchen."

The two men helped themselves and took their seats.

"It is very interesting to meet the man behind the legend," Lovell began.

Mike looked at the man over his steaming coffee cup. Riley said nothing.

What is the matter with this guy? He must realize that I am his superior officer and that he is assigned to my command. Is he trying to pick a fight? Keep calm, Drieborg. You don't need an enemy; you need this guy's cooperation.

"Dead men are sometimes called legends, Captain," Mike responded calmly. "There are few living legends I know about; General Custer maybe; Grant or the president. All I have done is survive and do what I have been ordered. And that is what is expected of you, to obey orders. Do we understand one another, Lovell?"

Lovell snapped ramrod straight in his camp chair. "Yes sir, we do."

"Fine," Mike continued. "Now, Captain, this legend wants to get on with the job here."

For the next hour, Mike reviewed the situation and the objectives of their mission. The three then discussed how Webster's cavalry troop would be involved in the operation.

At the conclusion of their planning, Captain Lovell rose to leave.

"Not so fast Captain," Mike cautioned. "I have been told that you've been ill for some time, but have refused treatment for whatever is wrong with you. I won't have your illness hampering this operation."

"The state of my health is none of your affair, Major," Lovell responded forcefully.

"You have been assigned to me, fella," Mike snapped. "As your superior officer, I order you to submit to an examination by the doctor in charge of this hospital. So sit down."

"Sgt. Riley," Mike ordered. "If you please; go to the next room down the hall and ask Dr. Woolworth to join us."

"Yes sir."

"But he's a Reb doctor," Lovell complained.

"He's saved the lives of hundreds of Union soldiers in the prison here. Just ask that ward full of Federal troops. Besides, until our doctors get here, he is the doctor who will examine you. You can have one of ours look you over later. But for now, he will be your doctor. And Captain, that's an order."

THE SUTLER STORE

The men talked while they were erecting the tent for their squad. As per Sgt. Riley's instructions, they had to be very precise setting up. It was pretty automatic after two years under his watchful eye.

"See that big tent outside the prison compound? The sign says it's a sutler's store. I'm heading over there first chance I get, " Dave Anderson told his mates.

"We haven't seen a sutler for weeks. I'll be glad to get a few things, like a beer." Stan added. "I just hope the other guys don't strip the place clean before Riley lets us go."

"I've still got some tokens from last fall when we were in the Shenandoah Valley. With all the fighting then, I never got a chance to use them all. Wonder if the guy at this store will honor them?"

"Bill, don't you beat all," Stan kidded. "You ran a retail store for years. Would you have ever given merchandise away in exchange for somebody else's tokens? I'd bet your wife would'a beat you upside of your head had you done it."

"Sometimes you're right, Stan. She probably would have. Since the government took all the coins out of circulation, these sutlers have issued their own money; usually no more than wooden tokens. Works fine when they and we are in the same place for a while. That's how I got stuck with a couple of dollars worth last fall. So I'll talk to the guy anyway. Who knows, he might not have a wife who would object."

"After I dismiss the troop yas are free to move about. I suggest ya keep your sidearms strapped to yas waist. If ya go inta the prison area, just remember, be respectful. Those guys have gone through a lot.

"At the sutler store, no shoplifting. I won't have it. I've talked to the man and told him he can collect any money due him from you at the pay table next week. He has beer for sale. Just don't overdo. Ya know how I feel about drunks. Troop, dismissed."

"My Lord," Dave muttered. "Not ten minutes since Riley dismissed the troop and there's a line a mile long. And look at those prices, Bill. Would you have ever charged five cents for a molasses cookie?"

"No Dave, I wouldn't have. But keep in mind the risks these guys take from bandits on the road getting here. Back home, all I had to worry about was some kid slipping a jawbreaker into his pocket. These guys have some pretty slick customers trying to steal their goods. That's why they let only one soldier into their tent at a time. Besides that, what if one of us gets killed owing them money? No, I don't think that's too much for a cookie; nor is the fifteen cents for a sweet potato. Out here, I'd pay seventy-five-cents for a can of condensed milk any day."

"All right already," Stan cut in. "Seems like highway robbery to me. You sure he isn't giving you a discount to defend these high prices?"

"Stan," Swede added, "I don't vorry about da price. I jus hope he has some tings left by da time he lets us into his tent. It's been a long time since I had a beer too, don't ya know."

GRAND RAPIDS, MICHIGAN

The Federal court house was located in downtown Grand Rapids, alongside the river that ran through the city. It shared jail and courtroom facilities with the municipal and state judges. This day, Harvey Bacon of Lowell was on trial. He was charged with conspiring to kill an officer in the Army of the United States.

It is wartime: Traditional rights were often waived. Freedoms normally guarded by the courts were now routinely ignored. Freedom of speech aside, there were several hundred citizens in the Federal prison at Detroit for speaking against the war. Others were kept in Northern jails for extended periods without charges or trial, just on suspicion of being Confederate sympathizers.

In this atmosphere, Federal judges exercised great latitude. They were judge and jury on most everything affecting the security of the United States. Judge Woodrow Yared presided over the case of the United States vs. Harvey Bacon.

"Harvey," whispered his defense attorney, Charles Calkins. "Keep your mouth shut during the proceedings. Woodrow Yared is the judge in your case. He is known as a real stickler for decorum. He'll be fair, but he will not tolerate any nonsense. You have something to say, tell me."

"You just get these charges dismissed," Bacon snapped back. "I'm paying you enough."

"All stand! The court of the Honorable Judge Woodrow Yared is now in session."

Judge Woodrow Yared got right down to business. "How do you plead to the charges, Mr. Bacon?" He asked.

"Not guilty, Your Honor," Bacon responded.

"Very well, Mr. Bacon; we will proceed. Will the district attorney present the evidence supporting the charge of conspiracy to kill an officer in the Army of the United States?"

"Your Honor, Exhibit One is a sworn statement by an assassin captured at the scene of the attack on Major Drieborg in Baltimore. In it, he stated that he received money sent from the Lowell Bank to kill Major Drieborg."

Bacon's attorney was on his feet protesting. "I have examined this statement, Your Honor. It was probably forced out of the assailant. Mr. Bacon has no knowledge of such a payment."

The prosecutor continued. "Exhibit Two is a sworn statement by Mr. Harvey Bacon's son Carl that his father sent this money to pay for the assassination of Major Drieborg."

Bacon's attorney protested again. "This is an obvious forgery, Your Honor. Carl Bacon is in Federal custody. How can he even know of such arrangements?"

"Please be seated, Mr. Calkins," Judge Yared snapped. "You'll have your opportunity to refute these charges and discredit the evidence presented by the prosecutor.

"Do you have anything else?" the Judge asked the district attorney.

"No sir. The prosecution rests its case."

"The defense may present its case."

"Your Honor," Bacon's attorney began. "My client is a respected member of the Lowell community. He is responsible for making it possible for hundreds of families to establish and run farms and businesses in that community. He has, in the past, loaned money to the Drieborg family; several times in fact; and all at standard rates of interest. He has no interest in pursuing assassinations."

"His position in the Lowell community is noted," Judge Yared stated. "But how do you account for the fact that his own son has sworn under oath that Harvey Bacon paid for the attempts on the life of Major Drieborg?"

"His son is at the mercy of his jailers. He was obviously forced to make this statement to survive their punishments. Besides, Mr. Bacon was never seen paying anyone to do anything; nor is there any evidence that he communicated by mail or telegraph with such individuals. I move that the charges against Harvey Bacon be dismissed."

Judge Yared ruled on that request immediately. "Motion denied, counselor. Do you have anything else?"

"No Your Honor," Bacon's attorney answered. "The defense rests."

"Very well," Judge Yared responded. "Mr. Bacon. Does the defendant have anything to say to this court before I pronounce the verdict?"

"Yes Your Honor, I do," Harvey Bacon jumped to his feet alongside his attorney. "These people, these Drieborgs are just immigrants living off our generosity. Were it not for my money they would not have anything. They have no gratitude for what this country and my money have allowed them. Despite all of this generosity, their son, this soldier you call a major, has tricked my son, who as a result in now in that Federal prison in Detroit. Not satisfied, they have seen to it that I am now in danger of joining him in prison.

"I have had nothing to do with any of this. I am not guilty."

"Mr. Bacon," Judge Yared began. "I have read the records very carefully. After your son Carl was expelled from the University of Michigan, you bought him a commission in the Army of the United States. Is that true?"

"I helped outfit an entire cavalry regiment to help defend the United States. My son was awarded a commission in that regiment based upon his background and horsemanship."

"I see," the Judge said.

"I also see from these documents that during training camp in the fall of 1862, it was proven at a military court martial that your son used his rank to order men under his control to attack this Drieborg when he was still a corporal. For that your son was dishonorably discharged. Is that true, Mr. Bacon?"

"That was a set-up. Some enlisted men turned on my son and falsely testified against him."

"I see," Judge Yared continued.

"After this incident, it appears that you foreclosed on the mortgage the Drieborg family had at your bank. Your own bank records show that at no time was Mr. Drieborg late in a payment on said mortgage. It seems then, that you were attempting to harm the family out of revenge."

"That is pure nonsense," shouted a red faced Bacon. "I had a buyer for that property. It was a simple business proposition."

"I see," Judge Yared went on.

"Last December, your son was arrested for an attempt on Michael Drieborg's life in Detroit. This was witnessed and sworn to by another assassin he hired to help him kill Major Drieborg. Your son was convicted of that crime and was sent to the Federal prison in Detroit, where he is presently serving his sentence. Is that true?"

"It is true he was convicted, but the witness was a former prisoner who was threatened with a return to prison if he didn't falsely testify against my son."

"I see," the Judge said. "But what of these other attacks, Mr. Bacon?"

"Two additional attempts on the life of Major Drieborg were made this past December; one in Cleveland and another in Baltimore. I am looking at a sworn statement from one surviving assassin that he was paid with funds from your bank to kill the major. I also have a sworn statement from your own son that you did just that; that you conspired to kill an officer on active duty in the Army of the United States during wartime."

"I never sent any money to anybody for that purpose. My son was forced to say that. They tortured him into doing it. He told me so."

"I see," Judge Yared commented. "Is there anything else the defense has to offer, Mr. Calklins?"

"No, Your Honor, we do not have anything else."

"Very well; I find you the defendant, Harvey Bacon, guilty as charged. Marshal Kalanquin, take him into custody to await sentencing."

"You can't do this to me," Bacon shouted as he was dragged out of the courtroom. "I'm the owner of the Lowell Bank. It's all the fault of those Drieborgs. None of this would have happened if not for them."

"Bailiff," Judge Yared ordered. "Bring the next case!"

LOWELL, MICHIGAN

Jake Drieborg was driving his wagon home from town. He was only one hundred yards away on Fulton Road when he saw the riderless horse standing in front of the house.

"Momma," he ordered. "Get into da back of da wagon. Susan, look toward da river. Tell me if you see any movement in dat direction. Something is wrong at da farm."

He urged his horse forward slowly until he directed it to pull the wagon into the yard in back of the house. That's when he saw the bodies in the snow.

"My God," he shouted. "Stay down Momma. Susan, get into the back with Momma and keep a lookout from the back of da wagon toward the road."

Then, he jumped down off the wagon with a shotgun in hand and went to the side of a bloody body laying face down in the snow. He took the dead man's pistol and looked around.

What has happened here? he thought. *This man was hit with a shotgun blast. Little Jake had his rifle; so it must have been Ann who killed this one. What of the other one?*

The second man was a few yards away, lying on his back. Clearly wounded, he was moaning and asking for help.

He's not armed and it doesn't look as though he can run away. Where are my children?

"Ann! Jacob! Where are you?" The only response was the late morning quiet.

"Papa! Is that you?" he heard.

"Stay in da house, Ann," he shouted. "Momma, Susan; go into da house with Ann. Where is Jacob, he shouted to his daughter?"

"The last time I saw him, he was in the barn loft, Papa," Ann shouted from inside the house.

"Ann, take your gun and stay at da kitchen window. Susan, you take your shotgun and go to da bedroom front window. Momma, you stay by da yard door."

Once the Drieborg women were inside the house, Jake moved to the barn. Inside, he looked around for a third intruder. Satisfied there was none, he called for his son. "Jacob, where are you, son?"

"Up here Papa," he heard. "I can't move very well. I was shot."

Jake climbed the ladder to the loft and found his son leaning against a bale of straw. There was blood on Jacob's shirt, just above the belt of his work pants.

"The guy's shot got me in my side, Papa. I think it went right through. But it hurts a lot."

Jake could see the perspiration on his son's face. His hands were shaking and he looked to be on the verge of tears.

"I'm sorry I didn't get a shot at him, Papa. After I fired a warning shot like you said, I must have leaned out too far to get a clearer shot. That's when one of them winged me. I'm lucky I didn't fall out the loft window. Does it look bad, Papa?"

"No, son," Jake assured him, not really knowing. "You'll be fine. I will help you down da ladder and Momma will take a look at it in da house."

"I recovered enough after he hit me to get off one shot with my pistol, Papa. That's when I saw Ann shoot one man clean off his horse. Then a lot of pain hit me and I got real dizzy and couldn't see very well. I'm sorry I couldn't help Ann. I'm sorry I didn't do better, Papa," Little Jake began to cry. "Is Ann all right?"

"You did fine son; and Ann too. She is not hurt. You both did just fine."

Once inside the house, Rose set up a pallet on the floor in front of the fireplace. She cleaned the wound and applied a bandage.

"You must eat this warm soup, Jacob. Wipe the perspiration off his face, girls. Give him water, too. I will clean the wound again later."

Jake entered the house with supplies from town.

"What of the men outside in the yard, Papa," Ann asked. "Did I kill them both?"

"I think one is still alive, Ann. I put him in da wagon all tied up. After dinner, I will go to town to get Dr. Peck. He will come back with me to treat Jacob's wound. I'll get Marshal Chapman for the prisoner, too. Ann, I want you to guard the man until I return."

"When will the Bacons leave us in peace, Papa?" Susan asked.

"Der is no way to tell, Susan. But I can tell you dat we Drieborgs have survived worse. We will survive dis, too. Enough talk now, girls.

"Momma is busy with Jacob. So you girls fix da dinner now while I go talk with da wounded man outside. Maybe I can convince him to tell me who is behind all of dis."

Back in the yard, Jake stood by the wagon and looked at the man he had tied up.

The man shouted at Jake. "Get me to a doctor, you pile of shit, before I bleed to death."

Jake pulled his skinning knife from its scabbard and held it out for the man to see.

"A few weeks ago I never believe I do dis. Back den, my son captured some of Bacon's hoodlums in Baltimore. He killed one and the other man did not want to tell who hired them to kill him. Then my son used his knife, like dis one, and had what he called a talk with da man. He cut da man here on dis leg and did another cut on da other leg. Guess what? Da man decided to tell.

"I think we have a conversation like dat too. Who paid you to attack us?"

"Go to hell, you pile of shit."

Jake shoved the knife into the man's wounded thigh.

"Damn!" the man grunted.

"Der is a lot of you for me to hurt yet. Who paid you?"

"I'll kill you first chance I get, Drieborg; and no one will have to pay me."

Jake twisted the blade and widened the wound in the man's leg.

The man jerked against his bonds, but said nothing.

"Maybe you remember now? Or would you like me to start on your right hand."

Jake gripped the man's tied hand and cut the skin with his knife.

"I think I start with da thumb. Do you think you could shoot a pistol without da thumb on dis hand?"

"You pile of shit," the man shouted in pain. "It was Bacon who paid me. I met him in the Grand Rapids jail. He offered $100 to anyone who would kill you and $50 for each member of your family. It was easy money, and I needed it."

"I write dis on paper and you will sign it. Yes?"

"All right I will. But you promise to get me to a doctor. Yes?"

"I'm going to town to fetch the doctor for my son, and da marshal for you. Maybe I tell the doctor about da-wounded man I have tied up out in da barn. But you better be good."

"Now I have my dinner; and den I take care of your horse. I go to town after dat."

"Wait a minute! You can't just leave me here. I'm still bleeding. I'll freeze."

"Yes I can. All dat shouting, you will bleed more."

"Who the hell shot me? I waited until you left for town this morning; and I shot the kid in the barn loft."

Jake walked back to the wagon. He smiled as he told the wounded man,

"A sixteen-year-old girl shot you; killed your partner too. Seeing her brother wounded, she's mad you are still alive. But you had better be quiet or I'll let her finish da job. She wants to, you know."

After dinner, Jake went to the road to examine the horse Ann wounded. After slowly approaching it, he took the reins and walked the animal into his barn's extra stall. There, he removed the saddle and other leather tack before he watered and fed the horse.

Ann will be pleased that da horse is not too badly wounded. It took some buckshot and bled some, but it should survive. I'll ask da doc to take a look at it.

Bacon has made my worst fear come true. What will be next? Whatever it is, with God's help, we will be prepared to face it. Lord, help my family to survive dis.

DANVILLE PRISON, SAVANNAH

Mike was reviewing the paperwork that had been sent him from Washington. There was a knock on the door of his hospital office.

"Come in."

A Union officer opened the door. He wore a cavalryman's slouch hat and had the insignia of the medical corps on the lapel of his greatcoat.

"I'm Major Harald Van Eycken, a doctor actually. I've been assigned to your project."

Mike stood and motioned to him. "Come in Major," Mike told him. The two men shook hands. "Welcome to Camp Danville. Take off your coat and have a seat doctor.

"Call me Hal. I'll sit, but I don't plan on staying long, so I'll leave the coat on."

"What makes you think that you will be leaving that soon, Major?"

"Look Drieborg," Van Eycken began. "I'm an expert battlefield surgeon. I know nothing about treating men who are malnourished, suffering from dysentery, scurvy, diarrhea, and various infections and overexposure. I can't even remember what my medical school textbooks said about these problems."

"I asked General Sherman to send me a good doctor," Mike told him. "I am glad to hear that he did just that."

"I'm afraid you didn't hear me, Major," Van Eycken repeated heatedly. "I belong near the scene of a battle, saving lives. I belong in a field hospital, not playing nursemaid to your prison survivors."

"So you're too good for my prisoners, eh?"

"Come on Drieborg," Van Eycken snapped. "I'm being truthful here, not arrogant. I'm telling you that I'm better suited to working on wounded men after a battle."

"If you're so damned good, Hal," Mike snapped back. "Why did they send you to me? Why didn't they keep you where you say you are so effective?"

"Sherman ordered his medical staff to pick a doctor and assign him to your project. My immediate superiors jumped at the chance to get rid of me."

"Why?"

"They happily sent me because I have embarrassed them. My patients survive in too large a number to ignore, when compared to the high rate of death most of the other doctors experience with theirs."

"For your information, Hal," Mike interrupted. "At Gettysburg, I had the privilege of experiencing first hand a full range of medical treatment; first on the battlefield; then at the field and regimental hospitals, all the way to Washington. My wound wasn't all that bad. But the aftereffects of the treatment damn near killed me. What did you do that made your approach so effective?"

"It's simple enough, Mike," Van Eycken responded. "The surgical literature from Europe told me that there are germs everywhere; and that they cause infection and death especially after surgery. These studies also claim that cleanliness can reduce the chance of post-surgery infection.

"So I wash my instruments and scrub my hands between surgeries. I clean my operating table with strong soap and water after each use, too. My colleagues do none of these things. They argue that since they cannot see germs, they don't exist; that at the battlefront, speed is of the essence. Therefore, they do not take the time to wash their hands, instruments or operating table.

"They also insist that shock is the greatest danger to wounded men. They believe that water can cause shock and that whiskey can protect men from it. So they give their wounded all the whiskey they want, but no water; not a drop. I don't believe in that. I give my wounded water; all they can hold down. As a consequence, few of my patients suffer from dehydration, while that condition is common with theirs.

"They give out addictive drugs like morphine, like they do whiskey. They give the wounded men all they want. I use drugs too, for pain, but monitor its use so men do not become addicts.

"My surgical practices and my post-surgical treatment result in higher survival rates for my patients. But I was an embarrassment to them. Worse, I kept good records and sent everyone in Washington copies. Of course, I also told everyone who would listen about it. That's why my superiors were especially happy to get rid of me. Sherman's order provided them with that opportunity.

"You see why I don't belong here, don't you? I need you to reject my services so that I can return to work that I'm good at."

"Not a chance, buddy," Mike chuckled. "If your medical superiors had wanted to help these poor men here, they could have done so before I got here. In the six weeks Sherman's medical people have been in this area, not once did any of them even visit here.

"You may consider yourself a fish out of water here, Hal. But doctor, you are my fish. The faster you help this hospital staff, get my prisoners ready for travel north, the faster I'll get you out of here. Do we have an understanding?"

"If that's the best you can do, Mike, I can accept that. But I want you to understand something. Once we are clear on what has to be done, I will not put up with incompetence or foot-dragging. Let's put together a plan of action right now, today; and get on with whatever has to be done. Do you agree with that?"

"Having a medical plan laid out for all to see is an excellent suggestion. The hospital director here, Dr. Woolworth, and his chief nurse, Sister Mary have both worked with our former prisoners since last fall. We had best include them in the planning stage."

"That's fine with me, Mike. You're the boss. I think I'll include my aide, Sgt. Barney Geltz too. He's been with me since I joined Sherman's march last fall. I operated on Barney's wound back in Tennessee. During his recovery he became so valuable in the operating room that I had him assigned to me. He's a sharp guy who used to make umbrellas back in Pennsylvania someplace. In surgery he's better than most doctors I've seen. Do you have any objections?"

"None at all, Hal. Mike assured him. "Clara Barton and some of her nurses arrived just yesterday, so let's include them, too. I'll get Dr. Woolworth, Sister Mary, Barton and her people in here right now."

"That's fine with me. But one last thing, Mike," Van Eycken insisted. "Once we complete our work, I'm out of here with your blessing; right?"

"Before I answer that, Hal, keep in mind that there are three hospital ships in Savannah harbor waiting to load our sick soldiers and take them to Baltimore. A doctor will be assigned to each ship. The fourth must accompany the healthier former prisoners west to Atlanta.

"You are one of the four doctors assigned to this project. I don't care how you assign this duty. You can return to hacking off limbs with Sherman's army as soon as our patients that are on the ships arrive in Baltimore, and the others arrive in Atlanta."

"We'll get the job done, Mike, believe me," Hal responded. "And my three colleagues will love to get away from combat duty and party with the shady ladies of Baltimore. In the meantime, I don't want to be housed in some dog tent or in one of those lean-tos out in the old prison compound. I want a real room, a bed with a soft mattress and a door I can close for privacy."

"I'll see what I can do Hal. By the way, we have a baseball game scheduled this afternoon; just a pick-up game, mind you. Ever play the game?"

"Every spare minute I had before this war, I spent on a sailboat. You can't match the thrill of sailing with the sea spray in your face. I really miss it. I played a lot of tennis too. But to answer your question, I used to watch the New York team called the Knickerbockers play. So yes, I know the game. I think Dr. Gersch would like to play. He and I have played tennis whenever we got the chance. So I know he's a good athlete. What time this afternoon?"

Dayton, Maryland

It was early Sunday afternoon before the Hecht family arrived in the village. The horses carrying the dead soldiers had been set loose in a stand of trees a few of miles out of town. Ruben parked his wagon in the livery and took his family to the town's boarding house. They had missed church.

After supper that evening the family sat around the table.

"Much has happened today, I know," Ruben began. "It has been very upsetting for all of us. Does anyone have anything to say, or a question to ask?"

Julia began. "Where are we going, Papa?"

"Last fall, when we were with da Drieborgs in Washington, Jake told me dere were many farms in his area mit good land und buildings dat had been abandoned. Da Papa had gone to war and maybe was killed; or da mamma couldn't manage alone. So da bank took da farms. Anyway, ve will go dere and buy one of dose places vhere it is safe for us."

"But Papa," Kenny objected. "We're Marylanders."

Ruben quickly responded. "No Kenny, not anymore. We're Americans. President Lincoln fought dis war for dat reason. We have thirty-four states, but der is only one country. So ve may live in Michigan or Maryland, but ve are Americans first."

Kenny wasn't done with his questions. "I thought this war was fought to free the slaves, Papa."

"Some might believe dat. But President Lincoln fought dis war to save da Union. When ve were in Washington last fall; remember when Michael received his medal at da White House? After da ceremony, the president took Jake and me all around dat building. Dat is vhen he told me dose things, Kenny."

"Starting from scratch though, Papa; that sounds terrible," Julia complained.

Emma chuckled at that. "Think of what you're saying, Julia; is it terrible that you and Michael are going to start with nothing after you marry?

"Listen to your Papa children," Emma continued. "He and I must do what we must to keep the family safe. So we go to Michigan. Besides, Julia; after you marry, isn't that where you and little Robert will go to live?"

"I'm not little anymore, Grandma," Robert protested.

"Dat is right, Robert," Ruben laughed for the first time today. "Come sit on Grandpa's lap and help me drive da wagon. Ve listen to Grandma."

"Baby Eleanor will be there, and your own children too, Julia."

Julia blushed at this comment.

"Papa and I would like to be close to you all. Wouldn't you want us to live near you?"

"Of course I would, Momma," Julia assured them. "It just seems so sad to leave everything I've known behind like this."

"War can change things quickly, children," Ruben told them. "We found dat out today, didn't we? Da men you and Momma killed, Kenny probably told others dat dey were going back to see dat pretty farm girl. What would stop da other soldiers from looking for dem? Should we stay to find out? I don't tink so."

"Papa and I left Germany years ago," Emma told her children. "We have not told you much about that. The nobles, who owned the land there, fought one another all the time. People like us were always caught in the middle of such warfare; our men were forced to fight in the armies, and the women were often abused or killed just like almost happened to you today, Julia.

"Just like Papa and me now, our parents were determined that we would survive that and have a better life. So when we were young they sent us to America. The farm we just left, we built with hard work. We will survive leaving that. And, we will build a new farm and a new life in Michigan. Won't we, Papa?"

"Ya, Momma," Ruben assured them all. "Ve will survive."

"It is getting late, children. And, it's past Robert's bedtime. We have a busy day tomorrow."

"Yes, Momma."

✳   ✳   ✳   ✳

After breakfast Monday morning Ruben and Emma went to the office of the town's only lawyer, Richard Sullivan. Although he was a young fellow, Ruben trusted him.

When they entered the office, Sullivan stood up and came around his desk to greet them. He was at least six feet tall, had black hair and a bright smile.

"What brings the Hechts to town on a weekday?"

Ruben told him what had happened at their farm Saturday. He did not tell Brady about killing two Confederate soldiers on Sunday. He knew that some Marylanders were supporters of the Southern cause and he didn't know how Brady felt about the issue. So he held back that information.

"Sorry to hear that, Ruben," he responded. "I know it doesn't help, but you are not the first farm family visited in this manner. I'm just glad to hear that no one was hurt. How can I help?"

"We want you to arrange da sale of our place," Ruben told him.

"My goodness, Ruben, that's a drastic reaction. Are you sure you want to do this?"

Ruben did not even answer the question. "Can you handle dis for us, Mr. Sullivan?"

"Of course I can. I just need to discuss a few things about the property with you first. Since I visited you a year ago to finish up your will, has much changed outside of the barn and outbuildings burned by the raiders?"

"No. Da house and all da furniture are still dere. My son and I cleared five more acres for da planting dis spring. And we left da two milk cows at da Bierleins' on our way here today. Dey will stop in and pay you in a week or two. Today we will sell the grain we have at da elevator along with our wagon and horse. So we hope you can find someone to give us a fair price for our land and house."

"I'll get the word out. You have good ground and a nice house. There shouldn't be much trouble. As I remember it, you didn't have much of a mortgage left at the bank."

"Dat's true. We would like to stop der next. Dey may have a farmer in mind already to buy our place. I want them to know you are handling things for us. Could you go with us now to see dem?"

"Yes, I can do that. Where can I contact you after today?"

"I'll send you our new address when we get der. Will dat be all right with you Mr. Sullivan?"

"That will be fine, Mr. Hecht. Would you allow me to give some advice though?"

"Of course."

"You and your family have been through a very upsetting event. But with this war coming to an end, it will probably never be repeated. Wouldn't it be better for you to wait a bit before you take this step? It would be a real loss for this community to lose you."

"Thank you, sir." Emma Hecht finally spoke up. "That was nice of you to say. But Papa has decided. We cannot stay."

That same afternoon, they hired a wagon and horse at the local livery and were driven to the Baltimore train depot. Once train tickets were purchased, Ruben telegraphed Jake Drieborg in Michigan.

✳   ✳   ✳   ✳

"Jacob: I have sold everything and I am bringing my family to Lowell. Our train will arrive in Grand Rapids from Detroit this Wednesday in the afternoon. I'm not sure of the time of our arrival, so we will stay at a hotel that night. On Thursday morning, the five of us will travel to your farm in Lowell. I hope you can put us up until we can find our own place. Ruben Hecht."

✳   ✳   ✳   ✳

"How will Michael know what has become of us, Papa?" Julia asked.

"When we reach Grand Rapids, Julia, we will go to Congressman Kellogg's office in that town. His people there will tell Michael where he can reach us."

Julia was still upset. "How will we get married this Easter, Momma?" she complained.

"Julia," her mother snapped. "That's enough whining. We'll worry about that after we get settled in Michigan," Emma snapped. "Right now, you concentrate on being a Momma to Robert. Do you understand what I'm telling you, Julia?"

"Yes, Momma."

"While we have a few minutes," Emma continued. "Write a letter to Michael. We can mail it before the train leaves for Cleveland. I'll watch Robert for you."

"Yes, Momma."

Julia had her letter ready to mail in a few minutes. She also sent a telegram to Mr. Young, the manager at the Waddell Hotel in Cleveland.

✳   ✳   ✳   ✳

Cleveland, Ohio

"Mr. Young, this telegram for you just arrived."

"Thanks Tommy. Well, well; remember that couple some hooligans attacked in our hotel in December? It seems we are to have a visit from the young lady and her family."

Dear Mr. Young: You might remember that Major Michael Drieborg and I were guests at your hotel earlier this year. You urged us to consider staying at your hotel the next time we were in Cleveland. My parents, brother and nephew are going to be stopping in your city tonight. If you could put us up for the night it would be appreciated. I think that our train should arrive between four and five o'clock today.

Respectfully,

Julia Hecht.

"Tommy," Mr. Young directed. "Once you know the arrival time of the train from Baltimore, have the boys meet the Hecht family at the station. Prepare a suite for them and make a dinner reservation for around five this evening. Notify Chief Haynes that they are coming to Cleveland and their arrival time. And yes, be sure to tell me when they arrive in the hotel."

SAVANNAH

"Good afternoon, everyone," Mike began. He was addressing Dr. Woolworth and his staff of nurses, Clara Barton and her four nurses, as well as Dr. Van Eycken and his three doctors.

"We have a great deal of work to do here. Before we formulate our plan, allow me to introduce everyone."

"Sister Mary is in charge of nursing care in this hospital. She is a nurse and a member of the Sisters of Charity. Many members of her order of nuns serve in military hospitals in the North too. She had been assigned here before the war began. And here she has stayed serving the community and the wounded and sick of both armies. The way I understand it, Dr. Woolworth is the doctor in charge but she runs the place."

"Sister, will you introduce your team, please?"

"Thank you, Major. But first let me assure all of you that Doctor Woolworth is the director of this hospital. We sisters insist on a few things, but generally we just follow his direction." She identified her associates and returned the meeting over to Mike.

"Moving on," Mike continued. "Miss Clara Barton arrived here yesterday with four nurses. They will assist Sister Mary and her team. Like Sister Mary, Ms. Barton brings a reputation for not taking "no" for an answer when the welfare of soldiers is at stake. She too is a take-charge person."

"Ms. Barton, will you introduce your team, please?"

"Of course, Major Drieborg; every one of these nurses has demonstrated unbelievable courage on the battlefield. Annie Etheridge had her horse shot out from under her during one battle and was awarded the Kearny Cross for bravery after another. Susan Wheelock was wounded at Chancellorsville. Arabella Barlow has worked with contagious patients despite obvious dangers, contracting typhoid fever in the process. And Katherine Wormeley attended the wounded on several battlefields during the fighting. In fact, she had to replace her dress for all the bullet holes. Believe me, Major, these women don't take any guff from officers or doctors who get in the way of treating the sick and wounded."

"Thank you Ms. Barton. Major Van Eycken, please introduce the team of doctors who are with you, please."

"Let me first tell you how privileged we doctors feel to be working with such a dedicated and distinguished group of medical professionals found in this room today. I assure you that we will give you our complete cooperation. Toward that end, we will do whatever is needed to get these men ready for travel."

"That's good to hear, Doctor," Mike assured him. "Sister Mary has suggested a plan to do just that. She and her colleagues have kept a file on each soldier in this hospital. She and Ms. Barton discussed it this morning, and they suggest you assign a group of the sick to each doctor. One of Ms. Barton's and one of Sister Mary's nurses will be assigned in that manner as well. Keep in mind that Dr. Woolworth is in charge of overall patient care and will review all recommendations the teams make for each patient.

"When your teams have completed their work in the hospital, you will turn your attention to the general prison population. The medical teams will give each soldier there a complete physical examination before travel arrangements are made for them.

"This morning, Sister Mary and Ms. Barton identified the teams and assigned the patients. So if there are no questions, I will leave you to your work. I suggest, Doctors, that you first meet your nurses and begin reviewing the records of your patients. The sooner you move on to actually examining your patients, the faster this phase of the operation will be completed. The ships are waiting in Savannah Harbor. So we have no time to lose."

"As soon as you get your team going Hal," Mike continued. "Please come to my office. I have something that needs your immediate attention."

A few minutes later, Dr. Van Eycken virtually stormed into Mike's small office.

"What's so damnable important that I have to leave my team, Drieborg?"

"I have a very sick officer in the other room. He's the commander of the cavalry troop that arrived here the other day. The way I hear it, he has refused treatment for the past few weeks. Whatever is wrong with him, it looks pretty serious to me. He virtually collapsed yesterday when we were going over what I needed his men to do here. I had to order him into bed. Dr. Woolworth looked him over and thinks he is suffering from dysentery; pretty bad case, he thinks. "

"Why do you need me, then?"

"The guy doesn't trust Woolworth because he's a Southerner. I just need you to check out the diagnosis."

"Well, let's take a look. Damn it all, I've got that entire team waiting for me in the other room, you know."

After an examination and a brief conversation with Dr. Woolworth, Van Eycken came back to Mike's office.

"Woolworth was right Mike. Captain Lovell is suffering from dysentery. It's pretty advanced, I'm afraid. He certainly is in no shape to resume command of his troop. The nurses here are doing the right things for him, but I believe he should be shipped north with the other sick men, as soon as possible.

"Now, can I get back to my team?"

*   *   *   *

Alone again, Mike opened the mail packet, which had been delivered that morning from Sherman's headquarters. Congressman

Kellogg's office in Washington had sent Mike paperwork; included was a letter from Julia.

My dearest Michael,

You will not believe what happened to us since I last wrote you. Just three days ago, some Reb cavalrymen raided our farm of all our food. Their officer said that our cavalry had burned all their homes and killed all the animals in the Shenandoah Valley of Virginia. So he ordered his men to burn our barn and other buildings, take our feed and kill most of our stock. He left us our house, wagon, the two cows and our old plow horse.

But that is not the worst of it. Two of those awful men returned the next day and tried to attack me. Kenny killed one and Momma shot the other dead. I'd tell you more about it, but I only have a few minutes to finish this letter. I'll write more, later.

It all happened so fast. Is that how the fighting happens in battles?

Right then, without even talking to Momma first, Papa told us we had to leave the farm. So after we visited Eleanor's grave, we loaded up and left; Papa says, for the last time.

It was so sad. As we rode away from our home, Kenny and I both cried. But Papa and Momma never looked back. I have never known them to be so quiet or seen them so stern looking not even when Eleanor died.

The other surprising thing about all of this I have to tell you Michael, is that Papa decided we are going to live in Lowell. Imagine; both of our families in the same town. Right now we are in Baltimore, waiting to board a train for Cleveland.

I remember the terrible experience when we were attacked here. But I also remember the wonderful feel of your lips. Just thinking about it makes me weak with longing for you. That's all for now, my darling, the train is about to leave and I want to mail this letter. Don't worry about me now. You just take care of yourself so you can return to me safe and sound.

I miss you and love you so.

Julia

✳   ✳   ✳   ✳

My God! I feel so helpless. Look after them, Lord.

Fuming in frustration, Mike stormed out of the building and walked up and down the nearby road. Still agitated, he sought out Sgt. Riley.

"Do you have a few minutes, Sarge? I need to talk with you in private." As they walked side by side down the road, Mike told him what had happened to the Hechts.

"What that Reb officer told yer girl Julia? I'm afraid tis true, lad," Sgt. Riley told him.

"Ya see son, the Shenandoah Valley he was talking about was sort of the breadbasket of Virginia. It ain't any more; let me tell ya. Our orders were ta destroy it. So last summer we did just that. The farmers there will not be able to support the Rebellion this year. We burned buildings, grain and feed and killed all the animals we could. Crops in the fields were fired as well. In the process, a lot of homes were set afire and destroyed, too.

"I'm not too proud'a what we done, son," Riley continued. "But non'a my boys took advantage of any woman like some troopers from other units did. An no one in this troop stole personal stuff from the homes, neither. Still, the memory of families watching their farms destroyed in front of their very eyes haunts me to this day."

"Knowing that, Sarge, I'm surprised the Hecht home wasn't burned, too." Mike decided.

"Seems ta me that they were just lucky to have run inta a Reb officer with some character about'm.

"What we did in Virginia wasn't nothing compared to what Sherman's army did in Georgia, believe me," Riley continued. "On the fight toward Savannah, we were on the north flank. We were fightin off attacks from Reb cavalry most of the time. But when we'd get relief an go south a few miles, we saw what was going on. Whole towns were burned to the ground, including churches of every religion; schools and store buildings, too. Mile after mile of countryside was empty of folks.

"It's a fact; as we rode east the only sign of where people had lived were the chimneys of their burn-down homes, the carcasses of all the dead animals and the ashes of the villages in between. The people of Savannah are lucky we needed their city as a port, or it would have been destroyed too, I think.

"I'm sure that the folks in South Carolina are in fer a rough ride too, now that Sherman's headed north."

"How'd you get so smart, Sarge?" Mike kidded.

"I always knew what was going on, lad. You didn't notice because you was so busy hearing me bark at ya, sos you'd learn ta survive sickness and battle."

"When I returned from leave last month, I told Julia that this war was almost over. But with all the destruction I see that we've brought to the people in the South, I don't think it will be forgotten or forgiven soon at all."

"Put in their place," Riley agreed, "I'd be bitter some, myself."

"By the way, Major," Riley continued. "I want ta thank ya for getting medical treatment for the captain. Unless I miss my guess, he's probably got the dysentery. He let it go so long, I'm afraid he's done for."

"The doctors who examined him earlier today diagnosed just tha, Sarge." Mike confirmed. "I asked one of our military doctors to put his findings in writing. As soon as the doc gives them to me, I'll telegraph them on to your division HQ; tomorrow, probably."

"Then, I wouldn't be a bit surprised if a new troop commander didn't show up any day."

"You think highly of this Dr. Woolworth, don't ya," Riley observed.

"Yes, I do. When we were moved here from Andersonville, he and his staff came right out to the field where our guards had the trains drop us and began saving lives. One of my messmates was near dead. His life was one of those saved. This man is a Southerner and maybe even a Reb; but he is a doctor first and foremost. I respect that."

"By the way, Sarge," Mike asked. "Do the men still call me the Dutchman?"

"Know about that, do ya, laddie?"

"Since we fought at Gettysburg and I was a very green lieutenant."

"Its' cause they were proud of ya, don't ya know. Twas there way of braggin about ya."

*   *   *   *

Back at the hospital, the medical teams were driven by Van Eycken to accomplish their tasks. At the end of the first afternoon an entire ward of sick had been examined. That same evening, recommendations were completed for each of the sick men.

It was dark, almost ten o'clock; alone in the room now, Van Eycken and nurse Etheridge were having a cup of coffee.

"What's a married woman doing working in combat, Mrs. Etheridge?" he asked.

"Actually Doctor, I'm not married. Back in Wisconsin I divorced Mr. Etheridge before the war. Quite a scandal at the time; it seems that no woman around there had ever done that. But he was a cruel son of a bitch. I just decided that I was not going to put up with that any longer. I had a number of witnesses. So it was not a problem getting a judge to grant my request.

"As far as why I work so close to the lines," she continued. "It's pretty simple Doctor; that's where the men get wounded But that's where the need for treatment is greatest. The sooner you get to a wounded man, the better chance you have of saving his life. I've worked so close to the fighting that, truth be told, I've had to do a bit of killing Rebs, too; just to defend myself and my wounded."

"My Lord," Van Eycken exclaimed. "What a woman you are. And, may I say, a very good looking one at that?"

"You may, Doctor. And let me tell you that you are not the first to pay me that compliment. So don't think this lady will get all-atwitter with such sweet talk from a doctor, no less. I'll admit though, it's still nice to hear. Now that we've gotten these issues out of the way, why don't you call me Anna?"

"I'd be honored, but only if you will call me Harald; when we are alone, that is."

"Oh? We're going to be alone?"

"We are right now, aren't we, Anna?"

"That's true, Harald. But I was thinking alone meant something rather more private."

A few minutes later, the couple could be seen entering Van Eycken's private room.

PORT OF SAVANNAH

The men of I Troop were all over the three supply ships. A cavalry officer on each ship was checking the manifest against the cargo. The platoon sergeants were directing their men, who were unloading the cargo. Other troopers were guarding the wagons full of scarce food and other supplies.

Several squads had been assigned the task of herding the cattle through downtown Savannah to the camp on the outskirts. One of Mike's advisors back in Washington had suggested that the best way to get good beef to his freed prisoners was on the hoof. The navy was a bit taken aback, but agreed. They only lost one animal on the short sea voyage south. One of the beasts died on the journey. Rather than just dumping it overboard, the sailors salvaged the meat.

"Just between you and me though," Bill Anderson said. "One of the sailors spilled the beans. Somehow, a hammer fell on the head of that steer, killed it instantly it seems."

"Sounds like something one of us would have thought of," Dave Steward commented.

"I imagine this is quite a curiosity, a small herd of cattle being driven right through Savannah's downtown." Bill added.

"I'll bet people in this city haven't seen cattle, much less a small herd, for a long time. It was a good we're guarding it." Dave concluded.

Back at the compound, Mike read a private dispatch from Congressman Kellogg.

Michael:

You reports have been well received by the Committee on the Conduct of the War. I also had an opportunity to visit privately with the president. You should know that he is pleased as well.

There is a problem however. It has to do with one Captain Taft, most recently a Lt. Col. on General Sherman's staff. His family back in Ohio has a great deal of influence in this town. They are raising all kinds of fuss here with the Ohio delegation and through them, the president.

On my recent visit, he asked about this matter. After I explained that you had nothing to do with Taft's demotion or his being assigned to the prison project, the president assured me that he would not interfere but would refer the matter to General Sherman.

That should have ended the matter. But this Taft family won't stop complaining. I think Secretary of War Stanton is their next target. He doesn't like Sherman anyway and might use this issue to embarrass the General if he can.

I just want you to be aware. I know you will continue to handle the situation.

Kellogg

PRISON COMPOUND SAVANNAH

Big Pete McCullough and Sam were talking about the food supplies just delivered to the camp from the Federal ships in Savannah Harbor. Pete was looking at crates made of tin, marked, "desecrated vegetables". He had opened one of the crates.

"What did ya say this stuff was?"

"I didn't, ya big lug. But the cavalry guys who brought this stuff here knew some about it. This stuff is called desecrated vegetables. Comes in sheets, would you believe. Seems that the folks who make this stuff throw in all sorts of things sposed ta be good for ya; turnips, beans, onions, carrots, cabbage and potatoes. Somehow they get all of the juice out'a them and press it all inta these hard two foot by two foot sheets. Then, they put the sheets inta these tins. Easy to store and ship, I would guess. I heard some about this stuff before I was captured. But the guys said it wasn't used much because it takes so long to prepare. But I guess it wasn't used much in the field.

"Anyway, we're supposed to dump this stuff inta boiling water for awhile. Makes pretty good soup, I'm told. We'll find out soon enough. Sister Mary says that vegetables are real important in a person's diet, that without 'em ya could get scurvy. Once that happens she says ya get real weak, have loose teeth an ya bleed real easy. Lord knows we didn't get any vegetables at Andersonville. Since we been here, the Sisters have given us the same share as they get. But I still see all kinds of guys with bad teeth and weak as lambs, even now. But this stuff should be good for us."

"One thing for sure," Pete added. "The cattle they put in that pen over there is more beef than I've seen since I joined up. I know that stuff's good for ya. Didn't get much of that at Andersonville Prison, or here either, truth be told. Can't say the nuns here had any, either. Won't the taste of a good steak be welcome?"

"You bet! Drieborg said that we're going to roast one tonight to celebrate. The nuns are going to bake a lot of fresh bread with the flour just delivered, too. It should be quite a feast. The only catch is that Sister Mary said each man had to finish a bowl of this soup before he got his steak. Maybe you could hand down a decision from your courtroom against that."

"You must be kidding me, Sam. I don't have a death wish. That lady is one tough cookie. She reminds me more of my mother all the time. Besides, that concoction she's got you brewing can't hurt us. Lord knows we've had much worse as prisoners. So you'll get no such ruling from me.

"Are you going to be in the baseball game this afternoon? It's us against the cavalry boys who just arrived. Drieborg set it up for right before we eat. The winner gets an extra portion of beef."

"How does he expect us to compete against those healthy guys?" Sam complained. "Sounds like a setup ta me."

"Naw, I don't think But Sam. Drieborg changed the rules of the game some. We get four strikes each time at bat, they get the regular three. Our batter gets on base if their pitcher throws two out of the strike zone; we can throw four out of the strike zone before their guy gets on first base. Oh yes, he and a couple of the doctors are going to play for our side, too. Even the Reb doc, Woolworth, is playing for our side.

"Those cavalry guys remember Mike as a pretty good player when he was with them; taught 'em the game, they say. He's out in that field over there right now, laying out the playing field; calls it a baseball diamond. He said the bases had to be ninety feet from one another."

"I'm not up ta playing in that game," Sam informed Mac. " Last fall he invited me to join him and escaped from this place. I was too weak from the diarrhea back then. He took an Indian fellow named Battist with him instead. Besides, right now I'm in charge of this soup and getting that cow cooked."

"I know you're a city boy, Sam," Pete chuckled. But that animal over there is a steer. We farmers milked cows. We raised cattle for beef."

"Thank you very much for the education, Pete. Whatever it's called will be cooked and ready to serve after the baseball game."

✳   ✳   ✳   ✳

"How can Drieborg believe we could lose to that bunch of half-crippled and sick prisoners?" Stan commented.

The nine members of the cavalry team were lined up along the first-base line looking over at the prison team lined up along the third-base line.

The prison team was made up of eleven players. This included Mike, Dr. Van Eycken, who claimed that tennis was his real passion, Capt. Robert Taft, Dr. George Gersch and Dr. Woolworth. Big Pete was their team captain. Taft wasn't happy to see the hospital director included. "My God, Drieborg; the man's a Reb after all. And you have two Reb hospital patients on the team as well."

"Stop that kind of talk, Taft," Mike ordered. "That doctor probably saved hundreds of our soldiers. As for the other two Rebs, they are hospital orderlies. It so happens they have waited hand and foot on our sick men long before we captured this place. If they want to join our baseball team, they're welcome. You want to play or not?"

"Don't get so hot, Major. I'll play."

The nuns had followed Mike's instructions and fashioned a ball of sorts out of twine, and covered it with tape. Because it was pretty soft, it could probably not be hit far; but it would have to do. Sam made several bats from old pine planks and carved out one end for the batter to grip it.

Not all of the other players on the Federal cavalry side were happy, either. "Drieborg sure changed the rules in their favor," observed Dave."He also allowed them two extra players to play the outfield. Besides, he and those rather healthy looking doctors are playing, and he is pitching. I think he evened up things a lot."

"I'd hate to lose to this bunch," Stan Killeen responded. "What if the other guys in the regiment hear of it? We'll never live it down. Teams from every unit would want to take on the guys who lost to these sickly prisoners and out'a shape doctors. We had better win, that's all there is to it."

Despite the chill in the air, several of the nuns, the visiting nurses and a good number of the sick came from the hospital to watch the game. Of course, hundreds of former prisoners left the stockade area to watch, too.

In the first two innings Drieborg and the two doctors made the only hits for the prison team. Taft got a base on balls and was batted home. Going into the third inning, they led the cavalry team, three runs to two. For the most part, though, the prisoners couldn't hit the ball out of the infield.

The source of cheering from the sidelines was a surprise. The nuns clapped every time a member of the prison team came to bat.

"At-away batter," shouted one of the nuns. "Hit it out'a the infield."

The others, even the prisoners, joined in the clapping and cheering.

"Did that shout come from one of those Reb nuns?" Taft asked.

"That nun you're calling a Reb, is from Boston, Taft," Dr. Woolworth retorted. "Her superiors assigned her to this hospital before the war. She couldn't get out once it began. She's more of a Yankee than you."

The cavalrymen spectators countered with cheers of their own.

Forgetting rank, they shouted. "Mow them troopers down, Mike. And, 'come on, hit that ball, soldier', or 'we're depending on ya batter'." With most of the nuns and nurses present, the language was pretty tame. But every once and awhile, you could hear a, "excuse me Ma'am" or "sorry Sister."

In the top of the third inning, the cavalry scored a run after infield errors made by the prisoners. Then they got a rare walk out of Mike's pitching. That put Killeen on first base and Dave at bat. He hit a soft fly ball that fell between first and second base into short right field. Killeen made it to second and took third when the prison outfielder threw the ball over the third baseman's head. Now, with men on second and third, the next cavalryman batter hit a slow roller toward third base. By the time Mike came off the pitcher's mound to field it, Killeen had scored from third.

The cavalry onlookers cheered wildly.

In the bottom of the third inning, the prison team could not score, so the game was now four to three in favor of the cavalrymen going into the fourth and final inning.

If his team were to have a chance, Mike had to stop the cavalrymen from scoring. The first batter flied out to Dr. George Gersch, playing second base. The second batter, Stan Killeen, struck out. So with two down, the old man of the cavalry team, Bill Anderson came to bat. In his forties, he didn't look like much of an athlete, but somehow he had gotten on base twice and scored once this day.

He startled everyone when he hit the first pitch down the left field line. "That'a way Bill," his teammates shouted. It looked like a home run from the time it left his bat. But by the time he reached first base it had curved foul. There were quite a few "excuse me Ma'ams" and "sorry for the language, Sisters" when that happened.

With the count three balls and two strikes, he swung and missed. The side went down. The score was still Cavalry 4, Hospital/Prison team 3.

It was the last chance for the prison/hospital team. The first two batters went down swinging. The third batter, Harald Van Eycken earned a walk. The fourth man at the plate was Captain Taft. He hit the first pitch over the pitcher's head into short center field.

Van Eycken left first base before the ball even landed on the ground, rounded second and headed for third, ninety feet away. Halfway there he saw that the third baseman had been thrown the ball and was waiting to tag him out. That would end the game.

Damn it all; the guy's smiling. Not so fast, buddy. This game's not over yet. Van Eycken thought.

"Tag that guy out, trooper," One of the cheering cavalrymen shouted.

But Van just picked up speed, lowered his shoulder and plowed into the guy with the ball. The third baseman went ass over teakettle, the ball went flying into the crowd, and Van went flying home with the tying run.

Van Eycken was mobbed by his teammates. All the spectators were on their feet cheering, even the cavalry guys.

"One more out and the game will end a tie," Killeen reminded his cavalry teammates.

With Capt. Taft on second base and two out, the next batter, Dr. Gersch, hit a high fly ball. The second baseman caught it and the game was over; a tie.

"That's tha first time I seen a team led by Drieborg not win a contest," Sgt. Riley commented to no one in particular. "But them prisoners didn't lose when they should'a. So I guess that's a win'a sorts.

"I don't know how you did it, Major" he continued. "But with no loser, everybody wins. Who gets the extra ration?"

"Why, Sergeant," Mike said in mock surprise. "Everyone does. I thought you would know that I planned this outcome before the first pitch was thrown." Both men had a good laugh at that comment.

"Tis truly good ta be back with ya, young fella."

Because of the lateness of the day and the chill in the air, the meal was served in one of the hospital wards. There was plenty for everyone. Even the locals, who were being treated in the hospital at the time, ate heartedly.

"You know," Sam commented to no one in particular. "This vegetable soup is pretty good. Think I'll toss in some of the bones from this cow for tomorrow's soup. Won't that be a treat?"

"Didn't I tell ya that this is not a cow?" Mac teased Sam.

"I know I'm a city boy, Mac. But are you telling me that meat from a cow is going to taste different than from a steer like this?"

"Only us farm folk can tell the difference, my man," Mac chuckled.

ON THE MOVE

By the end of the week, the entire hospital population of Union patients had been prepared for travel north. The three ships in the harbor, that had brought supplies to Savannah for the prisoners, now were to be hospital ships taking the sick north to Baltimore.

Dr. Harald Van Eycken and nurse Etheridge were looking over one of them with Mike.

Van Eycken began. "I remember hearing about this ship. A couple of years ago, the Sanitary Commission was given a cargo ship and outfitted it as a floating hospital. Now that I look it over, I can see that it is an excellent ship. It's as good a hospital on water as any land hospital I've seen. Better than most, in fact. They named the ship the 'Daniel Webster'."

"The other two ships are well equipped for our purpose as well," nurse Sarah Etheridge commented.

A nurse and a doctor had been assigned to each of the other two ships, and were there to welcome the wagonloads of sick that were escorted to the dock by the cavalry boys. Soup, bread and meat had been prepared for the short journey north.

"I hear that you're going on one of the ships, Hal." Mike observed. "I thought you were itching to return to battlefield surgery once these ships left Savannah for Baltimore. Seem ta me that you're scratching another itch by taking nurse Ethridge with you. You even commandeered a private cabin."

"Does the Dutchman object?"

"So you heard the nickname my troopers gave me years ago."

"But to answer your question, I don't object. If the nuns could ignore it when she spent her nights with you in that private room you had back at the hospital, why shouldn't I? All I ever cared about, Hal, was that your medical team took proper care of the men. I couldn't care a wit about your private life. By the way, which doctor is assigned to go on the train to Atlanta with the able-bodied soldiers?"

"I asked George, Dr. Gersch, to take that responsibility. He's not as good a surgeon as I am. But he is better at patient care. Before we were sent here, he and I used to play tennis whenever we got the chance. He was a pretty good player for a country doctor."

"The men need a good doctor, Hal, not a good tennis player."

"Then you'll be pleased; because he is that."

"Good. I'll talk with him." The two men shook hands. "Take care, Hal. And God bless."

Now, the rest of the men need to get on the trains for Atlanta, and then home.

✳   ✳   ✳   ✳

"Hey, Mike," John Ransom shouted. "I was afraid our train was going to leave before we could say thank you."

"I'd never let you guys go without wishing you well." Mike gave him a bear hug. The other men of his old Andersonville Prison group gathered around: Phil Lewis, George Hendryx, Joe Sergeant and of course Sam Hutton. Each one gave Mike a hug.

"Sorry I doubted you, Mike," Sam cut in. "I should have know'd you'd come through. After being lied to and ignored by Sherman's big shots I wasn't ready to believe anyone, not even you. But you pulled it off. Thanks."

"Sam," Mike chuckled. "You would be the classic doubting Thomas whatever the situation. But I happen to know that your doubts were justified by the conduct of that crowd. I hope you know that even if it weren't my duty to pull this operation off properly, I would bust my butt for you guys. You saved my life back at Andersonville. I didn't forget that."

Sam cut in, "I seem to remember that it worked both ways, don't you fellows? Remember when this brash young guy pulled us all out of our feeling defeated and sorry for ourselves? He convinced us that we could take on that outlaw bunch of prisoners who preyed on us. And we did. You were also the guy who got the prison commandant to allow us to govern ourselves. We all had a better chance at surviving then. You saved a lot of lives back there; you did, Mike. We don't forget that, either."

"Yaw." added Sam, "An don't forget how we carried you to the train, John, with that Reb guard yelling at us to leave you behind cause you couldn't walk on your own."

Big Mac interrupted. "What about you, Major? What will become of you now that this assignment is over?"

"It appears that my prison rescue days are over, fellows. Just this morning, I received orders to appear at Sherman's headquarters for assignment, as soon as these trains leave for Atlanta. The word is that since Captain Lovell of I Troop is too ill to continue, I'll be given that command and attached to one of the regiments in Kilpatrick's Division for the push into South Carolina. It looks as though I'm back in the thick of things."

"Do you have any idea how we're to get home from Atlanta, Mike?"

"Those arrangements are not complete yet, Sam. But I suspect you will go north by train. The other possibility is to go by train to a port on the Mississippi. A boat named the Sultana is being used to take men north as far as Cincinnati, Ohio. One way or another, you'll get home before I will."

"God bless you, Mike. You take care of yourself. When this is all over and you get back to Michigan, look us up, will you?"

"You can count on that."

LOWELL

Ruben Hecht was helping Jake Drieborg with morning chores.

"Jake," Ruben began. "Ve have been here almost three weeks. I tink it is time ve moved into one of dose abandoned farm houses da bank has for sale."

"Der is no need to rush, Ruben. Do you agree that there are two pretty good farms available?"

"Ya. Da Pulte place and da Kline farm are da best. Both have pretty good land about 100 acres cleared and a good stand of trees. Da Kline place has frontage on da river, but does not have good out-buildings. Da Pulte farm has good buildings, but I vorry about access to vater."

"Well, you know, Ruben. We can fix da buildings a lot easier dan we can a bad water situation. But before you and Emma decide, how about we go look dem both over again?"

"Ya. After breakfast vould be good."

*   *   *   *

Back in the house, the men told their wives what they had decided.

"You may have decided we had to leave Maryland and move to Michigan, Papa. But now that we are in Lowell, I will be part of the decision of which farm to buy."

"You see, Jake, vhat I have to put up mit. Ya Momma, you are right. So you vant to come mit Jake and me dis morning to take anoder look?"

"Wait a minute," Rose interrupted. "If you three think you're going off without me, you've got another think coming."

"Anoder country heard from, eh Ruben?"

"Fine, ladies," Jake concluded. "Ruben and I will hitch up Old Blue to da wagon. Don't forget to put da pistol in your purse Rose. Ann, you stay in da house, so get your shotgun ready. Jacob, you and Kenny go out into the loft. Take your rifle and da uder pistol."

"Oh! Papa," Rose lamented. "Can't we just once stop worrying about the Bacons attacking us again?"

"No Momma, we can't! Now do as I say, children."

"What about me, Mr. Drieborg?" Julia piped in. "I know I haven't killed anybody yet, but I'm capable of helping defend the farm, too. Sorry, Ann. I didn't mean to suggest what you did was bad or anything."

"Get this straight Julia," Ann snapped. "The man I killed was fixin to kill Jacob. The other hoodlum who attacked us testified against Harvey Bacon in court, so I guess I'm glad he lived. But I'll not hesitate to kill anyone who tries to harm this family."

My daughter is one determined lady, Jake thought. *I wonder if Joseph Deeb realizes what a tough wife he will have?*

Jake addressed Julia's complaint. "I'm sure you are, Julia," Jake told her. "I am sorry for not giving you a job, too. Ann and Jacob have been through dis before. But now we have two little ones to worry about. So your job is to look after da children. If deer is an attack while we are gone, you are to take dem into your bedroom at the front of da house. Get them behind da bed until Ann tells you it is all right to come out."

"I am not little, Grampa Drieborg," Robert nearly shouted. "Mike told me I'm big now."

"I can see dat is true, Robert." Ruben interrupted. "But Julia vill need some help protecting baby Eleanor. Vill you do dat until I come back?"

"Sure, Grampa," he beamed. "I can do that. Will Jacob play marbles with me in the barn?"

"How can you help protect da baby here in da house if you are in da barn, Robert?" Jake asked.

"Can he play with me after you get back?"

"Dat's good, Robert; after we get back."

✳   ✳   ✳   ✳

They reached the Kline place first. It was just a couple of miles down Fulton Street, east of the Drieborg place but west of Lowell. Laid out pretty much the same as Jake and Rose's farm, the house and farm buildings were on the north side of the road. The fields were on the south, between the road and the river. The icehouse was on that side of the river, too.

The ladies went into the house. The two men went into the barn.

"Dis building's foundation is secure and da framing is sound, but it still needs a good deal of repair, Jake."

"Nothing we can't do with some help. Da men of da church and some of da uder famers along Fulton Street will help. We will provide the lumber and other supplies and da ladies will cook da noon meal. With five or six other guys, don't you think we could fix up dis barn in one full day?"

"Probably, Jake; but first, let's decide just vat need to be fixed. Den ve make a list of da supplies we need."

"All right Ruben," Jake suggested. "Let's start at the front of the barn on the ground floor."

In another hour the men had gone over the entire single story structure. First, they made a list of all needed repairs. Then, they wrote down those features they would want added to the structure.

"So Jake; do ve agree? Da barn's main opening should be videned mit twin doors installed that open out. A third stall could go over dere, und anoder door should exit on da pig pen. Ve need a floor installed on top of da beams to add a loft. Up dere, ve could store hay und oder feed. Dat's vhere ve should build da farm vorker's room. Da hay and grain vill be lifted on through double doors on da front of da barn, up der on da loft."

Then they spent some time looking at the hen house, pig pen, corn crib and ice house, such as they were.

"I think we have covered everything. Let's join da ladies and find out what changes dey want in the farm house."

"I'm almost afraid to ask dem, Jake."

They didn't have to wait long. Upon entering the house Emma greeted them. "Come in, boys. If we were to buy this place, Papa, we need many changes."

"Vy am I not surprised." Ruben whispered under his breath.

"I heard that, Papa." Emma snapped sharply. "I will wager that the list of things you think need to be done in the barn and the other buildings is much longer than the list I have for inside the house. Are the animals to live better than our family? But sit and let's talk."

"Fine, Momma; talk already."

Emma took a good deep breath and began. "The outside painting can wait until spring. But the inside painting must be done before we move in. Some of the windows won't open and others won't shut securely. All the window frames are loose and let in cold air. The doors don't fit properly, either. I can tell that the roof leaks, too. So we will need to put a tarp over that part of the roof until spring.

"Also in the spring, I want a water pump put on the sink over there. But before we move in you must build an entryway like Rose has at her place. It must be big enough to have a water closet on one side and a stairway to the basement on the other. And it must have a place to hang up our coats and hats and store our boots.

"As for furnishings, Papa," she continued. "We had to leave everything behind in Maryland. So we will need to shop for furniture, throw rugs, dishes, silverwear, pots and pans. Rose said she will help make the curtains and bed coverings; but we need to buy the material.

"What have you and Jake decided about the buildings?"

"I am so exhausted just listening to you talk about da inside of dis house, I can't even remember vat ve decided. You tell da ladies, Jake."

When he finished, Rose had a suggestion. "Let us go home boys. You have some chores and we need to fix dinner for the family. And tomorrow morning we can go to the other farm, the Pulte place."

Nobody objected. But they returned to the Drieborg home.

The next morning the four went to the Pulte farm and repeated the inspection and evaluation process they had conducted the previous day at the Kline place.

Back at the Drieborgs' after the noon meal, Ruben was smoking his pipe and the other three adults were finishing their coffee.

"Well, Ruben," Jake began. "Are you and Emma any closer to making a decision?"

"I tink dat ve have decided on the Kline place. Eh, Momma?"

"Yes," Emma agreed. "We think you are right, Jake. Having water close by is more important than buying a farm with buildings that have been kept up better. Besides, with the help you offered, we can fix up the Kline buildings without too much difficulty. We also think that the bank will probably expect less for that farm because of its present condition. What do you think, Rose? Which place would you choose?"

"The Pulte place is in better condition," Rose answered. "You could move in without doing much of anything. But water could be a big issue one day; one never knows.

"Besides, just look around us Emma. There are two healthy men and two strapping big boys living right in this house who will perform the work needed to fix that farm up. After chores they just sit around, anyway.

"Be good for them to get their elbows off my table and do some work. I know several other farmwomen who will volunteer their husbands, too. So the changes and repairs you need to make at Kline's should offer no problem. I think your choice makes sense."

"Get my elbows off da table?" Jake retorted. "You should not talk about me like dat in from of da children. Watch your tongue, woman!"

Ruben interrupted quietly, and asked. "So ve go tomorrow to see Mr. Deeb at da bank in Lowell. Would you two go mit us?"

"It is settled then, eh Ruben," Jake announced. "We go with you into town tomorrow after da breakfast and we see Joseph."

"Of course, Papa," Rose said softly. "Anything you say."

By Lord! Look at dat smile on her face. She's probably mocking me in my own house. I'm da Papa, but I don't think I can win dis one. Best to drop it.

SHERMAN'S HEADQUARTERS

Mike stood at attention in front of Sherman's desk.

"My staff usually takes care of this type of thing, Drieborg. But I promised a Congressman from Michigan that I would see to it personally. So here it is. You might as well sit down; it may take me awhile.

"The next part of your prison project was to be the one at Salisbury in North Carolina. The prisoners there are going to have to take care of themselves, because you are being given another assignment.

"There has been a lot of pressure on the Congressional delegation from Ohio by a prominent family on behalf of one Captain Taft. They believe that you were responsible for his demotion in rank and the loss of his favored position on my staff.

"How did they come to this belief, you might ask? That little shithead has used his considerable wealth to gain access to my telegraph lines and send messages and dispatches so he could whine about his current assignment. He has blamed you for every bad thing that has happened to mankind since the Garden of Eden. Thus, his family has decided that by punishing you they rescue him.

"I'm not blind, Drieborg," Sherman continued. "You pulled this assignment off magnificently. You did this with no help from Taft. He's been hanging around here complaining and moaning about you ever since you first met with some Reb doctor at that hospital near the old prison camp. Claims you're a Reb sympathizer. I know better. But as long as his money and booze was offered, he has had many listeners."

"So what is to become of me, sir now that my Salisbury Prison project has been canceled?

"You are to be given command of I Troop formerly of Michigan's 6th Cavalry Regiment and the Michigan Brigade. I know that a major rates a slot on the regimental staff. But I need someone to lead this troop and you need an assignment. Sort of ironic, isn't it, Drieborg? You asked that I assign this unit to you, and now they've got you. Maybe it's a win for both of us. We'll see.

"Any comments, Major?"

"Yes, General."

"First allow me to thank you for your assessment of the prison project. I consider that all those involved should be complimented, including the supervisor at the hospital, Dr. Woolworth and his nursing staff of Catholic nuns. Long before you or I arrived in the Savannah area, they had cared for our sick prisoners with as much concern as any Reb soldier in their care.

"I know this because when the Rebs moved thousands of us from Andersonville to that site last year these medical people were waiting in Savannah when the trains arrived, to help our sick prisoners. One of the men in my prison mess was near death. They saved his life.

"Besides, all one has to do is listen to our guys at the prison praise them. They say the nuns fed them when even your staff did not. This is all in my reports, sir.

"The medical staff people you sent were excellent as well. The only fly in the ointment was that spoiled brat you assigned me, Captain Taft.

"But I have kept that between you and me General. I have kept Congressman Kellogg and the Committee on the Conduct of the War apprised of the project, as they demanded. So in all my dispatches I have always given high praise for the support you have given this project. I have not had good things to say about – what did you call Taft – that little shit-head?

"There is a saying I heard often in Washington. To survive, 'Keep your enemies close to you,' But Taft was so inept he angered everyone he worked with and screwed up the simplest assignment. I ended up telling him to stay away.

"As for the new assignment you have just given me, General," Mike continued. "I wanted a combat command all along. This prison project was the president's idea. As far as being a troop commander is concerned, I'm fine with that, sir. I will serve in any capacity you believe I can best assist your command. Besides, sir, I began with this troop as a private back in September of '62. I know most of these men, and am glad to be with them once again."

"Well said, major. I saw your reports. I know you had virtually a direct line to the President himself. You could have hurt me with him and that bunch of bureaucrats in Washington. But you never complained about me or any member of my staff. In fact, you were always careful to praise us. I appreciate that.

"There's another reason I've taken this time with you. I want to assign a young Lieutenant to your troop. He's not entirely green; he spent some time as an enlisted man up north. I want him to serve under someone whose values I respect. That's why I want him to serve with you. But I won't force him on you son. Will you take him?"

"As a favor to you General, of course. My troop happens to be short a platoon leader anyway. If having him assigned to I Troop helps you out, that's fine with me."

"Thank you. I appreciate that, so will his mother. She's my sister, by the way. I promised her that he would serve under a man of good character. Now that you know he's related, will you still take him?"

Mike stopped his laughter long enough to answer. "General, I wouldn't miss this for the world."

"Good. Now, you are to report to General Burbidge. He's part of General Kilpatrick's Division. A lot has changed since early 1864, when you last led a troop. But you might find his treatment of civilian supporters of Rebellion somewhat harsh. But his approach has the support of this command and General Grant.

"And one thing more," Sherman continued. "Just as a heads-up to you, I'm assigning Taft to command an Ohio cavalry troop. He'll be in Burbridge's Division as well. You might look out for him.

"I wish you well, son," Sherman concluded. "Anything else?"

"Yes sir. What is your nephew's name?"

"Henry Austry. He's waiting for you right outside."

"Why am I not surprised with that, sir?"

Both men laughed as they turned away from one another.

✳   ✳   ✳   ✳

Why would Sherman make such a point of the methods used by my new superio,r General Burbridge? He knows about all that Reb sympathizer trash from Taft. So he's probably just letting me know what will be expected of me, and what I must order my men to do. I've got to get my mind around this.

Sergeant Riley told me some of the things he saw done to civilians in the Shenandoah Valley and recently in Georgia. He'll be willing to talk openly with me about this.

"It's a real problem, Major, no question about it," Riley began. "Can I speak freely, sir?"

"Please do."

"A few weeks ago, when ya was frettin about what happened to the young lass Julia back in Maryland, I told ya a few things. Do ya remember, sir?"

"You told me about our destruction of farms and towns back in the Shenandoah Valley and in Georgia during Sherman's march from Atlanta to Savannah. I remember."

"Back then, we was told that our Congress passed a law that said we were ta destroy anything that supported the Rebellion. Makes sense, don't it, sir?"

"It does."

"Well sir. Picture yerself in the yard of some Georgia farmer. It's late last fall and the harvest is over. He's got a few pigs ready for slaughter; a milk cow or two; some chickens; a nag fer plowing and maybe even a riding horse. A'corse, he's got corn in his crib an grain and hay in his barn fer all these animals too. In the smokehouse he's got some hams and such. In his root cellar there are sweet potatoes, carrots and onions fer the winter. And his wife just finished canning chicken. Not much different than yer pa's farm, I would guess."

"You would guess right, Sergeant."

"Our supplies haven't caught up with us here yet. So we need to find grain for our houses, chickens, hams, and vegetables for our cooking pots. That's about all we can carry anyway, ya see. During a war that's called living off'en tha land. Any trouble with that so far, sir?"

"None at all."

"Do we leave all that other food we find but can't carry? What about all the farm animals an their winter-feed? Do ya leave what we can't actually use? Does all that stuff support tha Rebellion against tha Union? You're tha leader of our troop now, Major. What would you order us ta do?"

"I have the impression that I will be expected to destroy all of it. So the question I have to answer is, will I follow orders I believe are unnecessarily harsh?"

"That's about it. Believe me, laddie, we will face this situation, and soon. So I'll ask ya again. What will you order tha men of your troop ta do?"

"If orders are given to destroy what we couldn't carry off, I will order it done. But I'll not allow men of my troop to attack civilians, pillage their belongings, or burn their homes."

"I have some more ta say, sir if'n it's all right."

"Whom else can I talk to about this, Riley? If you have more to say, for God's sake, spit it out."

"What you jus told me you would order would have been fine six months or so ago. But a lot'a water has gone over tha dam. Most'a tha men in this troop have been away from home comin on three years now. They've fought their way south from Tennessee to Atlanta and west clear across Georgia to Savannah. They have fought their way through swamps and lived off'n tha land tha whole time. So they're not a happy bunch right now; and they wanna take it out on these Southerns; believe me.

"On top'a that, you musta heard tell that General Sherman wants to make the people of South Carolina pay fer startin this war. I heard that he said what we did in Georgia would be nothin compared ta what we would be doing in Carolina."

"Yup. You heard right, Sarge. I've been at his staff meetings when he said those very things."

Riley continued. "As a top sergeant, sir, I hear all sorts'a things up at regiment. Fer one, this Burbridge comes with a reputation of burning and killin back in Kentucky that would make our march through Gerogia seem like a Sunday school picnic.

"So I'm thinking that this general will expect us to leave no building standin on our route of march through South Carolina. That means, we burn every barn; every house; every bridge; every town, and church and school. That means we kill every animal we don't carry off; pillage every farm house before we burn it; leave tha population with nothin but the clothing on their backs in tha dead'a winter."

"Can you do that, sir? Can you sit high on yer horse an watch yer men do those things on yer orders?"

"Whew! When I was in prison at Andersonville, I grew to hate the Rebs. But I never thought I would be asked to do the things you talk about, to civilians.

"Besides, it doesn't make sense to me for us to do those things now. We have this war won. I know the Confederates have Johnston's army of about 35,000 somewhere north of us. But they're running, not fighting. If they did decide to fight, we could cut them up like a hot knife through butter. So we don't need to do these things to the civilian population at this point.

"What we do need is their ability after the war to buy goods made in the North. And if we're ever going to unite this country properly, we will need their good will, not their hatred."

"I think it's my turn to ask you, sir; when did you become so smart?"

"Put that thought on hold, Sarge. We've got to find this General Burbidge somewhere north of here in South Carolina, and pronto. Then we'll see how smart I am."

"Shouldn't be hard, I'm thinking, sir," Riley observed. "Alls we hav ta do is follow tha trail of burnt out barns and houses and dead animal carcasses."

✳   ✳   ✳   ✳

"Before I forget," Mike added. "We've been assigned another officer; name's Henry Austry. He's served some time in an infantry unit with the Army of Tennessee; but he's somewhat new to the cavalry. He handled his mount quite well on our ride here from Sherman's headquarters. Which platoon sergeant do you think would work with him best?"

"I have two suggestions, sir," Riley responded. "First, I'm a' thinking Killeen and Steward are a bit too impatient and direct for a rookie platoon leader. Bill Anderson would be better cause he's the calmest and least critical.

"Second, you and Lt. White should have a conversation with this man. Since he's served, he knows that the platoon sergeant actually runs a platoon, even though tha platoon leader is in charge. Lt. White has that system down pretty well."

"Fine, Sarge," Mike decided. "I'll take your suggestion on both counts. Tonight, Phineas and I will have a talk with Henry. You be there too. We'll get Anderson to join us after a while. In the meantime, I'll have Henry ride with you and me during today's march. We need to get on with this. Any other thoughts?"

"No sir, I think that should cover the matter, for now."

Carolinas Campaign

The Carolinas Campaign

South Carolina:
February 1865

Mike's Troop had just crossed the Savannah River into South Carolina.

"The main body has a three day head start on us, gentlemen." Mike reminded his officers and Sgt. Riley. "We have enough provisions so we won't have to forage for several days. We should be able to move right along unless there's a swamp ahead we don't know about. But from the looks of the burned buildings and dead animals we've come across, our troops aren't too far ahead.

"It hasn't been many days since these animals were butchered or these buildings torched. Keep an eye out for bushwhackers, Sergeant. Some of those irregulars might have slipped behind our forces."

"Yes sir," Riley replied. "The Point is out a good hundred yards. And I'll keep checking the flanks."

Riley was right about the destruction. So far, nothing lives and no building stands as far as I can see to the horizon on the east, the west and the north. All I have seen are smoking embers and animal carcasses.

On the evening of the second day out, Mike's troop rode into the barnyard of a small farm. Union solders were ransacking the house. Pots and pans were being thrown out of the kitchen window. They watched a man dragging a feather mattress out the front door of the house.

In the yard, plates were being tossed into the air for target practice. Other soldiers were chasing chickens and ducks. Flames could be seen licking at the barn's roof. The frightened cries of farm animals left in the burning building caught Mike's attention.

"Sgt. Riley. Get those animals out of the barn, quickly."

"Yes sir! Crawford, take Fenning and Connolly. Get those animals out'a the barn."

The three men needed no further direction. They jumped off their mounts and rushed into the barn. The two cows inside welcomed their rescuers, but the old plow horse wasn't about to come easily. In fact, led almost out of the barn, the horse bolted free and ran back inside the burning building.

Everyone could hear the awful cries of the doomed horse.

"Crawford," Riley shouted. "Let the animal go."

"But Sarge. We can't just let it burn alive!"

"Tis too late for tha poor animal, son. You tried. Stand down."

A sergeant came out of the house, a bed pillow under one arm and a framed mirror under the other. He looked around at Mike's troop ringing the yard.

"What the hell is going on out here?"

Sitting a 'top of his horse, Sgt. Riley looked down at the surly soldier. "Just saving those milk cows and their wonderful milk wouldn't ya know. Wouldn't want that beef all charred up in the barn fire now, would we?"

"You can shove yer smart talk, you red haired Irish bastard. I'm in charge of this foraging operation. General Burbridge's orders are for us to take or destroy anything that could aide the Rebels. Who are you to interfere with us carrying out his orders?"

"How do dinner plates and bed pillows aide the Rebel cause, boyo?" Riley asked.

"None' a yer damn business, you pile of shit."

"Now, now, Sergeant; calm yourself. No need to lose yer temper.

"See that major sitting on that horse over there? He's making it his business. And he's telling me to tell you to bundle up whatever it tis yer stealing from these poor farm folk and skedaddle. Is that so hard for ya ta understand, now?"

"The general wants these Rebels punished for startin' this war."

"Fought a pitched battle with this family, did ya now?"

"You smart ass Mick piece of trash. You got us outnumbered this time. So we'll go. But we'll meet again. You best watch your back. And I'm going to report that you stopped us from foraging for the army."

Mike rode up alongside Riley. "You do that, Sergeant. When you do, be sure to get my name right; its Drieborg; Major Michael Drieborg. Now you and your scavengers collect your loot and get out of here."

"What are you thinking, Sergeant?" Mike asked.

"It would appear, sir, that you have decided not to burn people out of their homes or kill their stock without cause."

"It seems that I have, Sergeant," Mike responded. "Problem?"

"None a'tall sir. Just ta be clear about it, though, I'm thinking that you don't want our men to pillage. But we will take food we need for ourselves and feed we need for our horses. Is that about it, sir?"

"That's about it, Sergeant. Please tell the men before we arrive at the next farm."

"Right away, sir. It's good to know the drill early on."

"Do you approve?"

"While tis not for me to be judgin one way or a' tuther, Major, I believe you made a decision I'm not ashamed ta carry out."

"How long do you think it will take for word to spread up to headquarters about what we did here today?"

"By this time tomorrow is my guess, sir."

"Carry on, Sergeant."

Riley called his non-commissioned officers together for instructions.

"Make sure your men understand just what we're doing here in South Carolina. We're lookin ta fight Confederate soldiers and end this damn war. We're not here to abuse civilians. We will confiscate the food and the feed we need, but we will not loot. When we run into more foragers like that scum we just run off, follow my lead. Hold your weapons at the ready, but no killing unless I give yas tha word.

"By the way, before we leave here, have each of your men fill his canteen an water his horse. Swede, stay with me. Off with the rest of yas, now. We leave in fifteen minutes."

"Swede," Riley continued. "You know the drill, Sergeant. Look at tha horses that have been giving us trouble. I don't want any'a them turning up lame. Report back ta me when you're done with your inspection."

"I'll be back, Sergeant." The Swede, as he was called by all the men, had been with this troop since it was formed in Grand Rapids, back in 1862. He had been brought over from Sweden a year earlier to handle the animals used in the copper mines of the Upper Peninsula of Michigan. Now, he looked after the mounts for the men of I Troop.

Then Riley rode alongside his troop Commander. "Major Drieborg, if I could have a word, sir. The family what lives here? They want to thank ya personally, sir. But they're afraid to approach. If ya could spare a minute inside the house?"

"Of course, Sergeant. I don't think I should enter their house alone though. Have Bill Anderson join me."

Inside the house, the farmer, his wife and two children greeted the two men.

"We just wanted to thank you, Major, for what you did today. The men you chased off were angry because we didn't have much of value for them to take. From what they said, I am sure they would have set fire to our house. God bless you and your men, sir."

"You're most welcome. Our duty is to find, engage and defeat your army, certainly not to harm you or destroy your property without cause. My hope is that soon this war will end and we will be able to live together as one nation."

They shook hands with the farmer. His wife curtsied. The children just clung to their mother's skirts.

As the troop rode back to the road north, the men could see smoke rising into the sky ahead of them.

"That next farm is sure not far away," Stan Killeen observed. He was a platoon sergeant now. Once he had refused to even consider becoming a corporal in charge of five other men in a squad.

He refused back then because, "I'm not ever going to be in the position of ordering a man to do anything that might cause his death."

But Stan had great confidence in his own abilities and even less patience for incompetent leadership. So he finally accepted the rank of sergeant and responsibility for a platoon of thirty men. He may have been the shortest cavalryman in that platoon; but he was the most feared.

"If what that bunch of looters was doing back there is any example of what we'll have to deal with ahead, we'll spend more of our time protecting Reb farmers than fighting Reb soldiers."

Bill Anderson was another platoon sergeant. He too had been a member of the original squad Mike Drieborg led back in '62. In his mid forties, he was the old man of the troop.

"Made me feel sort' a proud chasing those foragers off that farm. I know Sherman's army has to live off the land an all. But those soldiers were just looters, pure and simple. The stuff I saw them carry off would be of no use to their army. I expect we'll see a whole bunch of it by the side of the road when they get tired of luggin it around.

"I've fought tooth an nail against the best cavalry the Rebs can throw at us: and I'll do it again if necessary. But I won't abuse civilians. I hope Mike can keep us from being ordered ta do that sort of thing."

"Amen ta that, old man," Stan Killeen echoed.

As Mike's troop approached the next farm, they saw Union foragers ride out of the barnyard. The barn and house were already ablaze. Farm animals lay dead in the yard.

"Probably that same bunch we chased off the last place," Mike observed.

"Not much for us to do here, sir," Riley responded. "If we ride on by, we might catch up to the lead elements and our orders before sunset, sir."

"Sounds good to me, Sergeant; keep the men moving."

As it turned out, it was another day before they caught up with Division Headquarters and General Burbridge.

✳   ✳   ✳   ✳

Mike reported to Division Headquarters early in the morning. This was his troop's third day out of Savannah.

He handed his orders to a captain sitting at a desk in front of a field tent.

"Major Drieborg reporting for duty Captain."

"Welcome to our humble home, Major. I'll give your orders to the general. He's in a meeting right now, but he should be done shortly. I'll call you as soon as he can see you. You can find coffee, bread and some fruit on that table over there. Help yourself."

"Thank you, Captain. I will." Mike joined several other officers at the breakfast table.

Several of them were called to the general's tent. He was coffeed out by the time he heard his name called.

"You must have done a good job for General Sherman, Drieborg. He recommends you highly. Quite a twist of fate that you would regain command of your original troop, isn't it."

"Yes sir. They are a fine group of men."

"What's this report my staff received of you interfering with my foragers a couple of days ago? Stopped them from carrying out their responsibilities, did you?"

"That depends on what you call their responsibilities, sir," Mike responded carefully.

"Before the invasion of South Carolina, General Sherman told us at his last staff meeting in Savannah that he would not tolerate looting. He wanted us to pass the word and do what was necessary to prevent if possible, and punish if necessary, that unauthorized activity.

"On our second day after crossing the Savannah River, my troop came across a small farm. It was just a few acres, a couple of milk cows and an old plow horse. The men of the forage detail had already taken all the foodstuffs that were available; at least there was nothing left for us that my men could find. By the time we rode in, the foragers had already torched the barn and were simply destroying the house furnishings they couldn't carry off. I ordered them to pack up whatever they had decided to take and move on.

"In my opinion, sir, these men had gone beyond foraging and were looting. I did not attempt to punish them as, General Sherman suggested we do when such a thing is witnessed. But I did stop them from what I observed was unauthorized looting."

"That's not what the sergeant in charge of the foraging detail said. He was most insistent that his men were not looting."

"No disrespect intended, sir," Mike responded. "But is it customary in your command to take the word of a sergeant over that of a major?"

"Are you arguing with me, Drieborg?"

"Not at all, sir. I'm simply asking for clarification."

Agitated and somewhat red in the face, the general stood on his side of the camp desk. Hands on the table, he leaned forward toward Drieborg, who was seated a few feet in front of the desk.

"Need I remind you mister Medal of Honor winner, that you are no longer in Washington at some fancy dinner party? You are on active duty in a war zone. You are in South Carolina, the heart of Rebellion.

"Need I remind you that all these people supported treason? These people caused a war that has claimed thousands and thousands of our troops. They need to be punished, sir, not coddled. This army is the instrument of punishment. I intend to see that retribution is delivered in such a harsh manner that these people will never again even think of repeating their treason.

"If some of my foragers are a little overzealous, that's the price these traitors must endure. If you want clarity, sir, I suggest you read my General Order #59. In that I authorized a policy of retaliation against Rebel sympathizers for attacks on our soldiers.

"What do you have to say for yourself, sir?"

Mike rose from his campstool and stood at attention. "Sir, General Sherman gave me a copy of that general order. So I am already familiar with its contents. I have no problem carrying out this order for as long as I serve in your command.

"In the absence of such attacks, however, I will follow the directive of the Secretary of War and General Sherman, as stated quite clearly in General Order #10, part of which states that burning of private property is strictly prohibited; and further that looting will not be tolerated under any circumstances. The general has even gone so far as ordering our troops to stay out of private homes entirely unless our mission requires it.

"Consequently, sir, while I will direct the troopers in my command to forage for food and feed, I will not allow any of them to loot under any circumstance or to destroy civilian property without cause, when it is in my power to prevent either.

"Is the general suggesting to me that looting and the destruction of civilian property is always necessary?"

"Don't you be impertinent with me, Major! I expect that you will follow my orders.

"It would still be helpful, sir, if you could tell me exactly what your orders are with regard to stealing private property and the burning of people's homes. After all, Major General Blair as well as Major General Howard are both about to court martial a good number of officers for not stopping their soldiers from looting?"

"Major Drieborg," Burbridge concluded. "You will report to my secretary after today's noon meal. He will have your orders. You are dismissed."

"Yes sir." Mike responded. He did an about face and walked out of the tent.

Whew! I pushed that one pretty far; maybe too far. Based upon his General Order59 and the reputation he earned in Kentucky, I know what he wants me to have my men do. He wants us to burn and pillage. I'll bet that if I complied, he would throw me to the dogs the first time someone in higher authority called him on the carpet for it.

Virtually all the written orders prohibit looting and burning homes. But it seems to me that everyone from Sherman down looks the other way when it happens. Despite all the public pronouncements to the contrary, our leaders want to punish Southerners, from the big plantation slave owners to the little farmer. Make them all shudder at the prospect of opposing the central government ever again. Guys like Burbridge are their instrument.

Guys like me are caught in the middle. By damn, I'll not play their ugly game. If they drag me before a court martial, I'll expose their contradiction to the Northern press.

$$* \qquad * \qquad * \qquad *$$

"How did it go, sir?" Sgt. Riley asked.

"I'm afraid that I made the General very angry. He all but threw me out."

"Would you be telling me how you did that, Major?"

"First, I defended the actions we took against those looters we came across the other day.

"Second, I told him pretty much the same thing I ordered you to tell our men; no looting or burning of homes.

"Third, I quoted him chapter and verse from Sherman's own orders prohibiting what I believe Burbidge wants us to do, loot and burn without distinction.

"Fourth, I insisted that he give me direct orders of just what I am to have my men do."

"Where does that leave us, sir?"

"I'm to report to his office after noon chow today for orders," Mike chuckled. "Tell you after that, Sergeant."

GRAND RAPIDS, MICHIGAN

Jake Drieborg, his wife, Rose, and their daughter Susan were riding in their wagon east on Fulton Street. Ruben Hecht and his wife, Emma, followed in another wagon. The five were headed toward the bakery in Grand Rapids that George Neal, Susan's fiancé had just purchased. The men were going to help with building repairs. The ladies were going to fix up the apartment above the bakery.

Established in the early 1850s, its last owner had been caught up in the war fever of 1861 and joined the Union army. His wife had George to help when he left. But then George, a healthy young man, was pressured by locals into joining as well. He finally gave in and volunteered for the cavalry in mid-1862.

Without skilled help, the owner's wife simply could not handle the bakery and her young family. The final straw was when she was notified that her husband had been killed in December 1864. She closed the bakery and put it up for sale.

"It was a good thing what George started when he and Michael were in training camp, eh, Papa?"

"If you mean when he opened dat savings account at da Old Kent Bank and sent money to it every month?"

"Yes, Momma. It was a smart thing for him to do. So when he asked dat bank to help him buy da bakery dey, already knew he was a good saver, and dat he didn't throw his money away on drink or gambling when he was in da army.

"So I was not surprised when dey approved his loan."

"Of course, when you stood up for him, that helped too, Papa. The bank people remembered that you helped them get started with the farmers in Lowell. You talked to a lot of them about leaving Bacon's bank and switching their mortgage and operating loans to them when they opened a branch there. In fact, Papa, I think you were the first to do so."

"Maybe, Momma. But when I talked to Congressman Kellogg about George, dat helped even more. He's a director of dat bank, you know."

"When George came to our door last month, sick and weak with the dysentery, we welcomed him because he was Michael's friend from the cavalry; and, of course, because he and Susan had been writing one another ever since the boys were in training camp together two years ago already. Besides, he had no one else. And remember Papa; he helped you around the farm as soon as he had some strength."

"Ya, Momma," It was only last month. How could I forget? He turned out to be a hard worker, too."

"So I wasn't too surprised when he and Susan asked us if they could marry. But I worried about how he would provide for her. He is no farmer, you know."

"Dat is true, Momma. He was an apprentice dere before he joined the cavalry at da same time Michael did. So he knows about dis business. He is better suited for da bakery. But it may be tough for a while because it has been closed for over a month. So it might take him some time to get it going again. We will help dem for awhile."

When George sought help from the Drieborgs, he had just been given a medical discharge in January 1865. Now, he was going to marry Susan at Easter and was looking to return to productive civilian life. What could be better than to take over the very bakery he had learned to run before the war?

Lowell, Michigan

"It is hard to believe that you actually shot two men, Ann," Julia commented. "Would you do it again?"

"You're darn right, I would. Given half the chance, those thugs I shot would have killed my brother Jacob. No telling what they would have done to me. That's why Papa taught me to use this shotgun. I'll use it again in a minute.

"After what you went through in Maryland, wouldn't you do the same?"

"I'm not sure I could actually pull the trigger."

"Your Momma didn't hesitate, though."

"No, she didn't. She knew that soldier would kill Kenny for sure. She didn't hesitate to kill that man, not for a minute."

"Well, we're ready for any intruders, believe me. The boys are out in the barn loft. They have Jacob's squirrel gun and a pistol. I have my shotgun by the kitchen window.

"Remember, Julia. If we are attacked, you take the children into the front bedroom. There is a loaded pistol by my bed. Wait there until the shooting is over. If thugs get by me and the boys, I hope you will use that gun to at least protect the children."

South Carolina

Mike called his officers Lt. White and Lt. Austry together with Sgt. Riley and the non-commissioned officers together.

"Well, gentlemen," Mike began. "We have our orders.

"Our regiment is to lead the division north. In addition, the general has directed that our troop act as the Point on that march. It is very unusual for division to meddle in such a detail as that. That assignment is usually leave it up to us and is rotated among the various troops.

"But I fear that General Burbridge has taken a special interest in me, and thus in I Troop. I suppose that means he will be watching how we treat the civilians we come across.

"So let there be no misunderstanding; despite the pressure to the contrary, I will not allow the killing of civilians unless they take arms against us. Nor will I allow looting or the burning of homes or barns. But we will take whatever food and feed we need to sustain our march.

"I have directed Sgt. Riley to find us a wagon and a horse to carry supplies we confiscate along the way. We may even take a steer or two for our later use. We will not wantonly kill livestock and flocks we decide not to take.

"Are there any questions about these orders?"

Lt. Phineas White was from Lapeer, Michigan, a small farm village much like Mike's hometown of Lowell. He spoke first. He had been assigned the troop some six months earlier. Sgt. Riley thought he was a good officer. High praise Mike thought. Not much over five-foot-five and one hundred forty pounds, he was of ideal size for a cavalryman. Phineas was the oldest child in a farmer's family, just like Mike, too.

"At the officers mess last night, General Burbridge dropped in for a drink. You were there too, sir. I think he made it clear what he expected of all of us. How did he put it?

"If they think Georgia was bad, these folks in South Carolina will think they're in the bowels of hell before we're done with them. They started this war. They're all traitors. So don't bother to try sorting them out. What you can't carry, burn. Ashes, chimneys and carcasses are all I want to see left to mark our path."

"Couldn't be clearer, it seems ta me, sir."

"I heard that too, Phineas," Mike responded. "I have no problem with making the Rebs pay. In case you think I'm contradicting myself by saying that, let me explain what I mean.

"Most of the small farm families we run across probably have the husband, a son and plenty of kin fighting in a Confederate unit somewhere. Adult men we find at home are probably there because of wounds they received in some battle against us, or they are too young, old or sick to fight.

"If these men try to fight us, we treat them as combatants as our Congress has directed its Army to do. Then we will follow Burbridge's Order #49. Otherwise, I will have our men obey Sherman's Order #10, which prohibits looting or indiscriminate burning of homes.

"All the rest'a that talk you heard last night is bombastic crap.

"A question, sir," Henry Austry asked. Of typical stature for a cavalryman, he stood about five foot six and was some on hundred fifty pounds. He had plenty of black hair. The pencil thin mustache he wore gave him a sinister look. But that impression was soon corrected with his ready smile and his soft manner of speaking.

"Yes Henry," Mike said. "What is it?"

"I understand that Burbridge's Order #49, authorized the killing of six people for every soldier killed by a bushwhacker. Are you going to order us to do that?"

"Actually Lieutenant," Mike corrected. "That general order authorizes the killing of four Confederate prisoners of war for each of our soldiers killed. However, in Kentucky, things got out of hand and civilians were killed, too. We're not going to do either. We'll treat prisoners with the same respect we would expect from them if the situation were reversed. And we will respect the non-combatant status of civilians. Any killing will be of bushwhackers and marauders, if we can catch'em.

"But as soon as I return from regiment, I will call you together to go over our Plan of March. I expect that we will head out first thing in the morning. I suggest you alert your men and have them prepare three days supply of food, feed and water."

"If there are no more questions, you may return to your duties."

✳   ✳   ✳   ✳

Stan Killeen, another of the platoon sergeants was always ready to voice his opinion.

"The Dutchman has only been back with us for a couple of weeks, but it looks as though he has got us into a hell of a pickle. The last time he led us, we got volunteered for that damn Richmond raid of Kilpatrick's. In the middle of winter we forced marched right up to the outskirts of Richmond; we could even hear the church bells ringing. And what does our high and mighty general do, but call for a retreat? That's when Mike got himself captured on our march back to our lines. Was a miracle any of us made it back.

"Now Mike's principles have got us on the general's bad side fer sure. Burbridge wants us to burn everything in sight and the Dutchman wants us to play nicey-nice with these traitors. I've been away from home, a warm bed and a full belly goin' on three years. I've slopped my way through swamps all the way from Atlanta. Poor food, wet an cold all the time; and I'm supposed to treat these people with respect. Like hell I say! We ought to do what Burbridge and Sherman is telling us; teach these secesh a lesson they'll never forget. Burn everything. They'll never even think of doing this again, by God."

Another platoon sergeant spoke up. "I'm divided on the issue," Bill Anderson volunteered. "I can see the point you're making, Stan, and actually I feel much the same hatred for what these people have put us through. After all, for over two years now, we have lived out of doors, been wet and cold or hot and sticky. And, we've been shot at and seen some of our friends wounded and killed.

"But on the other hand, I agree with Mike that we should not punish civilians, especially small farmers who had nothing to do with starting all of this killing. So I think I'll come down on the side of respecting folks more than hating them."

"I might expect that attitude from you, old man," Stan snapped.

What about you Swede?" Dave Steward asked. "Any comment?"

"I tink I go mit what Mike said. I still trust him more dan some general who doesn't give a damn about anybody else."

"What do ya think of tha new guy, Austry, Bill?" Dave Steward asked.

"Seems pretty level headed ta me, Dave. Met with him and Mike the other night. He seems to be getting the picture of how a platoon is best run. It's only been two days though. But I'm thinking he'll work out alright."

"I have my doubts," Stan offered. "Never seen a foot solder, like he used ta be, who wasn't a slacker. We lucked out with White. Now that we're in a war zone, we'll see how this new guy does."

"Always looking at the half empty part of the glass, aren't you, Stan. Good thing Mike assigned Austry to Anderson's platoon."

"Well, Steward," Stan shot back. "At least we agree on one thing."

✳   ✳   ✳   ✳

At regimental headquarters, Mike reported as instructed.

Col. Kidd was hunched over a map table with several other officers looking on.

"Come on in, Major. We were just talking about you," he chuckled. "Appears that you've become Burbridge's bad boy."

"It does seem as though I have earned his disapproval, sir."

"After word of the speech he gave last night gets around our camp, I doubt if any officer will have an easy time of controlling his men. I expect it will be pillage, burn and damn the consequences."

"I expect that's true, sir. All we can do is try to maintain discipline."

"Let me assure you, Mike." The colonel added. "This command will not tolerate that loot and burn approach. The Michigan Brigade is made up of soldiers, not messengers of revenge.

"Anyway, my boy, welcome back to the regiment. You've had quite an adventure since you were with us last in '64."

"Thank you, sir. It is good to be back with you."

"Now let's see about these orders of yours. I understand that the general intended that your troop absorb the brunt of any Confederate attack. But we at Regiment object to that kind of meddling with how we run things. So I think we'll have several troops out front, rather than just one. He can't object to that do, you think?"

"Whatever you say, sir."

By the time Mike left, the Plan of March was established and he had his orders for the morning.

LOWELL

Julia Hecht's face was red with anger. She could hardly contain herself as she grabbed her coat and burst out of the house to the barn. Ann Drieborg was the first to notice.

"What in heaven's name is wrong with her?"

"I certainly don't know," Julia's mother Emma said. "I just gave her a letter that Papa brought from town. I think it is from Michael. I've never seen her react this way. She usually goes off by herself. But this time she seems angry about something. Just leave her alone for awhile, Ann. She'll calm down eventually."

And eventually Julia did return to the house. But she didn't seem the least bit calm, even after an hour or more alone in the barn. Now, back in the house, she stood with the letter in her hand, looking at everyone seated at the kitchen table.

"Can you believe it?" she started. "He promised me that the war was almost over, that he would not be in any more fighting. He promised!"

"What are you talking about, child?" her mother asked in some confusion.

"Michael has been assigned to his old cavalry troop. In fact, he's part of Sherman's army invading South Carolina. And just from the way he told me in this letter, I think he is enjoying it. He promised!"

"Oh, my Lord, Papa," Rose Drieborg exclaimed. "I also thought Michael was done with the fighting. If Julia is right, he could be killed."

"If Michael is back in da fighting, ya, Momma, he could be killed," Jake agreed. "But remember, he is an officer in da army. So he does not control his fate. He must do as he is ordered. All we can do is pray for his safe return."

South Carolina

It didn't take long for Mike and the men of I Troop to encounter their first challenge.

Mike was riding with the Point Squad, several hundred yards in front of the main body.

"I though we were the lead Troop of the Regiment sir,"

"As far as I know, Corporal, we are."

"Then what's all that smoke up ahead?"

"I don't know. But we will find out soon enough. Alert your men on the flanks to be on the lookout, Corporal, and send someone back to inform Lt. White with the main body."

After the main body had joined the Point Squad, men were sent out to scout the flanks for Confederate soldiers. Once the area was secured, guards were posted on the perimeter of the farm. Only then did Mike allow his men to enter the yard of the small farm.

The barn and outbuildings were piles of smoldering ashes. All that was standing of the house was the stone chimney. Household goods were scattered all over the yard. The remains of the family milk cow and an old plow horse lay in the dirt near the ashes of the barn.

Sgt. Boyer shouted. "Over here sir."

Mike rode over to the trooper. His officers joined him. They gathered around the still body of an adult white haired male. He lay at the base of a shade tree. He had a slip- knotted rope around his neck. Near him lay the near-naked body of a white-haired woman.

The trooper gave Mike his assessment. "I believe the foragers who hit this place believed this family hid valuables somewhere. Appears to me, sir, that they were trying to convince him to tell where the valuables was hid. My guess is, they overdone it some, and they killed him. Don't know what happened to the woman; they might have tortured her some though."

"Not much we can do here now. Sgt. Riley, send out a squad to the Point and get the troop back on the road. We've got a ways to go before we camp for the night."

"Yes sir," Riley responded. He turned to his platoon sergeants.

"Stop yer gawking. Get back to yer platoons. Anderson, send out one of yer squads to the Point. Off with yas now. I want yas all on the road right now."

To his officers, Mike shared another point of view.

"This could have been the work of marauders. They told me at regiment that law and order has broken down in this area. We can expect groups of Southern deserters and hoodlums raiding all over the state; maybe some Federal deserters too. If we come across any of these types, believe me, we will deal with them quickly and harshly."

*   *   *   *

Sure enough, not too far ahead the troop's Point Squad spied a group of men in a grove of trees. They withdrew out of sight and sent word back to the troop. Mike sent a platoon forward under Lt. White.

Shots could be heard, but by the time the rest of the troop came up, the issue had been decided.

"Report, Lt. White." Mike directed.

"Sir. We captured seven men. It appears they were having a heated discussion about loot when we surprised them. They claim to be

Confederate soldiers spying for General Johnston's army. I believe them to be the marauders whose work we came across down the road."

"Thank you for that report, lieutenant.

"Sergeant Riley!"

"Yes sir."

"Have the men of the First Platoon take charge of three of these captives. Using a slipknot like the one they killed that farmer with, hang'em.

"Lt. Austry."

"Yes Sir."

"Take charge of the other three captives. Use a slipknot on the ropes, and hang'em."

"Just like that sir, hang'em?"

Mike wanted to laugh at the look on his new lieutenant's face.

I'm afraid my new officer is surprised that the first order he received in I Troop is one to kill three men in cold blood. I wonder if his uncle General Sherman would be upset at what this man of character has ordered his nephew to do. Someone has to do it though; might just as well be Austry.

"You have your orders Henry. Carry them out."

"Yes sir."

"What of the seventh captive, sir? White asked."

"Bring him to me; any one of them will do."

One of the marauders was brought to Mike

"You mean you're not going ta kill me?" The man asked somewhat surprised.

"That will depend on you. For now, I want you to watch the other scum hang."

It wasn't long before the six marauders were swinging from trees in the grove.

"Riley," Mike shouted.

"Yes sir."

"Have the troop formed."

"Some of you want to vent your anger on the people of South Carolina. Some of you want revenge. You got it today, but against men who earned it. They were killers and thieves. In case you thought I would be soft, this is what will happen to all bushwhackers and marauders we find. I spared this man so he can carry the message to others like him that they best not be caught by the Dutchman and this troop of avengers."

Then, in front of the entire troop, Mike performed an act that no one who knew him would ever have thought him willing to do.

Alongside of Mike the seventh thief was bound and sitting upright on his horse. Mike unsheathed a knife, and without hesitation thrust the blade into the man's right knee. Then he pulled the man off his saddle. The wounded man writhed on the ground and screamed in pain.

Mike calmly sheathed his knife and returned his attention to the assembled troop.

"We will take this man to the town of Pocataligo a few miles ahead and turn him in to the authorities, whoever they may be. He'll spread the word for us.

"Sgt. Riley, get some treatment for this man's wound. When he stops screaming, tell him that I will cripple the other leg unless he tells us where we can find the rest of his band."

"Lt. White, see to it that the weapons of those killers are collected. Put them in the supply wagon. Round up their horses as well. We'll take them along with us. But throw their loot, saddles and other gear into the grove where we hung them. And, Lieutenant, get the troop moving."

"Yes sir."

On the march, Lt. White rode alongside of Mike for a spell.

"My God, Mike, was all that necessary?"

"Our men needed to know I'm not just some softie or Confederate sympathizer. You needed to know that too, I think, Phineas.

"And much more importantly, when we run across the next farm, and I stop our men from looting, burning and killing the defenseless civilians there, they will remember what I ordered them to do today to killers and thieves. Then they may begin to realize the difference and channel their hate and take out their revenge on those who have really earned it."

"I can see your point, Mike," Phineas responded. "But I doubt General Burbridge will recognize the difference."

*   *   *   *

Later that day a rider from the Point Squad reported a very large house ahead.

Once again, Mike ordered six man squads to the flanks to search for Confederate soldiers or bushwhackers. The main body moved cautiously toward the reported sighting.

By the time Mike arrived his advance party had checked the area and secured the buildings. This was the largest home they had yet encountered. A man and woman were seated on the front porch. Two Negro adults, one male and the other female, were standing on the porch behind the seated whites.

"This place is no small operation, Major," Riley commented.

"Have a squad search the outbuildings, Sergeant. I'll speak to the owners."

"Good afternoon sir," Mike said as he strode up the steps of the porch. "We mean you no harm, but my men must look for provisions."

The man stood and faced Mike. "I understand, Major," the man said. "But I hope the members of my family and my slaves will be safe during your stay here."

"Rest assured, sir, no harm will come your way as long as you cooperate."

"Just what do you mean by cooperation, Major?"

"We are in South Carolina without provisions. So we must live off the land. Therefore sir, my men will search your home and buildings for food for us and our horses. An officer will accompany any of my troopers who enter your home.

"I can assure you that we are not here to take personal possessions."

"What of our slaves, Major?"

"Since President Lincoln's Emancipation Proclamation, they are considered contraband, sir," Mike informed the man. "That means we are to set them free."

"Are you going to take responsibility for them, Major?"

"If you are asking me if my men will provide food, housing, transportation and protection for them as you have, the answer is no. We will provide none of that."

"The two people you see with us on this porch are all that is left of our slaves. The field hands ran off, with much of our smokehouse too. These two have been house servants; with us since they were youngsters. I doubt they would survive long on the road by themselves. Nevertheless, we talked with them about leaving along with the others, but they felt safer staying. Certainly, you can talk to them again about leaving."

"Before we leave, we will have a private talk with them. For the time being, though, we will camp in your yard for the night. My men will need to have a latrine; if you would point out an area away from the buildings, we will set one up."

"Lt. White," Mike called out.

"Yes sir."

"See that the perimeter is secure. And have the men set up camp for the night."

When they left the next morning, their provision wagon was full of feed, dressed chickens and a few ducks. Behind the wagon, a good-sized steer was being pulled along. Plenty of time later to slaughter something that could walk until it was needed. The two house slaves were still to be seen on the front porch with their former master.

Sgt. Bill Anderson had been delegated to talk to them. Sgt. Riley was explaining his lack of success to Major Drieborg.

"Sir, I sent him ta talk to the darkies cause he's the most fatherly lookin fella we have in the troop. Talks real soft, too. I figured Killeen or me would frighten them ta death."

"You're probably right. So what happened?"

"Bill said tha two'a them decided to stay where they was, sir."

"You sure he explained everything to them?"

"You know Bill, sir." Riley insisted. "Couldn't be a more soothing guy in the troop."

"All right Sergeant. Get this troop on the road."

"Yes sir."

Back at the main house, Mike had some parting words with the plantation owner.

"Thank you for your cooperation, sir."

"You have my gratitude for not burning my buildings, Major Drieborg. They are very old and sadly in need of serious repair anyway. But they are all that I have left. My wife was worried sick that you would destroy our home. Word had preceded you that all would be destroyed as a matter of policy. Fortunately for us, you are the first gentleman in a blue uniform we have encountered."

"You're welcome. And I wish you a good day, sir."

Down the road a bit, Lt. White continued to express amazement.

"One day you hang six men and personally cripple another; the next you leave two slaves with their plantation master and don't even burn one outbuilding. You are a puzzlement for sure, Major."

"You're right, Phineas, I am truly that. By the time we reach Charleston, I may have this thing figured out. What do ya think?"

"You might, Mike," White retorted with a chuckle. "But you'll probably still keep me guessing."

*   *   *   *

Before the end of the day, the captive Mike had crippled the previous day led them to an area a few miles south of the town of Pocataligo.

Mike checked with Lt. White and Sergeant Riley. "You've grilled this guy real good?"

"Yes sir. And, he understands you promised to ruin his other leg if he's led us into a trap or this is a wild goose chase. How did he put it to us, Sergeant?"

"He almost wailed when he said,"

'*Don't let that crazy Dutchman near me again!*'

"I believe he is truly terrified of you, sir."

"Good. He should be."

"Phineas, do you and Henry have a plan of attack developed yet?"

"Yes sir. We suggest that three squads move in the direction of the marauders' camp. According to our captive, it should be about three miles to the northeast; almost directly south of Pocataligo, actually.

"Our Point Squad will send back a messenger when the camp is sighted. They will remain in place until the main body attacks right past them.

"We plan to leave the flanking squads in place during the attack, to snatch up any of the hoodlums who try to escape their way. Our man says that their camp backs up to the river over there, so a fourth squad has already moved across and will block any escape in that direction.

"Unless the camp has been moved, we should make contact shortly, sir."

"That sounds good, Phineas. All we can do now is to move in the direction of our advance squads. Who is going to lead the attacking squad?"

"I suggest Austry sir."

"Fine Lieutenant. Let's get on with it gentlemen."

It wasn't long before a rider from the Point Squad arrived to report.

Then, the entire troop moved forward with White leading the way.

When they reached the Point, Lt. White asked for a report.

"The target is less than a mile forward, sir. We counted fifteen men. There were a few darkies moving around, acting like servants, it appears. A couple of Negro women come and go out of the tents. We couldn't see any guards posted, so security is pretty lax. We could ride straight in, seems to me, sir."

"All right Corporal; good report."

"Major, I suggest that we allow the corporal's squad to lead the way for the attacking squad to within a hundred yards or so and then charge the camp."

"Carry on, Lieutenant."

White and Austry left to make arrangements and Mike turned to Sgt. Riley.

"Sergeant, take a squad of men and remain with me in the rear with our captive. Make sure he is tied and gagged."

"Yes sir. Come here, me bucko. Ya wouldn't want me ta turn yas over to tha Dutchman now, would ya?"

Staying in the rear wasn't the most pleasing assignment for Sgt. Riley. But it wasn't long before he heard the bugle sound the charge, followed by shouts and gunshots.

*I hope tis my boys doin the shooting, h*e thought

It didn't last but a few minutes, before everything was quiet and a messenger soon appeared with the report that the target was secured.

As soon as Mike arrived he addressed Lt. Autsry.

"Report, Lieutenant."

"The camp has been secured with no casualties, sir. Our troopers have searched and tied up all the males; Negro men included. Weapons have been collected and thrown into that pile. Tents have been torn down, saddles, and all the crap the hostiles had collected have been put into that pile over there. The horses have been secured. The two Negro women have been told to get dressed and are under guard in that one remaining tent. The flanking squads report that none of the hostiles came their way, so it would appear that we bagged them all."

"Thank you, Lieutenant. Good job."

"Thank you sir."

"You know what we do with marauders and bushwhackers Henry. Use their ropes this time."

"The Negro men too, sir?"

"Not until we have had a chance to question them. Maybe one of the bushwhackers will tell us something about them. It's pretty obvious why the women are in their camp."

Troopers from Austry's platoon began to drag men kicking and cursing toward the trees. It took three or four troopers to handle each captive; but all twelve men were hung within an hour. They hadn't hung the thirteenth man, because he said he could help them find other bushwhackers in this area.

"What information did you get from him?"

"He said they found the Negroes on the road just sittin' there. Said they run off from some plantation, but had no place to go. But he and his mates took 'em for servants. Tha women they just took for pleasure."

"What about other groups of bushwhackers in this area?"

"He knows there are some, sir. But he says he's too scared to rat on the others. They might find him and kill him."

"Sgt. Riley. Form the troop. Tie this fellow behind his horse, please. Lets see if he can be made more afraid of me that the other bushwhackers."

Mounted before the troop, Mike turned toward the remaining killer and grabbed the halter of his horse. He spurred his horse to a gallop, pulling the bound man behind. He rode twice around the formation, dragging the reluctant man in the dirt.

After Mike stopped, the man lay on the ground barley moving. "Sergeant, ask our friend again if he will tell us where the other marauders can be found."

After a moment Sgt. Riley reported. "I'm thinking that he's willin, sir."

"Good. Give him some water and put him on a horse. Let's get on with it Sergeant."

"Lt. White. Detail a squad to collect their weapons. Free the Negro men. We leave in thirty minutes."

"Question, sir?" White asked.

"What is it?"

"One of the Negroes, a man named Ben, says he and his friend want to go with us. He says he's good with horses and his friend named Amos is a good cook. Will you allow them along, sir?"

"Make it clear to both men that we will drop them by the road the first time they cause trouble. Assign the man who is good with horses to Swede. The other fellow can cook for the non-commissioned officers. Inform Sgt. Riley to get each of them a horse and saddle."

"What about the two women?"

"Put them in the supply wagon. We will drop them off in the first town we come to. Until we do, Lieutenant, put them under guard."

Pocataligo, South Carolina

"What in hell is this all about?"

Corporal T.M. Boyer watched as several horsemen rode toward his Point Squad. The rider in the lead carried a white flag.

"Billy, move off to my right a few yards. Tom, you move to the left. Watch for anyone trying to flank us. Jacob, you and Willie stay by my side. Have your Spencer carbines out and cocked, just in case. We'll see what these birds have to say."

"Stay some behind me, you two." Austry nudged his horse ahead to meet the man carrying the white flag.

"Soldier," the man began. "Are you leading this force of men?"

"Yes sir, I am. What can I do for you?"

"I'm the mayor of Pocataligo, son. The men with me and I have ridden out to tell you that the people of our town mean you no harm. We are in hopes that you will not harm us, either. We would like to talk with your commanding officer."

"Well, sir," Boyer said. "I'll send a trooper back to the main body with that message.

The rest of my men and I will stay right here. Willie, ride back and tell the Dutchman what you just heard."

"We have heard of this Dutchman. Is he your commanding officer?"

"Yes he is, sir."

"You came upon a plantation south of here a few days ago. The owner was much impressed with how you and the men of your troop conducted themselves. He thought the man you call the Dutchman was a gentleman."

"May be, mister, but a coupl'a days ago that gentleman had us hang six bushwhackers we had captured. An' he personally used a knife on the seventh man in that bunch to convince him to lead us to another band of killers. When we found them we hung another twelve of the sorry bastards. If that makes him a gentleman, then I'm a monkey's uncle."

"Well, son," The mayor responded. "Because any semblance of law around here has disappeared, your Dutchman has done us a favor. We're thankful to be rid of those killers. He is a gentleman to us, I assure you."

"We'll see how thankful you are after he gets here."

It was a good hour before Willie returned with the Major and a platoon of men.

Corporal Austry rode back to meet them.

"What's the story, Corporal?" Mike asked.

Austry explained the situation.

"Ask the good mayor and his escort to join me back here Corporal. Remain to the rear of their group with your squad, just in case."

"Yes sir."

"Lieutenant, post men on the flanks and to our rear. Have Sergeant Steward join me here."

When the envoys from the town arrived, Mike addressed them.

"First, I must ask you gentlemen. Are you armed?"

"No, Major. We come in peace in hopes of saving the people and property of our town any unnecessary destruction. Will that be possible?"

"We are not here to seek revenge, sir." Mike assured him. "The men of my troop are not looters. Nor do we seek to harm anyone in your town. Your women and your homes are safe.

"Having said that, however, I want you to know that we will destroy any establishment that we believe supports your war against the government of the United States. In addition, sir, we are far ahead of our supply lines, so I will order my men to confiscate food for themselves and feed for our horses."

"We are just a small town whose merchants and service people support the farm economy around here. We do have a small railroad terminal here to move cotton to the port of Charleston. Beyond that, we don't have any factories."

"As long as your citizens are peaceful and offer no resistance, they will not be harmed in any way. It will be necessary, however, for us to tear up some rail track to disable the terminal.

"Do you have any storage buildings at the terminal?"

"There are two buildings, Major. But neither is much larger than a good size shed."

"I'll take a look. We will burn any building that could serve as a warehouse. If we have to do that, I suggest you have your fire control people stand by. We don't want fire to spread to nearby buildings."

"Can I make a suggestion, Major?"

"Of course; I would welcome it, sir."

"I think it would be helpful if you would allow my party to precede you into the town. Our people are very agitated right now. All of us have heard what happened to small towns like Allendale and Barnwell a few days ago. No resistance was offered there either, but your general sacked and burned those towns, anyway.

"So we're fearful of what you and your troops might do here. I would like to give them the assurances you have given me. Once I have a talk with them, I believe you will be given no trouble."

"Very well, sir. I'll hold my men at the outskirts of your town for one hour. Will that be enough time for you mayor?"

"Yes, that should do nicely, Major. As soon as I can, I'll ride out and lead you into the town."

When the mayor and his party left, Mike saw to his men.

"Sgt. Steward."

"Yes sir?"

"Have the bugler sound Officer's Call."

Once together, Mike explained the situation.

"The mayor seems to be determined to avoid trouble. But we will approach the town as though we expect resistance. So tell each trooper to have his Spencer at the ready, but don't have the hammer in firing position. In the meantime, we'll remain here until the mayor returns to escort us into the town."

"Lt. White. "

"Yes sir."

"Secure this area. Have the rest of the men dismount. But they must stay by their mounts."

The officers and non-commissioned officers returned to their platoons. The security squads sped to their posts on the perimeter of the troop. All the troopers watched for any hostile activity.

Back with the main body, Sgt. Riley talked with his troop commander.

"Ya think this will go all right, boyo?"

"Can't be sure, Sarge. We're in South Carolina. So we should expect that there's some serious Yankee haters in town. And even though I do believe the mayor is serious about trying to keep a lid on any disturbance from his townspeople, we must be on the alert. I'll take you and a squad into the town with the mayor. The rest of the troop will remain outside of town and seal off the approaches. I want the men to remain mounted, with their Spencers at the ready. Any disruption, we will respond aggressively."

"Yes sir."

Troopers of the Michigan Brigade had been equipped with Spencer carbines since they arrived in Washington back in December of 1862.

With this weapon, a trooper could get off seven shots without taking the carbine from his shoulder. Reloading was done quickly, too. The trooper accomplished this by extracting a metal tube from the stock of the weapon and inserting another tube containing a fresh seven rounds.

With this weapon the ninety-two men of Mike's troop could deliver a deadly barrage of bullets with reasonable accuracy at two hundred yards. At Gettysburg, Jeb Stuart's cavalry were the first Rebs to face this weapon. The fire was so deadly then, Stuart's men named the troopers of the Michigan Brigade the Michigan Devils.

Unlike most officers, Major Drieborg carried a Spencer, just like his troopers.

"It shouldn't be long before the mayor returns. Then we'll see."

LOWELL, MICHIGAN

The Hecht family was all packed. Ruben had helped Jake with the morning chores and they were just finishing their last breakfast at the Drieborg home.

"I was surprised, Papa," Emma told him. "that Mr. Sullivan found a buyer for our farm so quickly."

"I expected da Bierleins to be interested, Momma." Ruben told her. "Remember, dey have two boys who are Kenny's age. Warren and Brian are too young yet for da var. I tink dose boys are going to be good farmers; and our land is right next to them, too. Our land is perfect for dem."

"Did we get a good price, Papa?"

"Ya. I tink ve got a fair price, Momma; and for da two milk cows, too. Now ve don't owe a mortgage to da bank here in Lowell. So I tink God looked after da Hechts. I vish you didn't spend so much on tings for da house, though."

"Oh you don't do you!" Emma snapped back. "I noticed you didn't skimp on the repairs to the barn and the other buildings. My heavens, Papa; the animals will be more comfortable in their house than we will be in ours."

"See vhat I have to put up mit, Jake?"

"Put up with?" Emma continued. "How would you like to sleep out in that palace you call a barn for awhile, Ruben Hecht?"

"I think you're in trouble now, Ruben." Jake chuckled.

"Ya Jake, I'm afraid you're right. Come, Momma, let's move into our new palace, eh?"

Both the Drieborgs' wagon and the new Hecht wagon were loaded. Their new home was only a couple of miles away, so it would not take them long to complete the move.

"Dat lumber we got from Walter Bauer was really good stuff, don't you think, Ruben?"

"Ya it vas. Und his sawmill is only down da road from my place too. Since ve used trees from my place, it was easy to get them to him, too. That stream on the hill above his place gives him the power he needs to run his saws."

"You're right, Ruben. All things considered, you got the lumber you needed pretty cheap. The Bauers are a nice family, too."

"Yes dey are, Jake."

"Julia," Jake Drieborg began. "Your Papa told me you just received a letter from Michael. Is der anything you can share with his Momma and me?"

"Oh, I'm sorry. With all the excitement of moving, I forgot to tell you. He says that he and his men are in South Carolina, and headed north. He is well and assures me that this war is nearing its end. The way things are going down there, he figures he will be home by this June at the latest."

"Thank you, Julia. I'll tell his Momma what you said."

Pocataligo,
South Carolina

Mike's troop had secured the perimeter of the settlement. Then, he, Sergeant Riley and Corporal Boyer's squad followed the mayor into the town. They were led to the center of town.

As they began to dismount, a shot rang out. Sergeant Boyer was literally blown off his horse. He landed on his back in the middle of the road, his chest covered with blood. The startled horses pulled on their reins, bucked and turned. The troopers let their horses go and turned toward the sound. They knelt in the street, weapons up and ready.

"Between the buildings," one trooper shouted. "Someone's there with a shotgun!"

A hail of bullets flew in that direction.

"The shooter's down," another trooper yelled. Two men rushed in that direction.

A moment later they were looking down at the body of a boy, shotgun at his side.

"This kid's not even a teenager."

"Maybe he's not; but Boyer's just as dead."

Mike grabbed the mayor by his coat and pushed the barrel of his pistol under his chin.

" Mr. Mayor, you assured me that this would not happen. Tell me now, why I shouldn't burn the entire town to the ground."

"Because the rest of the townspeople are not causing any trouble, because it was the act of only one hate-filled little boy. That's why, Major."

"Take me to this boy's house. Now!"

Mike and his squad arrived at the boy's home on the outskirts of town. He shouted for anyone inside to come out. A lady and a man on crutches came out on the porch.

A trooper carried the body of the dead boy and threw it on the porch.

"Your boy killed one of my men. Now he's dead, thanks to the hate you filled him with. Instead of punishing the whole town, I intend to burn your home to the ground.

"Lt. Austry. Escort the lady into the house so she can pack a bag. Take two troopers with you; Lord only knows she might take a notion to attack you inside."

The lady on the porch heard him. She walked into the yard toward Mike, and looked defiantly up at him sitting astride his horse.

"We heard what you thieves did over in Georgia. Lots of us got kin over that way. Other blue bellies pillaged and burned Barnwell and other villages to the west of us, too. So I know we can't stop you from burnin' this poor excuse for a house. But I want you to know where our boy's hatred come from.

The little boy you just killed had his older brother starved and frozen to death in your Yankee prison up in Illinois. His other brother just went off with General Johnston. You'll probably kill him, too. My husband, the boy's father, was so badly crippled at Gettysburg he can't even tend our small garden.

"Your Momma would be ashamed' a you if she knew you were attacking people like us and burning our homes. I'd try ta kill ya myself if my husband could care for himself alone."

"Yes ma'am. Sgt. Riley,"

"Yes sir."

"Move these people out and burn this house immediately, Sergeant.

"Mayor, I will order a platoon of my men into town. You will escort them to each house and building. They will remove every person they find and confiscate any weapons found. These men will be under orders to burn any building in which anyone resists. Do I make myself clear, sir?"

The mayor sat slumped on his horse. Tears ran down his face as he watched the old wooden house burst into flame..

"Sir, I asked you a question."

"Yes, Major. I understand. Will you burn the rest of the town, too?"

"Look over to your left, Mr. Mayor. Do you see that smoke rising to the sky? That's the home of that boy who killed my trooper. The answer to your question is, not yet. But be careful, sir. Any more difficulty and my men will leave your town a pile of ashes."

While Mike stayed with a squad in the center of town, the mayor led Lt. White and his men from building to building. Anyone they found inside was sent into the street where Lt. Austry and his platoon placed them under guard.

The search for weapons continued for hours. It seemed as though there were weapons of one sort or another in every building; old swords, an ancient pistol, and more than a few shotguns and squirrel guns. All of them were thrown on a pile in the street and set ablaze.

"Sgt. Riley. Bring up the supply wagon. Take a squad and forage for food and feed through the town. You know what we need. Don't allow the men to pillage, though."

"Yes sir."

"Lt. White. Now that you're done with the search of the town, detail a squad to move the townspeople to that field over there. Have them all sit down and post a guard over them."

Yes sir."

"Sgt. Killeen. Take a squad over to the rail terminal. Start a fire. We'll create some bow ties of the rail tracks before we leave. If you find any cotton or other goods waiting shipment, set it on fire."

"Yes sir."

"Sgt. Swede. Take a look in the livery and in the various sheds behind these buildings for horses and livestock. Round up any you think would be useful to us."

"Yes sir.

Turning to the mayor, Mike reminded him. "I trusted you, sir. Now you can trust me to do what I threatened to do if your people did not cooperate. Remember what I told you? We would treat your people and your town with respect unless you couldn't control your people and resistance was shown us. Well, sir, one of my men was killed. So you didn't control your people.

"I will still not allow my men to loot or harm anyone. But we will take more supplies and stock than we otherwise would have. And I will order my men to do much worse if anyone else in this town allows their hate of us to overcome their good sense."

"May I speak, Major?"

"Yes, you may."

"I can't find the words to express my shock and regret at the death of your trooper. Please keep in mind, sir, a mere child caused his death. It would be an honor if you would allow us to bury your dead trooper in our own cemetery."

Mike couldn't help but laugh out loud. "Excuse my cynicism Mr. Mayor; but I don't think my men would allow that, even if I would. Once, I thought you spoke for your people. I will not make that mistake again. No sir. We will take care of Sergeant Boyer's body in our own way.

"I suggest, Mr. Mayor, that you join your fellow townspeople in that field over there. We should be done and gone before long, unless you have more surprises for us."

GRAND RAPIDS

With help from the Drieborgs and the Hechts, George was able to open his bakery by late February. Rose Drieborg and her daughter Susan stayed in one of the two bedrooms of the upstairs living quarters, while they worked at the bakery with George.

With their help, George was able to keep the bakery open while he visited the hotels and restaurants. He took them samples of his bread, biscuits and sweet rolls. His pitch to those in charge was simple.

"Why do you spend all that money to keep a full bakery staff, when I can supply you with most of what you need?"

The answer he always got to his question was: "I wouldn't if I could depend on you to deliver tasty baked goods, on time, every day. Right now, my bakery crew does that. Can you?"

"Tell you what. Before you lay anybody off, try my bread and biscuits. I'll provide these items for your lunch crowd for one week at no cost to you, and a second week at half the normal price. You can cancel my deliveries any time during this trial period, of course.

"After that, if you decide to buy my goods every day, you can lay off your baker. Then you might take your payroll savings and hire a pastry chef. That person will make your restaurant unique."

Eventually, with his tasty breads and rolls, low prices and timely deliveries, George's marketing efforts succeeded. He began to provide one item or another to each of the three hotels in town: the Rathburn

House, the Eagle Hotel, as well as the Hindsill Hotel. In fact, his goods were in such demand; he hired a baker who had been let go from the kitchen at the Hindsill Hotel.

At supper one evening George talked with Susan and Rose Drieborg about how things were going. "Susan, you and your mother have been staying here for three weeks now. The two of you have really impressed the daily shoppers."

For the daily street customers, Rose and Susan baked sweet rolls and pies. While George was out working with the hotels, they were at the bakery giving away free slices of pie and bits of rolls. After two weeks giving away samples, they began to sell out every day.

Susan had a suggestion. "Now that things are going well with the hotels, George, I think you should take some of our coffee rolls to the restaurants. If you go to one of the coffee shops at a time, it might not be too much for us to handle the increased demand."

"Sounds good, Susan. Why don't we start with some of your cinnamon rolls? How about you cut each of them in half for samples, so more men will get a taste? Would that work?"

Rose Drieborg got into the conversation. "Today is Thursday. Give us until Monday George. That will give you a few days to line up the first coffee shop, and us time to get organized. Besides, we're just breaking in the new baker you hired this week."

"That sounds good to me, Rose. Is that all right with you, Susan?"

"Oh! Good." She gushed. "I'm so excited, I know I'll have trouble going to sleep tonight."

So one of the downtown restaurants that had a good morning and afternoon coffee crowd would be their next target. Sweet rolls would be the hook to land them as clients, one at a time. Another hire might be necessary. This time, George thought, he would talk with a baker fired from the Eagle Hotel.

South Carolina

"Why are we camped in this damn field when we could be bunked in one of those dry and warm houses back in Pocataligo?" Stan Killeen complained.

"You mean because the Dutchman did not trust anyone back there? Maybe he thought someone would slit your throat while you slept in one of their soft beds tonight; or poisoned the food you forced them to cook for you," Bill Anderson retorted.

"After Boyer was shot by that damn little kid, you'd think we at least would've burned the town; like we heard Kilpatrick did to Barnwell and Allendale; Sherman left hardly a town standing in Georgia. But no, our gentleman major won't have any'a that."

"Can't have it both ways, Stan; hot eats and a nice bed in a warm house, or burn it?"

"We got neither you old fool. But we could've. Enjoy the place, then burn it I say. Instead what we got is hardtack, weak coffee and hard ground to sleep on!"

"Ya got a point there, my man. But in the morning, Amos will fix us a good breakfast with those eggs we found in town. Think of that while you sleep on this cold ground."

Dave Steward joined the conversation. "Finding that freed slave was the best thing that happened to us in a long time. I haven't et so good since I was home last. He can make something tasty out of practically nothing. We haven't had biscuits that good since George got a medical discharge."

"I suppose you're goin' to credit the Dutchman with getting Amos for us, too," Stan snapped, still irritated.

Dave continued to speak on the subject. "Could've kept the man for himself don't ya know; as a cook or a servant maybe. Instead he assigned him to us. Seems ta' me we should give him at least an "atta-boy" for that. Don't you?"

"Now you've got a point, Steward," Stan admitted.

"Oh ya. Did you hear about that arithmetic book one' a the guys found when we was searching the school building back in Pocatalico?"

When no one said they had, Dave continued.

"Well it's the darndest thing I ever heard. In this schoolbook, the kids were asked arithmetic questions like,

"If one confederate soldier can kill seven of the invading Yankees, how many can seven confederate soldiers kill?

"Another question was,

"If the invading Yankees can burn five homes in one day, how many can they burn in six days?"

Swede was the first to respond. "So vat is da answer, Dave?"

"I don't really care what the answer to the arithmetic problem is; that's not the point I'm trying to make."

"But vy you tell us dis den?"

"I'm telling ya because it's interesting that they are using school lessons to teach their little kids to hate us Yankees."

"I don't much care if it is interesting," Stan interrupted. "I'm more interested in why our cook has not rustled up some tasty grub tonight."

"Speaking of Amos," Bill Anderson asked. "Seems ta me I saw him sulking around that stand of trees over there. What in heaven's name is wrong with him?"

"The other day, I heard him mumbling 'bout some ghost or other. Could that be what's got him worked up?"

"Hey, Amos!" Stan shouted toward the tree line. "Get your big ass over here."

Shortly, the big fellow walked into the light of the campfire.

"Yes massa?"

"Stop calling me that! You're a free man now. Call me Sergeant, you hear?"

"Yes massa."

"I give up. You find out what's bothering this dumb shit, Anderson."

"Why you hiding in those trees, Amos?" Bill asked him.

"I don't wants da phantom rider lady ta gets me. Dat's why."

"If you're talking about that lady who is said to ride a white palomino horse at night, that's up in North Carolina. That's a hundred miles away or more, Amos. So there's no need for you to hide from her here."

"Maybe, massa. But a nigger over in G Troop tol me we's gots one too. He said he saw a woman ride a big white stallion right through their camp a few nights ago; yeller hair flying an shrieking like a mad woman. She turned around and rode through again. Some men shot at her; their bullets when right through her. Some others jumped on their horses an chased her. Theys ain't came back yet.'

"Oh, my Lord!" Stan chuckled. "You are as dumb as a stump. If there was such a rider it must have been real, cause there isn't no such thing as a ghost. Besides those troopers of G Troop couldn't hit a barn if they were inside with the doors shut. I'll bet the men who rode off are probably just gone on picket duty; be back after their relief gets to em."

"If'n you says so, massa Stan. But all the same, I'm goin ta sleep in that bunch'a trees yonder, if'n ya'll don't mind."

"Sleep where you want Amos." Dave Steward told him. "Just make sure you're up to fix breakfast for us at sunup."

"Yes sir. Thank ya, massa."

South of Columbia, South Carolina

At his regimental headquarters, Mike joined the other troop commanders at Officer's Call.

"We've received orders from Division to step up our advance toward Columbia. General Sherman has decided to go directly for the capital of South Carolina instead of taking Charleston first.

"Our navy has had that city blockaded for some time and artillery batteries on Morris Island have been shelling the city at will, most every night for over a year. They can shell it to rubble any time they want. So it's ours for the taking whenever we choose. To the east of us, General Sherman sent units out that way only as a diversion.

General Kilpatrick has units to the west of us. We are to spearhead a drive straight north to Columbia. General Burbridge has joined us to lead that movement.

"Gentlemen," Burbridge began. "Our march north through this den of Rebels has gone swiftly. We have driven a stake into the heart of the Confederacy. The city of Columbia is the place where secession first took place in December of 1860. We will teach the people there the consequences of their treason.

"You will receive your orders through the usual channels, gentlemen. You are dismissed."

As the troop commanders began to disperse, an aide to the general approached Mike.

"Major, a word, sir."

"Yes Captain. How can I help you?"

"The general wishes a word with you, sir."

"Of course. Lead the way, Captain."

"Major Drieborg reporting as ordered General." Mike said, standing at attention in front of the general's desk.

"Take a chair, Major."

"According to the reports you have filed with your regimental headquarters, you have been very careful since our last discussion."

"I don't quite know what you mean, by careful, sir."

"I see you aggressively pursued bushwhackers and hung any you captured, but you hesitated to burn civilian property."

"Thus far, my men have hung nineteen marauders. We have taken provisions we needed for ourselves and our mounts. We burned storage buildings, tore up railroad tracks, confiscated weapons in the hands of civilians and took care of former slaves we came across. As you might have seen in the report, we did burn one home in retaliation for the killing of one of my men."

"Yes Major, I did notice. That was in the town of Pocataligo, was it not?"

"Yes it was, general."

"Your response to the killing of a trooper in the service of the United States was in my opinion totally inadequate. Consequently, the Ohio cavalry moving in your rear was ordered to take corrective action."

"May I ask what corrective measures were ordered, sir?"

"Oh, you need not ask, Major. In hope that you will not be remiss in the future, I want you to know what was ordered. That cavalry troop was ordered to burn every building in the town; homes, churches, businesses; every single one. And further, they were ordered to kill every animal that they didn't take with them.

"I want every Rebel son of a bitch in South Carolina to know what will happen if one of our men is killed or even attacked when we enter a town. You did not leave that message.

"Instead, Major, it appears that you coddled these people. It was reported by that Ohio troop commander that the traitors in that town referred to you as the Gentleman Major. You evidently forgot that they are our enemies. I am here to remind you of that fact and to insist that you will treat them as such in the future.

"It would appear that I did not make myself clear the last time we discussed this issue. Are you hearing me clearly this time?"

"Yes sir."

"Believe me, Drieborg, if it was in my power at this moment, I would strip you of command and place you in charge of regimental latrines. You can be assured that if I see any more of this coddling of traitors from you, I will bring you before a military court- martial on charges of disobeying a direct order.

"By the way, the troop commander of that Ohio unit told me personally that you are a Confederate sympathizer. He worked with you in Savannah; remember Captain Robert Taft? He appears to have you pegged; and so do I."

*   *   *   *

Back in his troop area, Mike called Lieutenants White and Austry along with Sgt. Riley to his tent. He told them of his encounter with General Burbridge.

"Can I speak freely, Major?" White asked.

"Of course you can, Phineas. What are your thoughts?"

"After your first meeting with Burbridge, you can't be surprised at his reaction to what you've had our troop do thus far in South Carolina. His reputation from Kentucky is that he is a vengeance man. You applied a reasonable standard for our actions to this point. He doesn't want reasonable. He wants retribution.

"Do you disagree with my assessment?"

"No I don't, Phineas."

"Are you prepared to give him the uncompromising vengeance he wants?" Austry asked.

"No, I am not Henry. I will continue to apply what you referred to as a reasonable standard to the actions of this troop. This war is virtually over. Who knows, maybe it will end before he catches up with me on this issue."

"You're a good leader, Phineas. I don't want to drag you down, too. If you wish I will approve your transfer to another troop."

"Thanks, Mike. But I don't want out of your command. Actually, I'm all for your approach to the treatment of civilians and their property here. I just wanted to be clear about what lies ahead. Truth be told, it's sort of exciting walking that thin line the Gentleman Major has drawn in the sand."

"Thanks, Phineas. I appreciate that."

"And you Henry. How do you feel about my decision?"

"Recently, I heard a very important man, a general, truth be known, say that you are a man of good character. So I think I'll trust his judgment and throw in with you sir; if you'll have me that is."

'Glad to have you Henry."

"How about you, Sergeant Riley; do you have any thoughts on the matter?"

"Laddie, I've been watchin ya since ya was an eighteen-ear-old private. I'd' a been surprised and disappointed if ya had given the lieutenants here any other answer. Ya don hafta worry about me. I'll stand aside ya to hell an back."

"Thank you my friend. If my judgment of Burbridge is near accurate, it may just come to that.

"For now though, I'm off to regiment to get our orders. I expect they'll want us to move north quickly. So have the men get ready for an early start. Prepare three days rations and feed. Have the Swede and his new Negro helper check all the mounts. I'll get back to you later."

"By the way, sir," Sgt. Riley said. "During yer meeting with the General we had mail call. This one came for you, sir."

"Thanks Sergeant. I could use some cheerful news right now."

✳   ✳   ✳   ✳

As soon as the others left his tent, Mike sat down and opened his letter; it was from Julia.

My Dearest Michael.

I hope this letter finds you well. Everyone here is fine. Except, we Marylanders are having a hard time adjusting to the weather in Michigan. I can't believe all this snow and ice. As you know, we used to get snow; sometimes a lot of it. But it usually melted in a few days. Not here. It just keeps coming. It's piled as high as my windowsill, and it's only February. When does it go away?

When I am in bed at night and hear the cold winter wind roaring outside, I imagine you holding me close like you did in Baltimore. What a delicious feeling..

I received your last letter and am glad to hear that you have not been in any battles. You said you have to live off the land. I find it hard to believe that you order your men to steal food from the farmers you encounter on your march through South Carolina. Remember when our farm in Maryland was raided? Those terrible men took most everything we had. And because we supported the Union, they killed most of our animals that they didn't take. Then they burned our barn for good measure. Do you have your men do that because the people support the Confederacy? At least I hope you don't let your men attack the women.

Whatever you are doing, I don't think I want to know about it. You men and your war! I hate it! Just keep yourself safe and come home to me. I can't write anymore, I'm too upset just thinking about what your army is probably doing to those poor farmers just for what their leaders did. But I love you anyway.

With all my love,

Julia

*   *   *   *

Phew! What a woman. Hundreds of miles away, she lets me have it, both barrels. At least she is safe in Michigan. But I am not. So I best get about the business of helping to end this war. I'll write her later.

ANOTHER CONFRONTATION

"What the hell is this?" General Burbridge asked, outraged.

Lt. Col. Kidd, Regimental Executive officer, responded in the only way he could.

"It's a report form Major Drieborg, sir. He has sent a Sergeant McCarty, under guard to the provost, for the crime of rape. All the signed testimony from eyewitnesses is there too, sir."

"I can see that, Colonel. Don't get cute with me. I've got one smart ass in this Drieborg to contend with, I don't need another."

"Yes sir."

"At the earliest, I want Drieborg to explain his action in this matter. Do you understand Colonel?"

"Yes sir. I'll get him back here as soon as possible."

It took a full day, but Mike reported to the general.

"Major Drieborg reporting as ordered, sir."

"Sit down, Major. No, don't sit down. This will only take me a minute.

"I believe you trumped up this whole damn thing about one of my foragers raping some Southern trash just to irritate me. I talked to Sgt. McCarty. He insists that the girl lured him on and she consented to the act. He says that you put your men up to those statements they signed against him. What do you have to say in your defense, Major?"

"I don't have to defend my actions, sir. McCarty's the one who has to defend his. My men saw what they saw. In the paperwork, I also included statements from the parents of the girl. They witnessed the rape. The fact that her clothing was in tatters might suggest that the act was far from consensual, sir."

"You might want to look at the signature of the arresting officer on that report, sir. It happens to be that of a Lt. Henry Austry. General Sherman might not be amused if you take the word of a rapist over that of his nephew.

"As for intentionally irritating you, sir; I don't even think about you at all General. I just follow the rules. Rape is a crime, even in a war zone."

Burbridge virtually leaped across his field desk to stand in front of Drieborg. Several inches taller, Mike had to bend his head down in order to look the fuming general in the eye.

"This is war, not a Washington tea party, mister. You may have won this round, but I expect the Gentleman Major will trip up soon, and I'll be waiting with a hanging party. Now get out of my sight. Confederate sympathizers like you sicken me."

COLUMBIA, SOUTH CAROLINA

On February 16 Sherman's forces reached the southern bank of the Congaree River, within sight of Columbia. Mayor Thomas Goodwyn and a delegation met the lead elements of Sherman's army and surrendered the city. They were given the promise of protection for the citizens of the city and their property.

Nevertheless, Union artillery units were ordered to fire on Columbia. Over three hundred shells were fired into the city. Only following this bombardment were troops sent to occupy the town.

"You know the drill, Sergeant," Mike reminded him. "Spencer carbines at the ready; spread our column on either side of the road. Look out for snipers. Remind the men that we're here to secure the city, not destroy it or to kill civilians."

"Yes sir."

"Any thoughts, Phineas?" Mike asked

"This is the biggest city I've seen since we were in Savannah. That place was spared the torch; but I have a bad feeling about this operation. It appears to me that firing shells for almost an hour into a city that is not being defended, and in fact had been surrendered, does not bode well. Are you sure General Burbridge is not in charge of this operation?"

Mike had to chuckle at that last remark. "Don't know about that, Phineas. All we can do is be alert and ready for anything. We can only control our own behavior. Let's see if we can at least do that."

As it turned out, Mike's troop found thousands of Union troops already in the city. In broad daylight, looting by hooligans and Federals, white and Negro alike, had already begun. Buildings were burning on every street.

"Major," Sergeant Riley shouted. "We've got some troops carrying pails of whiskey out'a that building down the street. Do we stop'em?"

"Our orders are pretty vague, Sergeant; they don't mention whiskey. As long you keep it out of our boys' hands, I'm inclined to ignore it. Be like trying to stop the flow of a river, seems to me. It might help us, though, if we move out of this area at a bit faster pace, Sergeant."

"Yes sir."

Further on they came upon a building with barred windows. The front doors were open and scruffy looking men in the tattered remnants of blue uniforms lounged on the front steps.

"Sir, I think those men over there are wearin' whats' left'a uniforms. With your permission, I'll check it out."

"By all means, Sergeant."

"Ya ought ta talk to these fellas sir. They be Union soldiers kept prisoner in that building; the city insane asylum. They've had it pretty bad, it appears."

"Lt. White, secure the area. I'm going to talk with these men. Have Corporal Robinson join me. He's the closest thing to a doctor we have. Maybe we can help these men."

While Mike and Cpl. Robinson were talking with them, Lt. Little was alerted by screams coming from down the street.

"Sgt. Riley, stay with the main body," he ordered. "I'm going to take the 1st Platoon and investigate that screaming."

"Yes sir."

It wasn't long before he returned with four rather drunk Union soldiers, all under guard.

"Major, may I have a moment, sir?"

"Of course. What is it Phineas?"

White gave Mike the background information. "So I ordered these four disarmed and arrested on the charge of rape. Now what do we do?"

"We take them to the nearest provost marshal and let his people take care of the matter. Is there anything else?"

"Yes sir. The lady who says she owns the house where this took place wants to talk to you."

Mike rode up the street with an escort. Intending to knock, he noticed that the door had been knocked clear off its hinges. He rapped on the doorframe rather than just barging into the house.

"My goodness; a Yankee with manners," he heard someone inside say.

Oh my goodness! He thought, surprised at the person who stood before him.

"Didn't expect to see a Negro lady, did you? What kind of officer are you, anyway?"

"I'm a major in the United States Cavalry, ma'am."

"Polite too? My, oh my.

"Well, Major. I'm a free Negro lady who makes dresses for the most important women of this town; at least I did before your army got here The lady standing beside me whose clothing is so torn is my assistant. Your four soldiers raped her and me. Probably would've killed us when they got drunker and tired of us. But your men saved us from that fate. Thank you for that, Major."

"You're welcome, ma'am. Those four soldiers are not in my command. None of my men would do such a thing. Rape is a serious offense even for us Yankees, ma'am."

"Even the rape of Negro women, Major?"

"Yes ma'am. I'm not aware of any exceptions in our rules of conduct on this matter."

"What will happen to the men you apprehended?"

"We will turn them over to our provost marshal. He will read the statements made by my men and decide what to do with them. It would help if you would write a statement for you and your servant to sign. I'll turn in with ours."

"Excuse me, Major. But I learned long ago that the word of a Negro is not worth much in a white man's court. So I have a different punishment to suggest. As a dressmaker, I am very good with sharp scissors. Allow me a few minutes with each of the four men. I'll let them know how much I enjoyed their attention. You will have no need for a provost marshal. They would probably need a doctor, though. "

"As much as that solution appeals to me, ma'am, it would be against regulations. What I can do, though, is get a couple of my men to repair your front door. I can't leave men to guard you and your home. But I can take you to a safe place. I'm told there is a Catholic convent up the road some. I'm sure they would welcome you."

"I earned my freedom, Major, and paid for this house out of my own earnings. I used to own my helper here. She is a free person now and she chooses to stay with me and work for wages. But I'm not a foolish woman. I'll accept your offer to fix my front door and your offer to find us a safe place to wait for the end of your army's pillage of my city."

"Yes ma'am. While I'm seeing to that would you write out that statement I mentioned for my provost marshal and pack a valise? I do need to move along."

On his way out the door Mike snapped. "Killeen, get someone to fix this door, pronto. Then find a wagon and escort the women of this house to it."

Before long both tasks were completed. The only problem remaining was to find a horse and harnesses for the wagon.

"The Dutchman's not going to snap my head off again," Killeen said to no one in particular. "You prisoners will have the honor of pulling the wagon that will carry these fine ladies to safety."

"Tie these drunks to the wagon tongue." After some jostling and over their loud complaints, the prisoners were tied in place.

"Listen up, you louts," Killeen warned. "I'm going ta be the one driving this wagon. Any problem with you and I'll whip the shirt off yer back. Or, this fella alongside me might just shoot you dead. The sooner you get ta pulling, the sooner we get where we're going."

When they reached the convent, they found it a smoldering ruin.

"Sorry, ladies," Mike offered. "Do you know of another place where I might take you?"

"I think it would be best if you allowed us to return to my home. Could you send an escort to see us safely there?"

"I can do that if you insist, ma'am." She did.

"Lt. Austry. Take your platoon and escort these ladies back to their home. Leave the wagon here. Sorry, ma'am, you and your helper will have to ride a horse back to your place."

"That's all right, Major. Thank you for your help. Believe me, we appreciated it."

"Sgt. Steward, get me two horses from your platoon. You'll have them back shortly."

Before the ladies left with their escort, Mike slipped a loaded pistol into each woman's valise.

They may need these before this night is over.

"Sgt. Riley. Have the men dismount and secure the area. We'll wait here until Lt. Austry and his detail return."

"Yes sir."

Provost Marshal

It was near dawn before Mike's exhausted men found a provost marshal and turned over the four prisoners.

"We'll put these birds with the others we have in custody. But I'm so short of men I may just have to turn them loose. What did you say you arrested them for?"

"Rape, Captain. I'd sure be sorry to see them released."

"I hope we don't have to, Major. There's a fresh brigade of infantry due in the city this morning to help us stop all the looting. These hooligans set two new fires for each one firefighters get under control. Then the wind picks it up and fire spreads to another part of town. I'll bet half this damn city is in ashes, or will soon be.

"Could you stay and help me here until that brigade of soldiers arrive, Major?"

"I wouldn't mind helping out, but I have orders to rendezvous with my regiment north of the city. We lost a lot of time looking for you to drop off these four rapists. Sorry to leave, but we have to be on our way."

LEAVING SOUTH CAROLINA

At Regimental Officers Call, Col. Kidd revealed the plans to move into North Carolina.

"Now that Columbia has been captured, there's only mop up duty from there, north to the southern border of North Carolina. We're being sent ahead to lead General Kilpatrick's cavalry into that state. Our orders are to move quickly, so there will be no wagon trains carrying supplies for the regiment. Each troop will be responsible for its own provisions.

"We've lived off the land before; you know the drill. But let me remind you what General Sherman said. And this is a quote, gentlemen: "...deal as moderately and fairly by North Carolina as possible". Caution you men again, no looting; my staff will inspect your troop supply wagon from time to time; trooper knapsacks, too.

"Enough of that for now. We leave tomorrow morning at daybreak, so let's look at the maps."

*   *   *   *

Back with his men, Mike reviewed the situation.

"Gentlemen, we leave at five in the morning. Three days of rations."

"How are the mounts, Swede?"

"Most are good, sir. A few are a bit lame. A few days rest would be goot for dem."

"We don't have a few days, Sergeant."

"I vill manage dem, sir. In da morning ve be ready."

"See to it. How is your helper Ben working out, Sergeant?"

"He knows animals, sir. He's a big help."

"Lt. White. Pick a squad for the Point. We need to make twenty miles tomorrow."

"Yes sir."

"Lt. Austry. Select squads from your platoon and send one to each flank. Tell them to keep the main body in sight at all times."

"Yes sir."

✳   ✳   ✳   ✳

The troop got under way without incident the following morning. The sun was soon high in the sky and Mike was with the main body.

I was told that this map is very accurate. The open country ahead will help us avoid ambushes. It was good news that the colonel was told to crack down on looting. No problem for my command. I wonder if the other units will pay any attention to the order?

I can see a rider galloping back from the Point.

"Sir. There is a group of buildings ahead. The Point awaits instructions."

"Lt. White. Take the First Platoon and investigate."

"Yes sir."

"Halt the troop, Sergeant Riley. Inform the flank squads."

"Yes Sir."

The troopers knew enough to take advantage of the opportunity and dismount, check their horse blanket for wrinkles, and tighten the synch again. Each man then stood by his mount on the left side and held his horse by its bridle. Spencer rifle in hand, they faced the flank, ready to remount and move out or even return fire if necessary.

"Lt. Austry."

"Yes sir."

"Move forward right now on the right flank with your third squad. Clear the approach to the buildings from that side. I'll go with the third platoon on the left flank and clear the approach to the left of the buildings. Lt. White will enter the area from its south. Move at a trot. Keep an eye to your flank, Lieutenant."

"Yes sir."

It wasn't long before men from all three elements of Mike's troop were inspecting the buildings.

"Phineas, did you secure the perimeter?"

"Yes sir. Henry's with the Point right now."

"Sgt. Riley. Take a squad and our supply wagon. You know what we need."

"Yes sir."

"Phineas. You stay with the main body. Send a squad and Sgt. Killeen with me to find someone I can talk with."

They entered what appeared to be the main house.

"What do you think Stan? Is this a town or a good sized plantation?'

"Can't rightly tell, Mike. Whatever it tis, where are the people?"

"We're not that far from Columbia. After word about what happened there got up this way, I wouldn't blame them if they were hiding. Maybe they're in that stand of trees on the other side of that field."

"Want us to go an search out there, sir?"

"No. Just go through all the buildings. Be careful, Stan. Keep your men in pairs. You stay by the front door as they go through each building. You know the drill."

It took a good hour to carefully inspect all the structures. Mike met with White and Riley afterwards.

"We found some food in the smokehouse and grain in the barn. Enough for a couple of meals," Riley reported. There's a few milkers in that barn; pigs too. We're leavin them, sir. But we're takin some chickens in the supply wagon."

"Good, Sergeant," Mike responded. "Killeen's crew didn't find much in the buildings. The stove in the main house over there was warm. So I expect the inhabitants saw our Point men and fled. Their blacksmith's place had a hot fire going, too."

"Want us to check out those woods, sir?"

"If we found the people over there, even slaves, what would we accomplish with that Phineas? We've taken all the supplies we need and our orders are to move north quickly. No, I think we let the units that follow us solve the mystery of the missing people."

"No, I think we move out. It's only ten in the morning, so we'll take advantage of the daylight. Form up the troop, Phineas, and send word out to Henry to move out with his Point Squad."

"Yes sir."

"Sgt. Riley."

"As soon as we clear these buildings, send out the flank squads. Let's move now, Sergeant."

"Yes sir."

That search went well. The men seem to know their business. Unless we run into a Confederate force we'll get our twenty miles in during daylight today. In a couple of hours I'll start looking for a place to camp for the night. According to this map, there's an open spot with a river running through, I just about where we should stop for the night. We'll need water for our mounts and wood for our cooking fires. I'll see.

*   *   *   *

That evening, Mike met with his non-coms and his officers.

"Well," he began. "Any observations you want to share since we left Columbia?"

Bill Anderson spoke first. "After what we seen in Columbia, it sure was peaceful. I could go for this kind of ride all the way to Michigan."

"Well, my friend," Stan judged. "We're not even out of South Carolina yet, bucko. No telling what the Rebs have in store for us down the road; maybe tomorrow, even."

"He's right about that, lads," Riley agreed. "Check on yer guard mount tonight. And warn yer men to be special alert tomorrow. According to the map tha major has, we move through some hills filled with trees soon. Good place for an ambush."

"Now that you mention it, Sarge, I've got the map right here. Let's all take a look.

"Right now, we're about here, I figure; still in South Carolina. We bypassed this town of Camden to our west and we are now southeast of the town of Cheraw, right here. If we make good time tomorrow, we should be at the border of North Carolina in two days time; over here, probably.

"All that space just over the North Carolina border doesn't look like open ground, does it, Mike?"

"No, it doesn't, Henry. These shadings represent vegetation and trees. These squiggly circles show us hills with valleys in between. The more squiggles, the steeper the hill."

Dave Steward jumped into the discussion. " So it looks like a lot of ground ahead will have good spots for an ambush."

"Good observation, Dave," Lt. White observed.

"If Regiment leaves us out front, we will move into North Carolina day after tomorrow. We'll be heading northeast toward Fayetteville. I can't imagine the Rebs just letting us take a Sunday afternoon stroll all the way there. After all, Johnston has thirty thousand men or more out front of us somewhere. He's bound to use them at some point."

"Shouldn't ve run inta dem before anybody else, Mike?" Swede asked.

"Lucky us," Stan interrupted. "I can hardly wait."

"That's the general idea of us out here in front, Swede. But I'm told that Johnston's a wily old bird. He could stamp us out like a boot on a bug, but then he would alert our main force of his presence. So instead, he might just let us go by and wait to attack Kilpatrick's force behind us.

"Keep in mind what Stan and the sarge just said," Mike concluded. "We will review the situation at least once a day and check this map, too. But the key to our survival is to keep the men on their toes. Keep them alert."

"If there is nothing else, I'll see you men at 5AM tomorrow."

$$*   *   *   *$$

Over the next two days in South Carolina, Mike's troop came upon many small farms and two or three good-sized rice-growing operations.

The first rice field they came across, Stan observed, "Can you imagine bending over in this sun and wallowing around in all that muck up to yer knees all day just to grow some rice? Better be a good market to get me doing that."

Dave Steward, the fruit farmer from Newaygo responded. "Mike told me that he learned a bit about rice growing when he was with the Congressman in Washington. Says, there is a big demand for it overseas. Says it's a big cash crop; like wheat has become in our West."

"Think you're going ta grow it on that rocky ground at your place? You're lucky the frost don't get your fruit trees every spring."

"No, Stan, I'm not going to try growing it. The climate's not right in Michigan. But I like to find out about new things, especially stuff about farming. I find it interesting. You ever tasted rice?"

"No, and it doesn't appeal to me in the least."

"We got a bag of it at that last farm. Amos knows how to fix it. He's going to boil some up tonight; throw in some chicken and greens. Says it tastes real good. That's all we're having with our bread, so you'd better try some."

"Amos, you scoundrel." Stan shouted over at him. "What's this rice business you fixin tonight?"

"Good stuff, massa Stan. You love my rice gumbo. I knows you will, fer sure."

"I'd better like it, my man; I'd better."

✳   ✳   ✳   ✳

"Those are shots I hear off to the right flank. You hear'em, Stan?"

"You bet I did. My boys are out there, Dave. Here comes a rider. We'll soon know."

The trooper galloped into the formation.

"What is it, lad?" Riley asked.

"We got fired on from the woods to our right, Sarge. They took off when we returned fire. I think we got one' a them though. The boys are checking that out right now."

"Not regulars?"

"I don't think so, Sarge. Might be Home Guards. Or they could be bushwhackers we just stumbled on. You can tell the Dutchman, there's some good trees back there fer hangin."

"Anderson," Riley ordered. "Take yer platoon and support the flank squad."

Shortly, the second platoon returned with three men tied to horses.

"Who are these birds, Bill?" Riley asked.

"There're just marauders stealing from defenseless folk around here. They got all kinds of loot back in the woods where we found'em. They probably deserted from Johnston's army."

"What do ya want done, sir?"

"You know what we do with this scum, Sergeant. Lieutenant White, go with Anderson's platoon, find some stout trees and send these three to their just reward in hell. I'll keep the troop here until you complete your assignment."

Contact in North Carolina

Mike and Riley sat in their saddles and looked down at the valley before them.

"Can you imagine, Sergeant," Mike mused. "We're about to ride into North Carolina; the last state to leave the Union?"

"An, I think it will be tha last state in the Confederacy to be conquered by our forces."

"We're getting closer to the end every day it seems."

"I truly hope so, lad."

"Last night, we laid out our Route of March for today. We need to ride right through that valley beyond those trees. It appears to me an ideal place for an ambush."

"May be, sir. But we gotta go that way. We have Lt. White with our Point Squad. And we have two squads on each flank. Austry's with one'a them, an I'm about ta join the other. All of'em are moving slow, sir. We should be able to flush out any Rebs hiding in wait fer us."

"I hope so. Shall we join the men, Sergeant?"

The two men urged their mounts down the slope and across the small creek that Mike thought marked their entry into North Carolina.

He moved forward to join the fifty or so troopers that made up the main body of his troop. Riley went to the right and joined the squads that patrolled the slope on that side of the valley.

The hills on both sides of this valley are no surprise. But I didn't think the floor at the bottom would be so long; we're almost an hour into North Carolina. Shots ahead!

"Sgt. Anderson."

"Yes sir."

"Take a squad and ride to the sound of that firing. Get word back to me as soon as you can about what's going on."

"Right away, sir."

These are the first shots I've heard fired in combat since I was captured after the Richmond back in March of 1864. Whew! Calm yourself, Drieborg. These men have been through this type of thing before. Don't you panic. Just let them do their jobs.

A rider rode at a gallop from the Point.

"Sir," the rider began, pulling his horse to a sudden stop.

"Sgt. Anderson says that there are trees felled over the valley floor, blocking our route of march. When the men of the Point Squad began to pull the trees away, they were brought under fire from the slopes on each flank. So now our men are pinned down behind the trees."

"Thank you, Corporal. Good report. Tell Sgt. Anderson to hold his position. When he observes our flanking squads bringing the enemy under fire, he is to attack up the slope to his right. Troopers from the reserve will move to his position and attack up the slope to your left. You have all of that?"

"Yes sir."

"Swede, Mike continued."

"Yes sir?"

"Ride to Riley on our right. Tell him to move forward to the sound of the firing. Tell him that there are Rebs on the slope below him. He is to dismount and bring them under fire."

"Yes sir."

Mike wasn't done. "Sgt. Steward."

"Yes sir?"

"Ride to Killeen on our left. Tell him to move forward aggressively to the sound of the firing. Tell him there are Rebs on the slope below him. He is to dismount and bring them under fire."

"Lt. Austry."

"Yes sir?"

"You will stay here with the reserve. Move forward at a trot. Observe the area to our rear, Henry. Remember, we have removed your flank protection as well. Alert your men to be watchful in those directions, too. I am moving forward with a squad to join Anderson.

"Questions?"

"No sir."

As soon as Mike's small force reached Anderson's squad, he dismounted.

"Bill. What is your estimate of the situation?"

"We got some Rebs on both flanks, sir. Probably not more than a few, judging by the rate of fire. But they're pretty well positioned using muzzleloaders with good range, I'd guess.

"About one hundred yards forward, our Point Squad is pinned down. If we could attack those birds from a 'top the slope and rush them from here at the same time, we'd roust them sure."

"I agree, Bill. I've ordered Riley on our right and Killeen on the left to do just that. When we hear their attack beginning, I want you to go forward against the Reb positions up that slope to your right. I'll lead these other men to the left. Questions?"

"No sir. We'll be ready."

It didn't take long for Anderson to be proved correct.

"Report, Sgt. Riley."

"We killed two and captured one. I think one or two slipped away. No casualties for us, sir."

"Killeen?"

"I don't know, sir whether the Rebs on our side'a the valley were more stupid or just stubborn. Not one of them surrendered. Had ta kill'em all, sir. We had one trooper twisted his ankle in our run down the slope."

"Bring the captive along, Sergeant. Wait for Lt. Austry and the main body. I'll be up forward with Lt. White and the Point."

"Yes sir."

When Mike arrived forward he asked, "Phineas. What's your situation?"

"We got pinned down here when we dismounted and started removing these trees that blocked our path. We have not received any fire forward, so I can't tell you what's on the other side.

"I've got a man down, Mike. He was the first to be hit after we encountered these trees blocking the trail. It's a belly wound, I'm afraid. We can't give him any water, hot as it is. But I was able to get some morphine into him. So he's resting some now. But I don't think he'll last long."

"Pull your men back, Phineas. I'll send a fresh squad forward. We need to find out what we're dealing with before we walk into another ambush. Can we get around these trees without removing them?"

"Small groups can, Mike. But we'll need to pull them aside to get the formation through."

"Lt. Austry, "Mike called."

"Yes sir?"

"Take two squads from your platoon and move up the slope to the crest on our right. I need to know if there is a force waiting for us beyond this point. Questions?"

"No sir."

"Sgt. Steward."

"Yes sir."

"Take two squads and move up the slope to the crest on our right. Keep a sharp eye out for a force down the valley. Questions, Dave?"

"No sir."

And so it went, mile after mile; a few shots from several hundred yards forced Mike to deploy his troop until the shooter was rousted or simply disappeared into the dense undergrowth of the hills.

It took longer after another ambush. So before Mike and his troop had traveled an additional five miles into North Carolina it was late in the day and getting dark.

Sgt. Riley made the rounds of his platoons. "No fires tonight, lads. That tis why you cooked rations for three days a'fore we left the last encampment area."

The trooper who had taken a bullet in the stomach died. The men of his platoon collected his identification tag and buried him before they ate their cold rations that evening.

"I'll write his people next chance I get," Mike promised. "You too, Phineas?"

"Of course, sir."

LOWELL, MICHIGAN

"Your barn looks good, Ruben. If I say so myself, with the help your neighbors gave us last week, it turned out well. Don't you agree?"

"Ya, Jake. I tink so too. Better dan da one ve had in Maryland; but don't tell Momma. She already calls dis a palace."

Jake chuckled, remembering how Ruben's wife first used that term to describe this barn.

"Your house is pretty fine too, Ruben. When da earth warms dis spring, we will be able to lay pipe and bring well water directly into your home. And I think dat you've got da only Shaker stove in our area, too."

"Maybe so. But Momma's not too sure she likes dat new-fangled cooking device. She knows it's safer and quicker. But ya know, she is used to her open hearth cooking methods. I saw her using da fireplace to bake bread da udder day, instead of da new Shaker stove."

"It vill take a little time, I suppose. Right now, I'm getting anxious for spring to come. Dis ground hasn't been planted in two years, already. It needs to be cultivated. My bank account needs a harvest too, Jake."

"Ruben, I hope you know that Rose and I will help until you get your first harvest in."

"I do not forget, Jake. Neider does Emma. But we are used to managing for ourselves. It is goot of you just da same. I hope ve don't need to call on da Drieborgs for more help. So do not vorry about us being too proud. If ve need help to get through to da next harvest, I vill ask."

"Be sure, Ruben. You and Emma are more than friends. You are family. Rose and I would be hurt if you needed for anything and did not allow us to help."

"Tank you, my dear friend. Not to vorry. If it comes to dat, you vill be asked.

"Come into da house now. Ve have some hot cider and a nice meal."

The hung their coats and left their boots in the entryway. No sooner had they opened the barn side door to the house than Emma Hecht greeted them.

"Ah! We were wondering where you boys had gone. Out in that animal palace of yours, Ruben? Rose and I have been sipping hot cider waiting for you. Your mugs are probably cold already."

"Vat do I do mit dis woman, Jake? She never talked to me like dat in Maryland. Could it be da ice and snow here in Michigan dat makes her so sharp mit da tongue? Maybe it's da vater here."

"Momma, could you varm up our cider, please? It is cold, like you said."

"You poor fellows. You stayed out in the cold too long. You need something hot to warm you. We had better heat up their cider, Rose."

"By the way, boys," Rose told them. " While you were out in the barn, we sent the children to our place for the night. We'll stay here, Jacob."

"Alone?" Jacob responded, surprised. "We've never left da children along like dat before, Momma."

"They'll be fine. The girls are old enough to manage; so are the boys."

"But what of baby Eleanor and Robert?"

"Papa," Rose snapped. "If our girls and Julia are not capable of handling those children, they should not be getting married soon. Besides, they'll probably have more fun tonight without us."

"Who knows; without them around, we might have some fun tonight, too. Eh Jacob?"

Jake choked on the hot cider. Ruben only smiled.

*   *   *   *

Back at the Drieborg place, the girls were getting ready for a night without their parents.

"Who wants to take care of getting Eleanor ready for bed?" Susan asked. "You, Ann? Fine. You handle Robert, Julia? Great. That means I'll fix the popcorn."

"Be sure you make enough for us," Jacob added.

"Ya," Kenny piped in. "We each want a whole bowl."

"What do you think this is, you two, restaurant? I'm not your servant, ya know."

"Come on, Sue. Just this once?" her brother pleaded.

"On one condition."

"What's that?"

"That you, Jacob Drieborg, play two games of checkers with Robert. Agreed?"

"He takes so long to move a checker, it drives me crazy."

"Popcorn, Jacob?"

"Oh! All right."

"As for you, Kenny Hecht."

"What?"

"You must play soldiers for fifteen minutes with Robert. And you must let him be the Union soldiers."

"He never wants to be the Rebels; not fai, Susan."

"Popcorn, Kenny?"

"I've never known you to be mean before, Susan; reminds me of my sister, Julia."

"What's your answer? Rebel soldier or no popcorn?"

"Rebel soldier."

While Ann was changing Eleanor's diaper and putting on the baby's nightclothes, she asked, "Are you boys going to stay inside tonight or are you going to sleep out in the hired man's barn room?"

"Where could we sleep inside?"

"Momma and Papa are staying at the Hechts' home tonight. I suppose you could use their room."

"I wouldn't want to sleep in their bed. Sounds strange. Would you, Kenny?"

"Not on your life. It's our usual bed in the barn or by the fireplace here inside."

"Inside sounds great. That way we can be closer to the popcorn, too. Let's get pillows and blankets for the floor."

"No popcorn until you finish with Robert," Julia reminded them both.

"Your sister is really getting mean, Kenny."

"That's nothing new. She's been that way for the longest time; real bossy."

Then Robert complained too. "That's not fair, Julia."

"What's not fair?"

"Kenny and Jacob can stay up later than me. Grampa said I wasn't a baby anymore. So I don't have to go to bed the same time as baby Eleanor. Besides, we just started to play war a minute ago."

"Robert. Listen to me. The boys are much older than you, so they can stay up later. You aren't going to bed the same time as Eleanor. She went to bed a long time ago.

"And you stayed up and played war with Kenny for the fifteen minutes he promised after Jacob played two games of checkers with you. You've had some popcorn and cider, so it's time for bed."

"Oh! Julia. That's still not fair."

"Robert. Go to bed, now!"

The boys were done with their part of the bargain; Susan had fixed their popcorn and poured their cider. Ann and Julia had changed into their bedclothes and Susan was about to do the same.

Ann had a suggestion. "Since the boys want to stay out here by the fire and the babies are in our bedroom, we should use Momma's room so we can be alone. We never get a chance to talk."

"Bring the popcorn, Susan. I'll get the cider. Come on, Julia, follow me."

The girls were on the big bed, wolfing down the warm popcorn, when Ann swallowed a mouthful, paused, and looked directly at Julia.

"Well, Julia," she virtually demanded. "Did you?"

"Did I what, Ann?"

"Remember, before you left our place for Maryland last December, you told us that you were going to get Michael in bed with you on the trip back. That's the 'did you' I'm asking about."

"Oh that. Yes, twice as a matter of fact. We slept together twice on the way back."

"Oh, my Lord. You did it with Michael the first night after you left here?"

"Not exactly. The first night we stopped was in Cleveland. Michael and I had a suite at the very best hotel in that city. He took me to their exclusive restaurant for supper. I wore my best dowdy church dress and he had on his dress uniform; sword, medals and all. Afterward we had our picture taken before returned to our room.

"I was sitting on his lap and we were just getting started kissing, when an explosion blew in the door of our room and much of the wall. He put me behind a table, grabbed his pistol and rushed out into the hall. I couldn't hear very well and I was really dizzy; so I don't remember much else. But when Michael returned, I was shaking and crying, telling him to hold me and not to leave.

"Well, after all the police left and we were moved to another suite, I don't remember much of anything. When I awoke in the morning, I was in bed with Michael and someone was knocking on our door.

"After we ate breakfast in our room, he admitted that he had undressed and put on my nightdress. He insisted that he slept with me only to protect me and that nothing else happened. So, girls, that's the almost time."

"That was in Cleveland," Susan probed. "What happened the next night in Baltimore?"

"We had police with us on the train all the way there. Then a squad of soldiers guarded us all night. Michael insisted on another three-room suite. After we put our things away we sat in the sitting room of this suite and began to kiss and touch. While he was kissing me one of our soldier guards pounded on the door to announce supper.

"We ate right there in that same sitting room. Neither of us hardly spoke or ate anything. I think we were both still aroused. After a while, I got tired of staring at my plate so I stood up and came around the table. I stood in from of Michael, and began to unbutton my dress. I intended to take everything off right there in front of him."

"Oh my God," Ann shouted. "You wouldn't?"

Michael's sisters had fallen back on the bed. Ann had her hand over her mouth. Susan had her arm over her eyes. The popcorn had spilled but no one paid any attention.

Regaining her composure, Ann picked up the questioning." So you wore the poor boy down? What the devil happened Julia?"

"You know your brother. He stopped me of course. I was furious. But he wouldn't allow it to go any further."

"Julia either you didn't sleep with Michael that night or you did. Which is it?"

"After that experience in Cleveland, Michael understood that I wasn't about to sleep alone. But yes, we slept in the same bed that night too. Once or twice that night I thought he was about to give in.

But before I could get him to do more than hold me close, there was another attack."

"You faker. You had us believing that Michael made love to you. All the while you were just teasing us."

"I had you going though, didn't I?"

The three girls erupted in laughter as they pelted one another with popcorn.

North Carolina
Guerrillas

At Regimental Officers Call, Mike explained the situation his troop had faced in the preceding few days.

"As you can see from this map, Colonel, the terrain along our route of march is such that just a few shooters can force us to stop and deploy. At this rate we've made less than ten miles a day.

"An additional concern is that as we clear the road to the northeast, it would still be easy for Reb units to circle around behind us undetected in those trees and dense vegetation to harass our main force."

"Mike," Col. Kidd began in response. "It appears that you are facing a small force using guerrilla tactics. We could walk arm in arm through the entire state of North Carolina and guerrillas could slip around us. There is simply no way for us to completely clear this country of units using this tactic.

"So what do we do about it? We continue moving toward Fayetteville and the heart of this state. It General Johnston wants to confront us with his army, he certainly can do so. In fact, we would welcome the opportunity because his force of 30,000 troops is a third our size, poorly equipped and made up mostly of boys and old men. I believe we will crush his army in a head-on confrontation.

"If his intelligence is current, he knows that General Schofield's force of some 40,000 seasoned men is soon to join us from Atlanta. So

I expect Johnston will attack us before that happens. He will probably target the weakest part of our line; right down the center against us.

"When that happens, and I expect it soon, we must hold his advance long enough for our two wings to converge and crush his army.

"Let's look over our maps. Possibly the terrain can tell us where he will stage his attack. The line along which your troop is marching, Mike, is right here. Where does it offer the best ground for Johnston?"

"North of us some, sir," Mike began. "I think the town is called Averasborough. This map shows some pretty good ground a mile or so southwest of that town. If he sets up entrenchments there it might be tough to dislodge him in a frontal attack. And if Johnston has enough cavalry to block off Kilpatrick to the west, he might be able to effectively hammer Sherman's force to our east."

"Thank you, Mike. Our orders are to continue northwest and draw Johnston's attention.

"Your orders then, Mike, are to continue moving your troop toward Fayetteville. The rest of the brigade will be in support. If Johnston should rise to the bait, we'll establish a line and hold it until Kilpatrick can come up from the west and Sherman moves in from the east."

"If there are no questions, gentlemen, you can return to your units."

"Mike, I'd like a word with you."

"Yes sir."

"Just between you and me, you should know that General Burbridge has reviewed each of your action reports personally. I think he's looking for justification to relieve you of command and bring you up on charges."

"Thank you, sir. The last time he ordered me to report, he made it very clear that he didn't approve of my methods. I told him that I would confiscate needed food and forage we found, but that I would not allow my men to loot. We would destroy what I felt would support the Rebellion, but we would not kill farm stock we could not use, nor would we burn homes and barns without cause. My conduct and that of my troopers reflect exactly this approach.

"We have and we will continue to hang all bushwhackers we capture, but we will not kill civilians unless it is absolutely necessary."

"I know your position, Mike, and you know that I support it without exception. Just be careful, son.

"One more thing. General Sherman asked me how his nephew was doing. What's that all about?"

"When I last met with the general in Savannah, he asked me if I would take his sister's son, a Lieutenant Austry, into I Troop. He could have just have had the young man assigned, but he asked instead. I appreciated that. But we needed a platoon leader, so I agreed.

Henry has fit in very well. He turned a bit green around the gills when I ordered him to hang three bushwhackers a while back, but all in all I believe he will make a fine officer."

"I'm glad to hear it. If you don't mind, I'll tell the general next time I see him."

"By the way, Colonel," Mike continued. "None of the men in my troop know that Sherman is Henry's uncle. You know how things get around and how knowledge of that relationship could hurt him. He's under enough pressure, being a green lieutenant, without that, too."

"I agree. Aside from my communication with Sherman, this information will not leave this room."

"Thank you, sir. If that's all, I'll join my unit."

Interesting that Sherman is worried about his nephew. I can't think of any reason he should be, Henry is coming along real well. He and Sgt. Anderson work well together and he has tackled every assignment I've given him enthusiastically. I'm glad he is in my troop.

"Lt. Austry,' Mike shouted. "Have you and Sgt. Riley finished your business here?"

"Yes sir," he replied. "We have all the supplies we're entitled to and have picked up the mail. We can leave as soon as you're ready, Major."

"Fine. Gather your men, Lieutenant; let's leave."

*   *   *   *

During the ride back to their camp, Mike had a conversation with Austry.

"What did you think of the scene back at Regimental Headquarters Henry?"

"It certainly was fascinating, sir. I learned a great deal as well."

"That's one reason I ordered you along. Riley could have easily taken care of this detail. But I wanted you to experience it."

"Tell me what you observed."

"I was really confused right off when Sgt. Riley bought three bottles of whiskey from the sutler's store. I'd never seen him or any of the other platoon sergeants drink, but I assumed if was for him. Wrong! Those bottles were for the supply people. The sergeant knew just whom he had to give each bottle. After he did that, we had no problem getting all the stuff the troop needed. He even picked up some extra things and canned food that's not authorized."

"Oh my," Mike laughed right out loud. "I don't want to know what those items are Henry. And you had better forget you even saw Riley take'em, if you know what's good for you."

"I've sort of figured that out for myself, sir. I know you're in charge, Major, but First Sergeant Riley runs the troop, seems'ta me. The platoon sergeants look at their platoon as their kingdoms, too. All of them follow orders from us officers, but they run the platoons just the same. As long as we respect that and don't cause confrontations, things will run smoothly."

"You're a quick learner, Henry. It helps that Riley and the platoon sergeants are pretty good teachers. If you heard that Riley trained us all as raw assed recruits, you heard correctly. Our platoon sergeants, Swede and I were in the same squad back in '62. So we have a personal relationship that's a bit unusual. I'm still learning from Riley."

"I am too, sir. That's fer sure."

*   *   *   *

"At daybreak we move out, gentlemen," Mike told his officers at Officer's Call.

"At the rate we've been moving, Regiment figures we'll be hit by a good sized force sometime in the next forty-eight hours. No more of that hit-and-run stuff that we have encountered thus far in North Carolina.

"That means, Phineas, that you have to increase your patrols during the day and your guard mount at night. Work with Riley on that. Not much sleep for you either, Harvey. I need you to rotate into this mix, too. Watch closely in the next twenty-four hours, and stay close to Phineas, because on the second rotation you'll be expected to fully participate. Understand Lieutenant?"

"Yes sir."

"Gather around the map now. First, I want us to identify likely areas of ambush between our position and this town of Averasborough."

"I think this site off to the right of tomorrow's route would be a spot we should worry about."

Riley looked at it. "I'd can see that as a good possibility. See any others, lads?"

Several were identified.

"All right. I'm getting tired of the Rebs' guerrilla tactics. Let's see if we can turn the tables on them for a change. I want a special force of maybe two squads to attack each of these sites before our main body even gets there. You organize it the first attack, Phineas. You will handle the second one, Harvey.

"Pick the men from your own platoon. I want you to include your platoon sergeant in the attack force. Be out of here before dark tonight, Phineas. Leave your horses two hundred yards back of the target and attack on foot just before first light. Leave your swords and anything else that could make a noise with your horses. Take only carbines, pistols and knives. If it works out, bring back a prisoner or two. Might like to question him. You're out there, Phineas; no support, ya understand. Any questions?"

Several were asked and answered. "You best get on with it, Lieutenant."

"Yes sir."

These boys seem enthusiastic about my plan to take it to the Rebs like this. I'd like to go on this first attack. Might be fun.

*   *   *   *

"Well, Sergeant," Mike began. "Phineas and his men should be in place by now. I gave him pieces of those white sheets you got from the regimental quartermaster today. He'll find them handy. If each of his men ties one around his head, they should be able to recognize one another in the dark."

"You didn't tell me where you came on ta that little idea, lad."

"At Andersonville Prison; my men used rather dirty white rags when we attacked rogue prisoners in the middle of the night. We called those men Raiders. They preyed upon the other prisoners, stole food, clothing and anything else they wanted. They even killed fellow prisoners. We had to break their hold on the prison, or die. So I organized squads of men to attack them at night. We killed a bunch and hung some others. That took care of them pretty much.

"We were so successful that the camp commandant allowed us to organize the camp some. We had rules enforced by a police force called the Regulators, and a court to hear disputes, try cases and hand out judgments. It worked quite well. It didn't improve the amount of food we got or the quality of the water we were forced to drink, but it returned a degree of safety and dignity to our lives and it gave us a better chance of survival."

"Sounds ta me like ya was a leader, even in that hell hole of a prison too."

"Well, I was the only commissioned officer there, as far as I knew. The Rebs at the officers' Libby Prison in Richmond sent me to this enlisted man's prison because they tagged me as a troublemaker. I had been part of the first bunch to ever escape from there. They recaptured me in sight of our own lines."

"I finally made it to our lines when they moved a lot of us to from Andersonville to Savannah's Danville Prison. From there, I escaped with a Sioux Indian named Battist who had helped me destroy the Raiders back at Andersonville.

"He led the way. He was a wonder, Sarge. He could smell farmhouse smoke a mile away, I swear. He steered us away from any such place because of farm dogs, he said. I thought I was moving pretty quietly, but at one point he told me that being a white man I made as much noise walking as a buffalo would going through a forest. He was with some unit from Wisconsin. I wonder what happened to him? Good man, Battist."

"Changing subjects on you, Sarge. How did you ever get the guys in my old squad to take on the responsibility for a platoon? You even got Killeen to step up. As I remember, he was opposed to being even a squad leader."

"Well, Mike," Riley began. "It went something like this. When George Neal got tha dysentery, poor fella, and had to leave, somethin had ta be done, don't ya know. I was the top sergeant by then, so it was up ta me to advise tha captain on who should step in. Ya see, we were down to two platoons and needed a platoon sergeant fer each a them as well.

"First I called on Steward and took him fer a little walk. By the time we returned he was a platoon sergeant. Killeen was next; and he was the hard case. We went for our walk and he started all that business of not wanting to give an order that would cost someone his life. I said that was fine with me, but then I would transfer him to tha regimental aide station and burial detail, permanent. That includes horses nowadays, if ya didn't know, sir. Right about then Stanley had a change a heart, and accepted a platoon. I knew I could talk him inta it."

By this time, Mike had tears in his eyes from laughing so hard.

"I had Anderson promoted to sergeant and assigned to the Headquarters Platoon. Swede was promoted, too, and assigned to me; in charge of horses, a course. Then as soon as we got some replacements, I gave them to Anderson and the third platoon was his.

"And your CO went along with all of this?"

"Captain Lovell was a sweet man, bless his heart. I hope he's recovering from his dysentery someplace nice an safe. He was sorely sick when you got him sent to the hospital back in Savannah. I know he was angry with ya at the time, but when he's got his children around him he'll thank ya, I'm sure."

"Maybe so. My gosh, two hours have passed since the first guard mount. We'd better check on the relief for them. Austry is in charge tonight."

"Yes sir. Let's see that everything's going well."

A SURPRISE

"Lieutenant," Killeen nudged his platoon leader, Lt. White. "There's movement on the floor of the valley. In the moonlight, I can see dark figures all over the place."

"Point it out, Stan. Guess your eyes are better than mine."

White sighted down Stan's arm to his pointing finger.

"Oh ya. I see what ya mean. My Lord, Rebs are down there in at least platoon strength. Too many for us to attack as we planned. You take a few of our men back to the horses. I'll wait a few minutes and bring the rest along. Tell the men not to talk at all and move real quiet."

"Yes sir."

It was the middle of the night before White and his men returned to Mike's camp.

"If you're sure of the numbers, that's no ambush detail. Those are skirmishers, the vanguard of a larger force.

"Phineas, I want you and two of your men to ride back to Regiment and give Colonel Kidd the word. Take our map and show him where you saw that forward Reb unit. Ask him for instructions. Tell him I'm having my troop deploy on that slope back of us a hundred yards or so. Get fresh mounts, and off with ya."

"Sgt. Riley, break camp if you please. Lieutenant Austry, mount up, you're with me.

"You'll just be in the platoon sergeant's way back there, Harvey. They know the drill."

"I understand, sir."

"No you don't, actually. But you're learning. Right now, I need help setting up our fields of fire and marking the trenches I want our men to dig; can't do it alone as fast as when I have help. You're my help. So let's get a move on."

Riley was the first to arrive at the site of the defensive line with his headquarters platoon.

"Sgt. Riley, take our right flank. I've shoved some stakes in the ground as a guide. Have Steward's men begin to dig trenches there. Send the Swede to me."

"Yes sir."

As the men of the other platoons arrived, Mike shouted out directions.

"Killeen, go on our left where Austry is. He'll show you where your men are to dig in.

"Yes sir."

"Steward, take your platoon to the right where Riley is. He'll give you direction."

"Yes sir."

"Anderson, you've got the center of our defensive line. I want a trench there, there and here. Get your men digging, and fast."

"Yes sir."

As soon as the Swede reported, Mike gave him instructions. "Those two barrels that Riley brought back from Regiment yesterday. He talked to you about their use, did he not?"

"Yes sir. He did."

"So you understand how to use the stuff in those barrels?"

"Yes sir, I do."

"Here's what I want you to do. Mount the barrels on the supply wagon, like he told you. Put the hand pump into each barrel. Drive the wagon to the base of this slope. Start at Stan's left over there and move to his right. Pump the stuff from one barrel on an area of ground about ten yards deep and ten wide. In front of his position."

"Understand so far Swede?"

"Yes Mike, I do."

"Good. Then I'll direct you on until you are to begin pumping again down to my right in front of where Steward's platoon is digging in. When the barrels are empty, bring the wagon back where your horses are tethered.

"Get on with it, my friend. Time's our enemy right now."

Riley and Austry had joined Mike by now.

"Well, gentlemen. We have two hours till dawn. That should give us enough time to establish ourselves pretty well."

"Mike, you are certainly an old fox." That was the first time Mike recalled that Austry had called him by his first name.

"Am I really? How do you figure, young fella?"

"I was there when Sgt. Riley got those white sheets and those barrels from the quartermaster. You let me believe the sergeant was doing something sinister, maybe even against regulations. All the time you knew."

"Well Harvey, welcome to the cavalry. To survive in this man's army a leader needs to improvise. What I asked the sergeant to do back there, bribing with whiskey and all was against regulations. Besides, a cavalry troop is not entitled to this stuff.

"What I do know Lieutenant is that this stuff's so new I don't think anybody even knows how to use it. I'm not too sure myself. I do know that the stuff in those barrels is highly flammable, burns a long time and won't be put out with water. In fact, it is so flammable, and those guys at quartermaster were so afraid it would explode on them, they were glad to get rid of it.

"Look to your left. See how Swede is having it pumped onto the ground at the base of the slope? We're covering an area from Stan's left to that stake toward the center of our line.

"Ride down and tell Swede to stop pumping there. Tell him to keep driving his wagon straight ahead. When he gets to the stake on the right, have him start pumping again."

"Yer givin tha boy quite an education, lad." Riley commented.

"Truth be known, Sarge, I'm getting one, too. I hope this works."

$$* \qquad * \qquad * \qquad *$$

Dawn was breaking. Mike had a kitchen set up to the rear and had Amos cook up some fried cakes and hot coffee. The men were sent back in turns by squad. Back on the forward slope, everyone kept digging between gulps of coffee and bites of bread.

"The deeper the trench and the higher the dirt in front the better yer chance of survivin boys," Riley chanted up and down the line. He also sent parties to search the forest for fallen logs. He had the men drag them in front of the trenches for added protection against enemy fire.

Mike ordered a detail to use their mounts and drag fallen trees out two hundred yards on the flanks into the valley, as additional obstacles to funnel the attackers to the center of Mike's fields of fire.

Just before dawn, skirmishers were sent out several hundred yards to the front. Their job was to give early warning of the enemy's advance. Hopefully, their fire would force the enemy to deploy much sooner and further away from the defensive line. It was a dangerous assignment. In the best of circumstances, only half the men in the detail would return to their lines unharmed.

Lt. White had just returned from Regimental Headquarters.

"The colonel said to hold as best you can Mike. It's up to Burbridge to move the brigade. Kidd can't even order the rest of the regiment forward without orders."

"All right Phineas. Good work. Get some breakfast. I think we're pretty much ready.

"Sergeant Riley. As soon as our skirmishers return, the Rebs should begin shelling our position. If they do, move the men to the back slope.

When the cannon fire stops, hustle back to our prepared positions. In the meantime, keep the men digging and improving their positions."

∗   ∗   ∗   ∗

Two recent replacements from the same Michigan town, Will Shaw and Moss Laurent were digging and throwing dirt to beat the band.

Stan Killeen, their platoon sergeant ,watched with amusement.

"Hold on, you two. Ya dig that hole too deep you'll not be able to see over the front. Take a look out there. Can you fire your Spencer? Do you have a clear field of fire?"

"How can Connolly sleep in his hole over there, Sarge? We got a battle comin? Ain't he worried?"

"He's been in these before, boys. He's seen the elephant. So he knows there's only so much he can do.

"We're in God's hands, fellas and we have little to say in the matter. When there's time like right now, some guys sleep; others whittle, write a letter or read their bible."

"This is our first battle, Sarge."

"I know it is, Will. You'll be fine, you'll see."

"Scared, Will?"

"I guess. Aren't you, Moss?"

"Probably as much as you; but I'll be damned if I'll show it."

"Me too, Moss. But if you think I'm goin ta panic an run, sock me or knock me down. I'd rather die than have anyone back home know I ran."

"You'll be fine, Will. We'll both be jus fine. Killeen says the Dutchman's got a surprise for these Rebs. You jus follow me following our sergeant."

"Are you hearing me, boy? I need to know that you're protecting my left side here in this trench. Are you with me on this?"

"You bet, Moss. You look after me and I'll do the same for you."

"That's my man."

And so it went, up and down the line.

*   *   *   *

Without warning, shooting began to the front of I troops' position.

"The curtain's goin-up, Sergeant. I hope we've done all we could."

"I believe we have, lad. But time will tell," Riley responded.

"Harvey, get off that horse," Mike ordered sharply. "We don't need a target like that for the Reb cannons. Besides, I need a live platoon leader. Take your position with your platoon, on firm ground. Your platoon sergeant's been through this before, watch him."

"Yes sir."

"I sure wish we had a battery of cannon on this slope. We could hold off a brigade or two of infantry with four of them and some canister."

"The Lord will answer yer prayers just as soon as He gives ya the moon, lad," Riley mused.

*   *   *   *

Just then, up the back slope came horses pulling four caissons each carrying four artillerymen with a cannon attached behind.

"Well I'll be a monkey's uncle. Your prayers are sure better'n mine."

"Captain Weber reporting from the 6th Regiment, sir."

When the men saw the first cannon pull over the crest, a cheer went up all along the line.

"Where do you want my babies, Major?"

"Depends, Captain. Did you bring canister?"

Mike was asking about a type of cannon shell that was fired at short range against attacking enemy infantry. The shell was just a round, sealed tin can holding fifty or so round metal balls about the size of small marbles. Shortly after the tin can was fired from the cannon, the tin casing of the shell dropped away and the metal balls were released, racing like fifty rifle shots toward the bodies of the oncoming enemy soldiers.

"You bet we have. We unloaded all our long-range stuff, because the colonel said to bring every canister shell we could carry. We have another wagon full following a few miles back. "

"Here is our situation, Weber" Mike explained his defensive position and his plan to funnel the attacking Rebs into the center.

"Let me try this plan on'ya, Major. Have your men dig me one platform there, another over there, one here and another there. I'll keep my babies in the rear of this hill until the Rebs stop their cannon fire and commit their infantry. Then I can run these beauties out and cut Johnny Reb to ribbons. Sound like it might work?"

"Sure it does.

"Sergeant Riley, get the men digging. The captain will give directions."

Troopers stumbled over each other to help dig. Shovels clanged and men were quickly covered with the flying dirt. The men of the cannon battery helped shape emplacements so that they could run their weapons in easily on the forward slope. They also dug several pits on the rear slope to protect their ammunition from enemy artillery shells. They covered them with logs. Swede held their horses in the rear.

Mike repositioned some of his men to keep them away from the forward blast of the cannon. It seemed as if it took only a few minutes before all was ready.

*   *   *   *

It was none too soon. Firing to the front increased. Looking through his binoculars, Mike could see his skirmishers falling slowly back.

"That 'a way, boys. Take your time. Make the Rebs earn every yard."

Captain Weber, stood alongside Mike, binoculars up.

"If they was to shell this position Major, they should be doing it now. They must think they can overrun you without using their cannon. A year ago, this hill would have disappeared by now, all the shells they would've thrown this way. We can thank the Lord for favors, cause they must be low on shells."

As he spoke, the surviving skirmishers came through Mike's position.

"Sgt. Crawford. Good job. Take your men to the rear for some breakfast. Afterward, join Sgt. Riley and the reserve squads."

"Yes sir. We had'ta leave a couple of our wounded boys out there, Major. The Rebs came on too fast fer us to get all of them out."

"I watched you since you made contact, John. You and your men did what you could. You did your job."

"Thank you, sir."

✳   ✳   ✳   ✳

There still had been no Reb artillery bombardment.

Thank you, Lord. They're walking right into our net. Come on you sons-a-bitches. Come-on a few more yards. Cluster in the center like I want you to. Almost time for us to light the Greek fire we put in the ground.

"Sgt. Swede. Set the valley on fire."

Down the far slope to the enemy's left, the supply wagon flew. The driver knelt in the bed where boards had been attached to the enemy's side for protection. When it reached the bed of the valley it turned left and sped along the front of the attacking Rebs. Another trooper in the bed kicked fire pots out onto the ground. With a whoosh, the entire area was on fire. The same action was repeated on the enemy's right, in front of Killeen's platoon. By the time the wagon turned up the slope, both the right and the left of the valley was a'fire. Only the center remained clear.

Good job, men. Mike thought. Come into my house, said the spider to the fly. By God! They're moving to the center. Thank you, Lord!

As soon as the Rebs committed to the center, Captain Weber ordered his cannon forward to their positions.

Troopers had already opened fire from the flanks into the tightly packed Rebel infantrymen. Effective as they were with their Spencer repeating rifles, hundred of Rebs still managed to survive and begin to charge up the slope. More soldiers in gray followed twenty or thirty yards behind.

"Looks like they committed a regiment to take this position, Captain." Mike estimated.

"I assure you, Major, no regiment of Rebs is going back down that hill. My four cannon will see to that. We're ready. A few more yards now."

Mike saw him raise his arm. "Fire." he shouted.

A deafening roar startled Mike. When the smoke cleared he could see clearly down the slope.

My God! There are hardly any Rebs left standing.

The ground was covered with the bodies of dead and dying attackers. The survivors began to move down the slope, only to be pushed back by another densely packed group of Rebs coming right behind.

"Fire at will," Weber shouted to his people.

One volley, and another, and yet another of canister sent hundreds of steel balls into the advancing Rebel infantry.

"There're breaking, Weber. Your cannon did it!"

The cannon stopped firing, and in the sudden quiet Mike could hear his men cheering and waving their hats at the retreating Rebs.

"Believe me, Major. It wouldn't have been that easy without you forcing them into the middle. Now we'll see if Johnny supports the next attack with cannon of his own. I'll move my battery to the rear slope until we find out. This engagement is probably not over, is my guess."

*   *   *   *

The platoon sergeants were already moving along the firing line, looking for casualties and checking on ammunition.

Killeen came to the two boys from Stronach, MI.

"Will is gone, Serge," Moss told him. "One minute we was firing ta beat the band an the next he jus slumped forward in the pit here. With all the cannon noise, I didn't even hear him cry out."

"It was his time, Moss. Nothing anybody could do," Killeen assured him.

"His Momma going to take this hard. His daddy was killed somewhere around Atlanta last fall. His sister and little brother are all that's left to tend the farm.

"He was so worried that he would run."

"He wasn't a shirker, Moss. Tell his Momma that he did his duty to the end."

"Can I keep him here a while, Sarge?"

"No, lad. You can keep Will's haversack with his personal things, but we need to move him to the rear and put one'a the troopers from the reserve in here with you. The Rebs are likely to attack again. Before I have him moved, take his ammo."

"Yes, Sarge."

*   *   *   *

"Sergeant Riley. A casualty report, please."

"Two men killed and one wounded from the Point Squad. Anderson lost two men. Killeen lost one and had two wounded. Those two can still fight on the line. Steward had no casualties.

"The problem is with ammunition for our Spencer rifles. The boys poured it to'em but it cost us dearly in ammo. Most' a the men are down to half of the eighty rounds they started with."

"It's not yet ten in the morning, so we can probably expect another attack," Mike predicted.

"Lt. White; take a squad to Regiment for ammunition. Use the supply wagon and take the wounded with you. Report to Colonel Kidd the results of the first attack. And, Phineas, be sure to thank him for Captain Weber and his battery of four cannons"

"Yes, sir."

"Make it fast, Phineas. We'll probably only be able to turn back one more attack like this one."

"I understand, Mike."

Sent to the Rear

As soon as the Reb bombardment began, Sgt. Riley moved his troopers to the rear slope; the precious cannon were already there. Shells timed to explode in the air showered the forward positions Mike's men had fought from earlier, with deadly hot metal. Other shells plowed into the ground, exploded and created holes as deep as any the Union troopers had dug.

It took only a few minutes for the Reb gunners to thoroughly tear up the positions Mike's troop had occupied. When it stopped, Reb infantry began to march forward to begin a new assault.

Mike had sent out skirmishers shortly after the first attack. They were now drawing fire from the forward elements of the Rebel formation. He watched his boys slowly retreat as they were trained to do.

"Riley! Get the boys back into position," Mike ordered.

No sooner had he given that command that the men of his troop came running over the crest to their positions on the forward slope. Weber waited with his cannon; just to be sure, he said. With his binoculars, Mike watched the attack unfold.

Here they come; still too far for effective fire from our Spencers though. Without the little surprise fire we had for them last time, they'll be able to spread out more when they reach the slope. Can't help that. We're short on ammo too, so I told Riley to have the men hold their fire longer this time. Thank God Weber's got plenty of canister left.

The Rebs are about one hundred yards out now. They're stopping, My God! They're tightening up their ranks. Those boys are no more'n a foot or two apart now, almost elbow-to-elbow. If our ammo holds out we'll slaughter them, packed in that tight.

What's this? Several flags are being brought forward, too. We must've impressed 'em the last attack; figure to inspire their men with those flags this time. We'll see what our canister will do to that inspiration.

"Captain Weber," Mike called.

"Yes Major, what is it?"

"Wouldn't your canister be more effective when the Rebs are packed in tight between the logs and brush we put fifty yards out on their flanks? Once they're on the slope where you hit them last time, they'll be more spread out, I expect."

"Think you're right. I'll engage them sooner, Major."

Before the Reb force had even begun to move forward, Weber ran his guns into position and had them loaded and sighted in for one hundred yards.

"With your permission, sir," he shouted to Mike.

"Fire when you're ready, Captain."

Again, Mike was startled at the sound of the first cannon volley.

"Continue to hold your fire, Riley."

"Yes sir. The men will wait."

The canister is hitting then out there. I can see gaps in the front ranks already. Don't matter; the man in the second rank just steps forward, and the entire column continues to march forward. Must be a couple of hundred men coming at us.

The cannon were firing at will now. Mike's troopers still held their fire. He continued to look through his binoculars at the field to his front.

Another twenty yards or so forward and they'll be out of that corridor we made 'em use. Then they'll be able to deploy. Give the canister to'em, Weber! Even though a few ranks are deploying to our left and some to our right, Weber is firing those steel balls of death down the center of their column of men still crammed within our corridor.

Hold on, Riley. Don't fire yet. He silently urged. The Rebs are still moving onto the plain at the base of the slope to our front. Their flags are in the center of the front rank. There are fewer attackers after Weber's cannon greeted them in that corridor. But those who made it through are locking bayonets. They're getting ready to charge. Looks like an officer out in front, saber raised above his head.

"For Carolina boys. Charge!" he shouted.

They hit the base of the slope at a run. As they did, Mike's troopers began to fire their seven shot Spencer repeating rifles. Anderson's men in the center of the defensive line laid down a murderous fire and the Reb flag bearers went down, flags with them. The Reb who picked one up was the new target, and his flag was on the ground before he had taken another step.

When some Rebs had gotten half way up the slope, Weber shouted "Fire!" And his four cannon covered the slope with hundreds of metal balls; again and yet again. But on the right the Rebs were into Mike's trenches, going at it hand to hand with his troopers. The cannon at that end of the defensive line was silenced, too.

"Riley, get the reserve forward in support of Steward!"

"Yes sir."

Come on boys stand firm. Damn, the Rebs are moving more men forward.

"Push'em back boys, Push'em back!" Mike shouted.

All four cannon were silent now. The Union soldiers had left their cannon and joined the troopers in their hand-to-hand fight on the slope. When the last of the Rebs had retreated down the slope, a fresh column of confederates could be seen running through the tree lined corridor to join the fight.

"Get three cannon firing again, Weber," Mike ordered. "Have the fourth pulled out and set up back at that hill we chose to the south of us."

Despite the devastating canister fire of the remaining three guns, Mike's men, for lack of ammunition, could not keep up an effective rate of fire against this fresh wave of Rebs.

"Riley, have the men withdraw to the crest behind the cannon," he shouted. "Send Killeen's men with the fourth cannon back to our secondary position.

"Swede, bring up the horses." Since the beginning of the battle each squad had assigned one of their number to hold the reins of their six horses. Previously, the horses had been tethered in the valley behind the hill. Now, they were brought up to the crest of the hill.

"Weber, pull your remaining guns to the rear and get back to those positions on the next hill. We'll lay down some fire to give you cover."

Hate to leave our wounded. But if I don't order this withdrawal, we'll all go down.

Weber's on his way, most of the men are mounted.

The remaining platoon of troopers were still firing at the advancing Rebs.

"Anderson," Mike shouted. "Pull your men out and follow me to our horses."

Mike was the last to mount and ride down the rear slope.

At the foot of the hill his horse stumbled and threw Mike forward into the air. He landed several yards in front. Dazed, he struggled to rise, only to feel pain shooting up his right leg. He fell, rolled over and sat up.

Damn it! I'm not going to any Southern prison. Not again.

Before he realized it, hands grabbed both his shoulders and dragged him between two horses up the slope of the next hill. Bullets slapped leaves and whizzed around the three men. The hands let Mike down on the crest of the hill.

"Well, I'll be darned." He was looking up at the smiling faces of Henry Austry and Stan Killeen.

"You haven't got the time to thank us properly Mike," Stan chuckled. "Them Rebs are hot on our trail, don't ya know. But if'n it's not too much trouble the Lieutenant here and me are going to get our boys in position to give them Rebs a warm welcome."

"But I thought we were out of ammo."

Killeen, not to miss an opportunity, continued.

"No disrespect, Major, but someone will tell ya all about it later; we're a mite busy, ya see. This here trooper will help ya to the rear, if you don't mind. It happens, you're in the way."

I love that man.

Once safely behind the crest, Mike could observe the preparations Stan had mentioned.

The cannon I ordered back here are almost in position; so is Killeen's platoon. Steward's and Anderson's men are digging like crazy. But without ammo, how are they going to stop the Reb attack; throw rocks?

"How bad is it, Mike?" Lt. White asked.

"Phineas! So that rascal Killeen was talking about you. You brought ammo."

"A whole bunch this time. In fact, I brought an entire troop as an advance party too; the rest of the regiment is not far behind. We'll have a real surprise for these Rebs when they come up this hill. Not as creative as your Greek Fire, Mike, but a surprise just the same."

"Well, I'll be. A few minutes ago I was in deep shit at the bottom of that hill. Now I have a great seat to watch our boys tear those Rebs up."

"Henry and Killeen appear to have been the first to see your horse go down Mike. If they hadn't gone after you, I believe the entire troop would have ridden down that hill to get you out, Reb fire or not. For some reason or other, you mean a lot to your men.

"By the way, I think that Austry boy is a keeper, Mike. But say. I gotta get back to the men. Someone's got to take your place, ya know. We'll talk later."

Damn. this leg hurts. No blood; so I'm not wounded. Broken or just bruised up some? Give it a minute. Then I'll try get up. What's with this?

Every time I've gotten involved in firefights during this war I get hurt. Julia will have my hide if she finds out.

The cannon began to roar and spit their deadly shells. Mike's troop, now supported by another 100 troopers with their repeating rifles, poured well directed fire down the slope into the advancing Rebels. It wasn't long before more men in blue dismounted and came up the hill.

"What are you doing sitting way back here, Mike?" Colonel Kidd asked showing more amusement than Mike thought proper.

"Horse threw me on the withdrawal from our previous position, sir. Landed wrong or something. I can't stand on my right leg at the moment. If it weren't for your arrival

Colonel, I don't believe we could have held here."

"That executive officer of yours, Lt. White, is a good man. He near embarrassed us into supporting you up here. Did you really have your men steal those barrels of Greek Fire the other day while you were talking to me at Officer's Call?"

"Yes sir," Mike admitted. "Your quartermaster people were glad to get rid of it, Colonel. They were downright afraid of the stuff. Works real well, though, let me tell you."

"White already did; amazing. You'll have to tell me about it sometime. Meantime, I'll have the regimental surgeon look you over."

"Thank you, sir."

"What! You want to send me to the rear, to some hospital with the wounded? You've said that nothing is broken; and there are no wounds. So just bandage it up and get me a crutch. I'll be fine."

"When you can walk without the leg giving way under you, Major, you can return to your unit. As a doctor, that's my decision. The sooner you get off that leg, the sooner you'll be back with your men."

"Damn! Damn!"

RECOVERY

"Here I am, miles from my men; and I'm not even wounded or sick," Mike complained to anyone who would listen. "They need me more than I need these crutches."

"That may be, Major," the doctor agreed. "But you still can't walk on that leg without it giving out on you. Until you can, you'll not be released. No release; no return."

Angry, Mike stormed out of the room. In the week since he'd been here, he'd gotten pretty good with these crutches. That wouldn't get him out of here though. Something was still wrong with the right leg. Whenever he put weight on it, there was pain. Whenever he stood up, it flat out gave way.

Earlier that week, Mike had seen someone from the Savannah hospital; Anna Etheridge.

"Well if it isn't Major Drieborg," she said. "Surprised to find you here. I just never pictured you wounded or hurt. Thought you could walk on water, actually."

"I'm just as surprised as you, Anna," Mike chuckled. "I thought I could, too.

"And here I thought you and Hal would still be in Baltimore, living it up."

"That gets a bit tiring, you know. Didn't take long to get all the soldiers from the boats settled in hospitals there. And we had some fun, but we missed the excitement and the challenge of field hospitals. so Hal is back doing what he is so good at, a battlefield operating table; and I'm working with soldiers who are trying to recover from wounds and the operations that follow. Why are you here?"

"I'm stuck here with a bum leg that doesn't want to stop acting up. All the doctor wants to do is give me laudanum to numb the pain. It works of course, but the more often I take it, the more often I seem to need it. The doc will give me all I want. But I heard Hal talk of soldiers becoming addicted to the stuff. I don't want that to happen to me."

"He's right, of course. Would you mind if I took a look at that leg?"

"I would welcome it."

"I don't need you to take off your pants, Major. But I do need you to lie back on your bed so I can work on your leg. I'll roll up your pants leg though. Will that be all right?"

"Sure."

She took the boot and sock off Mike's right foot, pushed up his pant leg above the knee; and began to probe with her fingers.

"Ow! Watch it, Anna. That hurts."

"Hey, crybaby. You want to get back on this leg or not?"

"Yes."

"Then lie back and let me do my work."

Etheridge probed, twisted, raised and bent Mike's leg. Most everything she did was greeted with a grunt, but no complaints.

After a half hour or so, she sat on the bedside chair and told Mike what she thought.

"I've read a bit since I began to nurse when this war started. The leg is a rather fragile structure. From hip to toe, there are all kinds of muscles holding large and small bones in place. The knee is wrapped in place by tissue that can stretch and tear. Healing can be very slow.

"I think you've torn muscle. Your knee is especially tender to the touch. The foot seems fine, so is your hip. The knee is the problem, seems'ta me."

"What can be done about it, Anna?"

"First, we need to get the soreness out. But we'll apply some grease on the knee and pack hot towels over and around. Afterwards I'll massage the muscles. In between these sessions, you need to move the knee while lying on your back. That will hurt some at first, so I'll help you with that for a while.

"Once we start though, I don't want to hear any bellyaching, Major. If you're up to this we'll start tomorrow morning after chow. Agreed?"

"If you think it will help, I'm game. Thank you, Anna."

My Lord! That hurts. Her massages are anything but tender. And when she bends my knee and pushes my leg all the way back to my chest, whew; I want to yell it hurts so much. Feels good when she stops, though. But four times a day?

At least I don't have to take laudanum any more. Maybe it is getting better.

"Major, we've been at this for three days. I think it is time for you to do some walking.

I've made sort of a path with six chairs on each side. You grip the backs and sort of shuffle along. Go as slowly as you want and grab a chair if you feel the knee giving out. Let's see how far you can get today."

"Two chairs before the knee felt weak. Not bad, Major, for the first try. Lie on your bed now so I can massage the knee a bit."

Three days later, Mike made it down and back without the knee giving way.

"You're making good progress. I'm proud of you. Just remember to keep it well wrapped when you're up and about, at least for a while."

"Thank you, Anna. Without you, I'd still be on crutches."

Back with the Troop

Mike rode into the I Troop camp and dismounted, carefully.

"Well, what have we here?" Stan announced. "Welcome, my man."

There were many hands shaken and backs slapped during the welcome.

"How does it go, Phineas?" Mike asked.

"These old squad mates of yours and Sgt. Riley have kept me and Henry in line."

"We've gotten fifteen men to replace the troopers who were killed or wounded when you were last here, Mike. The platoon sergeants will introduce you around once you get settled. We've had two pretty good run-ins with the Rebs since, too.

"Not long after you left, Kilpatrick's division ran into a trap of sorts that Johnston sprung. Had a rough time of it until all the units joined in. We just overwhelmed those Johnnys then. That was a bit south of Averasborough. .

"Then a few days later near Bentonville, Johnston tried another trap. This one almost worked. But after Sherman forced marched his men from the east, our forces were too much for the Rebs.

"As it turned out, we've been in a reserve role most of the time. So we haven't seen much action at all since you left; some skirmishing on the flanks and such. Nothing as serious as we experienced where you got hurt."

"When I was at the hospital, I heard about the killing of an entire herd of horses and mules near Fayetteville. What was that all about?"

"The way we hear the story is that men in one of Kilpatrick's units stumbled on a huge herd, several hundred horses and mules. They weren't farm animals, so's I guess they'd have to be intended for the Confederate military. Anyway, the troopers couldn't use many, so they just starting shooting the rest. Went a little nuts once the killing started."

"I'm glad you didn't have to be a part of that, Phineas."

"Me too, Mike."

Lt. White continued. "We've been told that we should be in Goldsboro day after tomorrow. There, we expect to be joined by Gen. Schofield's 40,000 men from Atlanta. We're supposed to be refitted some when we get there, and then head north to join up with Grant."

Bill Anderson interrupted. "Won't that be a wonder? Imagine, a quarter of a million men together in one place. I can't imagine any force standing up against that."

"I can just taste the end of this war," Added Dave Steward. "Can't you, Mike?"

The Road North

"Well, Phineas, you were right about reaching Goldsboro. Schofield arrived with all his troops too. But Grant won't need Sherman's army anymore, it appears."

"Why not? What have you heard?"

"That courier just brought me word from regiment. Lee has abandoned Petersburg and Richmond is a city open for the taking."

"Wow! Sure seems like this war is windin down, Mike."

"My guess," Mike offered, "is that Sherman will turn on Johnston now with everything he's got. He'll force his old West Point classmate to fight, surrender or skedaddle."

"We're going to move out tomorrow for Raleigh. Get the platoon sergeants, Riley and Austry, together, will you? Have them here in an hour."

"Yes sir."

At that meeting, Mike greeted the men seated with his right leg propped up on another chair.

"Leg giving you trouble, Mike?" asked Phineas.

"Whenever I overdo, it reminds me by swelling and getting sore. It will be all right."

"I was told at Officer's Call that the brigade's going to head toward Chapel Hill. We're going to join with Kilpatrick for the final push against Johnston. You know the drill, Sgt. Riley; three days rations and so on."

"Yes sir. We had mail call, sir. There's a letter for you."

"If that's all gentlemen, I'll leave you to your duties."

$*$ $*$ $*$ $*$

My Dearest Michael,

I just got your letter about your knee injury. You can joke all you want, misters smart aleck, like saying 'too bad I didn't fall on my head' or reminding me that it could happen doing farm work. This is not a laughing matter. You know how I worry. You're not even supposed to be in combat, remember?

You just wait until I see that Congressman of ours. He was supposed to keep you in Washington City. I'll give him a piece of my mind.

My Papa took yours to see our new neighbor, Walter Bauer. He operates a sawmill during the winter. Papa likes to speak German with him. Papa took trees from our new land to him and got a lot of the lumber to use when our barn was fixed up.

Anyway, our fathers cut trees on your property and skidded them over to Bauer's sawmill. It was easy, I guess, winter and all. So now Mr. Bauer is going to cut lumber for our house and barn. Isn't that great, our own trees providing all the lumber we need for our house? By the time you get home, that lumber will be waiting for us to begin building. I can hardly wait.

I can't wait, either, for us to begin our life together. I miss you so Michael. I watch your sister Susan getting ready for her Easter wedding to George Neal, and I want to cry. I am so jealous. We were going to be married this Easter. Remember? By the way, George bought the bakery over in Grand Rapids where he learned the business before the war. He has been doing really well, I'm told. Susan and you mother have spent time there helping him.

You sister Ann and Mr. Deeb, the attorney in Lowell, are now engaged. Darn it all, Michael Drieborg! You start being more careful; and get home to me soon.

Love you with all my heart.

Julia

CELEBRATION

"My Lord, Mike!" Phineas exclaimed. "Can it really be true? Lee has surrendered? That's the word spreading through the regiment. Can't you hear the cheering? This damn war is over, by God! We're going home."

"Seems like it, sir," Riley judged. "Feels strange though to think of where I last lived, back in Detroit, as home; this here army has become my home. Ya have any problems with the men celebrating, sir?"

"Let's celebrate, Riley. Tomorrow we can remind everyone that we still have to deal with Johnston's army of 30,000 men. He's somewhere around here. I'll celebrate to beat the band when he hands over his sword. Just roust everyone out's the sack as usual. Don't want them to form any bad habits."

"You're a hard one, Mike," Phineas chided him. "But for now, let's join the boys and cheer. Come-on."

"You're right. Where is that cane of mine? Oh, hell with it. Let's go."

Walking through the camp, Mike thought of his men.

These men have not had a lot to cheer about for a while. It's good for 'em. Many have been away from home since the fall of 1862, almost three years. They've lived out of doors in all kinds of weather, never knowing if they would even see another day. Let 'em celebrate.

Where did that jug of whiskey come from? Hardly an hour since we heard, and a sutler has gotten liquor into the camp. One jug passed around can't do much damage. Riley will keep it under control.

IT'S OVER

Sherman's army, all 100,000 men strong, was moving toward Raleigh, North Carolina and a confrontation with Johnston's army of 30,000 men. There were other Confederate units all over the South. But this was the largest.

"I had heard that Johnston was going to meet up with Lee and continue the war," Phineas told Mike.

"That might have been their plan, but Grant surrounded Lee and put a stop to that. In fact, Lee told Grant that his men were starving, and asked if he could spare some food for them. His army was down to less than 20,000 actives. Wasn't much else he could do but ask Grant for terms."

"Johnston can't be much better off, do'ya think, Mike?"

"We're going to find out in the next day or two."

$$* \quad * \quad * \quad *$$

Killeen stuck his head into Mike's tent. "Mike, have you heard? Johnston has asked for a cease fire."

"How do you hear about this stuff before I do, Killeen? You'd think big shots like me would be first to know."

Stan chuckled. "You know better than that, Mike. The men always know important stuff before you officers do."

"If you know so much, smart ass, will Sherman accept the truce and treat with his old buddy Johnston?"

"Crazy Bill is liable to do anything. The way he had urged us to destroy everything in sight just to, how did he say it? 'Teach these people a lesson they'll never forget.'

It's a toss-up what he'll do. What do you think will happen?"

"Now that Lee has surrendered, I'm guessing that Johnston will surrender. He's no fool. Fighting a pitched battle against a force our size would be suicidal. So he has two options, seems to me; disappear into the mountains around here and conduct a guerrilla war, or surrender."

Bill Anderson joined the conversation. "That hit-and-run stuff we faced a few weeks ago, was tough. The Rebs were there one minute and gone the next. And we only faced a few men at a time then. Can you imagine trying to chase thousands of those guys all over the hill country? Men like our General Burbridge would sure take it out on the civilians if Johnston did that. So I think he'll surrender."

"We'll see, Bill," Mike offered. "We'll see, and soon I think."

*　　*　　*　　*

Before that happened however, tragic news reached Mike and his men. President Lincoln had been assassinated.

"He was a good man," Mike told his men. "This was an act of a deranged killer. Lincoln wanted us to welcome the Rebs back into the Union. Punishing innocent civilians would only make matters worse. He wouldn't have wanted that."

"I don't know about that, Mike," Stan offered. "Seems to me that most'a these Southerns will cheer the news. I couldn't take that, believe me. It's long past the time I'll be turning the other cheek. I'm so angry right now, I want to sock someone."

"Stan," Mike began. "The last time I met with Mr. Lincoln, he asked about my father; remembered him by name too. So believe me, I understand your feelings. But we can't allow our men to run amok here. The authorities will catch the killer. I'd rather honor the memory of our president by doing what he wanted us to do.

"So we're going to maintain discipline. Each of you, meet with your men and calm them. It may be hard for you to do but that's what I'm asking you to do. This war is virtually over gentlemen; let's go home without the memory of being out of control at the very end."

Despite the shock and anger, the men of Sherman's command did not take it out on the property or persons of North Carolina. Instead, the men waited for Sherman to decide what to do about Johnston's Confederate army.

On April 26th, the surrender of Johnston's army marked the end of hostilities between the Federal government of the United States and the Confederate States of America.

ADDITIONAL DUTY

Toward the end of May, Sherman's Army of Tennessee, and the Michigan Brigade joined Grant's Army of the Potomac in a parade down Washington's Pennsylvania Avenue. Two hundred thousand soldiers celebrated the end of the War Between the States.

And while they were celebrating the end of their lives as soldiers, they were welcoming the resumption of their lives as civilians, too; but not the troopers of the Michigan Brigade. They just didn't know it as they marched on May 24th.

General Grant had decided that the military service of these experienced cavalrymen was needed a while longer. So while the Michiganders were celebrating the end of one conflict, they were about to be sent west to fight on in another conflict.

At 10 PM the night of the Grand March, almost all of the brigade's troopers, with their equipment and mounts, boarded waiting trains headed west. Most of the men were too excited to notice, but some questioned why they needed horses and equipment if they were going home. The non-commissioned officers of I Troop were among those who were questioning.

"I tell'ya," Stan Killeen insisted vehemently. "Somethin's wrong with this. First they try to get us to spend our pay for new uniforms, just ta look good for the parade. Now they send our horses an stuff with us. Somethin's up I tell'ya."

The usually quiet Bill Anderson joined in. "Stan's got a point, you know. I think there's something we're not being told."

"I got no place ta go, anyways. So it makes no difference ta me," the Swede mumbled.

"Ya, as long as you have your precious horses, you don't give a damn about anything else," spouted Stan.

"Back off, Stan, Dave Steward interrupted. "You know darn well if it weren't for Swede looking after our animals, we'd a been on foot half the time."

"What do you think, Riley?"

"Don't know fer sure, mind ya. But the scuttlebutt I heard at the parade today is that were headed for the Dakota Territory."

"By damn!" Stan exclaimed. "I knew something shitty was happening. That's Indian country. I signed up to fight Rebs, not Indians. Sides, the papers I signed back in the fall of "62 say that I would serve for thirty-six months or until the war ends. The war ended, by damn!"

"I don't remember what the hell I signed back then," Dave Steward added. "But I gotta agree with Stan on this one. The war with the Confederacy is over. We should be goin home with everybody else."

"Well, laddie," Riley piped in. "Somebody sure don't agree with ya. I'm thinking we'll be told soon enough. Fer now though, you birds keep a cool head. Tha men look ta you for leadership. So don't rile'em up. We'll have no mutiny in I Troop. Ya hear me, Killeen?"

"Why you pickin me out here, Riley? All of us are steamed about this."

"Cause you have tha habit of sayin what's on yer mind, lad. A good habit most times, but not right now. A good leader sometimes has ta hide his true feelings fer the good of tha group. This is one of those times.

"If I can't count on ya, I'll throw yer bloody ass off this movin train right now. So help me God I will. I'm askin yas; all of yas, not just Killeen. Can I count on you with this?"

"Right now, speak out; Anderson, are yas with me on this?"

"Yes, Sarge, I am."

"Steward, are yas with me on this?"

"Yes I am Sarge."

"Killeen, are yas with me on this?"

"Ya dumb mick Irishman, of course I am."

"Swede, are yas with me on this?"

"Ya, like alvays, Sarge."

"Now that's settled, we got to come up with the same story when we talk ta tha men. Lt. White an the Dutchman' ill join us as soon as their meeting with the other officers is over.

*   *   *   *

At Officers Call, orders were given and explained. Col. Kidd, the brigade's Executive Officer was sick, and was left behind in Washington to recover. In the meantime, General Stagg, his superior, had the responsibility of reporting the brigade to General Pope in St. Louis, MO.

"During the last year of the war, Washington stripped the west of troops to fight in the east. Now, it will take some months for a force of regular army personnel to be re-established out there. In the meantime Indian uprisings have been increasing and local militias are having a rough time controlling things. So there is an immediate need for seasoned cavalry to protect settlers and the routes of commerce.

"So Grant made a decision to send the Michigan Brigade to fill that void temporarily. Those members of the brigade whose enlistment has run out have already been discharged to return home. But the troopers on this train still have several months to serve on their enlistments. They may believe that their enlistment papers promised them a discharge if the war ended sooner. But their papers did not promise that. Instead, the language was 'unless sooner discharged'.

"My sense is that your men are angry about this situation. They expected to be discharged, just like tens of thousands of their comrades. This assignment might have been explained to them better. But here we are. And, gentlemen, I hold you responsible for handling your men. We will have no mutiny. All of us will report to General Pope in St. Louis, as ordered. I hope I have made myself clear. Are they any questions?"

After waiting a moment he concluded, "Since there are none, this meeting is over."

*   *   *   *

"He made that pretty clear," Mike said to Captain Osmer Cole of G Troop. "I signed the same enlistment papers as most of my men, and I expected to be heading for home right about now, too."

"Doesn't make any difference what we thought, does it, Mike? We're going west. By my calculation, I have another six months on the enlistment papers I signed. That would have me going home in October, about the same time as my men. How about you?"

"I signed my papers in the fall of 1862, too. That would get me discharged this fall, same as you, Osmer. Think you'll have trouble with your troopers?"

"As angry as they are right now, I believe they'll hang in there. So I'd say no to your question. I don't have a quitter in my bunch. You, Mike?"

"Same for me. My non-coms are stand-up guys. In the past, whatever the job, they've gotten it done. I believe they'll handle this, too. Phineas and I are going to meet with them right now."

*   *   *   *

"Sergeant Riley, boys. Where do we stand"?

"We're not a happy bunch, lad; but we're going ta hang together whatever this assignment demands, sir. Seems ta me we need to decide what we're goin ta tell the boys."

"According to this copy of the enlistment papers we all signed in the fall of '62, there was no guarantee of a discharge should the war end before we completed the 36 months we agreed to serve; it only said 'or unless sooner discharged'.

"So much as we all don't like what's happening, Grant has the right to assign us out west. I figure they'll keep us until late fall, when our 36 months is up."

"It's a pile of horseshit, if'n ya ask me, Mike," Killeen exploded.

"That's got nothing to do with it, Stan. The best way for all of us to survive this assignment and get home next fall sometime, is to set our anger aside and work together. Can each of you do that? Will they, Riley?"

"We've had a discussion about that very point, sir; and I think they can."

"Excuse me Sergeant," Mike insisted. "But will they do that?"

"Yes sir. They will."

"I hope you're right. If not, and if any of you show anger or disagreement with this assignment, we could have a mutiny on our hands." With one quick motion, Mike drew his pistol.

"The focus of us in this railroad car must be to do our duty and survive this business out west. If I find any one of you encouraging the men's anger, by our God in heaven, I'll shoot you myself." He turned his pistol toward Anderson.

"Hear me clearly, Bill. You have to show a firm and uncompromising attitude on this matter. If you even so much as sympathize with any of your men and let them know it, you endanger our mission. And as much as I love you, I'll kill you right now."

He then turned his pistol toward Killeen. "Be careful with this, Stan. If you show your men the anger you just showed me, you'll encourage mutiny. You'll be a dead man if I hear of it."

"What? No love fer me, Mike?" Stan shot back.

Mike roared in laughter and he reached out and slapped Killeen on the back.

"Ya, Stan; despite my love for you, too." That broke the tension.

"Are we all together on this now?" Mike asked.

He waited for their response. In the silence, all he could hear was the creaking of the old railroad car as it swayed back and forth and the click-ity-clack of the car's metal wheels on the tracks.

With one voice, Mike's comrades since training camp back in 1862, said:

"Agreed."

"Thank you, my friends. Now, Sgt. Riley. You might recall an old military custom practiced by non-coms when expecting recruits or replacements in their troop. The non-coms go over the list of names, trying to pick out potential troublemakers for special attention. In fact, if I recall correctly, I was one who was so identified when I reported for training camp back in '62. The private attention you and First Sgt. Williams gave me just about caused me to shit my pants."

"I remember that well, laddie."

"What do you men think about going over the platoon rosters? If we can identify and have a private discussion with each of the potential problem troopers, we might just avoid difficulty before it begins."

They started with Killeen's platoon.

Right off, they all had a good laugh when Dave Steward began by asking. "Who do we know in that platoon who whines a lot and is loud about it; aside from Stan, that is?"

There was little sleep that night. One by one, over a dozen men from the three platoons were awakened and brought back to be told the situation by Riley and his platoon sergeant. Then, before these men returned to their own railroad car, each one had a private moment with the Dutchman and his pistol. He made it very clear what would happen if they didn't cooperate. He was not a gentleman about it. Not one trooper refused his challenge.

Four days later the trains pulled into Parkersburg, West Virginia, where seven steamboats awaited them. The men of Mike's I Troop boarded with their horses and equipment without incident.

Thank God! Not one trooper even talked desertion. Mike realized. Everything went well. I had better mail this letter to Julia. She's probably fit to be tied.

My Darling Julia,

The war is over and tens of thousands of soldiers are returning home. But my love, I am sad to tell you that my troopers and I will not be discharged right now. I know this comes as a terrible shock to you; it was to me, too.

After the grand parade four days ago, most of the troopers in the Michigan Brigade were loaded on trains headed west. Right now we are loading on steamboats heading toward Cincinnati, Ohio.

It appears that General Grant decided he needed an experienced bunch of cavalrymen to protect settlers against the Indians in the Dakota Territory. He looked around and discovered that most of us in the 6th Cavalry Regiment of the Michigan Brigade had a few months left on our enlistment papers we signed back in the fall of 1862. So instead of letting us go home after the big parade in Washington, he had us shipped west.

I was told yesterday that we should be discharged sometime this fall. Sorry, honey. Why don't you make plans for a Thanksgiving wedding? Please be patien,t sweetheart. There is no use fretting over something neither of us can control. Remember always that I love you.

Forever yours,

Michael

Arrival in the West

Eight days out of Washington City, they reached St. Louis. The ship carrying the men of the 7th Cavalry Regiment had no sooner docked than dozens of them rushed the gangplank connecting their ship with the dock.

Their regimental commander, Col. Darling blocked their way. The angry men threw him into the Mississippi River and left the boat. They disappeared into the city never to be seen again.

Aside from the loud cheers that greeted the sight of the good colonel floundering in the muddy waters of the river, the men of the 6th Cavalry Regiment made no effort to escape during their forty-eight hour layover in St. Louis.

Before they left, Mike met with Lt. White and the other non-coms of his troop.

"I want to take this opportunity to recognize the work you have done with the men. It appears that they are handling the shock of this assignment very well. I believe you are responsible for their positive attitude.

"I have no idea what lies ahead; challenges aplenty, no doubt. But you have shown me that you are up to handling it. You have shown your men that you expect all of them to do their duty and work together to survive the assignment we have been given. Thank you, gentlemen."

Central Plains
Theater of Operations: 1865-66

FORT LEAVENWORTH, KANSAS

On June 7th, the men of the Michigan Brigade disembarked at the fort to set up camp.

"We've been assigned that area well away from the river, Sergeant. Prepare for the stay of a week or so."

"Yes sir. "

"Lt. White."

"Yes sir."

"The men and our mounts are sure to be rusty after this long a layoff. So set up a daily training and inspection routine. See that Riley and the other non-coms carry it out. Make sure the Swede inspects our mounts and tack before the drills begin."

"Yes sir. Right away." On a ride outside of camp, Mike had a chance to see some of the countryside.

So this is what the West looks like. Appears to be a different world altogether. One of the guides told us at Officer's Call that once we get to the prairie country, it will change completely again. He said that further west, when we see the buffalo on the move, we will think we are looking at a brown sea flowing through the prairie. That's hard to imagine.

He said that there's a desert out there, too; dry, with very little vegetation, just dust and wind blowing all the time.

＊　　＊　　＊　　＊

At a subsequent meeting with Lieutenants White and Austry, Sgt. Riley and the non-coms of the troop, Mike asked,

"How goes the training, gentleman?"

Lt. White spoke first.

"Fine, sir. The men have responded very well. All the tack has been repaired. The lame horses have recovered. Man and beast seem to be working well together once again."

"I see you worked some hunting and fishing time into the schedule. How was that received?"

Sgt. Dave Steward answered this time. "The men loved it. And we have had some really good venison to eat. The fish are a bit strange, though. In Michigan, we are used to eating mostly perch, bluegills and trout. Here we're catching what the locals call salmon. Their flesh is even pink. Tastes pretty good though."

"Do ya think ve vill find dis kind'a game after ve leave here, Mike?" Swede asked.

"The guides have told us that there is a great deal of game west of us. In fact, they said we would have no trouble filling our cooking pots and skillets every day if we wish. But I'm guessing that the answer is yes to your question, Swede."

"I hope the men and the mounts are rested, because we will be striking camp day after tomorrow. Slack off on the training a bit, but increase the inspections. When we're given the order, I don't want any problems. And yes, collect a letter home from each man; yet today if possible, tomorrow at the latest.

"As you probably have heard, several hundred troopers have managed to desert in just the week since we landed here. You can be proud that not one of your men is in that number."

"Sgt. Riley," Mike asked.

"Yes sir."

"Regiment has asked for muleskinners. Do we have any men who are qualified for that type of responsibility? Evidently the brigade has a dozen or more wagons fully loaded that will come along with us."

"Seems'ta me sir, that we do. I think we have a trooper in Lt. Austry's platoon that might be just the man. Sir, isn't that Wright fella always talking about his wagon and mules back home?"

"What about him, Bill?" Austry asked. "

"I think he'd do Sarge. Let me check it out with him. I'll get back to you after chow tonight."

"No need to wait, Bill," Mike interrupted. "If he's our guy and you think he can handle the job, send him over to Regimental Headquarters right after morning mess. Have him report to the quartermaster. Now if there is nothing more, I'll leave you gentlemen to your work."

On the Trail
to Fort Kearny

"You sure you can handle six ornery mules, Sheldon?" Bill Anderson inquired for the tenth time since Wright had been given that assignment.

"I tol ya that a' fore Sergeant. A course I kin handle this bunch. These here roads are tha worst I seen. Six inches' a sand, or rocks as big as boulders, up steep hills or down into gulleys. Pullin a full load for sixteen or more miles today, these poor animals will be wore out a' fore ya know it. All I need to make it perfect is a pouring-down rain.

"Just you leave me at my job. You handle yours. Is that a deal, Sergeant?"

"All right Sheldon. Good luck."

"Is he going to manage those mules, Sergeant?" Lt. Austry asked.

"My guess is that he'll do fine sir. Besides the quartermaster people are in charge of the wagons. Sheldon's been with me since Atlanta, so I guess I'm being a bit over-protective. I'll let them handle it."

"Good idea, Bill."

✳   ✳   ✳   ✳

"Are we having a problem with the column, Phineas?" Mike began. "Remember, we asked Regiment to be the lead unit. We need to pick up the pace if we're going to make sixteen miles today. If we don't today, tomorrow he'll replace us and we'll be in the rear eating another unit's dust."

"Right, sir. I'll ride up to the Point Squad and speed them up."

"Sgt. Riley."

"Yes sir."

"Get your three platoons moving at a better pace Sergeant. At the rate you're going the men will fall asleep in their saddles. We'll have the men walk their mounts in another forty-five minutes or so."

"Yes sir."

And so it went for mile after mile until they arrived at Fort Kearny on July 4th.

*   *   *   *

Hardly seems like celebrating this 4th, does it, Mike?"

"No, Henry, it doesn't. If I had thought about this holiday much, I'd a figured we'd be back home by now having a good old time; especially this year. After all, this is the first 4th since the war. I can just hear a band playing in the town park; maybe even some fire- works. Pistols would be fired for sure, just to make some noise."

"The same back in Illinois. Oh well, no sense crying over spilled milk. I spose we can be happy the men stuck with us on this business. I'd guess we're the only unit that's not lost even one man to desertion."

"By gosh, Henry, I think you're right. Let's go celebrate that, at least, and have some of the fish the boys are fryin up; fresh caught this morning."

Before the end of the day, the troop had its first mail call since it left St. Louis. That was worth celebrating, anyway. Mike had one letter from his family and another from Julia.

I'll bet Julia is really mad that I'm not home; save her letter for later.

Dear Michael,

We were surprised and sad to hear that the government sent you and your men west instead of letting you come home. It doesn't seem fair. Papa says that you have no choice in the matter. He says that you promised to serve for three years, and that won't be over until the fall. No sense our complaining; we'll see you in the fall. We pray for your safe return at every meal just like we did during the war.

Baby Eleanor is almost one year old. Can you believe it? Has she ever grown since you've last seen her! You'll not recognize her. She's crawling all over the place and gets into everything. Momma has put away all her special nicknacks for fear of Eleanor's curiosity. We show her your picture all the time, and when we talk of you to her she points to it. She calls our mother, "Momma", because we do, I suppose.

Papa wants me to tell you that the crops are looking good. He and Mr. Hecht have planted your ground this year, too. But he says, you should have some corn and grain waiting for you at the elevator when you return. Mr. Bauer has all the lumber from your trees waiting for you, too. The only bad news is that the end of the war has caused prices for everything to go down. The government is just not buying as much wheat, corn, and wool as it did when it had a huge army.

Susan and George are doing well at the bakery. George has turned out to be a very good salesman. He has all the hotels as customers already. Momma thinks that Susan is pregnant, too.

Joseph and I are planning a September wedding. We hope you will be back for it. I can hardly wait. I'm afraid Julia is a little jealous; she sure is lonely for you.

The Hechs' home is really nice. They have one of those new Shaker stoves, too. Wait till you see it. We get together with them often. They are very nice people. I can see why you have always felt comfortable with them.

That's all for now, Michael. Take care of yourself and God bless.

Love

Ann, for all the family

Mike sat back and thought about what Ann had told him.

I've been comfortable with the Hechts most of the time, Ann. You've just not seen Emma Hecht when she gets after you. That is definitely not comfortable.

All the timber we need cut already. That sounds great. Haven't thought of Eleanor much. I should write a little note to her. Where will I get the time? I'll just add a line to my next letter home.

Officers Call

"Major, a message."

"Yes, Sergeant. What is it?"

"Colonel Kidd wants ta see ya, sir."

I'll read Julia's letter later.

"It appears, gentlemen, that we've been selected to head for Fort Laramie. We're to leave next week. If you will look at these maps with me, I'll show you the route we've been ordered to take.

On the seventh, we set out for Fort Sedgwick. We'll gather supplies there and head northwest for Fort Laramie. All told, we've got a two hundred mile trek ahead of us."

Osmer Cole, G Troop commander, observed, "These maps don't show much detail do they, sir?"

"Not like maps we used in the late war; that's for sure, Osmer."

"Is all this area between Sedgwick and us here, just empty?" he continued to inquire.

"Can't tell from this map. Let's ask one of the men who will guide us. This is a Pawnee Indian named Soaring Eagle. Ask him."

"Here," and the Indian pointed to Fort Kearny where they were camped. "Is prairie full of grass and game. Out there," and he pointed to the trail ahead toward Fort Sedgwick. "Is desert; dry with little grass or game. Hot in day and cold in night. Always windy."

"Well, you heard him gentlemen. Sounds like the men and our mounts are in for a dusty ride. Check their canteens; no whiskey snuck in on this trip. Talk to them about conserving their water. If this Indian is right, troopers could be walking if they aren't careful to bring enough water for their mounts.

"Without trees I'm told we will use the droppings of buffalo. I know it sounds strange. But they say that these 'buffalo chips' work well as fuel. If there is nothing else, gentlemen you may return to your units."

*   *   *   *

"Doesn't this wind ever stop?" moaned Pvt. Shaw to Killeen. "If Moss were with us instead of pushing up daises in North Carolina, he'd complain yer head off fer sure."

"Complain all ya want, Will," his platoon sergeant told him. "Won't do a lick a good. Sides, every time ya do it, ya get a mouthful of sand."

"According to our trusty Indian scout, we only gat a couple'a more days a this desert till we get to Fort Sedgwick. Then we head north to the Dakota country. He says it turns real nice and green then with lots'a fresh, clean water."

"That sounds great, Sarge, I can't wait."

"I think you'll find that ya can, Will," Killeen chuckled. "Cause that's when the Indians start pestering us. This wind-driven sand might be sharp and tough on the skin, but it ain't anything as sharp as an Indian arrow."

"Wonderful. Thirsty or dead; what a great choice."

*   *   *   *

"Welcome to Julesburg and Fort Sedgwick, gentlemen," offered Brigadier General Kidd at the first Officer's Call.

"Congratulations to you, General, on your promotion." one of the officers offered. With that, all stood and clapped in agreement.

"Thank you. I'm guessing that the promotion is to get me to stop complaining, to shut up and follow General Connor's orders.

"Aside from the obvious problems we all encountered on the trail, is there anything in particular I need to address; please don't ask me when we're going home."

After his troop commanders and their execs stopped laughing, he continued.

"The next leg of our journey to Fort Laramie will begin on July 31st. That gives you and your men six days to refit and rest. I'm being badgered by Connor to speed it up. So once on the trail, we will move rapidly. Gather around the map table, gentlemen. Such as it is, this map is the best we've been given.

"As you can see, there is no post between Laramie and the Powder River. We of the 6th have been directed to erect a fort on that river not far northwest of the Oregon Trail. Check that a dozen axes are in each of your troop supply wagons. Hate to have to hack down trees with bayonets and Bowie knives.

"We're going to be joined by several more Pawnee scouts. They will guide us and also hunt game to supply us with fresh meat. After the march we've just finished, I'm certain we'll all welcome that.

"As far as whether or not these birds will fight alongside us should we encounter hostile Indians, I just don't know. I'm told that the traditional enemies of the Pawnee include the Sioux, Arapaho and the Cheyenne. But they're moody. Could turn on us, for all I know.

"We'll meet the night before we head north. In the meantime, my door is open to you. Don't hesitate to stop by. I'll let you know should something come up in the meantime. So gentlemen, if there is nothing else, you can return to your men."

*   *   *   *

"Well, what do ya think, Mike?" Phineas asked.

"We got into camp so late yesterday, I'm still too tired to think. I feel that awful dust in every crevice and opening of my body. I know I'm carrying a pound of it in my hair alone. Right now, I need to take a jump in the Platte River with a bar of soap. Afterwards, if I can find some underwear that's not full of sand, I'll feel like answering your question."

"Sorry I asked. I think I'll go talk with Killeen. Compared to you, that grouch is mister cheerful. See you later."

Sorry, Phineas. I know I'm a serious grouch. Don' meant to take it out on you. We haven't had any mail since Fort Kearny. But I haven't heard from Julia since we left there three weeks ago. Her last letter was a barnburner. When she heard of our assignment out west, she was really mad at me, too.

I know I have to write her, but frankly I'm just too tired to face it. What can I say that's different; be patient; Indians are lousy fighters, so I'm safe? What? She'll have to deal with the situation, just like I am. Anger won't solve anything.

Yep. That's it. I'll just tell her that. I'm be home when they let me go home. Not a day sooner. She has to accept that and get off my back about it. Maybe she could keep a journal and write all her anger into it. I'll suggest that to her.

What the hell! I'm tired of reading letters full of complaints. Tonight yet, I'm going to write that letter to her, while I'm still steamed and have the courage.

✳   ✳   ✳   ✳

Before the regiment left for the Powder River, the six troop commanders were invited to supper with General Kidd.

Before they ate, he stood, raised his glass of wine and said, "A toast, gentlemen; to the United States of America."

"Hear, hear, his officers responded." And they drank some wine.

Another officer stood, "The Union forever."

"Hear, hear," was the response. More wine was gulped.

"To home," another toasted.

"Hear, hear," and more wine was drunk.

Two orderlies began to put supper on the rough wood table. Deer venison, bison and fish were served with fresh bread and baked potatoes. Apple preserves were used to bake some apple pie, a real treat. Of course, hot coffee and wine aplenty, too.

During the course of the meal stories were remembered and told of exploits and disasters performed, or at least witnessed, during the recent war.

"Mike, tell us about how you hoodwinked that Greek Fire out of my quartermaster back in Carolina, and used it against the Rebs," the general urged. "Wait till you hear this story, gentlemen. I still chuckle when I remember it."

Already several glasses of wine into the evening, Mike found he wasn't shy about recounting this exploit of his. When he finished, they all laughed and clapped.

"Didn't I tell you? And he stole the stuff from right under my nose, ta boot! Doesn't that beat all?" the general pronounced.

Another officer, Captain Osmer Cole of G Troop, announced that he had a story about a different war in a different century. He challenged all to bet him that no one had ever heard this tale before. Money was thrown on to the table, and the officer began.

"Centuries ago," he began. "The French and the British fought many wars over land on the continent that the French claimed, but the British controlled. Most noblemen wore armor, rode what they called warhorses and carried long lances and big swords or axes. They were a fearsome sight, thundering across a field at their enemy.

"Well, there was not much a poor foot soldier could do against such an attacker; except run. So it seems that some Englishman developed what was called a longbow. It had a considerable range and good striking power. The French still depended on the crossbow; deadly at short range but quite limited over ten or twenty yards.

"I think it was at the battle of Crecy when the English bowmen used this weapon for the first time against the French. It is said that hundreds of armor-clad French horsemen were killed that day. In subsequent battles, the bowmen proved that their weapon was here to stay.

"At some point in this warfare, bowmen were captured. The French, being the creative sorts they were, would cut off the bowman's right index finger, making him unable to draw his longbow's string. Then they sent the live Englishman back so his mates could see what would happen to them, if captured.

"In a subsequent battle, the bowmen were important to the English victory. Afterwards, they let out a great cheer and raised their right hands in a defiant gesture toward the French lines; like this."

Cole stood and raised his right arm, but atop his fist he only raised the middle finger on his right hand.

The men roared and clapped their recognition; and everyone, even the general cheered while raising the middle finger of their right hands in the now universally used salutation.

"Hear, hear," they shouted. They all drained their glasses; and Cole collected the money.

When the dessert plates were cleared, the general brought out a not-yet-opened bottle.

"Gentlemen. I dragged this precious bottle of cognac all the way from St. Louis. I think it is appropriate to share it tonight."

Clapping and cheering greeted his announcement.

Even when I served in Washington City, I never had more than one or two glasses of wine. Tonight, I've already had several, and now cognac. Who cares? No one in this God-forsaken wilderness will know, or care.

"For those of you new to this brew, it is for sipping. That's why I'm only pouring a little amount in each glass. This is often called the 'nectar of the gods'. So beware, any officer I see gulping will be the Officer of the Guard tomorrow morning.

"Observe, gentlemen," he continued his instruction. "Raise the glass slowly until it is under the nose. Take short breaths. Take in the aroma. Now when you sip, keep the liquor on the surface of your tongue for a moment or two before swallowing. Then lower the glass and await my direction."

"Good so far?" He looked around the room. "Now just relax a moment before we begin again." And so it went over the next hour.

Phew! This cot sure feels good. I must confess, I've have been affected by all the wine and cognac I drank tonight. I'm what they call woozy, I think. Not sure, actually, since I've never felt this way before.

*   *   *   *

"Rise an shine, lad. Tis Reveille." Riley announced none too quietly.

"Can't be, Sergeant. I just got to sleep."

"Might be, sir. I wouldn't know; not having been invited ta that loud party tha whole camp heard last night. Judging by when the noise stopped, when the rest'a us could get to sleep, you were back in yer tent about two in the morning. Tis now five, sir. The troop is up and getting ready to leave. Are you goin with us this morning?"

"You are evil, Riley; evil." Mike almost shouted. He sat up, holding his head between two hands.

"Feet on the ground now, sir. That' a boy. Grab the tent pole now and stand; easy with the dizzy head now. Wouldn't want ya to hurt that knee of yours again now, would we. I'll be getting the men to tear down your tent, laddie. So ya best get a move on."

"All right Sgt. Riley. All right."

By 6AM, the six troops comprising Gen. Kidd's force had struck camp and were moving northwest toward the Powder River. Hardly a trooper in the formation didn't know about the general's party the night before. Throughout the day, the troop commanders received snide remarks from the officers in their troop, even from their non-commissioned officers.

Oh! My God. My head hurts so much. I think my horse is punishing me on purpose. Every time it takes a step, a stab of pain shoots across my head. It's the general's fault, and his cognac. Never again.

"An how would the major be feelin this fine day?" Killeen asked one time as he rode beside Mike.

Mike's silence did not deter a further observation.

"Having experienced the terrible day-after-the-party feeling, sir, I suggest strong coffee an rest. Should be fine in a few days."

"A few days! That long?" Mike eyed him ruefully. "How would you like guard duty for a week or so, Killeen?"

"I always knew you'd use your awful power to no good. An here's the man I saved from the very hands of the terrible Rebs. Risked me own life doing it. Turned on me already."

"Stop it, Killeen," Mike moaned. "It hurts too much to laugh. Does this always happen when you drink?"

"Only when I tip one too many, Mike. In your case, innocent lamb that you are, I'd say you tipped several too many."

"I think it was the cognac."

"No wonder you're in such condition. Not that I can afford that fine stuff. Mighty powerful brew, cognac is. One serving or two?"

"Three."

"Oh my Lord, Mike. No wonder every hair on your head is sore and your stomach wants to kick up anything that you try to put in it."

"You had these feelings then?"

"More than I want to admit. After I get over the pain, I tend to forget; and I overdo the next chance I get. It's the 'Failing', you know. Most of us Irish men have it in our genes, I'm told."

"But I can tell, I've exhausted ya with all this talk. I'll move along an leave ya to enjoy your misery."

Stan Killeen was right. After a couple of days of misery, Mike felt like he could hold a meal down, and his head didn't hurt; not too much, anyway.

✳   ✳   ✳   ✳

Kidd's force reached their destination on the Powder River on August 14th. After setting up camp, Kidd picked an area on the eastern bank of that river for a fort. His commander had already named it Fort Connor.

The next day, troopers were chopping trees for the fort. They applied their axes to trees at least eight inches across and eight feet high. Others used their mounts to drag them back to the site for other units to construct the walls.

Eventually, the supply within sight of the fort dwindled and they had to move further away from camp to cut trees for the structure. Cooking fuel became scarce close by, too, so firewood parties had to forage further and further away as well.

The Pawnee scouts went out each day and kept the troopers supplied with fresh meat. One evening they returned without meat, but proudly displayed human scalps. They claimed to have been in a fight with Sioux warriors who were going to attack one of the work parties. After they killed seven, they scalped them as traditional trophies of their victory. That same night they danced around a fire and chanted some victory song for hours.

The troopers were generally skeptical of their story and disgusted with the scalping.

$$* \quad * \quad * \quad *$$

"We've got less than an hour of daylight, men," Mike told his log-cutting detail. "One or two more logs and we best get back to the fort," Mike told his detail.

They had no sooner loaded the last log on their wagon when several Indians came swooping through their work party. Two horsemen snatched up Lt. Austry and rode off.

"To horse, men." Mike shouted. He and six others mounted and rode off in pursuit.

"I can see them just ahead. They're rounding that next hill."

Just as Mike's force followed, dozens of mounted Indians appeared in front blocking their path. Looking back, Mike saw another bunch blocking their escape.

Shit! We're trapped. Like a rookie, I led my men right into it.

"Hold your fire, men," Mike shouted. "Let's see if we can find Austry and get out of this mess somehow."

Several Indians walked among the troopers and disarmed them. Between two columns, the Indians led Mike and his troopers into the wilderness. Dark as it was, the column was led without pause throughout the night.

*   *   *   *

I see that Austry's already tied to a stake. His chin is down to his chest; looks unconscious. The other men are being tied to stakes, too. Me too, I guess. We found a trooper last week, a corporal from G Troop. The Indians had tied him to a wagon wheel and set him on fire. What a hell of a way to die.

Women and children came out of shelters nearby and rushed the tied men. They tore the trooper's shirts, took their caps and pulled down their pants. They spit, threw stones and poked the bound men with sharply pointed sticks; all the time keeping up a din of shrill sound.

The Indians who had brought them in just stood around watching and laughing at the entire scene. When a group of several Indians rode in, dismounted and walked toward them, the onlookers stood back and became silent. Even the women and children stopped their taunting and stepped back from the bound troopers.

One Indian began to walk from stake to stake looking over each trooper in turn. When he reached Mike, the two men looked at one another for a long moment. Something was said in a language Mike only knew as Sioux. Then he was untied.

"Fix your clothing and follow me," the man told Mike in English.

As they walked through the woods, the Indian talked with Mike.

"You knew me as Battist; my tribal name is Lone Wolf. I knew you as Drieborg. Keep silent unless I tell you to talk. You and I once fought together in the Great War. But you and your soldiers have invaded my country, so you have become my enemy."

Mike walked into an opening in the forest. Indians sat around a small fire smoking pipes and talking quietly. Battist sat and pointed to a spot behind him for Mike.

"These men are the leaders of my tribe. I am a war chief, but they must approve your release. I will tell them that you saved my life in the Southern prison. I will tell them that we escaped together and that you treated me well. If I must, I will tell them that you punished the Pawnee for killing and taking scalps of my brother warriors. Do not deny this lie. It is important that they feel they owe you something, too."

In a language Mike did not understand, his old friend began telling his story. Sometimes quietly, often very loud, the discussion went on between Lone Wolf and the others.

Is Battist, winning them over? Some of these men shout at him angrily, I think. Others just sit there nodding their head and puffing on their pipe. Sit up straight, Drieborg, and keep your face expressionless. Don't do anything that will attract attention, show weakness, or anger.

Why are they all so quiet? I didn't notice them taking a vote or anything like that.

"Follow me," Battist ordered.

"Because they understood how you and I are bound together by our service in the Great War, they will allow me to free you; but not your men. I know you, Drieborg. I know you will not accept this. So I told them the lie about the Pawnee. For this they will let you take your men with you."

"But understand this. As long as this war between your people and mine goes on, you and I are no longer brothers; we are now enemies.

"During the Great War, while many Sioux warriors like me fought for your government, my people were mistreated. And while I was in that prison with you, another war was fought in Minnesota between my people and your army. My chief, Little Crow, led an uprising because Lincoln and your government would not pay attention to their complaints. After the uprising they listened.

"Now you lead men here to build a fort that will house more soldiers. That means that prospectors will be protected as they invade the Black Hills searching for gold. This is an area sacred to my people. So we fight. Right now, Little Crow is to the north of us fighting more of your soldiers. I lead the fight here. Maybe your government will listen to my people this time, too."

Mike asked. "Can I speak?"

"Yes, but we must move on quickly."

"My men and I were ordered here. We did not volunteer to fight this fight. All we want is to return to our homes in Michigan. We obey like you. Thank you for what you did for my men and me. I will never forget. As one soldier to another, I will fight you if necessary, but you will always have my respect and my friendship."

"Come, Drieborg. We must go."

Mike and each of his men were blindfolded, put on a horse and led east through the forest. At daylight, the Indian escort quietly left them to find their way back to the fort on foot.

"Do you have any idea where we are, Mike?" Bill Anderson asked.

"The sun will tell us soon, Bill. For now let's keep moving along this path. I want to put some distance between us and those Indians in case they change their minds."

Mike walked alongside Austry.

"We need to move quickly, Henry. Do you need help?"

"I'll keep up Mike. I feel pretty tough right now, though. They roughed me up pretty well before you arrived. I think they busted a rib or two. I'm not spitting blood, so I guess my lungs are not damaged. I'll be all right; just mighty sore."

"Let me know if you absolutely have to stop."

Mike's group headed east for another hour, when the Pawnee scouts who had been sent to look for his group found them.

Back at the fort Mike was met by General Kidd. "We had about given up on you, Mike," he said in greeting. "After the doc looks you over, clean up and get something to eat. We'll talk then. I need an action report too."

"I'm going to see to my men first, sir. But I'll be along."

Sure is amazing that the boys are in such good shape. All of us have a lot of bruises and small wounds from the Indian women and kids, but otherwise all right. The doc says that Austry probably does have a broken rib or two. Bandaged him up and ordered him to bed rest. What an experience; came pretty close to never getting home. Thank you, Lord, for Battist. Wonder if we'll ever meet on a battlefield?

"Sit down, Mike," Gen. Kidd told him. "Get a cup of coffee and tell me what happened."

After Mike reviewed the episode, Kidd wanted him to organize some training for the other troop officers and non-coms.

"We need to be more aware of the tactics they used to capture you, Mike. It's easy to understand how you were tricked into following the bunch that took Austry. First, we will need to protect our work parties better. Second, we need to respond better to their baiting. No more chasing into the unknown.

"Get some rest today, Mike. But before any work parties leave this area again, you will have run some drills to better prepare them to respond to this sort of thing."

Mike met with the other troop leaders to review potential tactics they might use. It was decided that the core defense was to first protect the work party. If the Indians were denied access to the working troopers, the cause for pursuing them would be reduced considerably.

It was also decided to use the Pawnee on picket duty, patrolling in a wide circle well outside the work area. Within that circle would be another picket patrol of troopers. This technique was practiced again and again within sight of the camp. No work party was sent out for several days.

Using this tactic, the work parties resumed their work. There were no more successful Indian attacks, and Fort Connor was completed in a few weeks.

$$*\qquad*\qquad*\qquad*$$

"Mail call, Major."

"Great. I haven't heard from home for weeks."

My dearest Michael:

Everyone here is fine; we all hope you are too, especially me.

I guess you are right, darling. Since neither of us can do anything about the situation, we best accept it. It is hard for me not to be angry. I will work on that, though.

Everyone here is helping with the wheat harvest. Even Robert was out in the field yesterday helping to shock the cut sheave. Papa said that we had to get the wheat in quickly before it spouted, whatever that means. We started early in your father's field and then moved to Papa's. Tomorrow everyone will start on your field. In the afternoon we will do Mr. Bauer's wheat field. His son Bernie, who is about my brother's age, has been helping, too. We had a big meal this noon, for all the workers and another this evening. In a couple of days, the wheat will be dry enough to be threshed. So we'll go to the fields again to load and move it to the thresher.

Papa says that prices have dropped now that the war is over. As good as the harvest is here, the prices will be lower than last year for sure. The price we get for our oats and corn is down, too, he says. Since he sold our Maryland grain and farm when the war was still going on, he got a good price for everything. So he and Momma do not have a mortgage on this place.

Will we have to borrow funds to build our place? I hope not. It would worry me to have debts, even if the banker is your brother-in-law.

Robert is growing like a weed. You will hardly know him when you get home. He talks about you all the time. He keeps asking what you are doing out west. What does an Indian look like? Why are you there fighting them? You know Robert, he goes on and on with his questions. I have been teaching him his figures and some reading. Momma says it's good for me to practice on him, for when I must teach my own children.

Speaking of children, Mr. Drieborg; you get yourself home to me so that we can start having them. I miss you so, Michael. We all pray for your safe return.

With all my love:

Julia

GRAND RAPIDS

"I'll be fine, George," Susan insisted. "It's nice of you to worry. Remember, it's only September. I'm not due until February; I'm only three months along. I can deliver these rolls to the restaurant."

"You're sure?"

"We promised to deliver fresh rolls every day by seven in the morning. We don't want to lose this customer. It's only down the street a block. You finish that bread order. I'll be back in a few minutes."

"All right Sue. Just you be careful."

"Yes, George."

He's so sweet. But Smith's restaurant is only a block down Monroe St. Our sweet rolls are a big hit in town. Sure helps us make the monthly payment on the business. It might be tough without daily customers like this. Looks as if I'm just in time. Good crowd waiting for their coffee and rolls this morning.

"Good morning, Mr. Smith," Susan began. "Looks as if I'm just in time for your morning coffee drinkers."

"My customers agree with you, Mrs. Neal. But I'll not be buying your rolls today or any other day."

"Oh, my." Susan sort of gasped. "Is something wrong with them?"

"No, miss, not a thing. But that guy sitting over there has paid me not to buy your rolls."

"Why would he do that, for heaven's sake?"

"Don't know. All I know is that he is paying me more not to buy your great baked goods than I could ever make selling them to my morning coffee crowd. See that skinny fellow sitting alone over there? The one with the weasel face? He's the one. Ask him."

"Well, I never," she muttered to herself as she approached the table.

Moving toward the table, Susan immediately recognized the man Mr. Smith had pointed out.

Oh, my God. It's Carl Bacon.

"And a good morning to you too, missy."

Sue gasped, almost dropping her basket of sweet rolls.

"Careful now; wouldn't want you to drop all those goodies. I was thinking I might just open my own bakery here in town. Yours' might be for sale if you can't sell your baked goodies, might it not?"

"You are a horrid man," Susan shouted.

"My, my, you are still the feisty girl I remember from our school days together. I thought of you often when I was in that hellhole of a prison where your brother put me.

"They put me in a tiny cell with no light for long periods of time. They wouldn't let me wash. Instead I had to live in my own shit and vomit.

I can see she's beginning to tremble. This is marvelous.

"But I survived in part by thinking of my old school mate, you Susan. I thought of kidnapping you, stripping off your clothing and toying with you. Oh, I made up such delicious images. I even decided that you enjoyed my fun and games. Now it is your turn to suffer, missy."

Bacon's laughter ringing in her ears, Susan turned and ran.

Oh, this is so great. This is such fun, I couldn't ask for more. Run, little lady. Run home. I only wish I could be a little mouse in the corner and see your husband's reaction when you tell him.

Back at the bakery, Susan sat in the chair behind the counter. She hadn't even taken off her coat. To calm her shaking, she leaned forward and clutched the basket of rolls to her body.

I feel sick to my stomach. Lord, protect my baby. Help me calm down.

Just then her husband walked into the room with a tray of fresh bread.

"What's the matter, Susan?" he asked.

I wish I were as strong as my sister Ann. She would probably get a gun and shoot Bacon without a second thought. George will want to kill him, too. I can't allow that. I'd lose him to some prison; my baby needs a father.

So she only told him of Bacon's intention to ruin their business. She did not tell him of the comments the man had made about what he would like to do with her.

"What?" he shouted. "I knew the guy was crazy. He'll never be able to ruin us."

"Please, George, I can't stop shaking. Right now I need you to hold me."

The two stood behind the baked goods case and held one another.

"We'll manage all right Sue," George assured her. "He can't frighten all our customers. Remember, just yesterday, we got that contract to supply the Eagle Hotel with fresh bread three times each day. Combined with our daily store traffic, we'll be able to make our payment to the Old Kent Bank just fine. So don't worry, sweetheart. Why don't you go upstairs and rest a bit? I can handle the counter for awhile."

"Thank you, George. I think I will. He really upset me."

That bastard! If I run into him on a dark night, he'll pay for upsetting Susan.

*   *   *   *

A week later in Neal's Bakery, Rose Drieborg walked into the small shop.

"Mother Drieborg, what are you doing here?"

"Susan wrote me that she is not feeling well George. She said she did feel up to working in the bakery right now. So I'm here to help you."

"Thank you. But you were here for weeks right after we opened. You have a family of your own to take care of. Don't you need to be there?"

"My Ann will take care of the house. Little Jake and his father could do with some time to themselves, anyway. Be good for them. Ann will see to it that the boys don't starve. Now, put me to work."

"All right, if you insist; right this way. I'll put you back on preparing the sweet rolls while I finish the bread for the ovens. That bastard Bacon has bought off several of our best sweet roll customers. But we still have good walk-in traffic."

Later that day, a well-dressed woman came into the shop.

"Mr. Neal, I was just having tea at Mrs. McArthur's house. She told me you made the rolls she served. They were delicious."

"It's very nice to hear that, ma'am. Until tomorrow morning I'm afraid we're out of the most popular ones. But I do have some cinnamon left. They were fresh this morning."

"My husband has a sweet tooth, I'm afraid. He shouldn't, but he loves a late evening snack. Why don't you give me four of them for him to try?"

"Yes ma'am."

"Where is that sweet wife of yours; Susan, isn't it?"

"She had an upsetting experience last week. She hasn't been up to working in the bakery since; pregnant, you know." At this point Rose Drieborg came to the front of the shop.

"I didn't know she was expecting. But I did hear at church last Sunday that she had a nasty run-in with that Bacon fellow. Most of the ladies I know were appalled with his rude conduct. Please give her my good wishes."

"Thank you, I certainly will. And who may I tell her sends the good wishes?"

"How rude of me, Mr. Neal; I'm Mary Bacon, that rude man's mother."

George practically dropped the tray of unbaked bread he was about to slide into one of his ovens.

Oh, my God! he thought.

"Yes ma'am. I'll tell her."

Addressing Susan's mother, Mrs. Bacon asked.

"Are you an employee here?"

"No, Mrs. Bacon. I am Susan's mother. I'm Rose Drieborg, from Lowell. I'm helping George in the bakery for a bit."

"You can be proud of Mr. Neal and Susan, Mrs. Drieborg. They have taken this old rundown bakery and brought it back to life for the people of this town. They are to be congratulated for their hard work."

"With your son trying to ruin them, I am surprised to find you here, Mrs. Bacon," Rose responded coldly.

"Let me assure you, Mrs. Drieborg, I will do all that I can to help the young couple succeed here. With such tasty baked goods, they have made that task quite easy."

"Excuse me, ma'am," George interrupted. "While I am pleased to hear that, why don't you just tell your son to stop trying to ruin us?"

"I have no control over him Mr. Neal. But I do have some influence over many of the ladies in this town. I would like to see that they all are exposed to your fine baked goods. Will you allow me to help you in my small way?"

"Of course, Mrs. Bacon," George responded with some excitement. "You just let me know what kinds of things you need. With Mother Drieborg's help, we can bake most anything."

"Fine. I'll be in touch. I have an idea or two about this shop that you might like, too." As quietly as she had arrived, Mr. Bacon was out the door with her cinnamon rolls.

"Well, I'll be damned." George stammered. "Wait till Susan hears. If you weren't here to hear it, Rose, she wouldn't believe me."

"I wouldn't blame Susan for being cynical, George. After everything her husband and son have done to our family, it's hard for me to believe her, either. We'll see what happens. Let's get back to work. We have much to do if your afternoon deliveries are to be on time."

"That lady has a lot to prove before I trust her, believe me," Rose concluded as she walked back to the ovens.

HEADING HOME

General Kidd was reviewing dispatches just delivered.

"Well, I'll be darned! Sergeant, get the officers in here."

"Gentlemen," he began. "I am pleased to announce that we have been ordered to return to Fort Leavenworth and mustered out."

The officers sitting under his tent fly all jumped up in unison, cheering and clapping one another on the back. Troopers hearing the commotion began to walk toward the unusual revelry. Very quickly, quite a crowd had gathered.

The general turned to them. "Men of the 6th Cavalry Regiment," he shouted over the din. "We have just been ordered to start marching home to Michigan."

Home at last. Thank you, Lord, Mike thought. *You have looked after me all this time. Please, just a little while longer, God; just a little while longer.*

$$* \quad * \quad * \quad *$$

Within a few days, two hundred fifty men of the cavalry regiment were on their way east. It took them eleven days to reach Fort Laramie and another fourteen to reach Fort Leavenworth.

The trail east offered them the same challenges as had that same trail they had taken west, weeks ago. But this time, they didn't seem to mind. Their attention was focused on home and what they would do after they got there.

Still on the trail, Dave Steward was sitting with his friends around a campfire. It had been a few weeks shy of three years since he had been at his Michigan farm in Newaygo.

"All I'm thinking about is laying around for awhile; playing with my kids and having my woman fix me her great meals."

"I met your wife, Dave. The last time your were home was for Thanksgiving back in '62, remember? I don't recall her ever waiting on you then. I'll bet you'll be able to get away with that laying around for about a day, two at the most."

"Yer probably right, Stan. What about you?"

"I hate to go back to my pa's place. My four sisters will probably start pesterin me to death the minute I get home. I'm not up to that anymore. Think I'll look around some. Maybe I'll settle in Cadillac. Pretty town, Cadillac. We used to kick up our heels there, swimming in Lake Mitchell, drinkin beer and such. Work for someone to pass the time. Heck, maybe I'll be my own boss. We'll see."

"Hey, Bill. You keep telling us about all that money you got stashed away. What are ya going ta do with it?" Stan asked Bill Anderson.

"Yup, I do have some set aside, in that Grand Rapids bank I took you guys to a century or two ago. I kept sending em most my pay the last three years, too. The cash I got for selling my general store in Wyoming before I signed up is also deposited there. So I guess I don't have to do much for a while. Till I get bored, that is."

"Vhere are you going to stay vhile you're not doing much, Bill?" the Swede asked.

"Think I'll go to my daughter's farm. Her husband will probably welcome another pair of hands for a while. At least I'll earn my keep until we get tired of one another."

"I got some money in dat bank too Bill," Swede broke in. "Remember you took me dere back in training camp. So I tink I find a livery to buy in some small town dat needs someone goot mit animals. Maybe find me a goot voman, too."

"We all know what the Dutchman's going to do," Stan chuckled. "No mystery there."

"Yup," Swede agreed. "He's going ta build that farmhouse he's alvays talking about and marry Julia."

*   *   *   *

When they reached Fort Leavenworth, most all the men wanted to send telegraph messages home. Mike was no exception.

Julia: We are going to be discharged any day. I don't know exactly when, but I will telegraph you again when I reach Chicago and know when my train will get into Grand Rapids. Michael.

Mike and Riley were relaxing before reveille in the fading sun of a late September evening.

"What are you going to do, Sarge?"

"I've been talking about that very thing with General Kidd. Seems that there's a slot for a sergeant major in a troop being formed here for duty in the West. They want a seasoned man to shape the boys up. So far, the recruits are Eastern trash and former Confederate cavalrymen. I got nothing ta go back to in Detroit. I think I'll accept that sergeant major offer. Good pay an grub. Not a bad rank, either, to retire on in a few years."

"Well Sarge," Mike offered. "They're fortunate to get you as their leader. If it weren't for you, a whole bunch of us would never have made it through the war or this mess out west either. I'll never be able to thank you enough, for sure. I'll never forget you, either."

"It's been a pleasure serving with ya, lad. I'm thinking, ya did your duty, and ya did it with honor. I'm proud'a ya."

"Thank you Sarge. God go with you."

*   *   *   *

Before the end of October, the men of the Michigan Brigade who were being mustered out were on the trail to St. Louis. It was none too soon, either. On their heels was a terrific snowstorm that swept across Kansas.

"Nothing like some bad weather to get a spring in your step, is there?" Anderson joked.

"You're right, Bill." Stan agreed. "This is one time, though, I'm not complaining about making twenty-five miles a day on this horse. My arse is sore, but my head tells me to get a move on before that damn storm catches up with us."

"No question about it," Dave observed. "Another day at this pace and we'll be at the docks, loading up on a boat for St. Louis. Another hundred or so miles down the Missouri River, and then head north for home. By damn! Can't wait."

At the head of the column, Mike, Phineas White and Henry Austry were talking, too.

"I believe we're going to be in St. Louis ahead of schedule, gentlemen," Mike estimated.

"Good thing too, Mike," Phineas observed. "By moving along at a good pace, we beat that storm beating down on us from the north. You know, I was just thinking to turn around and say something to Riley when I realized he's still back at Leavenworth."

"Those recruits must think they've been sent a messenger from hell itself," Austry predicted. "Snowstorm or not, I'll bet he'll have them out taking care of their horses."

Mike chuckled at that comment. "I can hear him as clearly as it was yesterday, shouting at us recruits, "If it weren't fer yer horse yas all would be in the infantry, walking.""

"When his new charges complain or pretend to be ill and go to sick call, I know exactly what he'll tell them."

"If I catch yas at sick call you'll have me ta deal with. Then you'll be wishing the Indians had ya tied to a wagon wheel instead."

On and off through the day, the men exchanged stories about Riley.

"At some point, those recruits will realize that they're in good hands, as we did."

"Wonder how he'll deal with the former Confederates in his troop?"

Mike responded to Austry's question without a moment's hesitation.

"He'll treat them like any other trooper. He'll not hold a grudge. In fact, I'll bet he'll make some of those Rebs squad and even platoon leaders if he thinks they're good men."

*   *   *   *

When they reached the Missouri River, the troopers were directed to leave their horses in corrals and then marched to a storage barn where quartermaster personnel checked in their saddles, horse tack and other gear.

"Sure seems funny," Swede commented. "Dis is da first time in three years dat I don't have horses ta care for."

"You're righ, Swede," Dave Steward agreed. "It does seem strange. Hated to leave my Spencer carbine, too. That was a sweet weapon. Using my old squirrel gun back home will seem strange when I take it hunting again. My saddle was broken in real nice, too. At least they let me keep my side arm and sword. They'll make good souvenirs."

"Good riddance, I say." Stan chortled. "All the time you spent nursing yer horse and bouncing around on that saddle, I'd think you'd be thankful to be rid of both. Just think about it. Every single day, without exception, each of us spent hours taking care of some damn horse. Can you tell me honestly that you miss it?

"I know my hind quarters ain't gonna miss it a' tall."

"Maybe yer right, Stan," Dave laughed. "But what I'll really miss will be hearing your positive opinion about everything and everybody. It has been so refreshing over the past three years. Yup, I'll surely miss it. I hope you'll stop by the farm now and again just to keep me properly informed."

"You had better be careful what you wish for Dave," Bill warned. "Hell, he might just take you up on that."

Over the following three days, the men of the 6th Cavalry Regiment enjoyed the quiet passage south on the river.

In St. Louis, the troopers received their mustering out paperwork and pay. Some men decided to stay and celebrate in the city, but not Phineas White, Henry Austry, Mike and his old squad mates. They chose to hop the first available train north, and home.

These men had last ridden a train in December 1862. Of course, it was wartime then and the cars were jammed with troopers. It was so overcrowded that you were forced to sleep sitting up, sometimes standing up, if at all.

Passenger cars had been improved some since then, too. Instead of bare wooden seats, now they were padded with a rawhide covering. If the car wasn't too crowded you could fold down the seat back into a bed; not all the comforts of home, but at least you didn't have to sleep sitting upright. Some of the runs included a car where passengers could buy drinks and cold sandwiches. This was a run that did have such a car.

Their tickets took them northeast through central Illinois. As they entered and then left Springfield, and further through Bloomington, they enjoyed looking at the lush farm fields just waiting for harvest.

"The fields that are barren were probably in wheat," Mike observed. "There're ready for some kind of cover crop, clover maybe."

Dave added his two cents worth. "Corn looks ready, too."

"Up Northern Michigan way, I never saw corn grow tall as this. Season's shorter, I guess," Stan added.

"Hey, Mister Conductor, tell me something," Bill inquired. "We just left Bloomington. When will we get into Chicago?"

"When you wake up tomorrow, soldier boy," he answered and walked away down the aisle.

"Come back here, fella," Killeen motioned to him.

Stan's companions sat back wondering what he had in mind. Mike had a smirk on his face.

"I don't think I like the way you said that, buddy. This soldier boy just returned from months in the saddle on the western prairie protecting assholes like you from being scalped by wild Indians. In fact, those savages captured one of our buddies, tied him to a wagon wheel and set him afire."

All the while he was berating the conductor, Stan was fingering the sharp edge of a big knife he held in his right hand.

Stan continued. "I watched our Arapaho scouts scalp another Indian. He grabbed the hair of the dead man and, using a sharp knife just like this one, he slit off the scalp from back to front.

"Fer the rest of our time with you Mister Conductor, I expect a little more respect. Do we have an understanding?"

Mike looked around the car. The other passengers were very quiet.

"Yes sir. Sorry, sir," he answered and hurried out of the car.

"Nice going, Stan," Dave kidded. "Probably the last time we see that guy."

"Well, he was a snippy fart. Probably sat out the war somewhere. I'll bet he bought himself a substitute. I won't take that from a slacker."

Everyone just slapped their hands on their thighs and laughed.

"As much as I want to get home," Mike told them, "I'll miss you guys."

*   *   *   *

Snippy or not, the conductor was right. Their train was moving slowly through Chicago heading toward the central station on State Street in the city's business district.

They were going to lose a member of their group here, Austry. He would be heading to Virden, a little town south of Chicago, while the rest of the group would be continuing together for Michigan.

"Why don't we have lunch at a good restaurant with Austry before we head out?"

"Sounds fine. But let's check the train schedule to Michigan first."

"Looks like we can get out of here around one o'clock and arrive in Grand Rapids tonight around nine or ten. We can stay overnight in town and head out in the morning."

"Ya, Mike. Sounds to me like that would work," Dave Steward agreed. "After lunch we might wander around some. We've got time before our train will leave. I'd like to buy a little something for my wife. While you were checking out the trains, I asked at that information booth over there. They told me that there are a good number of stores just up State Street, restaurants too."

After several days of travel, they were eager for a good meal, a hot one. They stopped at the first restaurant they found. Meatloaf, ham or stew was offered with all sorts of side dishes. They had had enough stew for the rest of their lives. Meatloaf was the favorite this day. Plates containing mashed potatoes, gravy, fresh corn, red beets with freshly baked rolls covered the table. They hadn't seen butter for a long time, either. A lot of that was used on the rolls.

Over hot coffee and apple pie, everyone smoked a cigar; Bill enjoyed his pipe. Even Austry had a smoke.

"Henry," Stan chided. "Now that we're civilians and equals, you don't mind if I call you by your given name do, you?"

"Would it make any difference if I did, Stan?'

"Not in the least."

The other men started to laugh softly while they waited for Killeen and Henry to continue having fun with one another.

"Henry," Stan continued. "Did you smoke when you left home as a sprout?"

"No, I didn't. It is one of the evils I learned from you fellows."

"Tell your folks that, will you?"

"Definitely, Stan, and I will blame you in particular."

"You would do that, would you?"

"Without hesitation."

"Will you promise them to quit?"

"No, I think I earned the right to smoke a cigar when it pleases me."

"Good man, Henry. I was worried you might just wimp out and quit to avoid the criticism of your parents or your girlfriend. I'm just sorry that we didn't have the chance to corrupt you further."

The other men were really enjoying this back and forth. They really enjoyed it as these two continued the banter, each with a perfectly straight face. The laughter grew louder and the men rocked in their chairs and slapped one another on the back.

"What type of evil would you have exposed me to, Stan?"

"Drink and loose women, of course."

"I'm sorry I missed that part, Stan."

"The Dutchman here wouldn't let us have whiskey around. And Sherman ran us so hard out of Tennessee to Atlanta, Savannah and the Carolinas we never had the chance to introduce you to any loose ladies. Washington City was full of'em, I was told. But the generals whisked us out' a there to the West so fast we missed that, too.

"You have my apology, Henry, for leaving out that part of your education. I feel badly about it, too, since I can't imagine you'll learn once you get back to whatever that little town of yours is called."

"Apology accepted, Stan. But I shave now and thanks to you I smoke cigars. I expect I'll just have to learn the rest on my own."

Stan stood. "Good luck to ya, Henry. And may the good Lord see to it that your education continues."

The men were on their feet now, clapping. Everyone shook Austry's hand and gave him a hug before they left the restaurant for the train depot.

Underway toward Michigan, the men all agreed that Henry Austry had been a good addition to their troop. He had a likeable way about him, looked after his men and was a hard worker. Most of all, they had grown to trust him.

"Not a bad fellow for an officer," Stan decided. That was high praise indeed, coming from Killeen.

✳   ✳   ✳   ✳

That evening, they decided to have a last meal together and a few drinks to celebrate their return to the town where they first met and trained together. So they chose the Rathburn House, because it offered liquor. If they got a little tipsy, they wouldn't have far to go to their rooms.

On the way there they noticed that Houseman's Clothing Store was still open. That was the store they had all shopped at on the occasion of their first pass to town three years before. Now, they all needed civilian clothes. It was decided that they each needed a suit. What better opportunity?

When one of them would come out of the changing room to have the clothing measured for alterations, the rest of them hooted and laughed at the sight. You see, they had never seen one another out of uniform, at least not for three years.

"Bill," Mike teased. "I never would have imagined that you'd look like that. Are you sure you want to turn in your military clothing?"

Stan took the worst ribbing of all.

"That stuff will never do, Killeen. Put your uniform back on. You look awful in that civilian outfit."

The tailors at Houseman's were losing patience with these rowdy soldiers.

Still in the uniform of a major, Mike apologized for everyone. "We're not drunk, sir, just so happy to be home after three years that we're acting a little silly."

"Come on fellas, let's leave these men to serious shoppers. We can get clothing another time."

✳   ✳   ✳   ✳

The evening meal was as delicious as the one they had had back in Chicago. This time, though, they had red wine with it. Except for Mike, it had been virtually years since anyone had wine with a meal.

"You gonna get drunk tonight, Mike?" Bill Anderson asked.

"Not on your life. That time out west with the general's cognac was the first and last time, believe me. The morning after, I thought I would die. Later that day, I was worried that I would not. Oh, that was awful, Bill. Besides, how would it be if I greeted my family and Julia tomorrow morning with a hangover and smelling like a brewery? No thanks. I'm taking the pledge."

Even though they had all sworn they would not wake up with the sun, they did. In fact, all of them had breakfast together, well before seven o'clock.

"What time does your train leave for Lapeer, Phineas?"

"Nine this morning, Dave. I gave you my address last night, didn't I?"

"I remember that we all exchanged them."

"Any time you're around Lapeer, look me up. I'm going back to the room, shave and clean up for my train."

"My train north won't leave until ten. I might just go back to Houseman's for that suit you thought looked so funny on me. I sort of liked it."

The men needed to move on; their life together was over. But no one wanted to leave. They thought they had said their goodbyes the night before. But this time it was final, and it hurt.

Damn! I love these men. Mike realized. *We protected and looked after one another. We became family. I owe them so much.*

As each man left the dining room, he felt suddenly lonely. Not one of them could explain it, but they all felt it as they hugged one another.

Home at Last

Mike got his gear and walked to George Neal's bakery.

"Michael," his sister shouted as he entered the door of the shop.

She came running toward him. Right behind her came Julia.

"It's about time you got her, mister." The two hugged and kissed right in the middle of the shop.

When he could take a breath, he asked, "I didn't know you were here?"

"Yup. I've been here for two days, just waiting for you. If you had been any longer getting here, George and Susan would have worked me to death."

"Oh, come on, Julia. It wasn't all that bad. But we did appreciate the help."

"Let's have some coffee and sweet rolls. You've never tasted George's baked goods have you, Michael?" Julia asked.

"Yes I have, as a matter of fact. Not his sweet rolls, but his biscuits were part of our daily meals when he was still in the troop. Weren't they, George?"

Just then, four rather scruffy looking fellows in soldier uniforms rushed into the shop.

"Mike, you rascal. Why didn't you tell us George had a shop right downtown here?"

The four soldiers hugged George and roughed him up a bit.

"A businessman now, by God!" Stan shouted.

"Place looks good to me, George," Bill Anderson observed.

"Smells goot to me, George. Can I have some of your sveet roll ta taste?" the Swede asked.

"Sure you can, Swede. Sit down, Dave. All of you sit. Let me get you guys coffee too."

Off to the side some, Julia sat close to Mike and hugged his arm.

"When will my folks be here, sweetheart?"

"After chores and breakfast. I expect them around nine, in another hour or so. Come on, I want to show you Susan's home upstairs.

"Be right back, you guys." Mike said as he followed Julia into the back of the bakery.

"A likely story." Stan remarked. "Let me try one of those apple things. What do you call them, George?"

"Fritters."

$$*   *   *   *$$

Upstairs, as soon as Julia shut the stairway door behind them, she was in Mike's arms.

Ummm! I waited so long for the feel of him. At least he hasn't forgotten how I like him to kiss me. Yes, Michael, hug me close.

Mike pulled away some.

"Michael," Julia urged. "Please don't stop."

"We need to go downstairs, sweetheart. We'll have plenty of time together later."

"Oh! I need you Michael. Its' been so long."

"I need you two darling. Later alright?"

$$*   *   *   *$$

No sooner than Julia and Michael returned to the shop door opened again to Jake and Rose Drieborg. Then the cries of greeting, hugs and celebration began again.

"Introduce us to your army friends, Michael." Rose prodded him.

Michael did the honors for both his parents.

"I remember Mr. Swede," Rose said. "You were at my home one Thanksgiving. Nice to see you again Gustov."

"You remember, tank you missus," Swede replied. "You were goot to me back den."

Rose continued. "I want to thank you boys for looking after my Michael. We prayed for him, of course, but for each of you too. We will thank God for the safe return of every one of you."

Bill Anderson stood. "Thank you Mrs. Drieborg. Mike was a good leader. He did right by us. He never let us down."

"Whatever happened to Sgt. Riley?" Jake asked.

Stan answered. "That dumb Mick stayed out west training recruits to fight Indians. Couldn't talk him out of it."

"We would like to have met him too. We'll pray for him too, won't we Papa? Remember boys, you are always welcome at the Drieborg home." She assured them.

"Thank you Mrs. Drieborg," Stan responded, suddenly serious.

He had to leave for his train, Jake needed to get home for mid-day chores and George wanted to get moving on the baking for afternoon deliveries; so the gathering broke up with much hugging and the exchange of best wishes.

"You be sure to write, Drieborg. You wrote letters for damn near the entire troop, one time or another. You best have time to write at least one to me." demanded Stan.

"Will you invite us the wedding, Julia?"

"Every one of you will get an invitation. Will you be ready to come back the Saturday after Thanksgiving Stan?"

"Be careful, Mike," Dave cautioned. "She's serious about this."

"I am too Dave," Mike quipped.

"You better be, mister." Julia added.

LOWELL

"Come on Michael," Julia urged. "Finish up your good-bys. Your Papa needs to get back."

"All right, all right." I'm coming. Swede, meet us outside by Papa's wagon."

"Ya, I be right der."

Jake Drieborg drove their wagon along Fulton Street toward Lowell. Michael sat in the second seat with Julia close at his side. The Swede followed riding a horse he, just bought at the local livery. Michael explained to Julia.

"Swede has no place to go yet. So I asked him to join us for a while. He'll help with the corn harvest and with the chores. It will be good to have him. He'll use the hired man's room in Papa's barn."

"That's fine. Just as long as we have time for ourselves, mister."

"Don't you worry about that, sweetheart," Mike assured her. "He'll not interfere in the least."

Mike hadn't been paying much attention. So when Jake pulled up in front of a house Michael didn't remember, he didn't realize just where on Fulton they were.

"What's this, Papa?"

"This is our new house, darling," Julia said, all excited. "Let me show you the inside."

Mike just stood in the road looking at the house.

"Well, I'll be darned. You little sneak. When did you do all this?"

"After you were sent west," Jake told his son. "You told Julia in one of your letters to go ahead with da house. She told me, and I got some of da men from da church, Ruben and da Bauers together. We already had da lumber from da trees we cut last winter. Julia told us what she wanted, and here it is, son."

Julia was fit to be tied. "Don't just stand there, silly. Come on. Let me show you the inside."

Mike walked through the inside. "Its like being in my old house. Its' perfect, Julia; just like I imagined it would be."

"It has the most modern stove, ice box and water system there is, too. Look, I can stand inside and pump water from the well directly into my sink. Ice from our icehouse goes into this box and keeps our food cool, even in the summertime.

"But the best room is back here," she confided, pulling, him by the hand.

"Our bedroom. I can't wait to get you into this bed. Feel how soft it is. A down comforter, too."

"You did it, Julia. I'm proud of you. Couldn't have done any better myself. Now all we have to do is get married, so we can really enjoy that bed."

"That's being taken care of too, my dear." Julia said with that smile Mike had come to know might spell trouble for him.

"That, too?" he said in mock anger. "Am I already married?"

"No, silly," She chided. "But the bans have already been read at church. They'll be read the second time this coming Sunday. So if nobody objects before that, we can get married the Saturday after Thanksgiving."

"My Lord!" Mike exclaimed. "Have you planned the rest of my life, too?"

"As a matter of fact, yes," she shot back, hands on her hips. "You aren't any big shot hero of the war any more, Major Drieborg. You're mine for the rest of your life; got that?"

She was in his arms looking up at him, waiting for a reply and a kiss.

She got both.

First the agreement; "Yes ma'am. Forever, ma'am."

Then the kiss.

CIVILIAN LIFE

Over the next few weeks, time flew for Mike, as he had never remembered. At the bank he took out a small mortgage, then finished the barn and outbuildings, bought his animals and flocks. He didn't need too much equipment. He would be able to share equipment with his father, and with Ruben Hecht and Walter Bauer.

They all worked hard to finish harvesting the corn and planting the wheat on all three farms. Julia was busy, too, preparing for their wedding. They even saw the new lawyer in town to arrange the papers for the adoption of Robert. They would submit those to the court after they married.

"No, Michael," Julia insisted. "We're not having the two children at our house for a while. I've waited too long for you to have them underfoot. I intend to have you to myself until after Christmas. Besides, they're fine just where they are for now.

"I can see we need to have an understanding here and now."

"Oh, and what would that be, miss bossy?"

"I won't tell you how to manage the farm, you don't tell me how to run the house. Got it?"

Mike chuckled.

"Don't you laugh about this, mister. Do we have an understanding here or not?"

"Yes, sweetheart. We do."

My heavens! Is she like Emma Hecht or what? Seems to work for her and Ruben. Should work for us too.

✳   ✳   ✳   ✳

What a Thanksgiving weekend it was. All the men of his old squad showed up on Friday and stayed for the rest of the weekend. Stan, who was living in Cadillac now, and Dave the farmer from Newaygo, bunked with George at the bakery. Bill lived in the area at his daughter's farm in nearby Wyoming. The Swede was at Jake's farm in the hired man's room. Phineas White from Lapeer stayed at the Hecht farm.

Phineas brought a surprise guest with him for the weekend, Bob Lilley. Mike and Bob had traveled together in November of '64, going home to Michigan on leave. He was also a major, but in the infantry. He had been with Mike when Bacon attacked him in Detroit. He lived in Lapeer now, a farm boy like Mike.

"Well, I'll be. Look who the cat dragged in, Julia." He and Bob gave one another a big hug.

"I saved this tall galoot in Detroit a year ago when we got shot at. Poor country boy, he wouldn't have made it without me. Not used to a big town like Detroit, it appeared."

"Miss Julia," Bob countered. "Are you aware that this fella of yours has a poor memory. As it happened, my life was in danger just walking down the street with him."

"Now that he mentions it, Julia," Mike admitted. "He did help some."

That evening, the boys stayed at Mike's place. Julia would stay at her mother's until the wedding.

Mike introduced Bob and they both had a good time, sharing what had happened in Detroit a year earlier.

"What are you doing with yourself, Phineas?" Mike asked.

"I got a job teaching," he said. "My military training prepared me pretty well for managing these children, especially the older ones.

They remind me a lot of you, Stan; devious and always wanting to be somewhere else but in my classroom.

"The kids have already learned my Riley Rules."

That brought a lot of laughter.

"What the hell are Riley Rules, Phineas?" asked Stan.

"First off, they're rules that cannot be challenged. Like 'No talking when I am.'

"Actually, they are common sense rules just to maintain order in the classroom. Out of doors, the big rule is, 'No picking on other kids'."

"The older boys want to meet the Dutchman, Mike."

"Why me?"

"They never met a man whose wartime friend, an Indian, saved him from a terrible death. I might have exaggerated some, not having actually been in that Indian camp. My tale sure got their interest, though."

"More tale than fact I, expect." Mike challenged.

"You might be interested to know, fellows, that Bob here is a Baptist minister now. He's my minister, truth be known; the Hunter's Creek Baptist Church."

Bob explained. "My congregation is small right now, so its' only part time. I'm really a farmer, like my dad and his father before him. We have land much like this. Our crops are the same too; corn, wheat and oats."

"Have you got a lady picked out to marry, Bob?" Mike asked.

"Well, now that you mention it, I have my eye on a young woman. She visited us for a family reunion; sort of a welcome home for me, last summer. Her parents are cousins some three or four times removed. From Wisconsin; they stayed for two weeks. I got real fond of her.

"You'd be interested in this, Mike. She is a real good baseball player. She can hit the ball a mile; good at catching it, too. She was the star of our family games."

"From what I hear, Bob," Stan interrupted. "We have you to blame for saving this lad here back in Detroit, so he could return to us as our troop commander. Seems like he needed a bunch 'a help ta just walk down the street much less get through the war."

"Stan will never let Mike forget that down in North Carolina, he got Mike out of a jam."

"Snatched him right out of the Jaws' a death at the hands of the terrible Rebs, I did, fer sure." Stan insisted.

"Ya shore did that, Stan, I must admit," Mike admitted. "It was another prison for me if not for you and Austry."

"Where is that sprout? Illinois isn't the other side of the world, after all." Bill asked.

"He wrote that his father is ill; had to stay close to home."

"By the way, Drieborg, I'm getting bloated on all this cider. Haven't you got something a little stronger to celebrate with?"

"As a matter of fact, Stan, I do. A little red wine for the red blooded men of my troop."

"I'll pass, Mike," Bob said when offered. "I've taken the pledge. Cider is fine for me."

"Mike told us he was going to take that pledge too, Bob." Bill Anderson remembered.

"Let me tell this one, Bill," Stan interrupted. "When we were out west, General Kidd had the officers in for a special meal and some of his private stock. After feeding them wine, he gave them some white lightning stuff called cognac. A bunch of that later, this fine gentleman we called the Dutchman was flat out drunk."

"Oh come on, Stan. I wasn't that far gone."

Dave Steward jumped into the conversation at this point. "Mike was so drunk, Bob, that he couldn't hold any food for two days. He moaned and complained for three days about how much his head hurt. And, he promised to us, very loudly, that he would never take another drink again."

"Ya, I remember dat too, Mike," the Swede added. "I seen drunks before. Been drunk myself once or twice. You vere really drunk, Mike."

"Just don't tell my father. I promised him I would not do that. Besides, it just sort of snuck up on me that night. I didn't mean to do it."

Everyone laughed at that.

George Neal capped this part of the conversation with, "We've all experienced that, Mike. None of us ever means to get drunk, and we have all vowed never to do it again. Until the next time it sneaks up on us that is. Since I've been married to your sister, I've been good. Can't bake and drink, anyway."

"Well, I'm going to be good all the time. I remember how terrible I felt. Never again."

"Until the next time buddy." Everyone chanted and laughed.

WEDDING

Neighbors, townspeople, and Mike's army buddies filled St. Robert Catholic Church. Julia had planned the entire event. Father Dumphy had finally just given up reminding her that the ceremony was set in Catholic ritual. She had her own ideas; and she had things her way. The Catholic Mass she did not change, but that was about all.

She decided that her sisters-in-law, Ann and Susan, would stand up with her, and that Michael's brother Jacob and her brother Kenny would do so for him. Even Robert was involved as a ring bearer, much to the three year old's discomfort.

When she sent invitations to all of Mike's army comrades, she had asked that they bring their military swords.

"You guys actually brought them with you?"

"I saw the look in Julia's eye the day we met her at the bakery; before we went home, remember?" Stan reminded Mike.

"Me too," Dave agreed. "I didn't want to have to deal with her anger. So I just brought the damn thing."

"But that's not the whole 'a it, Mike," Stan added.

"Oh my God, what else?"

"We all brought our uniforms, too."

Mike laughed till tears ran down his cheeks. "That's my Julia, all right."

*   *   *   *

Julia's changes blended in beautifully with the traditional Catholic Mass and wedding ceremony. Everyone clapped and cheered when the priest told the groom, "You may kiss the bride."

On the way out of the church, she had the men standing in uniform on either side of the outside stairway, holding their swords over the stairs for Mike and Julia to walk under.

The day was balmy, so everyone sat outside at long tables for the wedding meal. Many of the guests had brought a dish or two to pass, just as they did after most Sunday morning services.

"Did you demand that God give us this pleasant weather too, Julia?" Mike asked teasingly.

"I mentioned it a time or two, yes."

Mike was saved from further comment when the audience hit their silverware against cups, signaling the couple to kiss.

All in all, it was quite an impressive production.

WEDDED BLISS

It was still dark outside when Mike threw the covers back and started to swing his legs out of bed.

"Where do you think you're going, mister?"

"Our cows don't care that we've just been married Julia. They need to be milked each morning at this time."

"True. But you don't have to worry about it, my dear husband. Jacob and Kenny agreed to do it this week, morning and afternoon.

"All you have to worry about is making love to me."

"Sweetheart, you've kept me up most of the night. I suppose it doesn't bother you that I'm almost exhausted."

"Don't give me that nonsense."

"What nonsense?"

"I've heard you and your 'boys' talk of long marches without sleep followed by big battles. You mean to tell me that making love to me is more exhausting? That's what I meant when I said nonsense."

"You've got a point there. Where were we when I fell asleep at whatever o'clock it was this morning?"

Later that morning the lovebirds heard a loud knocking at their door.

Mike pulled on some pants and a shirt.

"Just a minute; hold on, for heaven's sake."

Jacob and Kenny were standing in the vestibule, laughing at the sight of Mike.

"What's so funny, you two?"

"Our folks want you and Julia to come over for dinner and the opening of wedding presents. George and Susan are waiting to go back to the bakery, and all of your old army buddies are there, too. No one wants to leave until you two get there. What do we tell them?"

"We'll be along."

"Julia, we have no choice. Everyone is waiting. You might just as well be gracious about it. So stop complaining and get a move on, please."

"Just you remember, mister." She warned. "After they leave, you're all mine."

✳   ✳   ✳   ✳

It was great fun, even for Julia. Just as they were told, everyone had crowded into the Hecht home. Some of the food was left over from the wedding, but it was still delicious. George had brought a chocolate cake and of course, his famous rolls.

Mike's army buddies had chipped in and bought him a Spencer rifle.

"You guys knew I was going to get one of these first chance I got. This is so good of you."

"Look at the engraving on it, Michael," Julia urged.

"To the Dutchman – From your friends: Bill, Dave, Swede, Stan, Phineas.

Bob Lilley rescued Mike from shedding a tear in front of everyone by interrupting at this point.

"I know you and Julia are Catholics, but God's word is the same for people of all faiths. I hope you will accept this family bible from another friend."

"Of course, Bob. We will treasure it always. Won't we, Michael?" Julia said graciously.

"Look Michael!" Julia cried. "Our parents have given us $200. Oh, you shouldn't have. You already have done so much."

"We know you two need many things for the house," Julia's mother told her. "So we decided to let you pick them out."

"Don't forget us," Jacob said. "Kenny and me got something for you, too."

"How did you boys ever guess that we needed kitchen knives? There're perfect. Thanks guys."

Then Robert came up to them. "I have a present for you, Mike; you too, Julia."

"My goodness," Mike said. "That is so great. Can I open mine?"

"Ya. But Julia first, cause she's a girl."

"Wow!" Mike exclaimed. "A handkerchief. Just what I can use out in the cold and everything. Thank you, Robert."

"Thank you for mine too, sweetheart. Come here and let me give you a hug." Julia asked holding out her arms.

"Ugh! Hugs are for babies. Big boys don't need hugs, do they, Mike?"

"I sure enjoy it when Julia gives me a hug. You might want to get one. They're pretty nice, even for big guys like you and me."

"Oh all right. You can give me a hug, Julia."

"This is a wedding present from me, Julia," Mike said while handing her an envelope.

Inside was a card telling Julia that she and Mike would be guests at the Eagle Hotel in Grand Rapids for two nights this next week.

"Oh my! This is so wonderful, Michael. What a nice surprise."

"Maybe we'll shop some when we're in town," Mike suggested.

"Think you'll have the strength to leave the hotel, mister?" Julia shot back.

Mike actually blushed as most everyone laughed at his embarrassment.

✶   ✶   ✶   ✶

While they were in Grand Rapids, the newlyweds treated Susan and George to supper at the hotel.

"So these are your rolls that they serve here at the Eagle Hotel?"

"Yup. People love 'em. They make their own desserts here at this hotel, but all their bread and rolls come from our bakery."

Susan joined in, too. "We provide rolls and bread to all the hotels now. We even had to hire another baker and a delivery boy to help us."

"You'll never guess who is helping us, Mike."

"I don't know anyone in Grand Rapids, George. So I can't begin to guess."

"Mrs. Bacon, Carl's mother."

"We'll, I'll be. How did that ever happen?"

George explained her first visit to the bakery.

"Since then, she and her friends have had their mid-morning coffee and sweet rolls in our shop. She bought the little tables you saw there, too. They all buy rolls, pies and cakes to take home as well.

"The exciting part is that very soon we will move to a new location. We will continue to bake bread in the ovens at the present site, but there's a building on Monroe Street that's much bigger. We'll be able to serve many more customers for coffee and rolls.

"We're going to call it the Cosmopolitan. She even chose the name."

"But how can you manage all that expansion when you've been open for business such a short time?"

"That's the other part, Mike." George continued. "Mrs. Bacon owns the building we're moving into. She's sort of our silent partner."

"What will Harvey and Carl say when they get out of prison?"

"Heck, Mike," George responded. "The old man was let out months ago. Because he's supposed to be ill, he's under house arrest. But Carl was released in a general amnesty or something a couple of months ago."

"And neither of them object?"

"I don't know about that part. All I know is that she told your mother one time when they were in the bakery talking, that she was sorry for all the trouble those two had caused the Drieborgs. She said that she wanted to help Susan and me get the business going. She told me that she would take care of them in her own way."

"My goodness," Mike said. "God sure works in mysterious ways.

"Maybe the Bacons will leave the Drieborg family alone now."

"Then you won't have to carry your pistol with you all the time, Michael." Julia added.

"We can only hope, sweetheart," Mike said. "But time will tell."

December in Lowell

As winter settled onto the land, Julia finally got her wish. She could snuggle under her blankets in Michael's arms while she heard the wind whistle outside and the snow pelt against the window of their bedroom.

"After church this morning, we are bringing Robert home with us," Mike reminded Julia. He'll stay with us for a couple of days."

"Do we have to Michael," Julia whined "We've got such a comfortable routine. He'll just upset everything."

"He probably will, sweetheart. But he is going to be our son. So we have to involve him in our lives sooner or later."

"I vote for later."

"We promised he would begin to live with us, as our son, right after Christmas. So we should start getting used to it. It will be easier for him, and us, if we do it a day or so at a time."

"I know you're right Michael. I just don't want it to face it yet. I'm enjoying us too much."

"Once we're used to having Robert with us, we can start having Eleanor visit." Mike added.

"I did not need to hear that right now, Michael. In fact, I am not going to even think about that right now.

"What I want you to think about though, Mr. Drieborg, is this lady in your arms who needs some serious loving."

"Yes, ma'am."

CHRISTMAS

"Come on, Michael," Julia urged. "Finish washing up or we'll be late for Christmas Eve Mass."

"I had a couple of things to finish up in the barn," Julia. "I guess that I forgot the time."

Mike stood at the kitchen sink and poured some hot water into a shaving mug. He stripped off his shirt and lathered his face to shave.

"Michael?" he heard behind him.

Oh, my Lord! Where have I seen this before?

Julia stood in the bedroom doorway without a stitch of clothing on her very beautiful body. Her arms were outstretched and in each hand she held a dress.

"Which dress should I wear tonight, Major Drieborg?"

What a tease this woman of mine is. She's not thinking of church at all.

This time, Michael did not turn his back on her as he did in Cleveland, a year ago. This time, he took up her challenge.

They were late for church; very late.

✳   ✳   ✳   ✳

While they were getting ready to leave for the family Christmas Day dinner, Julia told Michael to sit down. She sat on his lap.

"I've got a surprise for you, sweetheart."

"What kind of surprise?" Michael implored.

"The kind that you must guess." Julia teased.

"Is it something that will be helpful to me in the barn?"

"Could be. One can never tell."

'Will it have to be fed?"

"Definitely, Michael. Feeding will be necessary. You're getting warmer."

"Is it something we will eventually eat?"

"Oh, no! You are so cold now."

"Will it last a long time?"

"You're getting back to warm now, Michael. This surprise will last a long time."

"I have exhausted all the possibilities, Julia," Mike protested. "You are now bordering on being cruel. I'll bet that you didn't give me the right answer to one of my questions."

"I don't want you to think me cruel. So I'll give you a clue. You helped me make this gift for you."

What in heaven's name can she be talking about? I helped her? With what? She won't let me touch a thing around this house.

"I'm stumped Julia. I haven't a single idea. Please, don't torture me any longer."

"Oh, all right, crybaby. Are you ready?"

"Yes, please."

"You're going to be a father, Michael."

"Oh, my God!" Mike exclaimed.

✳   ✳   ✳   ✳

The Drieborg, Hecht, Deeb and Neal families were already sitting at the dinner table when the newlyweds arrived.

"Nice of us to join us," Emma Hecht snapped. Your dinner is probably cold."

"Sorry Momma, it couldn't be helped," Julia insisted. "I had something special to tell Michael."

"What was so important that you would be late for dinner on this of all days?" Emma continued.

"I wanted Michael to know, before anyone else, that I'm pregnant."

Emma and her daughter hugged in celebration.

The men slapped Mike on the back.

The boys, Kenny and Jacob sort of shrugged their shoulders.

Robert wondered what all the fuss was about.

"Can we open presents now?" he asked.

✳   ✳   ✳   ✳

The Michigan winter continued. The men did their chores and worked on equipment in their barns. The daily routine was equally set for the women in the homes. They baked, cooked, cleaned and sewed. Weather permitting, the young people walked to school. When at home, they helped with chores.

Everyone waited impatiently for spring. The men were anxious to get seeds into the ground. The women wanted to start their gardens. The kids wanted to play outside.

The spring would bring the gift of new life for these families too. In March Susan Neal would give birth to her first child. Then Ann Deeb would welcome a child in July. Right before the fall harvest Julia Drieborg would have Michael's baby.

Julia and Michael Drieborg had legally adopted Robert. His daily presence in their home had upset things as Julia feared. But she was getting used to having him around the house. She was grateful for the time he spent with Michael in the barn.

"Sometimes, Michael, his questions drive me crazy."

She wasn't ready to bring Eleanor into her home.

FINAL RECKONING

It was cold and windy this Wednesday morning in early March. It was Ash Wednesday, the beginning of Lent. Morning chores were completed. The Drieborg and Hecht families were in church. Michael's mind wandered during the service.

I keep seeing Julia walking across the street tugging our three-year-old stepson Robert alongside. That image will be with me forever. I stood on the elevated sidewalk in front of Yared's General Store watching her cross the road toward me. She had been at the library to check out some books to read to the little fellow. Paying more attention to the three year old than the horse and wagon traffic on the street, she did not see two horsemen ride up on either side of her.

When I saw them each begin to swing a club toward her, I screamed, "Nooooo!" and ran into the street. I pulled my pistol as I ran, but did not fire for fear of hitting her or the boy. In an instant she was on the ground. As the attackers spurred their horses down the street, I got off a couple of shots; think I hit one of the men.

Then I was on my knees, holding Julia in my arms. Robert was on the ground at our side and did not stir.

My wife's head was covered with blood. One eye was swollen shut, the other fluttered open.

"Is Robert all right, Michael?" she asked.

"He is fine," I *assured he, even though I didn't know if he was or not.* I *picked her up and walked toward Doctor Peck's office.*

On the way I heard her whisper, "I love you Michael." *Then I felt her go limp in my arms.* "Please don't go, Julia." I *sobbed.* "Don't go."

I laid her down on the bed in the examining room of the doc's office. She was breathing, barely. Her mother Emma followed us and stood at my side. Ruben laid Robert on the other bed in the room.

I saw the doctor feel for his pulse. "The boy is gone, I'm afraid." *He turned toward Julia.*

"Can you save her Doc?"

"I'll try, Michael. I'll do the best I can."

Then he ushered me out of the room. "You too, madam," *he told* Mrs. Hecht.

"This is my daughter. I'm staying."

I sat for some time, waiting. My parents had come into the office by then, too, and my father stood at my side. Then Dr. Peck opened the door. By the look on his face I could tell that his news was not good. My father's hand tightened on my shoulder as the doctor spoke.

"We could not save the baby, Michael," he said first. "Julia has lost a good deal of blood and as a result is very weak. I can't tell you the extent of her head injuries. She is conscious right not and is asking for you, Michael."

I sat in a chair by her bed and held her hand. "Why are you crying, sweetheart?"

"Because I lost our baby. I'm so sorry, Michael."

"That's not your fault. Besides, we can have another as soon as you get better."

"Is Robert all right, Michael?"

For the second time, I lied. "He is still unconscious, so the doctor doesn't know much."

She closed her eyes and seemed to fall asleep. Her grip on my hand was firm and her breathing seemed steady. So I felt relieved some. Please Lord, help Julia. This is my fault not hers. She did nothing to deserve what has happened. Look after little Robert Lord. To have his life cut short like this is terrible. But I am sure that he is in heaven now with his mother Eleanor.

I remember putting my head down at Julia's side. I must have fallen asleep, because I awoke with a start at the feel of her hand on the top of my head. I heard her whisper, "I love you, Michael."

Then her hand slipped off my head.

"Doc, come quick," *I shouted.*

Once again he sent me out of the room when he shut the door behind me. Julia's mom was with him, too. Everyone from both families was awake now and waiting with me.

This time, only a few minutes passed before the door opened. But once again the doctor looked grim.

"Julia is still breathing," he told us.

"But she is in a coma, probably caused by the blows to her head. I have no idea if she will come out of it. All we can do is wait and pray."

I didn't know how much later it was, but when Father Dumphy went into Julia's room to give her the last rites of the Catholic Church, it seemed as though God had given up on her, too.

Before he left he put his hand on my shoulder and said, "I'll ask everyone at church tomorrow to pray for Julia, Mike."

When he left, I sat by her bed and held her hand; it felt cold and clammy.

"Get some sleep, Mike," *the doctor urged me.*

"Leave me alone," *I almost shouted.* "She'll be frightened if she wakes up and is alone. I must be here."

That was Saturday night. *I was still there Sunday afternoon when Julia joined our unborn baby and little Robert in heaven..*

✳   ✳   ✳   ✳

It was early Monday morning, milking time.

"Momma," Jake told her, "I'm done with da milking. So I'm going over to Michael's place to see if he needs any help."

"I worry about him too Papa. Take these slices of ham, these biscuits and this jar of gravy with you. He probably didn't have anything to eat this morning. Fix some coffee and heat up the gravy when you get there too, Jacob."

"Ya Momma, I'll see to it."

Down the road Jake found his son still at chores in his barn. Last December, Mike had only been home a few days when Jake had recruited other farmers to build this barn for his son.

Mike was sitting on a three-legged stool, milking his cow. "Morning Papa. You done with your chores already?"

"Your brother and I finished da milking. He can take care of da rest. Your Momma sent me over with some breakfast. Besides, I thought you might want some help dis morning."

"Thank you Papa," Mike responded. "I'm just moving around here in a daze, I think."

Mike leaned forward and rested his head against the side of the cow and began to cry. "I can't believe this has happened. I expect to hear Julia's voice calling me and to see little Robert running into this barn to pester me with his questions. Neither of them deserved to die Papa. The last thing she said to me was, 'I love you, Michael.' I'm so angry right now, I want to kill someone."

Jake moved about the new barn. He looked for other chores that needed to be done.

"Remember, Michael, we do not control much of what happens to us in dis life. I think dat you blame yourself for Julia's death. But did you bring da Hecht family here from Maryland? Of course you didn't. They decided to move to Lowell to escape da war.

"Are you responsible for da hate da Bacons have for us Drieborgs? Remember, we only have defended ourselves when dey attacked us. Dey is da sick people. You did not cause any of dis, Michael."

"Why did God let this happen Papa?"

"I think God allows all sorts of things to happen. It was bad when your Eleanor died. But it was good dat she gave our family your daughter.

"God doesn't stop evil men from doing bad things either, Michael. Just think of da War Between the States dat just ended. I don't believe God wanted dat to happen. But He allowed it and He let Americans kill thousands and thousands of udder Americans to settle da argument. He let a crazy person kill President Lincoln, too.

"I am sure dat if God had had His way, all of dat would have been settled without war and all da killing."

"I hadn't thought of it that way Papa. But in losing Julia, our unborn baby and Robert, I seem to have lost all purpose for my life. I feel so alone. My God, Papa; I miss her so."

"Michael, listen to me," Jake directed. "Over the years, we Drieborgs have not always gotten what we wanted. But we kept on, doing what we could. We never gave up; not one time, not one day even. You must look beyond dis, Michael. After da funeral Wednesday, you must begin again. Remember, you still have a daughter who needs her father."

"I know you are right Papa. But right now I'm so angry I can't even think straight. It seems that everything was killed along with Julia on that Lowell Street last Saturday."

"Enough, Michael!" Jake shouted from across the barn. "Take out your anger on da woodpile. But da day after da funeral, I will send your daughter Eleanor and your sister Ann to live with you. Den you must become a fader again. Now come into da house. Momma sent breakfast for us."

"Yes, Papa."

✳   ✳   ✳   ✳

So this was not your normal Ash Wednesday church service, signaling the beginning of Lent. It was the funeral service for Julia Drieborg and her adopted son Robert.

Several of Mike's old cavalry mates were in attendance. George Neal, Mike's brother-in-law, telegraphed them. Gustov Svenson, the Swede, owned a livery and operated a vet practice in nearby Hastings; Stan Killeen ran an elevator in Cadillac; Dave Steward was a farmer in Newaygo; and Bill Anderson was living at his daughter's farm in the nearby town of Wyoming; all were there to offer support. Sergeant Riley had remained out west, so he was not in attendance.

Congressman Kellogg and his daughter Patricia happened to be at their home in Grand Rapids then. So they were in the church audience as was Lowell's new bank manager Joseph Deeb, Mike's sister Ann's husband.

Once the service was over, everyone at the service followed the two caskets to the cemetery just outside the church. Prayers were said and the caskets were lowered into the cold ground. Afterward, as was the custom then, a potluck dinner was served inside the church.

Despite the solemn occasion children, normally in school were in and out of the building. They would be outside frolicking in the snow one minute and inside warming up the next. So no one noticed much when the door opened and a scruffy looking adult entered.

"Where can I find Mike Drieborg?" he asked the first adult he met.

"He's the fellow at the head of that table over there."

When the man was in front of Mike, he asked, "Are you Mike Drieborg?"

I don't know this guy. Never saw him before, either. He's got a pistol holster strapped outside his overcoat. What in the devil does he want here; today, of all times?

Mike took a pistol from inside his jacket and placed it on the table in front of the stranger.

"I'm sorry, folks," Mike said to those at his table. "But I'm not going to be taken by surprise again."

"Yes I am. Why do you want to know?"

"I mean you no harm, Drieborg. And I don't mean to disturb here. But I was promised $10 dollars in gold to deliver this to you while you were still at this church today. I know I don't belong here, but I needed the money bad. I don't get paid unless you sign this paper that you got the letter."

Mike picked up his pistol and pointed it at the messenger.

"I'll sign for you, mister," Mike responded. "But you understand something. Assassins probably paid by the same man who is paying you, killed my wife and son last Saturday. Who was it?"

"I don't rightly know. Some guy buying drinks at a bar in Grand Rapids last night. He said he would pay in gold for this to be delivered. Never did tell me his name. I just drank his liquor, took his letter and went on home."

"That may be, mister, but I'm pretty nervous around strangers right now. So I'm going to take your pistol, search you and sit you down at that table with those four men. They would like to have a little conversation with you. Our Lowell Marshal is sitting at that other table. I'll give him your pistol and stuff. He'll give your things back when he feels it's safe."

"Are you going to open the envelope here, Michael?' his father asked.

"This is not the place, Papa. It's probably from Bacon. I'll read it tonight. You and I can talk about it tomorrow during morning chores. Is that all right with you?"

"Yes son, dat would be fine."

∗   ∗   ∗   ∗

Most of the men in attendance at Julia's funeral had afternoon chores and their women had the evening meal to fix. So before long, everyone was on their way to their homes. Mike and his former comrades went to his farm for the night. After he finished his chores, Mike gathered with the five men for a supper of leftovers from the church dinner.

Stan Killeen finally broke the silence. "When are you going to read that damn letter?"

"Ya, Mike," Swede joined.

"Now's as good a time as any, isn't it?" Mike agreed as he opened the envelope.

Hi There Farm Boy

I heard of your wife's death. Very sad; she was pregnant too, I hear. Your child? The little boy was your adopted son, too. That was a bonus. Three Drieborgs sent to hell.

Now you are without a wife. Just like me. No good family will even receive me or invite me to any social event. The only women around here who will have anything to do with me, I have to pay. My father is so ill from his stay at the prison in Detroit, that the Marshal here has allowed him to serve his sentence at home instead of the jail cell your father's lies got him. Just like me, everyone here ignores him. It would appear that you have destroyed my family.

Now it is your turn. How does it feel, farm boy? I told you long ago that you could never escape me.

But don't worry, Drieborg, you won't be next. That would be too easy. You will be the last. I hope you will see all the members of your family die. Your sister Susan, now the baker's wife here in Grand Rapids; your sister Ann, who is married to the new Lowell bank manager; your brother Jacob; and of course your dear, dear parents will all meet in hell first. And how could I forget your child Eleanor? When will each of them will die?

No, you won't be next, not if I can help it. I want you to watch as each of the Drieborgs is put into the ground. I suspect that you will bury them all, just like you buried you wife today. It's too bad I can't be at each funeral.

Happy New Year old, Buddy,

Carl

＊　　　＊　　　＊　　　＊

"Holy shit," Dave Steward exclaimed. "I always thought this guy was a bit crazy; but he is sick."

Bill Anderson spoke next. "Remember when I told you to stay clear of this guy, Mike? Now, I think that's not possible. I think you have to take the battle right to him."

"Und da sooner da better, by damn!" Swede added.

"Well, by God," George interrupted. "If you don't do something to stop this guy, I will. He almost caused Susan to lose our baby last fall. I'm not going to sit by again. Unless he's stopped now, he'll get to my family eventually."

"Ya see, Mike," Stan said, smiling. "After you got yourself taken prisoner and then became a big hero, we had quite a time fighting a lot of battles. We didn't survive by being the whining wimps you might remember when we were with you. Quite the contrary, my friend; we learned to be very nasty. We learned to be angry and show no quarter. We learned to kill."

"You seem to have forgotten that I was with you in the Carolinas, Stan," Mike reminded him. "I think I caught up with you in the nasty department. Remember all those guys I ordered hung. But you might be ahead of me on killing experience.

"So if you're willing to help me overcome that fault, I'll welcome your help. Just keep in mind, before you agree to help, that I am out to solve this Bacon problem permanently."

"I'm with you," volunteered Stan. "Anyone want to leave in the morning?"

No one said a word.

"David," Stan said. "You have family on that nice little farm up by Newaygo. Don't you think you spent enough time away during the war? Aside from George here, you're the only married guy. Why don't you head home in the morning? The rest of us can take care of this problem."

"Just like you, Killeen," David responded. "You're always saving the fun for yourself. Farm life can be very boring for a hardened war veteran like me, don't ya know. Besides, Mike is my friend, too. No thanks, I'm in."

"All right, let's get down to it," Mike suggested.

He turned to George Neal first. "You tell your wife to stay at her parents' house for a few days. Tell her I want you to stay with me and the squad for the time being."

"We need to find Bacon. I suspect that won't be hard. Stan, David and Bill can ride into Grand Rapids tonight and hit the bars. From what that messenger told us today, Bacon buys company with liquor.

"Swede, George and I will go over to Hastings. Swede told me he heard a fellow at a bar there last Saturday night bragging about earning some easy gold for roughing up a couple of people in Lowell. We'll snatch him up if we can and bring him back here for a conversation."

George piped up, "I guarantee, he'll tell us who paid him and where we can find his partner."

Mike continued. "If you guys find Bacon, follow him out of the bar. He should be pretty liquored up. So grab him if he's alone. Gag him and tie a sack over his head. Wrap him in a tarp and tie him over the extra horse you'll have with you.

"If you can capture him alive, take him to the deserted farm just west of here. Leave him in the empty barn there. No lights. Keep the sack over his head and keep him tied and gagged. Come back here for the night. We'll deal with him in the morning. If there is no other way, kill him."

"Anything else?" Mike asked in conclusion.

None offered, Mike continued. "Before you go into Grand Rapids tonight, here's $10 dollars for each of you to use. Be careful. Don't take any chances. There's always another night. If need be, just watch. Don't push it."

In Hastings, the three men found one of the killers in the first bar they entered. They followed him out of town. The Swede rode a bit behind as Mike and George come up on either side of the man. They hit him with the clubs they carried and steered his mount off the road. Once his body was tied over his horse, they headed toward Lowell.

"Any ideas on how to get him to talk?" Mike asked.

During their service with Sheridan's cavalry in the Shenandoah Valley of Virginia, Mike's old squad mates had witnessed Union foragers hanging civilians repeatedly, until the person revealed where valuables were hidden. In South Carolina, they had found people who had been killed by marauders who used this method in their search for loot.

"I think we should use the old hanging method," George answered. "What do you think Swede?"

"Ya, George. I seen it used during da var."

Back in the abandoned barn west of Lowell, Mike watched as they used this persuasive technique.

"Be careful, you guys," Mike cautioned. "Don't want to kill this guy before he tells us what we want to know."

"Rest easy, brother-in-law," George retorted. "While you were being wined and dined at those fancy parties in Washington, we were in Virginia watching our army's best foragers convince Reb civilians to give up their valuables. The sarge would have skinned us alive if we had done any of that; but I think we remember how it was done. We'll get this guy to spill his guts without killing him."

They had the man's feet tied together and his hands bound behind him. A rope had been thrown over a barn beam and a noose was around the man's neck. They used a slipknot so that the man would be slowly choked. The rope was taut enough so that the man was on his tiptoes.

"Before we pull you off the ground, do you want to tell us who hired you to kill that lady in Lowell last week?" George asked him.

For an answer, the man spit at him.

"I pull dis time, George," Swede told him. "You tell me vhen to let him down."

George counted to ten. "Let him down Swede. Remember back in the Valley? Those guys used to count to ten the first time. Each time after, they would add a couple of counts. That seemed to work pretty good for them. Hear that you bastard? Are you ready to tell us who hired you?"

"Guess not, George," Swede commented. "Your turn ta pull. I count dis time."

They pulled the man off the ground three more times and got to a count of sixteen when he had had enough. He agreed to tell them who had hired him.

"Water; give me some water," he rasped.

"If I tell you what you want to know, are you still going to kill me?"

"What'ya say, Mike? Are we going to kill this child-killer?"

"Not if he tells us what we want to know. After all, we need him to testify in court, don't we?"

The man began to talk. "We were just hanging around some bar in Grand Rapids when we overheard this guy asking the man next to us if he had killed anyone during the war. My partner interrupted and said he had killed plenty of Rebs. Enjoyed it too, he said. The guy asking turned out to be named Bacon. He grabbed a full bottle and invited us to a corner table; said there was a Reb lover living over in Lowell who needed to be taught a lesson named, Drieborg. Said he had a southern wife too. He offered us fifty dollars in gold for each member of this guy's family we would kill. He really wanted us to start with the man's wife. We would get nothing if we killed the guy. We needed the money, so we agreed."

George jerked the man up on his toes again. "You agreed to kill a woman."

"If you were in the war, mister, you'd know we killed a lot of women in Virginia with Sheridan's boys. Got so it made no difference, soldier or not; we killed all the damn Southerners who looked cross-eyed at us."

"How were you going to do it?"

"We planned to kill Drieborg's people at his farm house after he left for town last Saturday. But the woman and a kid went with him, so we just followed. He was at the general store. So when she was crossing the street with the kid, it was easy to just run them down. Bacon paid us last Monday."

"Where is your partner?"

"He got shot as we were riding away. I'm not going to make it worse and rat on him. Anyway, I told you what you wanted to know."

This time the Swede pulled the rope and began the hanging torture all over again. "I'm not as goot a counter as my friend here, mister," Swede told him. "I forget da counting, so I start again; one, two."

After a count of ten, Swede lowered the man to the ground.

A few minutes later Mike said, "Count to ten again, George. If he hasn't told us the name of his friend, we'll just hang him again."

"No more," the man gasped. "I'll tell ya. His name is Varnor. He's holed up at Moore's rooming house in Hastings, room 10 on the second floor. He took a shot in the side last Saturday in Lowell. Lost a lot of blood; the doc said he might die even. I was on my way there with some food and whiskey when you grabbed me last night."

"We'll check it out tomorrow. So for now, you stay alive. Give him some water."

Afterward they gagged the man and put out the light. It was almost daylight, so they left him in the barn; after all, there were morning chores to do back at Mike's farm.

Back there, Swede helped milk the cows, feed and water the animals. George fixed biscuits. By the time they had fried eggs and bacon and brewed some coffee, their comrades who had gone to Grand Rapids had returned, without Bacon.

"Couldn't find him?" Mike asked.

"As a matter of fact, we did. But around midnight he left with a bunch of men for a local brothel. He was still there at daylight. We'll have to go into town again tonight. How about you? Find either of the attackers?"

George told them everything that had happened in Hastings and at the barn.

"Are you going after this Varnor tonight?" Bill inquired.

"Yes. We need to be in Hastings by dark. Just so no one in that town spots you, Swede, you go with Stan and Dave into Grand Rapids tonight. Bill can go with George and me to find this Varnor fellow in Hastings. For now, let's all get some sleep. We'll go over everything later."

* * * *

Behind the rooming house in Hastings, Bill stayed with the horses while Mike and George went up the back stairway. George tested the doorknob. The door was unlocked. As soon as he pushed the door open, Mike ran into the room, weapon raised. The room was small and the bed was only a couple of steps inside. Mike was on top of the wounded man before he could even sit up.

George closed the door while Mike pinned the man to the bed.

Knife in his hand, the point of the blade under the man's chin, Mike asked, "I have one question."

"Who hired you to kill that woman and little boy in Lowell last Saturday?"

"I don't know his name," the man gasped. "We were in a bar over in Grand Rapids and this guy fed us some whiskey and a sad story about being framed; offered us some gold if we would do this job. He had more gold for other killings later."

George almost shouted. "Didn't bother you to kill a woman or a little boy?"

"Needed the money. Besides, we did a lot of that when we rode with Sheridan during the war."

"You won't be earning any more of his money, mister," George told him. Mike nodded as George held a pillow over the man's face until he stopped struggling.

* * * *

Mike and his companions rode out of Hastings directly toward the abandoned Lowell barn.

"You killed that man without any hesitation, George. That's not the baker's assistant I met back in '62 when we joined up. You were even afraid of your horse back then."

"A lot has happened to me and all of the guys you knew then, Mike. Besides, my wife would probably been the next one killed by that guy. Right now I wouldn't hesitate to kill ten of them to protect her and my baby."

"George is right, Mike," added Bill. "If he hadn't done it, I would have."

"You may have that opportunity when we get back to the barn."

The three men continued to ride silently in the darkness.

When they arrived at the barn, they found the others already there with Bacon tied and gagged.

✳   ✳   ✳   ✳

"Is George still down at Michael's place, Susan?" Rose asked.

"As far as I know he is Momma. He's pretty fired up to do something about the Bacons. I wouldn't put anything past him at this point. Anyway, George told me to wait here for him."

"Da boys of Michael's old squad are still dere too, Momma." Jake added. "I think we leave dem alone for a day or two. But I might go over dere in da morning and help with chores, though."

Since Julia's funeral, Ann had been staying with her parents.

"I can't imagine the grief the Hecht's are going through right now," she said. "They lost little Eleanor's mother two years ago, heir farm back in Maryland a few months ago, and now they lost their daughter and little Robert too. They raised him from the time he was born. I'd want to go out and kill someone too, believe me. Do you think we are all still in danger from the Bacons, Papa?"

"I think so Ann. We will have to be on guard even more now. We'll keep our weapons loaded and nearby all da time. I think we'll stay out of town for a while too. Do you think Joseph will mind if you stay with us for a while longer?"

"He won't mind, papa. He likes Momma's cooking better than mine anyway. But this can't be allowed to go on forever."

THE BACON SOLUTION

"We didn't expect you'd be here this soon. What happened?" Mike asked.

"Tonight we decided to try something different. Instead of searching the bars, we watched his house. Funny, it's located just a few hundred yards or so east of our old training site. It was perfect, dark as a cave on that street.

"Anyway, just after dark Bacon left the house, alone. Stan was stationed in the horse barn back of the house. When Carl entered to get his horse, Stan hit him over the head rolled him up in a tarp, and tied him over his horse. After that we rode right here."

"He came to a few minutes ago; doesn't like being tied up, either."

Mike knelt beside Bacon and removed the gag.

"You had better let me go, Drieborg, if you know what is good for you."

"Like what your paid assassins did to my wife and son in town last Saturday? Let you go so that you can hire a few more to kill members of my family? I don't think so, Carl."

"What are we going to do with this piece of shit, Mike?"

"First, we are going to see how he likes the punishment his thugs gave my wife Julia and my son Robert. Here Swede, help me get him up. A rope around the neck with the other end thrown over that barn beam ought to hold him in place. Got that, George?"

"Well now, Carl," Mike continued. "Remember these men. In the middle of the night you marched down the company street back in '62. I think you called it a duck walk. Pretty painful, wasn't it, Bill? Later you ordered some troopers to attack George and me with tent stakes while we were all on maneuvers. George got broken fingers from that attack. I can forgive these things.

You drugged me in Washington, and tried to kill me in Detroit, again in Cleveland once more in Baltimore. I even forgave those attacks. But when your hired thugs killed my wife and son last week, I can't forgive that.

"And I cannot forget your promise to kill all the other members of my family. Can't allow that, Carl. Let you go? I'm afraid not."

"Turn and face the wall, guys," Mike ordered. "In case you're asked, I don't want you to have to lie about what you've seen."

As soon as everyone but George had turned away, Mike began to hit Bacon with a club. First he hit his arms, then his legs and back.

George grabbed Mike. "Let me have some time with this bastard, Mike."

"Was my wife Susan going to be next, Carl?" George shouted at him through clenched teeth. He too used the club on Bacon's arms and legs. "Were you going to have my bakery shop burned down, too?"

"That's enough for now, George," Mike ordered. He let Bacon down, removed his gag and used cold water to revive him.

"I wouldn't want you to sleep through all of this, Carl," Mike told him. "I have more in store for you this night."

"What do you intend to do, Mike?" Bill Anderson asked.

"I plan to hang him and his hired killer here. There's a good solid tree down the road some."

"Hey!" the prisoner tied up at the back of the barn shouted. "You promised not to kill me if I talked."

"Did I promise you that?" Mike mocked. "I guess I lied. Will one of you guys gag him?

"You all go to my house after we're done here. I'm going to end this vendetta tonight at his father's home in Grand Rapids."

"I want to go with you, Mike."

"Thanks, George. But you have to live and work in Grand Rapids. Besides, you need witnesses who can testify that you were nowhere near the city this night. I'll handle Harvey Bacon alone.

"Early tomorrow, I suggest that each of you leave this area and return to your homes. Back at my house are five documents. Each one states that we were all together at my place the entire evening. So before you leave in the morning, sign all of them and take one with you just in case you're questioned. I have already signed each one.

"George, after everyone signs my statement give it to my father to keep. Give him this letter, too, would you?"

"Sounds like you've got plans to be elsewhere when the shit hits the fan around here." George surmised.

"I can't live in this house. I see Julia everywhere. So I'm leaving. I'm not going to tell you where I'm going, so you won't have to lie if you are asked."

"We can't just leave you now, Mike." Stan objected. "How are you going to manage these two birds alone?"

"You haven't killed anyone yet, Stan. Neither have Bill, Dave or Swede. I'd like to keep it that way."

Bill Anderson offered a solution. "How about this, Mike? We help you get these two men on horseback ready for hanging. Every one of us takes a switch in his hand and all together hit each horse on the rump. That way, no one of us killed anybody."

Dave spoke up. "I like it, Bill. Anyone object?"

No one spoke up at first.

"I don't," Mike said. "That just means all of you killed these two guys."

"You got that right, Mike." Stan mocked. "Back in training camp you objected when we elected you squad leader. Everyone knew it was the best decision, except you that is. Seems that you haven't wised up yet."

Swede jumped into the conversation. "Ve talk enough. I say ve get on mit dis."

"All right," Mike agreed. "Thanks for helping me and George end this Bacon thing once and for all. Swede already checked the horses, so we didn't leave any distinctive shoe marks in the snow and mud outside. But let's be sure no one left anything inside that can identify us. Let's police the area. Each of you make sure that you still have your pocketknife and any other personal stuff. Check that you have your cap and both of your gloves. Does anyone leave any special marks in the snow with his shoes? "

"Sounds like he's commanding our troop again, doesn't it?" Stan quipped.

"You wanted to stay and help, Stan," snapped Bill Anderson. "Besides, better safe than sorry."

"Thanks, old man." Stan answered.

"What about it George?" Mike asked.

"Everyone checked out, Mike. And we looked over every nook and cranny of this barn. It's clean. I think we're ready to go."

"Put out the lanterns and let's get these two outside."

"The hired killer hangs first. I want Bacon to watch him die."

The horse that carried Julia's killer lurched forward when all the men hit its hind quarters. The rope around his neck jerked him off the horse. He fell until the rope stopped his feet from touching the ground. The slipknot used on the noose around his neck caused him to die slowly.

"See him struggle for air, Bacon?" George taunted. "Just think. You're next."

When the man's struggles stopped, Mike looked up at Carl. He was straining against his bonds and whining through his gag.

George laughed. "Listen to him cry. This is what happens to baby and child killers."

"See you in hell, Carl."

Bacon's horse jumped forward, leaving him swinging free, twisting against the rope closing around his neck.

"Leave them both hanging here. Fulton Street is only a few yards away. Someone will see them tomorrow, for sure.

"Don't use Fulton Street to go back to my house. You don't want to leave tracks from here directly back to my place. Ride the back trail. You know the one, George. Swede will see to the horses in my barn. After chores in the morning everyone should leave at the same time.

"George, join your wife at my parents' home. You'll need some people to vouch for your whereabouts until the mess at the Bacon home is discovered. So stay there for a couple of days. I'll take Bacon's horse and leave it in their barn."

Mike mounted the horse.

"We said our good bys in the barn, and I've got to go while it's still dark. God bless you all. And thanks again."

Then he rode into the night toward Grand Rapids.

THE DRIEBORG FAMILY

"What Momma? Why do you wake me?"

"Me wake you?" Rose retorted, sitting up. "You're the one who is moaning and talking in your sleep. The way you jerk your legs, it's a wonder I can sleep tonight at all."

"If you know I was talking, Momma, then I didn't wake you. So what did I say?"

"Don't get smart with me now, Jacob Drieborg. You are not the only one in this bed afraid for our family. Besides, the only word I could make out was the word "no", which by the way, you shouted loud enough to wake the entire house."

"I'm sorry Momma. I know you are worried, too. When I helped Michael with chores dis afternoon we talked about dis Bacon situation. I'm afraid he is going to do something violent against dem."

"I can't say that I would blame him, Papa. Even when they were in jail last winter, they paid men to attack him and us, too. I'm sure their money hired those men who killed Julia and little Robert last Saturday. Will the Bacons kill more of us?"

"He let me read da letter dat was delivered to him at da funeral. In it, Bacon promises to kill us all. Michael doesn't think Marshal Chapman in Lowell or da federal Marshal in Grand Rapids can do anything to stop him. So I believe Michael will take matters into his own hands.

I think he will kill both Harvey and Carl Bacon before dey kill any more of us."

"But what will become of Michael, Papa?"

"Come Momma. Come into my arms. Da Drieborgs will survive dis. Let us pray dat God will help Michael survive dis, too. Right now, we need to be strong for our children, and da Hechts." Jake hugged his wife close.

"Yes, Papa, I will be strong. But it is so hard."

Rose began to cry.

GRAND RAPIDS

Dear Lord, if there is any other way, help me to see it.

It's good that there is no moon tonight. I should be able to slip into town without being seen. The door to the horse shed at Bacon's place opens on the alleyway behind the house.

There's the shed. Good so far. All right fella. I'll bet you'll be glad to get this saddle off and the feedbag on.

There's no light on at the back of the house. Will Harvey be on the first or second floor, I wonder? Strange, the back door is not locked. I would think everyone who lives in a big city would lock their doors at night.

Move slowly, Drieborg. Don't bump into stuff in the dark. Get these boots off. Step quietly. There is a flickering light in the room beyond the kitchen. Ah yes. A fireplace is still going some. There's a wingback chair in front? I see blanket covered feet on the stool in from of the chair. Have to be sure its Harvey.

"Well hello, Mr. Bacon." Michael whispered.

"What?"

"Yes sir, that's the point of a very sharp knife you feel under your chin. Excuse me, sir. I've not properly introduced myself. I'm your son's old school chum, Mike Drieborg. That's right. I'm the one you paid to have killed in Cleveland last year. I'm the son of Jake Drieborg, whose family you tried to murder last year.

"A week ago, your son's hired killers murdered my wife and son in Lowell. Then, he promised to kill all the other members of my family. so tonight, I hung Carl and sent him to hell.

"But why am I here? Why am I here in the middle of the night with a knife at your throat? I am here to get you to sign this paper. It says what the courts have already decided; that you tried to kill me and my family; things you have claimed were not true. But we know you did them, don't we? Here we go now, slowly over to your desk.

"Please now, Mr. Bacon; no struggling. Just sit down, pick up your pen and sign the paper. Very good, sir. That will do nicely. Back to your chair in front of the fire. Just sit back, sir, and relax."

"I have done what you asked. What now?"

"Because you have admitted trying to kill me and sending killers to my father's farm to kill them, I believe you will try that again. So Mr. Bacon, I'm going to send you to meet your son in hell."

"Nooooo," Bacon moaned. Mike shut off his cry with a pillow held tightly against the old man's face.

He's stopped breathing.

"Is it over, Major Drieborg?" A lady in a nightdress stepped through the doorway into the light of the fireplace. "Must I be silenced too?"

"I hope that's not necessary, ma'am."

"We've never met, young man. I'm Mrs. Bacon. I heard you tell Harvey that our son is dead too."

"Yes, ma'am. He is."

"May God look after their souls." She sat before the fire. "When Mr. Bacon and I were much younger, we had a daughter. She was a delightful child. She still is. Mr. Bacon was much different then; a helping sort of man. Everyone liked him. Then we had Carl. Somehow whatever we had done right with our daughter, we did wrong with our son.

"As the boy caused trouble in town, with you and all the other youngsters, Harvey changed. He believed he had to always defend the boy and demand that everyone else accept the child's wild behavior. To have his way, he began to use the power of his bank to enforce his will on the people of the town. As Carl became worse, so did Harvey. You know the rest.

"I am so sorry about your wife and child. Harvey wouldn't allow me to attend the funeral."

"Thank you, ma'am. A minute ago you asked if this is over. Is it Mrs. Bacon?"

"As far as I'm concerned it is, Major. Unless, that is, I must die to satisfy you need for revenge."

"Please understand, ma'am," Mike interrupted. "Revenge was not my motive. Your son sent me a letter in which he promised to kill all the Drieborgs. He boasted that my wife Julia was only the first. I killed your son and Harvey to stop them from killing any more of my family. Revenge was never a consideration. So, ma'am, you tell me if this is over or not."

"Rest assured young man, it is over. Harvey's death will be explained as one of natural causes. Over the years I have become good at lying and making excuses; first for Carl's behavior, then for Harvey's. But my explanation will be accepted. Do we understand one another, Major?"

"Yes ma'am, we do."

"You should go, then. I need some time to prepare."

Mike moved toward the door.

Retrieve the note from the desk. Quietly now, leave the house. I'll change out of my farm clothing in the horse shed. Then I'll throw them, my boots and this knife into the river on my way to George's bakery. I'll wait there until my train leaves later this morning.

Lord, forgive me for what I have done.

LOWELL

After morning chores and breakfast, George told the Drieborgs he had been asked by Michael to read a letter to them and the Hechts together. So once both families had gathered at the Hecht home, he did as Mike had requested.

Dear Family,

The loss of Julia, our unborn child and little Robert has left me with a feeling of terrible despair. They would be alive at this moment if not for me. Nor is there anything I can say or do to lessen the guilt I feel over what has happened. Feeling sorry will not bring them back, nor will revenge on those who caused their deaths.

It's too painful for me to stay at the farm right now, so I'm leaving Lowell. I'll let you know where I am after I become settled.

In the meantime, see the lawyer and arrange for Kenny and Jacob to have ownership of my entire farm. I have left some funds in my account to get them started on the spring planting. Of course, I expect Ruben and Papa to oversee the operation. But I want the boys to jointly own the farm that Julia and I began, eventually.

Look after little Eleanor; and give her my love.

God bless you all. Love,

Michael

"Oh Papa," Rose moaned. "We have lost our Michael for good."

"We don't know dat, Momma. He is in God's hands now. Please everyone, pray with us for our son."

AFTERWORD

Just the other day, Papa told me that the Drieborg family did not run from adversity. He insisted that our family always looked life squarely in the eye, and did what was necessary; what was honorable.

So what am I doing on this train? Is the guilt I feel for what happened to Julia so strong that I cannot face the Hecht's or stay in Lowell? I should try to understand all of this before I go much further.

Mike got off the train when it pulled into the Lansing depot. He took his baggage and got a ticket for Flint, fifty miles or so to the East.

I need to talk this out with someone. Maybe Bob Lilley can help me shake my feeling of despair. Phineas lives in Lapeer too. Maybe he can help me. After my train arrives in Flint, I'll stay over and rent a horse first thing in the morning. Lapeer should be only a few hours ride east.

"Well, I'll be," Bob Lilley exclaimed when he found Mike standing in his doorway. "Come on in before you let all the cold in."

After they were settled in front of the fireplace with a mug of hot coffee, neither of them spoke.

"I suppose it would be a good idea if I told you why I'm here."

Lilley chuckled. "Must be some good reason you traveled over 100 miles in the dead of winter to knock on my door."

"The Saturday before Ash Wednesday, Julia and our adopted son Robert were killed on the streets of Lowell"

"Oh, my God Mike. A runaway wagon?"

"No Bob. I think I could live with that. Hired killers did it."

At this point, Mike dropped his head and sobbed. When he had gotten control of himself, he told Bob the story.

"So you, George, and the other men in your old squad killed four men."

"Yes. We killed the two who killed my wife and son; the man who paid them and promised to kill all my family members; and his father, who financed the vendetta. We killed them all."

"Mike. Would you join me in a prayer for your wife and son?"

"Gladly. Thank you, Bob"

The two men knelt by the fireplace and Bob began.

"Please Lord, welcome Julia, her unborn child and little Robert into your heavenly presence. They were snatched from this world in a most cruel manner. We ask that you help Mike accept their passing and forgive him for the vengeance he brought on those involved in the killing. We pray this in Jesus name, Amen."

"Thank you Bob. In the last couple of years I had gotten away from turning to God. I didn't realize how much I had missed it."

That afternoon, Mike helped Bob with chores in the barn. In the evening Bob led a prayer group at the Hunter's Creek Baptist Church. Mike joined the small congregation in prayer.

He slept well that night for the first time since Julia was killed.

"Why don't stay with me for a while, Mike." Bob suggested. "I could use your help around here, and you and I could talk some. Besides, if you rush off, you'll miss talking with Phineas. I know he would like to see you."

"Thanks Bob. As long as you allow me to work for my room and board, I'll stay. I do want to see Phineas, too."

Each evening, Bob read from the Bible. The two men talked of Christ's message of forgiveness at some length.

"How can I not blame myself? My problem with Bacon began long before I even met the Hechts. If I had reacted differently to him when we were in school together, none of this would have happened."

"You cannot know that; only God does."

"My father warned me from the start. I just didn't listen."

"You were a child who could not have known you were dealing with a sick schoolmate. Besides, the Lord does not expect the child you were then to have the wisdom of your father."

Bob told him repeatedly. "You did not cause the deaths of Julia, her child or Robert. A demented hate-filled man did. Whatever blame is yours, Christ has forgiven you, shouldn't you forgive yourself, too?"

And so it went over the days. They arose early for chores and some prayer. The afternoon was spent cutting trees and digging stumps to clear land.

As they swung their axes Bob exhorted Mike. "Take out all the hate you feel on the tree! Strike the tree harder Mike; and again. Do you feel the anger leaving you? Don't stop now, Mike. Swing the axe for God and cleanse your soul."

Then after early evening chores, they cleaned up and prepared their supper. Bob would read a passage from the Bible and they would talk about it. After a few days, Mike was able to pray, too.

"Thank you Lord for welcoming my wife Julia and our children into heaven. Look after them Lord," And, "Please forgive me the guilt I feel for their deaths."

Later, he was able to go further.

"Thank you, Jesus for forgiving me the vengeance I took on the killers of my family."

One night, just before they went to their rooms Bob commented.

"One day soon, Mike, you will recognize that Jesus has forgiven you the guilt you feel for all of it."

*   *   *   *

On two occasions after evening chores the men spent some time with Phineas, the Lapeer schoolteacher at his house by the school.

"How are things going Phineas?" Mike asked.

"Things are going well," he told them. "It sure beats living out of doors all the time and being shot at."

"Have the kids questioned you about the war?" Mike asked.

"During our study of history, they have. They find that a much more exciting topic than Rome or Greece. So they ask me a lot of questions about it. Most of them think war is all parades and harmless fireworks like they see on the 4th of July. I have tried not to glamorize it though.

"For example, I have reminded them of those people who are missing from this community because of the war. We have also talked of those men around here who have lost limbs, limp or walk with a cane or crutch. That sobers them up some.

"I also have told them of the devastation we saw, first in the Shenandoah Valley and later in Georgia and South Carolina. I even mentioned the name our troopers gave you, Mike. I can't remember why it came up. But they know about it."

*   *   *   *

After chores one morning, Mike and Bob went into Lapeer and visited Phineas at his school.

They sat in the back of the single room building and listened for a while.

"He's got this group under control, it seems to me," Bob whispered. "Even the older ones are quiet and pay attention.

"You can see that he has given the older kids the role of helping the younger ones. Even the boys seem to have welcomed that responsibility."

"Boys and girls," Phineas began. "For our history lesson today, we have a treat. In the back of the room, I'm sure you have seen the two very tall gentlemen watching us. They are farmers; one here in Lapeer, the other from the western part of our state near Lake Michigan.

"I asked them both here today to help us with our lesson. Since they both served in our army with distinction in the late war, they are very well qualified to lead our discussion. Major Robert Lilley was a regimental commander in the 4ᵗʰ Michigan Infantry Division. Major Michael Drieborg was a cavalry troop commander in the Michigan Cavalry Brigade. He was also awarded the Congressional Medal of Honor by President Lincoln himself. I had the honor of serving in his troop as his executive officer.

"Gentlemen, welcome to our school."

As soon as his teacher Mr. White stopped speaking, one of the boys blurted out a question.

"Which one of you was called The Dutchman?"

A bit surprised, neither man spoke right away. The children were suddenly quiet too.

Mike stood. "My men gave me that nickname."

"Why?"

"It was common for the men to make up such names for their leaders. They chose this name for me, I suppose because both my parents were of Dutch descent."

"What does descent mean?" a young student inquired.

"Do you know what country you parents came from son?"

"They came from England."

"That means that you are of English descent. Does anyone have parents who were born in some part of Germany?"

Several hands went up.

"That means that you are of German descent."

"In our troop, Mr. White and I had two sergeants whose parents came from Ireland. Anyone here have relatives from there?"

"So you three kids are of Irish descent. You all understand now?"

"What about you, Major Lilley?"

"My parents came from England. So I am of English descent. But remember kids, everyone in this room is an American now."

"What did your men nickname you sir?"

"My men called me the Minister. I think they chose that name because I used to lead Sunday service, and before battles, I read to my men from the bible."

One of the girls asked Mike another question.

"You were given another nickname though, weren't you, Major Drieborg?"

"Your teacher has been telling my secrets. But yes, that is a fact, young lady. Some people in South Carolina called me the Gentleman Major."

"Were these people our enemies?"

"Not really," Mike told the kids. "Some were farmers, like I am. Others lived in town like some of you. They all just wanted to be left alone and survive the war. But I didn't really consider them enemies, like soldiers with guns."

"But why did they call you that?" another student asked.

"First, you have to understand that my men and I had to live off the land. That meant we needed to take food for ourselves and feed for our horses from the people who lived in the area where we were operating.

"Picture this. I ride into your farmyard and order my men clean out your smokehouse, take your chickens and all the feed you had stored for your animals. In wartime, that is called living off the land. Now do you understand?"

Mike watched the little heads nod.

"Now the tough part; how much should I take from your farm? How much is enough? Would I take everything the farmer had stored up for the winter? Or would I take just what my men and I could use for the next few days? Come on, children. Think of your own farm now? In my shoes, how much would you have taken?"

The children began to argue some among themselves, but finally agreed on an answer for the question Mike had asked.

One of the older girls stood and gave the answer.

"We think that we would take what we needed and leave the rest."

"All right. Now I have a second important question for you to answer. Would you destroy what you didn't take because it might help the enemy?"

Another argument ensued among the students.

One of the older boys stood.

"Are you talking about killing cows, pigs and poultry; even our plow horse?"

"That's exactly what I'm talking about. Would you kill every living animal you did not take for your men?"

A much shorter discussion resulted.

The same boy stood.

"We decided not to kill all the animals we didn't take. We decided that it wouldn't be right."

"That's exactly what I decided. So that is why some of the farmers and townspeople there began to call me the Gentleman Major."

Another student made a comment. "If it was just you they called that, seems to me other cavalry officers decided to kill all the animals. Could that be right, Major?"

At this point, Mr. White jumped into the conversation.

"The major is probably too modest to say this, but many other officers in our army did just that. Evidently, the word spread that our troop only took what food and feed we needed; and that we did not kill all the animals or burn homes and buildings; thus the nickname Gentleman Major."

"Did you really read from the Bible before battles Major Lilley?"

"Yes I did, miss. Most of my men wanted me to. Each of us wanted to be at peace with God before we went into battle. Our prayer also reminded us that we were fighting the Lord's fight to make men free."

"Major Drieborg, were you really captured by wild Indians?"

"Yes, I was. My troop was sent to the Dakota Territory last summer. We were chopping trees for a fort when it happened."

"Mr. White told us that another Indian rescued you and your men."

"Yes, he did." Mike then explained what had happened.

The discussion went on much longer than the history lesson normally would have. But because the children, even the young ones, hung on every word, their teacher let it continue.

"Major Drieborg," a girl asked. "Do you have any children?"

Mike hesitated, taken by surprise with the question. "Yes, I do," he finally responded. "I have a little daughter."

"Where does she live?" The child continued.

"She is less than two years old and lives with my parents."

Phineas interrupted the exchange at this point.

"Children," he announced. "It appears that a real snowstorm has hit us this morning. It is best that we thank our guests and get on home."

✳　　✳　　✳　　✳

The three men remained behind, talking.

"Those kids are a smart bunch, Phineas." Bob judged.

"I believe they are pretty good students," Phineas agreed. "I especially like their inquisitive attitude. They ask good questions, like they did today. You two gave good answers. Thank you."

"And thank you for rescuing me from the questions that little girl was asking me about my daughter. I was getting very nervous about it."

"What about you, Mike? Now that you've left your farm to the boys, what are you going to do?"

"I really didn't know when I left Lowell, Phineas.

"I didn't even feel like a complete person then. I felt empty. I had no clear plan or destination either, because I wasn't thinking very clearly. So when I got off the train in Lansing, I just stood there and watched it pull out of the station. I don't even remember making a decision to go to Lapeer. I just sort of wandered in that direction.

"When Bob opened his door, I didn't know what to say at first. All I knew then was that I had to get away from all the painful memories back home. And I was carrying a load of guilt for everything that happened. Bob has helped me see things more clearly and has helped me reach out for the Lord's healing.

"In the process, Lilley has worked me half to death chopping trees and digging stumps at his place. There's probably a method to his madness, because I've had no time to feel sorry for myself; I'm too tired all the time."

"I was just helping you work out all that guilt you felt, Mike," Bob quipped. "The Lord told me to do it."

"I suppose the Lord wanted you to have enough firewood for at least two winters, too."

"Well Mike, the Lord does look after his own."

"You are so full of it, Lilley. That must be why you are such a good minister."

"I'll accept that as a compliment."

"To answer your question more directly, Phineas, I think I am ready now to head for Washington City."

"Why there?" Phineas asked. "Seems to me that if you're ready to go there, you're ready to head home. After all, your daughter Eleanor needs a father doesn't she?"

"You two don't let a guy off easily, do you?"

"If you were afraid of that little girl this morning asking about the family you left behind, maybe you're not ready.

"Bob may have worked you to death chopping trees and digging stumps, Mike." Phineas said. "But he evidently didn't challenge your fear of going home."

"I had to leave something for you, Phineas." Bob said in his defense.

"So, Mike," Phineas went on. "Didn't your father already tell you what he thought on this matter? Didn't he tell you that he believed you belonged in Lowell raising your daughter, Eleanor?"

"Yes he did, Phineas. Papa told me exactly that."

"So if Bob has helped you deal with your sense of guilt and you feel the Lord has forgiven what you did, what is keeping you from returning to your responsibilities in Lowell."

"Julia herself built our home. Everything there reminds me of her. How can I live there now?"

"Neither of us can put ourselves in your shoes, Mike," Bob offered. "And you need to work through your grief for the lose you feel. But right now you are still not seeing things very clearly. So I have a suggestion that would give your family hope and you an opportunity to recover."

"What would that be, Bob?"

"Go to this job in Washington. Take your grief out on this job as though you were still chopping trees at my place. But tell your folks that you intend to return to the farm. Tell them to plant your ground and maintain your home. Maybe your sister Ann and her husband would live in it until you return.

"But tell them that you intend to return; you just need some time to grieve. I believe you need to promise them that, Mike. I think you need that as a goal for yourself, too. "

"When did you two become so smart?"

"We've hung around some pretty smart people, Mr. Dutchman."

Thank you, Lord, for bringing me here. You led me to these two friends who have shown me a way out of my despair.

*   *   *   *

When you get to Washington, what will you do there?" Phineas asked.

"Back in December, Congressman Kellogg offered me a job working for him. He is deeply involved in what they are calling Reconstruction. He said that Congress is having a lot of trouble protecting the newly freed Negroes in the states of the former Confederacy. It appears that many of the Southern leaders who led their states out of the Union are re-establishing their control over the lives of the freedmen.

"There is a big fight looming between President Johnson and Congress over this matter too. Anyway, Congressman Kellogg asked me to help.

"I turned him down then. But with Julia gone now, I think it would be a good thing for me to do, for a while anyway.

"Would either of you be willing to give me a hand on this?"

"You mean go to Washington, or wherever, and work with you?"

"Yes."

Bob Lilley spoke first. "Thanks, Mike, but I have plans to marry and stay right here."

"How about you, Phineas?"

"Sounds like quite a challenge, Mike. I'd be the first to admit that this teaching job is boring compared to the years I spent in the saddle. How about this? You check out this job and get back to me. If there is an opportunity for me; send me a telegram and I'll be on the next train. All right?"

"That sounds good."

"So you think you're ready to leave here and live in Washington?" Bob asked.

"Thanks to you two, and the Lord, I think I am Bob. But there are no trees to chop in Washington. So I'll need to come up with a substitute for working off my grief. Maybe you could help me with that before I leave."

"Just remember what Richard told you at our last prayer meeting, Mike. He told you to stay in the Word: and the Lord will look after you.

"Find a prayer group in that city Mike. If you work as hard at staying with the Lord as you did on those trees and stumps, you'll be all right."

*   *   *   *

On his trip to Washington City, Mike didn't bother to stop overnight in Cleveland. Instead he changed trains there and continued on to Baltimore.

With your help, Lord, I'll be able to handle this new direction in my life. Your will be done.

Once in Baltimore he paid for a ride to Washington on a horse drawn passenger bus.

From long experience, Mike knew where Congressman Kellogg's office was located.

"Well, my goodness. Look what the cat dragged in. Mike, how the hell are you?" George Krupp, the Congressman's aide, shouted.

"Don't just stand there in the doorway, man. Come on in. The Congressman's waiting for you."

Cast of Characters

Drieborg Family:

Father Jake Drieborg, age 44

Mother Rose Drieborg, age 42

Son Michael Drieborg, age 21

Daughter Susan Drieborg, age 18

Daughter Ann Drieborg, age 16

Son Jacob Drieborg, age 14

Granddaughter Eleanor Drieborg, newborn

Hecht Family:

Father Ruben Hecht, age 42

Mother Emma Hecht, age 41

Daughter Julia Hecht, age 18

Son Kenny Hecht, age 15

Grandson Robert Bierlein, age 3

Kellogg Family:

Father William Kellogg, age 44

Daughter Patricia Kellogg, age 19

Village of Lowell MI:
Lowell Justice of the Peace Joseph F. Deeb
Town Marshal John Chapman
Lowell Bank Harvey Bacon, owner
Lowell General Store Jim Yared, owner

Military Personnel
Mess-Mates I Troop 6th MI Cavalry Regiment – Michigan Brigade
George Neal age 19, baker's apprentice, Grand Rapids MI
Stan Killeen age 22, farm worker/lumberman, Cadillac MI
Gustav Svenson age 22, mineworker, Houghton MI
Dave Steward age 26, fruit farmer, Newaygo MI
Bill Anderson age 37, retail store owner, Wyoming MI

Former Andersonville Prison-Mates
Phil Lewis 5th Michigan Cavalry
George Hendryx 9th Michigan Cavalry
Sam Hutton 9th Michigan Cavalry
Joe Sergeant 9th Michigan Cavalry
John Ransom 9th Michigan Cavalry
Battist 24th Wisconsin Infantry
Pete Mc Cullough 8th Missouri Volunteer Infantry

Lowell Schoolmate
Carl Bacon age 23, son of Lowell's banker

Other Military Personnel

Captain Don Lovell I Troop Commander, Grand Rapids MI

Sgt. Riley I Troop First Sergeant, Detroit, MI

Lt. Phineas White I Troop Executive Officer, Lapeer MI

Lt. Henry Austry I Troop Platoon Leader, Virden IL

General Henry Halleck Army Chief of Staff

General Kilpatrick U.S. Cavalry Division Commander

General Sherman Army of Tennessee Commander

General Burbridge Kilpatrick's Cavalry Division

Colonel Kidd MI 6th Cavalry Regiment Commander

Clara Barton Nurse with Sanitation Commission

Anna Ethridge Nurse with Sanitation Commission

Dr. Harald VanEycken Union Medical Doctor

Other Characters

Woodrow Yared Federal Judge

Richard Sullivan Dalton, MY Attny

Ron Kalanquin Federal Marshall

William Young Cleveland Hotel Mgr.

Craig R. Haynes Cleveland Police Chief

Congressman Kellogg's Aide Congressman's Kellogg Aide

Below, I have attached a last page announcement for Book Three, Honor Restored.

Honor Restored

Book Three

of the

Drieborg Chronicles

After four years of civil war, Lincoln's determination to keep the Union together had prevailed.

But then, a new conflict began, this time to decide the nature of that Union. Would the Northern victors allow the old Southern ruling class to regain control or would a new political and socio/economic structure based on Negro suffrage be imposed?

President Johnson and the Congress were at odds over that issue.

Michael Drieborg found himself in the midst of that struggle. Allied with Congressional Radicals, he became involved in Washington intrigues and South Carolina reconstruction.

Printed in the United States
127722LV00002B/130-300/P